The City In Darkness

A Stefan Gillespie Novel

Michael Russell

CONSTABLE • LONDON

CONSTABLE

First published in Great Britain in 2016 by Constable

This paperback edition published in 2017

1 3 5 7 9 10 8 6 4 2

A CIP catalogue record for this book
is available from the British Library.

ISBN: 978-1-47212-191-2

Typeset in Dante by SX Composing DTP, Rayleigh Essex
Printed and bound in Great Britain by Clays, St Ives plc

Papers used by Constable are from well-managed forests and
other responsible sources.

MIX
Paper from
responsible sources
FSC® C104740

Constable
An imprint of
Little, Brown Book Group
Carmelite House
50 Victoria Embankment
London EC4Y 0DZ

An Hachette UK Company
www.hachette.co.uk

www.littlebrown.co.uk

For my grandmother
Sarah Josephine Harvey
Moville, Donegal
1898

Still south I went and west and south again,
Through Wicklow from the morning till the night,
And far from cities, and the sights of men,
Lived with the sunshine and the moon's delight.

I knew the stars, the flowers, and the birds,
The gray and wintry sides of many glens,
And did but half remember human words,
In converse with the mountains, moors, and fens.

'Prelude' by J. M. Synge

BAY OF BISCAY

Bordeaux

FRANCE

N

Toulouse

Santander

ANDORRA

Oviedo • Pendueles Bilbao
Cantabrian Mountains

Santiago de
Compostela

Vigo

Burgos

Valladolid

Zaragoza

Barcelona

Porto

Salamanca

S P A I N

BALEARIC ISLANDS

Flying Boat to England?

Madrid

Jarama Valley

PORTUGAL

Caceres

Valencia

Lisbon

Córdoba

MEDITERRANEAN SEA

Seville

• Granada

ATLANTIC
OCEAN

Gibraltar

ALGERIA

MORROCO

0   100   200   300   400km

Part One

Hibernia Sancta

On Christmas Eve, in the season of peace and good-will, a postman goes about his works in a village in the Wicklow Mountains. He is seen in the afternoon in the company of a number of men and women, and is never seen again. His bicycle is found some miles away the next day, but the man might have vanished into thin air for all the trace there is of him. Now comes one of the strangest aspects of this remarkable case. Everyone knows the secretiveness of the Irish countryside, but surely the inhabitants of this village surpass all others in this respect. A man has vanished as if the earth had opened and swallowed him up, a phrase grimly suggestive of the subsequent suspicion, and not a word is said. Life goes on normally, there are brief paragraphs in the newspapers, and then everything is quiet again.

Irish Independent

1

The Upper Lake

Wicklow, August 1932

There was barely a whisper of mist on the Upper Lake, a softness in the air where the water rippled among reeds and lapped at the pebble beach at the eastern end. The sun was low in the sky, but the brightness of the morning gave the grey waters an unaccustomed tint of blue. It would be a fine day in the mountains. They rose on either side of the lake, a great amphitheatre folding round it. The tree-lined slopes climbed steeply out of the water, heavy with leaves, a hint of the turning year in the oaks and the yellowing needles of the Scots pines. Higher up heather and bare rock caught the sunlight more keenly. The mountains held the lake tightly on three sides; Camaderry and Turlough Hill to the north and west, Lugduff and Mullacor to the west and south. To the east, through the woods, were the ruins of the thousand-year-old monastery of St Kevin, the Round Tower and the tumbled stones of ancient churches and monastic cells. As morning wore on the buses and cars would come from Dublin to fill the valley with visitors. But for a few hours the only sounds would be the rooks and the chattering sparrows and, somewhere above, the high shriek of a peregrine hunting.

———

Back from the pebble shore a small green tent was pitched. Beside it were the ashes of a fire from the night before. Inside a woman and a man in their mid-twenties lay close together; between them a boy, not yet three. The man and boy were asleep. The woman lay on her back, looking up at the ridge of the tent. She had not slept well; in all the peace around her, in the slow breathing of her husband and son, and in the morning birdsong outside, she was not at peace. She sat up slowly. Her yellow hair fell over her shoulders. She pushed the blanket away from her and shivered.

She looked at the man and the boy, smiling. Troubled as she was, she felt her contentment; it was deeper and more solid than she had ever anticipated such things could be. What was wrong had nothing to do with this. It was something else and part of her simply wanted to walk away from it. What it would mean for people she cared about, people she had grown up with, was already hard to bear. But she had no choice. What she had discovered, so suddenly, so unexpectedly, could not be ignored. She looked down at her husband again. He would know what to do. He would help her find the strength she needed. And when it was done he would help her leave it behind. Only strong light would clear away the darkness.

She would tell him tonight, at his parents' farm across the mountains. She needed to be somewhere else to say it. But for now she wanted to fill her head with the new morning. She stretched across to a duffle bag and took a swimming costume, inching down the tent to the flaps, pulling it on with as little movement as possible. The man slowly opened his eyes.

'What are you doing?'

'A swim. It's a beautiful morning.'

'Jesus, it'll be cold enough in that water.'

'I've swum in that lake since I was four years old, summer and winter,' she laughed. 'My father always said, if you're cold swim faster!'

4

'Have you forgotten the day you begged me to take you away from your mad father and a lifetime's sentence of healthy exercise?'

She leant forward, her face over his and kissed him. As she did he could smell the scent of her body on her skin from the night before.

'There are better ways to warm up than swimming, Maeve.'

'I need to clear my head. Go back to sleep.'

As she got up he saw, momentarily, that her smile had gone.

'Are you all right?'

'I need to talk to you, that's all. When I have, I'll be grand.'

She smiled once more, then crawled out into the morning. He lay back. There was something wrong. She had been quiet the day before, for no real reason. It was only now it struck him. And last night, as they sat looking at the Upper Lake after making love, she had been tearful for a moment, in a way that was unlike her. Still, it couldn't be serious. It was only two days ago that she had talked long into the night about her happiness and about their simple, ordinary plans for the future. Stefan yawned, looking across at the face of the sleeping boy. He closed his eyes. He listened to the rooks, a blackbird singing overhead, the rhythmic, easy breathing of his son. And then almost immediately, he was asleep again.

The woman walked through the trees to the lake. She stood, looking up at the mountain slopes that enclosed this space she knew so well. It had seemed a simple idea; driving down from Dublin for a week with his parents at the farm outside Baltinglass; outings in the hired car they couldn't quite afford; a few quiet days by the Upper Lake where, until her marriage and her son, she had known her happiest times. Now it could never be the same again. Everything would change; everything in her childhood would be different. It could never be the refuge it was. But perhaps there had always been questions.

5

She was already wondering if the happiness she remembered had been real. And what she had discovered had somehow shocked her less than it should have done. It wasn't that she knew, even remotely, but she felt as if something had opened up in her that she should have sensed. There were uneasy things, uncomfortable things now, crowding in on her. She knew the darkness had been there all along.

'Shite!'

Her voice echoed back from the mountains. She waded into the water, wanting its coldness to drive it all from her mind. Then she swam. She swam hard, unaware how far she was going, pushing forward, stroke after stroke. She stopped and bobbed up, treading water. She felt the sun, warmer now, higher overhead. She was close to the craggy face below the sheer Spinc on the south side of the lake, where steep steps led up to the cave and the ruins that were called St Kevin's Bed. She lay on her back, kicking her legs very slowly, letting herself drift on towards the rock.

The legend came back into her head. She remembered the game they played as children. She was Kathleen of the Unholy Blue Eyes, trying to make the saint fall in love and forsake his sacred vows; Kevin and his monks had to chase her from the cave, throwing bunches of stinging nettles at her. In the gang of friends she spent her summers with the boys were Kevin's monks, the girls Kathleen's witches, stealing the saint's gold along with his virtue. The gold had been their own addition to a tale that was really no more than chasing and catching. But as they grew older the price the girls paid for capture turned from dodging the stinging nettles to forfeiting a kiss; it wasn't quite in accord with the triumph of St Kevin's sacred celibacy over the wiles of Kathleen and those unholy blue eyes.

She laughed, but somehow it seemed less innocent now; the cave in which those kisses were given felt blacker. She kept on treading water. She had to work it out, every detail of what she would tell her husband. If he didn't believe her, then who would? It was then that she saw the dinghy.

The boat had pulled out from the landing place below the steps to St Kevin's Bed. She knew it, old and battered now, the paint bleached and peeling; she knew it when it was new, fifteen years ago. It was the companion of a hundred lake adventures. And she knew the rower. He would have been fishing in the early morning when he had the lake to himself. She watched him row towards her, his back arched over the oars. He looked round, grinning, calling out with the voice of old familiarity.

'Long time since I caught a mermaid here!'

She smiled, still treading water. He must have seen her swimming towards the rock. But her smile stopped. She had forgotten, just forgotten, what was going to happen. He didn't know. None of them knew. How could she have an ordinary conversation? How could she laugh, joke, lie?

The man swung the boat round to face her and shipped the oars. She swam up to the boat and grabbed the side. She didn't know what to say.

'I thought I'd row over and see was any bacon frying, Maeve.'

'There's maybe a cup of tea and some bread and jam,' she said.

'They say a woman who puts a plate of bacon in front of her man every day need never fear he'll wander. A vaguely risqué metaphor trying to get out there, I guess. But anyway, beware of too much bread and jam!'

'I think we'll cope, with or without bacon.'

'Absolutely,' he said. 'I'm sure he doesn't go without.'

She looked at him, more puzzled than offended. It was unfunny in a way she never remembered him being unfunny; it felt unpleasant. Maybe he was trying too hard to make a joke. He grinned the warm, rather empty grin he always did. It had never before occurred to her it was empty, but that's what it was. There was nothing behind it. And it wasn't warm, in any way whatsoever; even as the word formed in her head she replaced it with cold.

'You're going back today?'

'To Baltinglass, but Stefan has to be in Dublin on Saturday.'

'Ah, a policeman's lot!'

She felt the sneer in his voice.

'Get in. I'll row you back across. If it's only tea and bread and jam, I'll take what's going, even if it does sound a bit like a prison breakfast.'

She realized how tired she was. She had swum a long way. She wanted to be with her husband and her son. She wanted to pack up and go.

'All right, can you pull me in so?'

She started to heave herself up into the boat. He didn't budge.

'I do need a hand.'

Her voice was sharper; she was no longer concerned about him. And maybe this was what would happen, she thought. This was the start. No one would come out of it unchanged or undamaged. Where there had been friendship and fond memory there would be guilt, accusation, anger. They would feel they should have known; they'd see faults, weaknesses, dislike.

He was staring at her quizzically, as if he knew what she was thinking. He leant forward, and suddenly his hands were on her, one holding her right arm, the other clasping her hard between her neck and shoulder. And he was pushing her, pushing her down, back into the water.

For a few seconds she thought it was a bad joke. He was strong; he had been even as a boy. She was struggling, fighting to get out of his grip. But his hands held her tightly. He wouldn't let go. As she thrashed in the water he was still bearing down on her. Her head went under, gasping, choking. All she could try to do was break away, but his grip never faltered.

Water filled her mouth and her nose. She pushed up, desperately trying to hit out. She tried to scream. Her cries barely echoed across the lake. She was already weak. He pushed down again, his arms in the water as she flailed and kicked and struggled. But in all that movement he was still, his eyes fixed on her. And then abruptly she stopped moving. He held her under the water. Strands of her fair hair floated delicately on the swell.

The lake was calm again. Finally, he let go. Her body sank. The last wisps of hair disappeared into the blackness. He gazed down into the depths. She was there, not far beneath the surface, but despite the blue sheen the day had given the water, it was too dark to see her now.

He moved back into the centre of the boat. He put out the oars and pulled back towards the Spinc and St Kevin's Bed. He felt a sense of satisfaction. It had worked better than he had imagined. He had been watching the tent since the previous afternoon, unsure what she knew, unsure if he was at risk, but knowing he could not let it go. He came closer after dark. He heard the two of them. Fucking. He hadn't expected that. It was unpleasant to listen to, unpleasant to think about. By morning he knew he must act. He remembered she swam every morning as a child; he thought she would still, as if this place still belonged to her somehow. As for what she did or didn't know, death resolved all doubt, all risk; that was the simple truth. And it had been so easy, so very easy, that he knew it was meant to be, like so many things in his life. Yet he would remember her more fondly now. In an odd way it was almost as if she had come home.

2

El Río Jarama

Jarama, Spain, February 1937

The guns stopped at almost the same time along the valley of low hills on either side of the Jarama River. All day the noise of battle had sounded; the roar and thud of artillery and tanks, the whine of aircraft, the rattle of machine guns, the staccato crack of rifles, and behind that the cries and the screams of men in all the various stages of fighting and killing and dying.

For the fifth day Generalissimo Francisco Franco's army had flung itself across the muddy, sluggish river at the soldiers of the Spanish Republic, battling its way up over parched earth and cracked stone, through the groves of shrapnel-splintered olives, over the bodies of the five days' dead. If the road through the valley was taken, Madrid would fall, and what remained of the hated Republic would be pushed into the Mediterranean.

Each day the Republic's line bent beneath the Nationalist onslaught. Hilltop positions were taken, held, lost, retaken, lost again. Each day that line held only by virtue of those who died to hold it. And each evening as the sun set, and the guns were quiet, and the sour smell of cordite faded, the last heat of the day filled the air with the smell of the decomposing dead. In the silence the engine-like buzz of millions of flies was a solid bass to the chattering cicadas. Along the Jarama the crows swarmed in black clouds for the carrion; the buzzards that had circled overhead all day sailed down to feed. Here and there a soldier fired a shot to chase the birds from the feast; sometimes a shallow trench was dug to keep the bodies whole. But there were always too many bodies, and there would only be more tomorrow.

On the bare brow the men of the Fifteenth International Brigade had christened Suicide Hill that day, an Irishman looked down at the river, smoking a thin, hand-rolled cigarette. He wore the uniform of a brigadier of the Spanish Republic's International Brigades. The men he commanded had come to Spain to fight for a collection of ideals that didn't always make easy bedfellows. They were big ideas: freedom, democracy, justice, socialism, communism. But what mattered was a common enemy. Here it was Franco's fascism, but that was no different to Mussolini's fascism; no different, above all, to Hitler's fascism. That was what united the 400 Englishmen and Irishmen who had marched to the hills above the Jarama River that morning; less than 150 were still alive.

Brigadier Frank Ryan watched a dozen of his men move among the bodies on the hillside, collecting guns and ammunition. On the Nationalist side the dead wore the desert fatigues of the Spanish Foreign Legion, the bright red fezzes and cloaks of the Moroccan infantry, the grey-green of the Falangist militia. The Republican dead mostly wore the tan-brown overalls of the International Brigades; their names were in Ryan's head, above all the names of the dead Irishmen he had led up Suicide Hill that day. Men he came from Ireland to Spain with. Men he had campaigned for Irish freedom with in the streets of Dublin. Men he had fought beside in the IRA in the Tipperary hills. He dropped his cigarette end and started to roll another.

From the olive grove behind came the sound of shovels hitting stony soil; trenches were being deepened. There was a smell of cooking; from pots of vegetable stew the scent of herbs someone had found, that smelt not of death and ideals but of being alive. There was laughter rising up out of words about nothing. It mattered that his men could laugh. Even staring at the dead he needed them to laugh, scream, cry, anything that had life in it. He heard his officers moving through the lines, making the lists that would soon come to him. The lists of the living; the longer lists of the dead.

On the farm track behind the olive grove a truck backfired. Frank Ryan looked round. On the canvas of the battered vehicle were the words 'Comisaría Política', on the cab roof a trumpet-like loud speaker. The distorted martial tones of the 'Internationale' blasted out. A voice crackled, enthusiastic, purposeful. The language was English, though the same words had been heard along the line in Spanish, French, German. They were words that few wanted when the bodies of their friends were still warm.

'Comrades, today's victory has pushed back the fascists again! A triumph for the people of Spain! The workers of Spain give thanks to the men of the International Brigades who stand shoulder to shoulder in the struggle. Where the people are united, we are invincible! No pasarán!'

Some dutiful comrades raised weary clenched fists and shouted 'No pasarán!' The 'Internationale' started up again and the truck disappeared.

Brigadier Ryan took the sheets of paper that had been handed to him by the young English lieutenant. He didn't bother to look at them.

'How many, Allen?'

'Two hundred and twenty dead. Thirty seriously wounded.'

'Jesus, we can't hold this place with a hundred men.'

Frank Ryan finally looked at the names. He was a thin man,

with sharp features. His face was lined; he seemed older than his thirty-five years. It was a face that was good at showing passion and enthusiasm, but not much else. It was no bad time not to show much. The men of the Fifteenth Brigade were watching; even for those who had been in the thickest of the fighting the cost of retaking Suicide Hill was only just sinking in. It wasn't Brigadier Ryan's business to show what he felt now; it was to prepare for the attack they all knew would come the next day.

'We'd better get to Brigade HQ. I'll shout, you beg. Now Commissar Klein has congratulated us, they need to know the price. No reinforcements, then Klein needn't come back tomorrow. We'll be feeding the crows too.'

Brigadier Frank Ryan and Lieutenant Allen Armstrong left Brigade HQ. What they brought away was only the vaguest possibility of reinforcements from the stretched French and Belgian battalion, and the boot and back seat of their commandeered Renault filled with bottles of red wine and brandy. It was the best HQ could offer. Well, wasn't there something to celebrate in the miracle of Suicide Hill? In the small white finca, surrounded by a thousand olive trees, Ryan had indeed shouted, cajoled and begged for reinforcements. The result had been yet more achingly sincere congratulations from Spanish officers and the International Brigades' political commissariat, still barely able to believe the line had resisted the Nationalist onslaught. The men of the Fifteenth Brigade, now dead for the most part, were the heroes of the hour. But the expectation that they could repeat what they had done tomorrow was a hope that trumped arithmetic. There would be no more troops. The Fifteenth Brigade's survivors would have to hold their line.

It was dark as the Renault rejoined the road along the eastern ridge of the Jarama Valley. The road was busy; columns of soldiers walking with the slow tread of men who had fought all day and would fight again with the daylight; trucks carrying ammunition and pulling artillery; carts ferrying the wounded and the dead. And while Frank Ryan chain-smoked, Allen Armstrong hunched over the wheel, weaving through the melee of men and vehicles, trying to avoid the potholes and craters that the traffic of war and constant shelling had created. Then suddenly he swerved off to the right.

'I'll take the road towards Belchite. We'll be half the night here.'

The car headed downhill on a track that ran close to the river and the front line before climbing up to the escarpment where the Fifteenth Brigade was camped. There were a few straggling soldiers, small camps and gun positions. But it was surprisingly quiet. With the light of the moon in the sky, Ryan found himself thinking of the winding roads of the west of Ireland at night. It didn't feel so different. He believed the war he was fighting here was the same war he had fought there. But the uneasiness that took him out of Ireland was never far away, even now, like an itch beneath beliefs that should have been as comfortable as old clothes. Fighting was fine if you didn't stop to think. But the silence had made him think of home. He felt as if he wanted to stay on that quiet road for a long time.

Rounding a bend, Armstrong's foot hit the brake. They lurched forward; the Renault skidded. Something dark thudded against the bonnet.

'You all right, Frank?'

'Apart from my head. I hit the fucking—'

'That's all right, we all know how hard your head is – sir.'

Frank Ryan got out. As the lieutenant did the same he unbuttoned the clip that held his revolver. A few yards away lay a man in uniform. Ryan crouched down. Armstrong pushed the pistol back into its holster and shone a torch on to the soldier's face; it was stained with sweat and dirt and dried blood. The uniform that could have been grey or khaki or green was filthy

14

and shredded; one sleeve was black, hardened with the same dried blood. It was a very young face; the soldier looked like he was still in his teens.

'Is he alive?' asked Lieutenant Armstrong.

'Jesus, Mary and Joseph!' The soldier gritted his teeth in pain.

Frank Ryan laughed. The accent, like the words, was unmistakable.

'Is he one of ours then?' Armstrong bent down.

A look of relief pushed away the pain in the soldier's face.

'I never thought I'd make it. I was hiding, running, hiding.' He tried to sit up. There were tears now. He was coughing. 'I didn't even know where I was half the time. Jesus, weren't they all round me, everywhere?'

'What's your company?' Ryan asked.

'I got hit when they started firing. I ran, I must've passed out. I took a bullet. We were cheering them on, then they fired, our own fucking side—'

Armstrong produced a canteen of water. The soldier drank thirstily. Frank Ryan watched him, frowning; there was something odd about him.

'Who's your sergeant, who are your officers?'

'Tommy O'Toole, sir. I think he was killed.' He crossed himself. 'He went down in front of me. When we marched over the river they thought the Bandera was Brigaders! The feckers wouldn't stop shooting at us!'

The last word, Bandera, left no doubt in Brigadier Ryan's mind.

'Christ!' he said quietly.

The Englishman nodded; there wasn't anything else to add.

Ryan shone the torch closer to the torn uniform. The grey-green colour was clear now. Something glittered on the collar, a small silver harp, an Irish harp. The young soldier was one of the men General Eoin O'Duffy had brought from Ireland to fight for Holy Spain and Holy Ireland against communism, atheism and darkness. They had come with the blessings of the Church in their ears, with rosaries and holy water, and all the saints in heaven looking down on their crusade. But the Irish Bandera had not lived up to its high ideals. O'Duffy's men, stronger on drinking, whoring and praying behind the lines than fighting, were an embarrassment even to Franco. Yet there were uneasy rumours that the fascists wanted to push their own Irish troops against the Irish Brigadistas. Despite the contempt for the Bandera on the Republican side, the Connolly Column soldiers knew there were old IRA men in their ranks, men they knew, men they fought beside against the Black and Tans, against the Free State in the Civil War.

'What's your name?'

'Private Mikey Hagan, sir.'

He saluted; he was trying to get up, shaky, still in pain.

'You need to look at my uniform, Mikey,' said Ryan.

The boy soldier frowned, not grasping what this meant.

'You're a prisoner. My name is Frank Ryan. I am a brigadier in the Fifteenth International Brigade. I'm sorry, you didn't make it back.'

The fear in Hagan's eyes was momentary. He was too tired not to feel this Irishman whose name he knew offered safety.

'I know you Mr Ryan, Brigadier Ryan. You'd know my father, Liam Hagan. He's a teacher, in Cashel. He was with you in the Galtee Mountains, in twenty-two it was, fighting the Free State. He always talks about you.'

He spoke as if they were somewhere else; a railway platform, a pub. He looked at the man whose prisoner he was with pride in the connection.

'And your father'd be pleased you're here, would he?'

'And why wouldn't he be when we're fighting God's war?'

The words were defiant. Then a deeper spasm of pain wracked Mikey Hagan, spreading from his arm into his body. He was unconscious.

'Get him into the car, Allen.'

They pulled open the back door; Armstrong shoved aside crates of wine and brandy. They pushed the Bandera private into the seat.

'The Sanidad Militar can sort him out. It's all we can do.'

'Or we could shoot him.'

'Is that supposed to be funny?'

'The Field Police will hand him to the Comisaría Política. When the party hacks have interrogated him, for sod all I'd say – they'll shoot him.'

Ryan said nothing; it was true.

'Still, all's fair,' continued the Englishman, 'and if the fascists got hold of us, well, they'd shoot us, so, quid pro quo! Buyer beware, etc.'

'We've our own men to keep alive, Allen.'

Lieutenant Armstrong looked at the young face through the car window. He looked at the night sky, conscious of the rare silence. There was no reason for what he was saying. It shouldn't matter. But there was more and more that didn't matter. It was arbitrary that this did, but it did.

'When you've just seen a dozen of your best friends die, having another man shot for no reason, even in the wrong uniform – pisses me off. That's all. It pisses me off.' He grinned. 'And you did know his father.'

'I never knew his father, for Christ's sake. What the fuck are those O'Duffy bastards doing here? It's Eoin O'Duffy who wants shooting. He doesn't give a shite about Spain, any more than the priests who sprinkled holy water over his men. All he wants is to go home a sainted hero. And there's his fucking martyr.' He looked at Mikey Hagan's unconscious face pressed against the glass. 'God, Ireland can produce some gobshites!'

'We'll pass the turn for Belchite,' said Armstrong. 'A kilometre from the Jarama. One of the Canadians said there's a doctor there. He could be patched up and pointed across the river. More chance than we can offer.'

'And what about the Republicans in Belchite?'

'He's just one of Frank Ryan's Irishmen with a bullet in his arm.'

'Fuck you, Lieutenant.'

'Thank you, sir.'

'Let's get him out of that uniform. And get a bottle of brandy.'

They opened the car door. As Mikey Hagan fell out, Ryan caught him. He started to unbutton the grey-green jacket. He turned to Armstrong.

'The brandy.'

'He's still unconscious. It'll choke him.'

'Did I say it was for him?'

The moonlight picked out the road into Belchite. There were patches of open ground and groves of olives and walnuts. Fires burned where Republican machine guns pointed towards the Nationalist lines. At the sentry posts, as Frank Ryan wound down the window and shouted out his name, they were waved through with the raised fists of the struggle. The militia men knew Brigadier Ryan. The story of Suicide Hill had swept along the line faster than Hermann Klein's propaganda truck. The thin Irishman and the men of the Fifteenth Brigade needed no papers or permits here.

In the town the battle that had pushed Belchite back and forward between the Republicans and the Nationalists all week had left its scars in the broken buildings and the pockmarked plaza. A fire, fuelled with the timber from damaged houses, burned across the square from the church, which had lost part of its white stucco façade from a shell; no one could remember which side fired it. Half a dozen Regulares sat round the fire.

As the Renault pulled into the plaza militia men were loading two dead Republican soldiers on to a cart. The bodies of three of Franco's Foreign Legionnaires stayed where they were.

Ryan and Armstrong got out. The lieutenant spoke in Spanish, addressing the sergeant of the Regulares.

'Lieutenant Armstrong, Brigadier Ryan, Fifteenth Brigade, Comrade. We've a wounded man losing blood. They said there might be a doctor.'

The sergeant smiled broadly and shook their hands.

'That was some fight, Comrades.'

They all agreed it had been some fight.

'The priest is a doctor of sorts. He's in the church.'

Armstrong pulled the Tipperary man from the car. He had drifted from unconsciousness into sleep; with waking the pain returned. He gritted his teeth, unaware of where he was. Frank Ryan's face came into focus.

'Can you understand what I'm saying, Mikey?'

'Yes, sir.'

'You're an Irish International Brigade man. Lieutenant Armstrong and I are your officers. We'll have a doctor look at you, then see if someone can get you out of the town, quietly, somewhere nearer your own lines.'

Private Hagan's head was clearer now; he could feel the danger.

'Will they shoot me, sir?'

Inside the church candles were burning. Against the walls there were wounded civilians and soldiers; three Regulares, one with a bloody, bandaged head, were playing cards. The priest was in his sixties, overweight, with a ruddy, bloated face. He was in shirtsleeves; he was stained with sweat and blood. His eyes, like soldiers all along the Jarama Valley, had the hollow gaze of a man who had not slept for many nights. He got up from where he knelt in prayer beside a dying old man.

'It's his arm, Father,' said Lieutenant Armstrong. 'I think there's still a bullet or some shrapnel in it. The bleeding did stop, but it's back . . .'

The priest took the arm gently and raised it into the light. Mikey Hagan looked into his face, and then clumsily, shaking slightly, got down on his knees in front of him. He stared up, with tears in his eyes.

'Bless me, Father.'

The priest made the sign of the cross. Hagan responded with his good arm. Frank Ryan crossed himself too. The priest looked at the International Brigade brigadier, already puzzled by something that didn't quite fit.

Brigadier Ryan and Lieutenant Armstrong sat on the steps of the church, a circle of nicotine-brown cigarette ends at the Irishman's feet. Ryan took a swig from the bottle of brandy. Across the square the Regulares were sleeping. The Brigadistas stood as the priest came out, lighting a cigarette. He looked at the plaza of his town with a weary familiarity, as if the broken buildings and the bodies had always been the view from the church steps.

'The bleeding has stopped,' he said in good English. 'But I can't do anything more for him now, Brigadier. The arm needs a surgeon to save it.'

'Thank you, Father,' said Ryan.

'And what now?' replied the priest. 'You brought him because you can't take him to your own hospital. He does know he'll probably be shot.'

'He told you who he is?'

'He's holding a rosary with a medallion on it offering a prayer for the crusade against the Red Terror. We've all heard about Franco's Irishmen.'

'I don't want to hand him over to Field Police,' said Ryan.

'So instead of being the Good Samaritan yourself, you want me to be the Good Samaritan. The Good Samaritan didn't get much thanks for it.'

'If someone can get him out of the town, towards his own lines . . .'

'Bullets and bombs from both sides have killed my people, women and children. Why should we give a damn if those bullets kill him, or you?'

'There's no reason why you should, Father.'

The priest shook his head. It was a statement that he had no choice.

'I'll do what I can to get him out of here. The best thing you can do to help is leave, now. Just drive away and they'll forget he was ever here.'

He turned without another word, back into the church.

The two officers walked towards the Renault. It was very quiet. Frank Ryan was aware he had dumped his problem on a man he didn't know. But he wanted to get the trusting face of the Bandera private out of his head. Perhaps he had known Mikey Hagan's father. He prided himself on his memory for old comrades but he had forgotten too many.

The stillness was broken as two motorcycles and a truck pulled into the square; the Comisaría Política's propaganda unit. When the truck stopped the men who jumped down from the back were communist Field Police, Brigade Commissar Hermann Klein's familiars. Klein himself stepped from the cab, short, wiry, bullet-headed, always neat in a uniform that no one else could make look anything but shapeless. He was surprised to find Frank Ryan in Belchite's plaza. He didn't much like surprises.

'Go into the church and get him away, Allen,' said Ryan quietly.

Lieutenant Armstrong walked back towards the church.

'Hardly your beat, Brigadier,' said the German commissar.

'Wrong turn. My lieutenant thought he could avoid the traffic. When I'd finished bollocking him, I thought we'd have a drink. Brigade can't give me troops tomorrow, but they did fill us up with booze. We can die happy.'

He held the brandy bottle towards Klein.

'You can leave me a bottle. I'm working now.'

Klein nodded to the Field Police. Two of them turned to the church.

'You do know how close to the river you are, Brigadier?'

'We'll find our way home, don't worry.'

'You're almost at the front. Intelligence says there are snipers.'

'I'll keep my eyes peeled then, Hermann.'

Lieutenant Armstrong strolled back out to the steps of the church, passing Klein's men on their way in. He walked down to the square.

'A beautiful evening, Commissar. Good to stop and look sometimes.'

'I didn't have you down as a church-goer, Lieutenant.'

'I was going to light candles for my dead comrades, Commissar, but there weren't enough. I'll need to find a bigger church, with more candles.'

Klein turned to Ryan. 'You know this is a fascist town?'

'Is it so? And I thought they had a pretty good spread of the dead when we drove in. Ours, theirs, and a few locals to even things out.'

Frank Ryan had no difficulty irritating Hermann Klein; taking his lieutenant's lead, it seemed a good idea to keep his attention away from what might be happening at the back of the church. But Commissar Klein had his own reason to be in Belchite. That reason was walking towards him now; the priest, with his arms held by the Field Policemen.

'Julio Costales?' said the commissar in Spanish.

'Yes, I'm Father Costales.'

'I'm glad to find you here.'

'This is my church. Where else would I be?'

'Information has come to the attention of Military Intelligence. You have provided medical assistance and comfort to renegades and fascists.'

'Soldiers have died here on both sides.'

22

'There is only one side,' said the commissar. 'When the Nationalists took the town, you gave the wounded water and the dying the last rites.'

'Isn't any man entitled to die in his faith?'

'It's not only that, Julio Costales, it's what's in your heart.'

Hermann Klein took out his pistol.

'This is mad,' shouted Ryan, 'can't a priest give the last rites?'

The commissar's pistol was pointing at Father Costales.

'Evidence proves you are a fascist sympathizer, a fascist spy.'

'What evidence is that?'

'The evidence is what you are. That's more than enough.'

Father Costales knew what was coming now; if he had not expected it he had, in the space of only a few seconds, accepted it.

'You won't do this,' said Frank Ryan.

'Get back to your battalion, Brigadier. You have no authority here.'

The Irishman pulled his own revolver out and pointed it at Klein.

'Frank, you can't!' said Allen Armstrong.

Hermann Klein looked round at the communist militia men standing behind him. Three rifles were already trained on Ryan and Armstrong.

'You don't need to do this, Brigadier Ryan.' The voice was the priest's. 'If there was a point I might encourage you. One more death will do for today.'

Suddenly the sergeant of the Regulares walked forward, smashing the butt of his rifle against Frank Ryan's wrist. The revolver fell to the ground. The sergeant picked it up, giving the Irishman an apologetic shrug.

Hermann Klein turned back to the priest and fired three rapid shots.

On Suicide Hill, Brigadier Ryan and Lieutenant Armstrong looked into the darkness of the Jarama Valley and drank a second bottle of brandy. Ryan was burying his anger in what the next day would bring. With the dawn his men would fight and die for Spain and freedom again. Hermann Klein didn't change that. He had seen enough innocent men die in Ireland to know the smell; nothing would ever quite get it out of his nostrils. He couldn't even say the commissar wasn't right, that Father Costales hadn't spied, hadn't collaborated. He was a believer too, but there were few priests, in Spain or Ireland, who wouldn't tell him he was fighting for the Antichrist and that Franco and his fascists were the saviours of civilization and faith. There was no room for the emotion he had shown. No one who had fought and killed as he had could be unaware that war was ugly and arbitrary, however just the cause. By the time the brandy was drunk he had put away his anger.

It was Lieutenant Armstrong whose doubts were not so easily buried, doubts about what had just happened, about what happened everywhere the Communist Party tightened its grip on any hint of heresy. But by afternoon Allen Armstrong's doubts would be laid to rest too, along with the little that Frank Ryan could find of his friend, after a fascist mortar landed on the stretcher party he was leading back into the olive groves of Suicide Hill.

Later that day, standing over a shallow grave, Frank Ryan reached into his pocket for tobacco. His fingers touched metal. It was the Irish harp from Mikey Hagan's Bandera uniform. It was likely the young Irishman was dead now too. He looked at the harp almost fondly, then dropped it into the earth of the Jarama Valley as it was shovelled over Allen Armstrong.

3

Crane Lane

Dublin, December 1939

Four days before Christmas, Dame Street was busy and aglow in the seven o'clock evening; the shops were still open even by Dublin Castle. The lights were bigger and brighter at the Trinity College end, where the shops were bigger and brighter too, bustling into Grafton Street and over the bridge to O'Connell Street; but just past the Palace Street entrance to the Castle the tree by the pillared portico of the City Hall blazed with 200 bulbs. Detective Inspector Stefan Gillespie glanced at it, as he did most nights, walking into Palace Street from the side gate to Dublin Castle.

He crossed Dame Street to the Olympia Theatre, where a line of people queued for the evening performance of *Cinderella*. The theatre too was full of light, with coloured bulbs strung along its flat front. There were always a lot of lights in Dublin at Christmas, but as he walked out of the Castle night after night he had felt there were more than usual. There was a kind of gaudy determination about all that brightness. It wasn't far across the Irish Sea, across the whole of Britain, and on across Europe itself, that there were no Christmas lights at all, because darkness was safer, because a city of lights, any city, could only be a shining target for the bombers. The lights of Dublin didn't

lend much in the way of Christmas spirit to Stefan Gillespie
now; not that he was indifferent to it, but all that brightness had
the effect of reminding him of what he was doing rather than
helping him forget it. In a city where people were uncomfortable
talking publicly about the war Ireland wasn't a part of, there
were aspects of that war that were his daily preoccupation. He
was far from easy with what that meant.

He turned off Dame Street into Crane Lane; the noise and
colour of Christmas stopped immediately. The narrow alley
down to Essex Street and the river was ill-lit because there was
little to light. He walked on to the black, boarded windows of
Farrelly's Bar at the end of the lane and went in.

The pub was packed with shop workers and Dublin Castle
civil servants and, as always, a group of Special Branch
detectives from the Castle's Police Yard. Farrelly's made few
concessions to Christmas; two strings of ancient paper chains
above the altar of gleaming spirit bottles behind the bar. The
lights were low; the bar and what there was of furniture were
dark; the floorboards were bare and black; the ceiling might
have been white once, but in living memory it had only been
a marbled tobacco-brown; there was a haze of smoke. Stefan
nodded to his Special Branch colleagues. They grinned, not
expecting him to sit down for a drink.

Stefan had joined the Special Branch as a detective three
months earlier, after two years back in uniform at home in
Baltinglass, not because he wanted to, but because Detective
Superintendent Terry Gregory, head of the Branch, decided he
needed him. He still felt an outsider, partly because he made
it his business to be; he didn't like where he was and made no
secret of it. At the same time the Special Branch officers in the
Police Yard were a close-knit bunch, suspicious of anyone who
didn't share their background and their history. There was no
real hostility towards him, but if he didn't really know why he
was there, they didn't either. They weren't easy with that, and

if nobody particularly disliked him nobody much liked him either.

He pushed his way to the bar and ordered a bottle of Guinness. He took out a cigarette and lit it with a taper from the gas flame on the bar, for the reason he always took out a cigarette; something to do. He fixed his eyes on the middle distance, between the gas flame and the glinting shelves of spirits. For ten minutes the noise of the bar was only a rumbling irritant to the anger that was too close to the front of his mind to be pushed out. Then he saw Gregory; the round, always flushed face with the wry smile that never changed, whatever his mood. It was a soft face that still spoke of a lazy mind to Stefan, even though he knew the truth was very different.

'We'll talk in the snug, Inspector.'

Farrelly's snug was no more than the end of the bar partitioned off by a wooden wall. A few feet of the bar took up one corner; there was space for a table, a bench and a couple of chairs. As well as the door from the bar there was another into the backyard and Essex Street. The snug was the property of Special Branch, open to Superintendent Gregory and his men day or night. Everyone who used the pub knew it; no one else went in there. It was access to the bustle of Temple Bar and the Quays, without going through the pub, that made it a place to meet those who didn't want to be seen with Special Branch officers. It was a conduit between the streets of the city and the Police Yard at Dublin Castle, and had been since the Special Branch men were British. Informers were still paid or blackmailed here, according to the particular circumstances, as they always had been.

Terry Gregory sat on the bench. Stefan pulled up a chair. Dermot Farrelly appeared and set down a bottle of Powers and two glasses. Gregory poured two whiskies; he pushed one towards Stefan, then drained his own.

'You're a pain the arse, Gillespie, you know that?'

'I have been working on it, sir.'

'You think if you tell me to fuck myself, and walk out of my office one more time, I'll kick you out? Not much of a plan for a clever feller.'

'I thought of trying something subtler. I wasn't sure you'd notice.'

'You work for me. That's all you're there for, all any of you are there for. You don't stop working for me till I decide I don't need you anymore.'

'What do you need me for at all?' Stefan's question was real.

'A clever feller like you? Why wouldn't I need you, Inspector?'

'I'm the best German speaker you have. I know a lot about what's going on in Germany and how they read Ireland. The men you've got watching the German community, the embassy, people who might be in touch with German agents, who might be German agents – they don't speak German, and most of them think the Nazis aren't such bad lads anyway—'

'We're a neutral country,' laughed Gregory, 'there are no bad lads.'

Stefan hadn't touched the whiskey; he drank it down now.

'You'd like to do all that then, would you, Gillespie?'

'Look, everyone knows men are leaving the country to join the British forces, thousands of them, and there'll be thousands more. What's the point listing them? Why worry if some feller says he's taken the boat for a job in England and joins the army? What's anybody going to do? I'm scrabbling about questioning friends, families, wives, girlfriends – why?'

'Because you're right, it's getting out of hand. A lot of people would call these men traitors. Is joining the British Army something any decent Irishman should be doing at any time, let alone when we could be facing a British invasion? That's not impossible. You know what's at stake for the English. If they've got their backs to the wall, which looks likely enough . . .'

Terry Gregory's voice had become more serious, but the smile didn't shift. Stefan felt the words were merely repeating other people's words, official words. The superintendent stopped, maybe unimpressed himself.

'Presumably you can recognize the seriousness of it when soldiers leave our own army, Guards leave the Gardaí. The word there is desertion.'

'If it's impossible for them to resign—'

'Bollocks! You know the expression – there's a fucking war on, isn't there? The fact that we're not fighting it doesn't mean we won't be. I don't know if anyone's coming after us. If they do it could be the English or the Germans. Say it's the Germans. Who's going to stop them if our army's gone AWOL to help out across the water – and all that's left is the IRA?'

'If the English can't stop them, I don't think we will, sir.'

Terry Gregory grinned. He refilled the glasses.

'I will take some shite in your reports, Gillespie, but don't push it.'

'Don't push what?'

'I don't blame Dessie MacMahon. I took him on as your sergeant because I thought he'd tell me what you were doing. A rare error of judgement. It doesn't matter. But I do have details of three Guards you didn't pass on information about, one now in the Lancashire Fusiliers, one in the Royal Artillery and one a gunner on HMS *Achilles*. Three Guards you worked with. Three deserters you didn't add to your last report.'

Stefan shrugged. 'If I'm not up to the job—'

'That's not a plan either, so don't bother. I'll take so much, but if it gets out of hand you won't be transferred, you'll be out on your arse.'

'It's not what I want, sir . . .' Stefan left a 'but' hovering.

'I don't know what you are yet, Inspector, but if you're not a Guard, I'm not sure you know what you are yourself. You won't be walking out.'

For just a moment the smile on the superintendent's lips disappeared. So far Stefan felt, as he always did, that words were being batted back and forward that didn't really say what Gregory meant, what he knew, what he wanted. With the last words there was, briefly, none of the deceptive softness in his face. He was saying something Stefan had never consciously thought, but something that somewhere he knew was true, or almost true.

'I can live with some selectiveness in what you give me, Gillespie. We all hold things back in this job, for all sorts of reasons. Usually it's self-preservation, but if you've got reasons you think are noble, what do I care? You're good at what you're doing. None of the other arseholes could give me half what you put together. Why? Because you know these people. You sympathize with them. I have no shortage of men who sympathize with the IRA. That's why they follow Republicans and you don't. You couldn't do it as well. They don't need a guide book, just their noses. Horses for courses.'

'And a test into the bargain,' said Stefan, watching his boss.

'What does that mean?'

'The dirtier we get our hands, the more you can rely on us.'

'You'll make a Special Branch officer yet, Inspector. But horses for courses doesn't mean I'm a one-trick pony. The less anyone knows about what goes on in my mind, the better I do my job. And that's what dear old Ireland needs from you, son, a job, not beliefs, not principles. You'll do what you're told. You're here for as long as all this shite lasts. Like me.'

The superintendent's voice was hard and flat. Stefan could almost believe these words expressed something that mattered. But he wouldn't have been surprised by a wink after 'Like me'. Gregory pushed the bottle across the table and stood up. He walked to the door, then he turned back.

'If you're wondering about the lists . . .'

Stefan had forgotten where the conversation had started.

'Our brave Irish boys in the British forces.'

Stefan nodded and looked at his boss.

'One day they'll be coming back. And God help them then.'

Gregory had made his point; he wasn't going to give Stefan any space to believe that his hands would be anything other than dirty, dirtier than he had told himself they were already. He sat for a moment feeling more a part of Special Branch than he had since arriving at Dublin Castle. He had a sense that the dirtier his hands got the more he would belong. He poured himself a glass of whiskey; he knew he would finish the bottle.

At the top of Crane Lane, in the now quiet night, Stefan stopped. It was gone midnight and Dublin was not a city that went late to bed. Whiskey was always a mistake. He needed something to clear the sourness out of his head, the sourness of the drink and what Terry Gregory had left behind. He needed to talk to Kate. She wouldn't be long home from the Gate Theatre now, at her parents' in Dún Laoghaire. Her parents didn't like him phoning late at night, but there wasn't much they liked about him anyway. The O'Donnells accepted he and their daughter were lovers in the way they accepted the war; they called it by another name and assumed that if they kept quiet it would go away. He had made considerable efforts to get on with Kate's mother and father, but they had not got past stiff politeness. Not waking the house up with a phone call at half-past midnight, after Kate got home, was normally an element in the protocol of strained coexistence, but the best part of a bottle of Powers wasn't much of a recipe for politeness.

The Special Branch offices were across the street along with a telephone. Kate would know he was the worse for drink. It would piss her off; it changed his personality in a way he didn't like himself. But he needed to hear her voice. He needed some of her light back in his head.

He crossed Dame Street and walked into the Castle through the Palace Street Gate. A stifled yawn hailed him as he passed the sentry box.

'Something on, Inspector?'

Garda Aidan Fogarty clasped a mug of tea.

'Not when I left Farrelly's, Aidan.'

'You should've brought me over one, sir!'

Stefan walked down the dark, cobbled street to the arch into the Police Yard. There was a light in the yard but as he headed to the Special Branch offices he was surprised to see a light inside. It didn't matter; at least not until he passed the doors of the garage and saw the black bonnet of a big Humber. It was Superintendent Gregory's car. That was what Fogarty meant. The last thing he wanted was another conversation with his boss. He was about to turn back when the light in the office went off. The door opened. He slipped into the shadows of another doorway, feeling foolish and knowing he would feel more foolish if Gregory saw him hiding.

He heard Terry Gregory's voice as the superintendent moved across the yard to his car; there was another man with him. Stefan didn't know the voice. The two spoke quietly, but their words were clear enough in the enclosed space.

'Three to four hours. Don't bank on any more,' said Gregory.

'It'll be plenty,' replied the other man.

'My men'll be half strength, less, and it'll be the same in every Garda station in the city. The culchees are already heading down the country for Christmas, and you can split what's left between the ones who'll be at home putting up the lights and the poor buggers on duty who'll be on the piss.'

The other man laughed.

'Four hours includes getting away, Cathal,' Gregory continued.

'We can shift a lot of ammunition in that time.'

Stefan was sober. Standing in the shadows seemed less foolish.

There was silence; feet on the cobbles, the car door opening. The engine started. Headlights blazed as Gregory drove the car out into the yard. Stefan saw the other man in the lights. He recognized him immediately, though he had never met him; his photograph was in the detectives' room. He was a man who had no place inside the Special Branch building, except for interrogation. He had no place having a whispered heart to heart with Detective Superintendent Gregory in the Police Yard. Cathal McCallister was a senior IRA man; the organization's Quartermaster, responsible for arms, ammunition, explosives, everything the IRA used in its struggle against Britain, in the North and across the water, and against the government of Ireland too.

The black Humber stopped. Gregory got out and opened one of the rear doors. Cathal McCallister walked to the car.

'Don't push your luck,' said Gregory, 'just get out with what you can. Whatever else, I don't want any shooting. I don't want anyone killed.'

'You're the boss,' said the IRA Quartermaster, laughing.

He got into the car and stretched across the back seat. Gregory threw a coat over him and shut the door. He got back in himself and lit a cigarette. Stefan could see his face before the interior light went out. There was no smile.

Stefan Gillespie waited until he could no longer hear the Humber's engine. He wanted Terry Gregory gone. Kate O'Donnell was not in his mind now. He had forgotten why he was there. He wanted to forget what he had heard too. He didn't know what it meant. It was dangerous information; it was dangerous he had it and more dangerous if anyone knew. If the head of Special Branch was working with the IRA who was there to trust? The price for knowing too much was a high one where the IRA was concerned. He came out of the shadows. At the Palace Street Gate Aidan Fogarty shouted something he didn't hear; he didn't even see him. Dublin was very still as he walked down Parliament Street to the bridge, along Wellington Quay to his rooms over Paddy Geary's tobacconist's. He should have left Terry Gregory's bottle of Powers alone. Whiskey was always a mistake.

4

Roly Poly

The next day was almost like every other day. Stefan Gillespie and Dessie MacMahon took a list of names from two government departments; men who had left civil service jobs and were suspected of joining the British Army. They also picked up a list of missing soldiers from the Military Police at Collins Barracks; these were deserters and as much information as possible was required. For the most part there was no doubt where the men were; they had told friends and families. Sometimes the tale was that the men had gone to look for work in England. But if facts weren't forthcoming from tight-lipped relatives, rumour and begrudgery often offered more. So did the Post Office Censorship Office where letters to and from Britain were opened and read. Stefan and Dessie spent two hours there. They drew a clear line under two men; letters from the War Office in London told the next of kin that they had been killed in action. It wasn't possible to chase up every man who had disappeared across the water and might or might not be in uniform, there were far too many, but civil servants mattered; they were employees of the state. And military personnel mattered above all; the Irish Army was haemorrhaging soldiers at the rate of hundreds every month.

By six o'clock the two detectives were putting together their work. Stefan had said little that wasn't about the job in hand; there were none of the gripes and complaints that got them through the day. Dessie knew there had been a set-to with the boss the night before, but the two men had known each other a long time. If something needed saying, it would be said.

'Get in here, Gillespie!'

Terry Gregory bellowed across the detectives' room.

Stefan got up and walked to the glass-partitioned office. He had no reason to think Gregory knew anything, but somehow he half-expected it.

'Tell me about this play.'

Stefan had no idea what he was talking about.

'At the Gate, *Roly Poly*, is that it?'

'Er, yes, sir.'

'Your other half's working there?'

'She's got a part-time job in the design—'

'You've seen it?'

'I was at the opening night, sir.'

'Very nice too. Enjoy it?'

'Yes.'

'Herr Hempel, the German ambassador, didn't.'

'Yes, sir, I've read the papers.'

'So what's this play about?'

'Well, it's based on a French story—'

'Just tell me what happens.'

'There's a war on. Some civilians from one side are trying to get through enemy lines to safety. They're stopped by an army officer who won't let them go, because of a woman he wants to sleep with. That's it.'

'Not *Cinderella* at the Olympia, but still a fucking pantomime.'

Stefan didn't know why they were discussing this.

'Is there a whore in it?'

'The woman is a prostitute.'

35

'The guardians of our morality are troubled by that, in Leinster House, the Ministry of Justice, even, I am informed, our beloved Prime Minister Mr de Valera. Dev is unconvinced what Mac Liammóir and Edwards are up to at the end of O'Connell Street is suitable for a nation that gets overheated dancing at the crossroads. So the lads need to take it off.'

'It's only been on three days!'

'You'll be at the Gate tonight. The last night. I want to know who's there, who says what. And if Mac Liammóir does what he's supposed to.'

It was the last thing Stefan wanted to do.

'I know people there, starting with Mr Mac Liammóir. With Kate—'

'Horses for courses. You'll remember that. Anyway, you scrub up better than the rest, and what would be the point me sending some gobshite detective who couldn't even be identified as a Special Branch man so?'

'But what does it matter, if it's coming off anyway?'

'Details always matter. There's never anything you don't need to know. That's all the job is. There are things it's not helpful to know, things it's not even wise to know, but you can't tell in advance. Instinct tells you what to jettison, what to forget. I think you're a man with good instincts.'

The last words were delivered with Superintendent Gregory's smile at its wryest. Stefan didn't know what that told him. He didn't know if it was a coda on the conversation in Farrelly's, whether it was amusement at sending him to do something else he didn't want to do, or whether Terry Gregory did know something about his presence in the Lower Castle Yard. They could have been idle words to wind him up, or maybe a warning.

36

For the second time in four days Stefan watched the army officer walk into the hotel foyer and regard the group of travellers with disdain. The officer was prepared to treat enemy civilians with courtesy, but the idea that they were innocent bystanders was an indulgence. He knew these travellers for what they were: rats. Yet he had made a mistake. He should have let the party go on its way. Instead he saw the woman. She was not a rat. He assumed he could have her, given the profession she clearly pursued. But she refused. He might have ignored it but as he realized why, he couldn't. Where the other travellers eyed him timidly, apologetically, she looked him in the face and told him he could force her, if that was the man he was, but she would not dishonour her country by sleeping with him. They all knew; his own men knew. He had lost face. It was as if his country had lost face, too, to a whore. The travellers had applauded her patriotism, but they were still rats. Once they realized the officer would only let them leave if the woman came to his bed, the applause would stop. He sensed their mood changing. Roly Poly was turning from heroine to whore again. What she refused for her country's sake her compatriots would soon insist she did for theirs. The officer need do nothing; the rats would do it all.

It was at this point, minutes before the end of the first act, that three men, a few rows back from the stage, stood up and pushed past other theatregoers, forcing them to stand too. The soldier stopped in mid-speech; other actors looked out to the auditorium. There was tutting and grunting. One of the men walking out looked at the audience around him and said, 'This is a disgrace.' His voice was accented; to make his point more forcefully he repeated himself in German, 'Das ist eine Schande.' In the lapel of his suit, better cut than any Irish suit there that evening, he wore a small circular buttonhole, red and black; the swastika of the Nazi Party.

The words 'disgrace' and 'shame' were thrown back at the departing figures, one of them the stiff-faced German ambassador to Ireland, Eduard Hempel. By now the soldier on stage had resumed intimidating the travellers as Roly Poly herself came on. She stopped, looking at the fellow countrymen who had so recently approved her patriotic virtue but were now watching her with the beginning of something like indignation. They turned away, all of them. Then there was loud applause. And the lights went up.

Stefan stood against the wall to one side of the bar. It was a small, crowded space, like everywhere at the Gate, stage and backstage, theatre and front of house. Faded wallpaper and muddy paint gave the feel of a Victorian drawing room that had seen better days, but the intimacy that lent the theatre its uniqueness had no appeal to him. When the interval came he wanted to go out to Cavendish Row for a cigarette, but he had a job to do, pointless as it was; watch and report. He was the only Special Branch officer known at the Gate. Even the barman who poured his Guinness knew him. The report of what happened, who said what, who did what, was incidental. He was intimidation, to remind the Gate's director, Micheál Mac Liammóir, that the play had to come off; if the theatre did not do what was unofficially demanded, there would be some very official consequences.

Stefan knew he would be challenged soon enough. The best he could hope for was getting out of the Gate before he encountered Kate O'Donnell.

The conversation in the bar wasn't about the play, but about Herr Hempel and his entourage, and everything that went with it, including the displeasure of Éamon de Valera and the Irish government. In the war now overtaking Europe, Ireland's neutrality was above all about appearances, both for the ever-watchful, ever-threatening belligerents and the people of Ireland. The Gate wasn't keeping up appearances by putting on a play about war, let alone a war in which people didn't behave

38

well. It wasn't what the German ambassador expected from Ireland, or what Berlin expected either.

'Ah, dear boy, what a surprise! Good to see you again so soon!'

Inevitably it was Micheál Mac Liammóir Stefan saw walking towards him, smiling more than he usually smiled. It was a smile cold enough to tell him the director's surprise was feigned. When Mac Liammóir was angry his voice became softer and quieter; his carefully enunciated words became ever more precise; the charm that was his stock-in-trade only increased with the contempt it could, when required, so effortlessly express. Stefan Gillespie did not know Mac Liammóir well, but he had seen that contempt directed at others; he was well aware it was now directed at him.

'So impressed by the first night that you had to come again. First as a guest, now as a secret policeman, a spy? I'm not sure of the word, but given the times that are in it, what more could we ask for? With all the excitement I feel the action has spilled out into the audience, even into the bar at the interval. I dare anyone to say we're not thoroughly experimental!'

'It's not my choice to be here, sir.'

It sounded as feeble to Stefan as he knew it did to the director.

'So are you here to shut us up, Inspector, or shut us down?'

Mac Liammóir's voice was louder; people were looking, listening. But that shift from private to public anger was a relief. It gave Stefan room to exchange awkwardness and embarrassment for something like irritation.

'As I understand it, shutting up will suffice,' he said quietly.

The artificial smile on Micheál Mac Liammóir's lips didn't relax but there was, for a moment, a glint in his eye, and Stefan knew that if he hadn't started to gather an audience, he might just have laughed.

'They were right to send you, Stefan. You play your role well. The reluctant secret policeman. Tragical-comical verging on tragical-farcical, but I'm afraid the comic performance of the evening has to go to dear Herr Hempel. None of that means I'm not pissed off in the extreme, but not so pissed off I want to see the Gate closed down. Of course, I will have to make some show of it. The play's the thing. I'm sure you won't mind.'

Stefan didn't know what the last words meant, but Mac Liammóir's anger had subsided. It had been easier than he had expected. He had forgotten that a few harsh words from the Gate's director were the least of his problems. But as the interval bell sounded and Mac Liammóir turned away with a shrug of acceptance, his next words brought reality home.

'Kate darling, you didn't say your feller was so wild about the play!'

He didn't know how long she had been there, but there was no smile on her face, feigned or otherwise. By now everyone at the Gate must know he was there to supervise the demise of *Roly Poly*. No one else would give the wry absolution of Mac Liammóir's near laugh, including Kate.

'Why you?'

'You'll have to ask Superintendent Gregory.'

'Do you think it's funny, Stefan?'

They looked at each other for a long moment. The bar was empty now, except for the barman, watching them as he slowly collected glasses.

'I've got friends here now. And I hoped I'd keep this job.'

'Nobody's going to take it out on you, Kate.'

'You think the conversations won't stop every time I walk in . . .'

He looked past her. The auditorium doors were closing.

'I have to go back in . . .'

'What happened to telling Gregory to stick his job?'

'It's not that easy . . .'

'You'll probably need a few more drinks first. I don't know

why you keep telling me you don't fit in as an informer. You seem to fit perfectly!'

The play concluded with thunderous and sustained applause. The news that this was the last time the curtain would fall on *Roly Poly*, after only four performances, had spread. Detective Inspector Gillespie stood and applauded with everyone else. The applause only died down as Micheál Mac Liammóir came on stage, in front of the cast, waiting for silence.

'Tomorrow you will hear that Hilton and I have reluctantly taken off our play for the sake of Ireland's soul. It seems the character we call Roly Poly is a danger to it, by virtue of her unvirtuous profession. I am not sure which of her sins is most damning, the fact that she is a prostitute or that a prostitute is the play's only virtuous character. Of course, none of this matters, because the reason the play is coming off has nothing to do with morality, as the presence of a guest from Garda Special Branch testifies.'

Stefan knew now what 'I'm sure you won't mind' meant. The lights were up and he was on the receiving end of laughter, glaring looks of disapproval, and hissed and whispered explanations of who he was.

'To talk about the real reason might see me incarcerated in Dublin Castle under the Emergency Powers Act, and my liberty is precious, almost as precious as the money the Gate is about to lose for the sake of the nation. If by chance the issue of neutrality enters your minds, not apropos of these events you understand, I believe passionately it is the only way for Ireland in the face of this war. But does neutrality mean we have decided there is no pain, no disease, no pleasure, no health, no desire, no war, no song, no women, and very little wine? Will we live in a waiting room for passengers to heaven, airless, claustrophobic, where we sit self-centred, refusing all news, all ideas, all perilous things from the outside world, denying freedom to protect freedom? If even the light in our head offends, is our only course to sit in the dark? But God forbid it has anything to do with *Roly Poly!*'

Stefan Gillespie stood outside the Gate Theatre. The audience was moving away, still full of the evening's events rather than the play itself. It was bitterly cold. There were flakes of snow in the air. Stefan had his collar pulled up and his hat pulled down, but it was more about the attention that had been drawn to him inside than about the weather. There were only a few stragglers coming out as Kate O'Donnell appeared. She looked at him, shaking her head. It wasn't about him; she knew that, but it still hurt.

'Everyone's very upset and very angry.'

'I'm sure they are.'

'You'll be writing a report about us all.'

'Hardly a report,' he laughed, 'it'll only be what's in the papers.'

It wasn't true; the papers wouldn't mention the German ambassador or what Micheál Mac Liammóir had said. Stefan was conscious not only that there were things he didn't tell Kate now, but that he was starting to learn to tell her lies as if they were simply their normal conversation.

'Most people are going for a drink,' she said.

'I wouldn't blame them,' said Stefan, smiling.

She took his arm and pulled herself against him. He kissed her.

'Go and have that drink with your friends.'

'I won't stay long. And I'll come back to Wellington Quay.'

'Yes, I think we both need that,' said Stefan.

A black Austin 10 pulled up. Dessie MacMahon got out. For a man who had made a career out of never being flustered, he looked flustered.

'The boss's called everyone in.'

'What's wrong?'

Dessie hesitated. He wasn't going to say it with Kate there.

'He's all yours, Dessie.' She kissed Stefan and walked away.

Dessie got back into the car; Stefan sat in beside him.

'So where are we going?'

'The Phoenix Park.' Dessie took out a Sweet Afton and lit it as he drove. 'The IRA raided the Magazine Fort tonight. Explosives, weapons, ammo. They got a dozen lorries in and out before the alarm was raised.'

Stefan nodded. As he looked through the windscreen snow was starting to fall quite heavily. Dessie talked and chain-smoked. Stefan said very little. At one point Dessie turned round, lighting another cigarette.

'You don't sound very surprised!'

He hadn't been surprised since Dessie's first words. He now knew what Terry Gregory and Cathal McCallister had been talking about in the Police Yard. He was on his way to investigate an IRA raid the head of Special Branch was instrumental in planning. It was possible his boss knew he knew that. The parting words in Gregory's office seemed suddenly bigger.

5

The Magazine Fort

As the black Austin pulled out of Capel Street and along the Quays, the snow was already lighter. The streets were muffled in that clear, clean silence that even a dusting of snow brings to a city at night.

The black and white stillness was broken as they approached the gates of the Phoenix Park. The four pillars that marked the main road through the 400 acres of grass and water and woodland were blocked on one side by a military Bedford truck and a police car. Next to the lodge a Rolls-Royce armoured car closed one gate so that anything coming in or going out had to go round it. A dozen soldiers stood with rifles slung on their backs. There was a huddle of uniformed Gardaí. Dessie steered round the armoured car. The Guards moved forward. Stefan wound down the window, but they had been recognized already. The uniformed sergeant grinned at them; someone else's mess was always entertaining.

'Here to see the stable door's properly shut, Inspector?'

'Something like that.' Stefan's enjoyment didn't come so easily.

'Can't be much to see. They cleared the place out. Still, there's dozens of your lot up there, along with assorted military brass.

They don't stop, the army fellers. In and out. You can't blame them. There is a sweep of the Park, though. They think there's a couple of IRA men left behind.'

The Guards stepped back and Dessie drove on.

'This is going to be a fucking waste of time.'

'Yes, it probably is,' said Stefan quietly.

The scattering of snow gave the Park a kind of luminosity, spreading undisturbed across the swathes of open grass. The obelisk of the Wellington Monument rose up out of the whiteness into the grey sky. As they approached the roundabout into Wellington Road there were soldiers ahead, walking in a line away from the unseen Magazine Fort, rifles unslung, some with torches. A Military Policeman waited by the roundabout, watching.

'Jesus, if we keep going we'll see the Marx Brothers next.'

Dessie was getting his money's worth out of this cock-up.

'Give the fags a rest, Dessie, for God's sake!'

'You're back with us then, Stevie?'

Dessie glanced round, still grinning, then slammed his foot on the brake. Across the windscreen shot the shovel-shaped antlers and mottled flanks of a fallow deer buck. They missed it by inches. Two smaller bucks, in a blur of speed, followed close beside. The car kept going, skidding across the road in the slush that had been churned up along the road to the Magazine Fort. It slid on to the grass, narrowly missing the trunk of a tree.

'Mother of God! They came out of nowhere!'

'Too busy lighting up to see where you're going, Dessie?'

Stefan looked back towards the Wellington Monument. He could see the white rumps of the bucks, disembodied in the darkness, still racing hard.

Dessie turned the key. The engine turned over once then stopped.

'I'll need the handle. This one's a bastard when it stalls.'

'Turn off the lights.'

'Eh?'

'Turn them off.'

Dessie switched off the headlamps. Stefan wound down the window.

'Not much sends deer running like that at night,' said Stefan. 'People, that's all they're afraid of. But they're used to people here. And they'd have been bedded down. Someone's stumbled right on to them.'

'The army's all over the place. They might not frighten the IRA much, but I'd say they could just scare the shite out of a bunch of deer.'

'You in a hurry to see Terry Gregory, Sergeant?'

'I'm in a hurry to get home.'

'Let's give it a couple of minutes.'

They sat in the darkness. The occasional snort from Sergeant MacMahon told what he thought of the exercise. But he was the one who saw the movement first. He touched Stefan's arm. Where Wellington Road turned up towards the Magazine Fort there was a patch of trees, thick from the pines that were scattered in among the leafless beeches and sycamores.

It was the snow at the edge of the thicket that showed up a man walking slowly towards the road. He stopped, looking up and down. The black Austin, hidden by the tree, was not in his line of sight. Two more men emerged behind him. They all crossed the road, heading for some more trees and the wall of the Park that ran along Conyngham Road. Stefan opened the glove compartment; he took out the Webley. As Dessie opened his door, Stefan methodically broke the revolver and checked the cylinder.

They looked across at the thicket the three men had entered. Beyond it lay a patch of tussocky grass and a sprawl of bushes abutting the Park's stone wall. That's where they would climb over. He handed Dessie the gun.

46

'I'll do the beating, you do the picking up.'

Dessie set off, almost noiselessly, at a pace that would have surprised anyone taking only a cursory glance at his size. Over the years he had surprised many people, a considerable number of them still in Irish prisons.

Stefan moved over the snow-covered grass more slowly. He took a silver police whistle from his pocket. He could hear the light crunch of his own footsteps on snow. There was the rumble of heavy vehicles on the Conyngham Road, army trucks from the barracks at Islandbridge. He turned his head back into the Park; there was a shout and an indistinct reply from the hill that hid the Magazine Fort; a sweep of lights showed a vehicle turning on to Wellington Road. He stopped as he reached the trees. Behind him the car passed, heading to the main gate. Then it slowed; he heard car doors, voices. They had seen the Austin 10. Now he heard movement among the trees. He put the whistle to his mouth and blew three blasts.

Bodies crashed through the undergrowth as the IRA men ran for the wall. Stefan walked at an even pace behind them, blowing rhythmically. As he came out of the trees he saw them, stumbling through the scrub and bushes. One tripped and fell. Two kept going; they were almost at the wall.

A shot rang out. The men stopped, unsure where it had come from. The whistle still sounded behind them. There were voices, coming closer, and torches as the soldiers from the car moved in. The fugitives made one more run; they were only yards from the wall. Another shot was fired in the air, but in their direction. They halted. Dessie MacMahon was in front of them, crouching behind a pile of cut timber, but they could see him now.

'I'm waiting for you lads!'

One of the men pulled a pistol from his pocket.

'Now is that a good idea with Christmas coming?'

Dessie blocked the men's way to the wall. They could see

Stefan behind them. And there were three soldiers running across the clearing towards them too. The IRA man dropped the gun.

On the ground in front of Stefan Gillespie was the third man, crawling forward, in pain; a twisted ankle, maybe a break.

'Get up!'

The man stopped; he didn't turn his head. He was shaking; there was a choking noise, a sob he wanted to hide. Stefan squatted down beside him.

'I said get up!'

He saw the face of a boy who was no more than fifteen years old.

'Don't shoot, mister. Mother of God, you won't kill me, will you?'

The Magazine Fort sat on a low rise to the south-east of the Phoenix Park, hidden from Islandbridge and the Liffey by a belt of woodland. It had been built in 1735 by the Lord Lieutenant of Ireland to store gunpowder. The slope up to the fort was an artificial glacis constructed to protect the walls from artillery and keep attackers under the defenders' fire. The grey-rendered walls were thick and clumsy, fronting the wide ditch that enclosed them, barely visible until you reached them; all that stood out, rising from the hillside, were the tall chimneys of the barrack blocks. Inside, the fort was a small courtyard of stone and brick buildings, and beyond that the cavernous underground stores that were the magazine. It had never been clear what it guarded; its storerooms had rarely held explosives. Its defences had never been put to the test; no shot had been fired at them in anger. Even when it was built it had been looked on as a kind of absurdity. Jonathan Swift watched its construction and saw a demonstration of the special folly that characterized Irish affairs in general and Irish military matters in particular. The British had gone; not much else had changed.

It was occupied on Easter Monday, 1916, when Republican Volunteers and Boy Scouts approached the sentry outside, kicking a football back and forth between them. Only when they reached the entrance did they produce a revolver. They walked through the otherwise unguarded gates and took the fort before anyone could pick up a rifle. The aim was to blow up the magazines as a spectacular beginning to the Easter Rising and a signal for an insurrection that had already been cancelled, but the storerooms contained no high explosives and barely any ammunition. Twenty-three years on, faced with the Magazine Fort's impregnable walls, the IRA had successfully re-run the same plan.

Superintendent Gregory sat on an upturned ammunition box in the artificial hill that was the business-end of the Magazine Fort. The lights that hung from the barrel-arched ceiling shone brightly, though not so brightly as to illuminate every dark corner of the great empty space beneath. And empty it was. Of the hundreds of wooden crates and ammunition boxes that had been stacked in the magazine only a few remained. A score or so of rifles, brand new and still heavily greased, lay on the ground; there were odd heaps of spilled cartridges. Two long-faced quartermaster sergeants turned sheets of paper on clipboards, still totting up what had been taken.

Terry Gregory's wry smile was especially broad. He looked at the two older IRA men in front of him with satisfaction. Behind them were Stefan Gillespie, Dessie MacMahon and two other Special Branch men.

'Did they forget you then, Anto?'

The man he spoke to didn't answer. He turned to the other man.

'And Gerry Rowe. Must be three, four years. I heard you

49

were in England. Leeds was it? You're probably better out of that. I'm surprised they didn't get you. Haven't they picked most of the Boys up over there?'

'You'd be the one to know. You'll have enough friends there.'

'Whatever kind of pig's arse you made of it across the water, it's some job tonight. A dozen lorries, right? In and out and away before anyone noticed. And they say there's no Santy. You'll all believe in him now, even if he has changed that old red and white yoke for an Irish Army uniform.'

Gerry Rowe did smile now.

'That's the trouble with us, Gerry. Give us a fecking magazine fort and we put stuff in it. It's asking for trouble. The English had better sense.'

He turned to the fifteen year old, holding on to the man called Anto.

'I was going to say that at least the army didn't have to suffer the indignity of having the Boy Scouts unleashed on them. No such luck.'

'He's just a kid, Mr Gregory.'

'He is, Anto, you're right.'

The boy glared at Gregory. He had to make up for the fear he had shown. The superintendent watched him with kindness, but it lasted only a second.

'Just a kid. That's what pisses me off.' Terry Gregory turned to his officers. 'Take them back to the Castle. See what you can get. It won't be much, but I doubt we'll need much. Tomorrow's another day altogether.'

Stefan looked at his boss. It was as if the superintendent had suddenly lost interest. As the Special Branch detectives escorted the IRA men out to the yard, Superintendent Gregory followed them.

'You may go home, lads. There's sod all to do here. We've shown our faces so. But I'll want everyone in at six. We may sort it out then.'

Stefan didn't know what the reaction of a man who knew about all this before it happened ought to be, but surely it wasn't this. Even for public consumption there should be some concern. It was an arms' raid on an unprecedented scale. Apart from the quantities of weapons and ammunition in the hands of the IRA, the incompetence of the Irish Army was more than a joke. Yet Gregory couldn't even pretend to get past the joke.

He laughed, slapping Stefan on the back with an odd familiarity.

'Ah, come on! Where the fuck are they going to put it all?'

Stefan walked into the courtyard of the Magazine Fort, brightly lit by its own harsh sodium lights and the headlamps of cars and lorries; engines were running, filling the yard with smoke as exhaust fumes pumped into the freezing air. Soldiers, Guards and Special Branch detectives stood in the slush of snow adding a haze of cigarette smoke. A line of shamefaced soldiers filed from the barrack block into the back of a Bedford truck. Each man gave his name and rank to a Military Policeman; each name was ticked off. It was the garrison. The last man was the commanding officer, Joseph Curran, his eyes down, avoiding any of the eyes that were fixed on him.

A senior army officer and a man in civvies were watching the truck as Superintendent Gregory passed them, heading towards his car.

'There'll be a court martial then, Jack?' said Gregory.

The two men turned. Colonel Jack Rowe was the commander of An Cór Póilíní Airm, the Military Police. Stefan didn't know the colonel, but he recognized the other man immediately as Commandant Geróid de Paor of G2, Military Intelligence. De Paor nodded a stiff greeting at him.

'In due course,' said Colonel Rowe.

'And you're a bit late, Geróid,' said the superintendent.

'No point saying it didn't take us by surprise, Terry. You too?'

Gregory shrugged and looked back at the colonel.

'I hear it couldn't have been Captain Curran's fault. Wasn't he away at confession when the Boys went in? I wish a few of my lads had more acquaintance with confessions than beating them out of fellers, but you can't always pick your men, can you? So was it an inside job then, Jack?'

'They certainly knew what was here.'

'There wouldn't be a pub either side of the river where there's not a feller could tell you where you keep your reserve ammo, Jack. Am I right the IRA man walked up to the gate with a parcel for Captain Curran, and your man on sentry said, "Jesus, it's good of you to deliver this time of night!" and let him in, along with the fifteen lads with the Thompsons?'

'I'm sure you know as much as I do at this stage, Terry.'

'I wouldn't say that. Chances are I'd already know more.'

'You'll appreciate we have a lot to do, Terry.'

'Good luck, Colonel.' Gregory looked at his watch. 'Brigadier Brennan must be waiting at the Department of Defence with the General Staff. A long night. Start with the parcel. A joke always breaks the ice.'

As the colonel's car door shut the superintendent walked on.

'I'll drop you home, Stefan,' said Dessie. 'I've got to get the car.'

'Don't worry, I could do with the air, Dessie.'

For a moment Stefan stood still as the truck containing the Magazine Fort garrison pulled away, followed by Colonel Rowe. Gregory was turning his car, blasting the horn at a group of soldiers standing aimlessly about.

'Your boss is right.'

Stefan turned to see Geróid de Paor beside him.

'Who needs an inside job when you can ring the doorbell?'

'So what did they get out?'

'Mostly ammunition, over a million rounds. And it is most of our reserve. It was ammunition they were after, especially

.45-calibre for their Thompsons. They've plenty of Tommies hidden away but not much ammo. Does that tally with what you've heard at Dublin Castle?'

'I'm not on the IRA side of things, but it makes sense.'

Stefan was as noncommittal as he could be.

'This took some organizing,' continued de Paor, 'and not a whisper.'

Stefan didn't reply. He had heard more than a whisper.

'Hundreds of IRA men. Getting the trucks, getting them in and out, dumps for more ordnance than they've ever seen. And some of their best people locked up in England. Look at the three you found – a fifteen year old! How did they keep it so tight? They're all over the place since Stephen Hayes took over from Seán Russell. It should have leaked like a sieve. But no excuses. It was our farce. Maybe when Terry Gregory's had his fill of rubbing that in we might all consider what went wrong. Your end as well as ours.'

'I'm sure there'll be a time for that, Geróid.'

'I'm not trying to pump you, Stefan.' De Paor laughed.

Stefan gave some sort of smile, but what puzzled the commandant wasn't unreasonable, nor were the questions he asked. Perhaps there was an explanation for Superintendent Gregory's behaviour. The more people ridiculed the army's incompetence, the more that was the issue, and the less likely anyone was to ask how the biggest IRA operation in decades had been planned with such meticulous secrecy. Geróid de Paor could have no suspicion about what Stefan knew, but he sensed the Intelligence officer, in the guise of thinking aloud, was fishing. He knew something smelt. Perhaps his instincts told him that the smell might be coming from somewhere in the Branch.

When Stefan arrived at the flat the lights were out. He could smell Kate's perfume. He turned on a lamp and looked into the bedroom. Her steady breathing told him she was asleep. There was nothing left of the night they had planned together. If her anger had subsided his own mood was darker. He didn't want to explain what had happened at the Magazine Fort; some of what he would say would be a lie. It was a grubby fact. It wasn't much of an aphrodisiac. If he woke her, he would sink deeper into deceit. He closed the bedroom door. He poured a whiskey.

He pulled open the curtains and looked out at the night, at the River Liffey, at Grattan Bridge, at the colonnaded dome of the Four Courts. Like everywhere in Dublin the Four Courts had another story to tell. It was where the Civil War started. Where the leaders of the new Free State used British artillery against men they had fought beside all their lives. In the bombardment and the fire that followed the building was almost destroyed. It took ten years to rebuild, but cement didn't disguise where the bullets and the shrapnel hit in the summer of 1922. Stefan drained the glass. The Four Courts had been rebuilt, but the battle wasn't over. And you still had to pick a side. He didn't really want another drink but he poured one anyway. For now, it was easier than sleep.

6

The Clarence

When Stefan reached Dublin Castle the next morning an armoured car sat where Dame Street met Palace Street, guarding the approach. The Gardaí at the gate carried rifles. It was early, just before six, but passers-by had stopped to discuss the night's events with the soldiers and Guards. The story was greeted with a mixture of surprise and amusement that was already its hallmark. Gall is always an admired quality in Ireland; directed at the establishment it rarely misses. And since the raid had been carried out without casualties, even the soldiers on the streets found it hard not to hand it to the Boys. But the good humour was a backhanded compliment for the IRA. In most countries the theft of the army's entire reserve of ammunition by an organization that aimed to replace the existing government would have led to the expectation of civil war. It was a measure of the relationship between Ireland and the IRA that no one expected anything to happen. Armed insurrection may have been on the agenda of Éamon de Valera and his cabinet that morning, but embarrassment came higher up the list.

Stefan hadn't wanted to wake Kate that morning but he couldn't leave without speaking to her. It didn't start well.

It wasn't that he had drunk very much, but he was drinking regularly, in a way that he never had before. It was a habit that echoed what Kate liked less and less about the job he was doing. But the Magazine Fort raid was enough to push it away. As she realized what he was saying, and grasped the full extent of it, as well as the absurdity of the way it had all happened, some laughter was inevitable.

She put his uneasiness down to the argument at the Gate and did her best to put that aside. It had been accepted at the theatre that *Roly Poly* might come into conflict with the state's show of neutrality; the weeping and gnashing of teeth disappeared quickly. Micheál Mac Liammóir made a point of talking to her in the pub. He couldn't keep her on in her job but he assured her she had not lost friends. As for Detective Inspector Gillespie, he said rumour had it the Abbey's management was furious that Ireland's national theatre had not been given its own Special Branch detective too. Kate was aware that the smile Stefan gave in response to this didn't go as deep as she hoped.

Superintendent Gregory was a different man that morning. The indulgent amusement of his Magazine Fort visit was gone. There was a sense of eagerness that Stefan felt as he entered the detectives' room. The full complement of Special Branch men stood around maps on blackboards and easels, or sat on desks talking fast and loud, some even, a rare occurrence, scribbling down notes. On one wall, beside the photographs of the most wanted IRA leaders, were lists of dozens more, with known haunts, details of friends, family, home, work addresses. It was a new day. And at the centre of it, holding several conversations at once, was a new Terry Gregory, looking as if he hadn't slept, which was true, yet newly energized.

Dessie MacMahon ran his finger down a list of IRA men as Stefan came in. He looked up, grinning, an unusual activity at six in the morning.

'Jesus, I don't know where the boss got his information but there's no shortage of it. He's right on this. So some bugger's talking somewhere.'

Gregory stepped into the centre of the room. The noise stopped.

'Right, lads. You'll be working in teams with the army and the Military Police. There's a blockade round the Pale since the early hours. Road blocks, patrols, armoured cars. There are spotter planes out. It's unlikely what was stolen got further than County Dublin, Kildare, Meath. It certainly won't go any further. Whatever the Boys planned in the way of dumps, the size of the haul hasn't made it easy. And they used all their surprises up last night. The IRA demonstrated they can put on a show. We can put on a better one. And ours is going to run a lot longer than theirs.'

Stefan Gillespie caught the wink that was directed at him.

'First job is recovering what they took. Easy and methodical's the game, and no one's going to get in the way now. You might remember when the Dáil brought in the Emergency Powers Act, people didn't like it. Our friend Mr Cosgrove criticized the government for asking for a blank cheque. It was decent of him to stand up for the Boys when they'd shoot him as soon as look at him, but there'll be no more of that shite. The Dáil will amend the Act to plug the holes, without a squeak. Mr Cosgrove and the bleeding hearts have an idea where some of the rounds may end up.'

There was laughter. Stefan watched Gregory. The boss was enjoying this. Another shift of mood that didn't relate to the conversation with the IRA Quartermaster. What the politicians in Leinster House were doing didn't interest many detectives, but Gregory wasn't really talking to them. He was talking to himself, and it went far deeper than stolen ordnance.

'I'm off to HQ to see the commissioner. Ned wants no cock-ups. Shorthand for if anyone's feeling frisky the only fellers who need dead IRA heroes are the Boys themselves. And that's straight from Dev. You won't be thanked. The success of this operation will be down to Special Branch. We know where to look. As for the army, whatever about the Phoenix Park farce, we're working with them. So no shooting, and keep off the subject of parcels. If they don't know what they're doing, let's show them we do.'

The day that followed was long. Stefan took charge of a group of Special Branch detectives, including Dessie MacMahon, and left for the barracks at Islandbridge where they picked up two truckloads of soldiers and drove west and south towards Kildare. Stefan made the journey in an army staff car; the lieutenant who sat in the back with him said little. They looked at the maps of the area they would be searching, but even though the lieutenant seemed to know the area beyond the Curragh and Newbridge better than Stefan, it was clear all the information to direct the search came on the lists he had brought from Dublin Castle. The officer's silence said he didn't much like it, yet there was no argument about who was in charge.

Between the ring of roadblocks closing off the city itself and an outer ring that sealed off the adjacent rural counties, the countryside had been divided into small areas that were broken up by more roadblocks, more Guards and more soldiers while they were searched. It was going to be done in a way that was, as Terry Gregory had said, easy and methodical.
Stefan Gillespie and his men were searching around Rathangan, on the Kildare–Offaly border, working out along the River Slate. Beyond the town, farm buildings were the focus, but every wood had to be swept, every ivy-clad ruin, every field and ditch, every quarry, the grounds of churches, chapels and schools, even graveyards. Every car, every cart, every pedestrian was stopped. It was a lot of work and it was productive.

As darkness closed in Stefan had found two arms' stashes and one major dump; 15,000 rounds of ammunition, 20 Lee-Enfield rifles and a dozen Thompson machine guns. The intelligence from Terry Gregory gave the search a direction Stefan quickly learned to trust. There were places as the day progressed where he moved his men on, and places where the information made him send them back to check they hadn't missed something. Even Special Branch men who dealt with the IRA and its informers all the time were surprised how easy it was. And the lieutenant who had started the day off with stiff-lipped sourness now expected another discovery round every corner. It was like clockwork. And by the end of the day Stefan was sure of one thing: the intelligence that came with the maps hadn't been put together in a couple of hours that morning. He already had the same level of detail for the next day's search in Kilcullen and Narraghmore. Nothing was haphazard. It felt like it had been planned for a long time.

When he returned to Dublin Castle detectives were already heading home, mud-, peat-, and dung-spattered from the day. They were all tired, but there was a sense of satisfaction, even camaraderie, that Stefan felt too. There was a cheerful competitiveness he couldn't help joining in with as he walked into the Police Yard, with Special Branch men all round him throwing out claims of how many thousand rounds they'd found and how.

'Mick Calloway's opened a book on it. There'll be the pot and a couple of bottles of whiskey for whoever finds most by Christmas Day.'

'And where are we, Dessie?' said Stefan.

'Thirty to one outsiders.'

'That's a bit rich. I thought we did all right!'

'We're stuck with an inspector who knows fuck all about the IRA.'

'Thanks very much!'

59

'Now if we were looking for subversive plays, we'd be odds on.'

When they entered the detectives' room from the Police Yard, Stefan was laughing. It had been hard not to take some pride in the operation. The sense from the army and the uniformed Guards that 'Whatever you think of these Special Branch lads, they know what they're doing' was strong. Special Branch wasn't much liked, even within the Gardaí. They were seen less as a weapon against the IRA's gunmen than as barely distinguishable from them. Stefan still carried that dislike. As he looked through the glass window into Gregory's office, watching the superintendent and his senior detectives drinking beer, talking and laughing over each other, he felt a little less comfortable with the fact that he was sharing the same feelings.

He caught his boss's eye suddenly. The superintendent raised his glass and smiled. Stefan was still no wiser as to what Terry Gregory's connection to the IRA Quartermaster meant. It had looked like betrayal but he wasn't convinced. Was Gregory giving information or getting information? Was he playing both sides? He had a reputation for guarding himself against all eventualities and not caring who he screwed in the process. Stefan had known that before he came into the Branch. But whatever the game was, he had already compromised himself; the decision to say nothing, do nothing, hadn't let him step away from anything; it had drawn him more deeply in.

'Your girl was in earlier, Stevie. There's a note for you.'

The words came from a detective on his way out. Stefan picked up a scribbled note from Kate. As he read it he felt a shift that took him out of the detectives' room, back to what he told himself was the real world. If the night before, looking out over the Quays, he had been uneasy with the idea that there were places in his head he needed to shut off from one another, today he was happy just to close the door and walk into another, brighter room.

Stefan crossed O'Connell Bridge and half-ran and half-walked to Clerys. There were two days till Christmas; the shops were open late. All along the first-floor windows of the department store there was a line of Christmas trees and coloured lights; below them windows were full of toys, clothes, gifts. There was an ordinariness about the crowded pavements and the good-natured jostling through the doors that was more than ordinary at Christmas. In a corner of Stefan's head it would always remind him of how it should have been and wasn't; of his son in Baltinglass with his grandparents and less and less time to see him; of Maeve who wasn't there and never could be. They weren't unhappy reflections; they were simply there. To enjoy Christmas without them would have been to diminish what it meant. Not that he knew what it meant now; he hadn't since he was little more than a child. But it was still about a better place to be; it touched at the heart of the things that still mattered and at the things he sometimes forgot.

As he raced up the escalators to the café he remembered what he had pushed from his mind all day. Two days till Christmas. All leave had been cancelled. For the Dublin men it would only take the daylight hours of Christmas Day away. For him and for Tom it would take away Christmas. He should have been going home on Christmas Eve, bringing Kate with him. It had been planned by Tom, who at eight was a great planner-ahead. There had never been a Christmas since Maeve's death that father and son had been apart. It had become important when Tom was three and four and Stefan was a detective in Dublin, but even after his return to West Wicklow Tom had never lost the sense that Christmas must be inviolable for them.

Kate was still in the café, starting to pack up her bags to go.

'Can we have some more tea, please?' She caught the waitress's eye, then grinned at Stefan. 'So, have you saved the nation? I hope so. It's been chaos in town all day. Anyway, it looks like it's taken it out of you so.'

'I've just run all the way from the Castle!'

'Oh, so you didn't save the nation?'

'Well, I should have it all sewn up soon.'

'Good, I thought you probably wouldn't make it, so I decided I'd better get some presents anyway. You haven't done anything, have you?'

'I wouldn't go as far as that.'

'Of course you haven't.' She pulled two carrier bags on to the table. 'This covers most things I think. Some bath salts and scent for your mam.'

Stefan looked; his response wasn't enthusiastic.

'You don't like bath salts or you don't like these bath salts?'

'It's not what I'd buy her.'

'Handkerchiefs?'

'What?'

'I'd guess you'd buy her some handkerchiefs normally?'

'No, that's what Pa usually gets her.'

'Take it from me, Stefan Gillespie, treating your mother as if she's a woman, not just a mother, won't go amiss. You should probably pass that on to your father too. She'll have a drawer full of those handkerchiefs.'

He laughed; she did have.

'And your dad wanted a new lighter.'

She took out a box that contained a square, chrome Colibri.

'That's not bad.'

'Does that mean it's all right?'

'It's not the same as the one he had before.'

'You mean the one the cow trod on? Perhaps you could stick it under a cow's hoof over Christmas, and flatten it out. If you want to change it . . .'

He leant across the table and kissed her. 'He'll love it. Ah, tea!'

The waitress put down the pot and another cup and saucer.

'And I got this for Tom, and a few bits and pieces besides.'

She took out a box of Meccano. Stefan sighed.

'For God's sake, what's the matter now? He likes making things.'

'And he's great at it. The trouble is he expects me to be as well.'

'You really do look like you've been dragged through a hedge.'

'Several, backwards and forwards. Look, I don't know what's going to happen, Kate.' He was serious now. 'Leave's been cancelled. There's every chance we'll be out after this fecking ordnance on Christmas Day.'

For a moment they said nothing. Kate shrugged.

'I'm going back to Dún Laoghaire tonight. I can go to Mass with Mam and Dad Christmas Eve morning. They're not happy me being in Baltinglass Christmas Day. And can we say that without the usual aside – the one where you say they wouldn't mind me being there so much if you weren't coming back with me afterwards?'

'Kate, you don't have to go down if I can't get home . . .'

'I want to. It might take Tom's mind off you not being there. I don't know him well, but I'm sure Christmas without you will be – quite hard.'

Stefan looked at her. He wished she wasn't going back to Dún Laoghaire; he wished they could finish what they were doing and go to the flat now. He took her hand.

'I'm sorry about last night.'

'It's okay. I guess we had enough on our plate without the IRA.'

'Stefan!'

He looked up at a tall man in an overcoat, slightly awkward about the moment of intimacy he knew he had just interrupted. It was the second time Stefan had seen Commandant Geróid de Paor in twenty-four hours.

'Christmas shopping?'

'I haven't had much time for it today. Kate has been.'

There was no reason the commandant shouldn't be doing some late shopping in Clerys a couple of days before Christmas, but given the day it had been, it seemed odd he didn't have more important things to do.

'Sorry, this is Kate O'Donnell. Kate, Commandant de Paor.'

'We have met, Stefan, remember? The Commandant was one of the officers who interrogated my sister when I brought her back from America.'

She stood up and shook de Paor's hand; he smiled.

'I hope she's put all that behind her. Is she somewhere in England?'

'That's right, somewhere,' said Kate more coldly. 'But I'll leave you two to it. I assume you're out scouring the bogs as well, Mr de Paor.'

'No, I'm happy to let Stefan and his colleagues do all that. After last night I'm keeping my head down. If I was walking along O'Connell Street in uniform, I'd be in serious danger of being mobbed by small boys asking me if they could deliver a parcel! I suppose he's told you about the—'

'The parcel? Yes, it's not exactly a state secret.'

'Well, at least we now have a plan if the Germans or the English come knocking on our door with a parcel to deliver – we won't answer it!'

Kate gathered up her bags.

'Stefan, if I don't run, I'll miss the train. Phone me in Dún Laoghaire. Whatever happens I will be getting the Baltinglass train on Christmas Eve.'

She kissed Stefan and left.

'I didn't mean to interrupt, Stefan.'

'No? I thought you did.'

'Well, I did follow you from the Castle,' de Paor laughed. 'Saw you over the road. I was looking for you. You took some keeping up with too.'

'Any particular reason?'

'Call it a Christmas drink.'

'No pumping intended then?'

'All right, I could see you were uneasy last night, at the fort.'

'Is that surprising, Geróid?'

'I'm uneasy too.' De Paor spoke more quietly. 'I think two people in our line of work who are uneasy should have a conversation. I've trusted you in the past. You've trusted me. We might not be friends, but we once had a friend in common. He trusted you too. I'd like you to listen to something. It doesn't amount to much. Probably nothing. Will you listen?'

As Stefan and de Paor crossed O'Connell Bridge for the Quays, the G2 man said how pleased everyone was with the search for the arms, though 'everyone' meant the government and the newspapers. The army wasn't so much pleased as relieved. There would be changes at the top. Michael Brennan, the Chief of Staff, would go. That would make the papers feel that firm action had been taken. He interspersed confidential asides with idle remarks about the weather and Christmas. He had a good memory. When he said his ten-year-old daughter was hoping for more snow he asked about Stefan's eight-year-old son as if they chatted about their families regularly. It led naturally to a memory of the first time they had met, six Christmases ago in de Paor's house in Fitzwilliam Square. The last time they had seen each other had been at a memorial service in Rathfarnham, three months ago, for the third man who was with them at Fitzwilliam Square, de Paor's colleague, John Cavendish, who had died in New York for no reason except that old hatreds still twisted Irish hearts and minds. That was their bond.

'I thought we'd try the Clarence. It's handy enough for you.'

They were walking past Paddy Geary's tobacconist's.

'Do you know every Special Branch man's address, Geróid?'

'Not all, no. But some addresses are more useful than others.'

The Clarence, only a few years ago a crumbling, rat-infested Georgian house calling itself a hotel, had a brand new building. With its bright limestone, its classical pillars, and a touch of art deco unusual in any Dublin buildings other than cinemas, it was a beacon of modernity between the still crumbling, rat-infested Georgian houses on either side. When Stefan rented some rooms a few doors along his landlord had said if there was one building without rats, he was in it. The noises at night were less reassuring, as was the rat Paddy Geary's cat had dropped at his door.

The octagonal cocktail bar of the Clarence was clamorous with the expectation of Christmas, but the waiter found them a table away from the crowd around the bar. He seemed disappointed the cocktail menu was unopened and the two men ordered beer. But it was a cocktail bar in which the barman wasn't often stretched beyond a port and lemon or a Martini.

'I don't warm to cocktail bars either,' said de Paor. 'But we're almost guaranteed not to see a Garda Síochána man, let alone Special Branch.'

'Is that important?'

'You must decide for yourself.'

'So no objection to me telling Gregory we had a drink?'

'Of course not.'

'You said you weren't pumping me last night, but if you want to pump me tonight, I'd say you'll be disappointed, whatever it's about.'

'I'm not a great one for pumping. Let's call it thinking aloud.' Stefan shrugged and sipped his beer.

'I'm looking into the Magazine Fort raid, which won't surprise you. After all, military regulations do require an inquiry into any loss over £5.'

'You're just over then,' said Stefan.

'There will be a court martial, but I've yet to see any indication it was an inside job as far as the army's concerned.

66

It might be easier to deal with it if it was. The IRA had plenty of information about the layout, and they knew what was there, but that's not so hard. As far as the garrison goes, I don't think the routine's changed from when the British were there.'

'Perhaps it should have done.'

'But you're the fellers with the gen on the IRA. Look at the way you've picked up our ordnance left right and centre. No complaints there. If there's a consolation, it's that the Boys' security's worse than the army's. But it's the speed that's impressive. We could be forgiven for thinking you had a fair inkling where the ammunition and guns were going to end up.'

'They were never going to get it very far, were they?'

'I think they got some of it further. Into the North.'

'I haven't heard that,' said Stefan.

'A whisper. From the RUC.'

'I don't get the whispers, Geróid.'

'Someone does. You lads have got some instincts when it comes to where to look.'

'Well, if you look in enough places—'

'But another thing that surprised me – arrests.'

'What arrests?'

'That's the question. The Dáil's pushed through legislation for you to arrest anyone, for anything, but Garda cells aren't exactly bursting at the seams.'

'Don't you want your ammo back first?'

'There were four senior IRA men in town last night. The Chief of Staff, Hayes, Jack McNeela, who's doing most of the planning as Hayes can't wipe his arse without someone to tell him how, McCallister, the Quartermaster, and Charlie McGlade, who's reorganized the Boys in Ulster and is dangerously close to knowing what he's doing. It was Charlie who got one lorry-load of guns over the border. McCallister's already gone, but not much further than Kildare. And Hayes and McNeela didn't leave Dublin till late this afternoon.'

'For a man who doesn't know much about the IRA, that's not bad.'

'If I knew they were there, you're not telling me you didn't.'

'In three months at Dublin Castle, I haven't been near the IRA. You'll have an idea what I've been doing. Spying on anyone in the British forces. That's the sum total of what I know right now. If you want a list of Óglaigh na hÉireann soldiers in the British Army, then I'm your man.'

De Paor smiled at the flash of anger, but the anger was as much about Stefan's discomfort as it was about the job he was doing. The mention of the IRA Quartermaster in particular was unsettling. The events of the day had relegated most of that to the back of his mind but they hadn't erased it.

'I get the lists too,' said de Paor

'If you've got a question about what's going on in Special Branch, ask Terry Gregory. I doubt he'll be amused that you're interrogating me.'

'Will you tell him I am?'

'Why wouldn't I?'

'Quite right. But we're working on this together, aren't we? No orders we shouldn't speak to each other. I know Terry's a cautious man, but what's there to be cautious about in friends reflecting on the day's work? Isn't there a war on, well, an Emergency anyway, and aren't we all in it?'

'I think we'd better leave it at that, Geróid.'

'The word I have, Stefan, is only a whisper, funnily enough from the RUC again. The word they have is that the IRA have a man in Special Branch.'

'Half the Branch are ex-IRA. It wouldn't be the first time.'

'No, it wouldn't, but it would be a dangerous game now.'

'Isn't it always a dangerous game?'

'It would be someone up the ladder, not your Constable Kelly.'

'You can't have it both ways. We're on the way to recovering virtually everything that was stolen from the Magazine Fort for you.'

'But not everything. Maybe we'll get back so much no one will care what's still out there. Meanwhile, no one noticed Stephen Hayes and the three musketeers having a fish supper in Cook's in Dorset Street.'

Stefan said nothing. Even the idlest evasion was a lie again.

'However, I gather arrests will start after Christmas. We're setting up military tribunals in the New Year to deal with it. There'll be plenty of room for the Boys in the Curragh. Just a pity you could have had half their General Staff last night.'

'I'm not the man to discuss this with, Geróid.'

'No, probably not. I wanted to pass it by you, though.'

'Pass what by, for God's sake?'

He checked himself, but de Paor could see his discomfort.

'I cast my bread upon the waters, Inspector, it's the best I can do.'

'Well, have a good Christmas.' Stefan stood up; he'd had enough.

'You too. I hope you get away. And if ever you feel uneasy about anything again, and there's no one you can talk to, you know where I am. It's not a one-way street. I may have information that's useful to you. Sometimes it might suit me to drop it into Special Branch without your elders and betters knowing the source. That wouldn't do you any harm.'

'You think I'm that easily used?'

'We're all being used, and we're all users. Only the results matter. And I think you've got too good a nose for this job not to do it properly.'

Stefan turned and walked out, through the hotel lobby to Wellington Quay. Shoppers and Christmas revellers still filled the street. He was sober enough, he had only one drink, but he was trembling a little as he took out his key to open the door to the flat. Paddy Geary was in the doorway to his tobacconist's shop, fat and red-faced as usual, but slightly the worse for wear tonight, and cheerfully offering the season's greetings to passers-by, whether he knew them or not. Stefan hadn't seen him there.

'Will you come in, Inspector? I've a bottle open.'

'I'll leave it, Paddy, thanks. It's been a long day.'

'Youse are giving the Boys the run-around now I'd say!' Paddy chuckled. 'Still, they gave youse the run-around first, fair play to them!'

Stefan slammed the street door behind him. He walked up the stairs without bothering to turn on the light. Something scurried across the landing in front of him. There was a high-pitched squeal. He turned on the light to unlock the door to his flat. Paddy Geary's fat tabby was staring up at him from the bottom of the next flight of stairs, a young rat still wriggling in its mouth. The cat didn't take its eyes off him, but it closed its teeth tighter and there was a faint crunch. The rat stopped wriggling.

7

Kilranelagh Graveyard

Stefan sat at a typewriter in the detectives' room, transferring lists of ordnance from notebook pages skewered on spikes. Two other detectives did the same. At intervals the door from the Police Yard opened; detectives came in and put more tallies on the spikes. Cars came and went. He heard the doors open and close, the voices outside. There was still laughter, but the good humour of the previous day was wearing thin as men came in from Kildare and Meath and County Dublin, fresh from the army convoys bringing weapons and ammunition back to Islandbridge. The job was tiring and repetitive; satisfaction in showing Special Branch could do it was still there, but now it was clear it would carry on all through Christmas and into the New Year – no one had the enthusiasm Terry Gregory still showed.

Stefan had been told to stay at the Castle and get on top of the paperwork that was piling up. No one knew why Superintendent Gregory wanted it recorded in such detail. The army was checking everything. They had inherited from the British a passion for double-entry bookkeeping and chit-issuing second to none; in the event of a German invasion their paperwork would run rings round the Wehrmacht. Nevertheless, the superintendent insisted on his own records; he didn't trust what others put down. In a man who often found it convenient to throw away statements from suspects and witnesses, and write what he felt was a more accurate reflection of events on their behalf, such attention to detail was unusual. But he wanted it done. He wanted the Special Branch's role to be crystal clear.

The few detectives who could do something that approximated typing had been pulled in to collate the tallies and pile them in the in-tray in Gregory's office. Stefan sat back and looked through the glass at his boss. The conversation with de Paor was in his head in a way it wouldn't have been if he was out searching the countryside. If recent events had left him confused about Gregory and the IRA Quartermaster, what the G2 man told him had compounded it. Yet that morning the superintendent enthusiastically announced changes to the Emergency Powers Act that meant they had free rein to arrest anyone they thought was an IRA member. And if they had no reason to believe a man was in the IRA, but didn't like the look of him, that would do just as well now. It got the laugh Gregory intended but it was true. He said they would start picking up the IRA men and their fellow travellers soon, in days not weeks. But Stefan had to wonder. Soon was still a delay. The IRA knew what was coming; senior men would disappear; the people they picked up would be the foot soldiers.

'I know it's boring, Inspector. It's a fuck sight warmer than Kildare.'

Superintendent Gregory was walking towards him.

'I'd still rather be outside, sir.'

'We'll never get the farm boy out of you, will we?'

'I did tell you I wanted to stay in Baltinglass.'

Gregory looked at him, half smiling; a questioning look.

'You've got a lad down there, haven't you?'

'Yes, sir.'

'You'd better piss off. If you don't go now, there won't be a train.'

Stefan didn't waste time. He took his coat, called his goodbyes and left. There was no reason Gregory should single him out for leave. He was unpredictable as always. It did go through his mind that he might want him out of the way. He hadn't lost the feeling that the superintendent suspected him of knowing something. But heading up to Kingsbridge Station the streets were busy with the noise of Christmas. All that could wait for another day.

Darkness was creeping into the scruffy graveyard that sprawled along the side of Kilranelagh Hill. It was a place of tumbled, cracked headstones and tufted grass, bordered by leafless trees, skeleton-like against the grey sky. Now, in the dusk, there were pockets of white between the gravestones, but the snow that had swept the hilltops two days earlier had almost gone. It was an uneasy place in the dark. Strangers would have seen only a disused cemetery, unkempt and abandoned, but it wasn't abandoned for those whose families lay here. They liked its isolation, as they liked the ancient stones that rose over the headstones, marking it as a place where the dead and the living had met long centuries before Christianity came to Ireland.

On this Christmas Eve, Kilranelagh echoed to the cawing of rooks, flying in to the stands of beech and oak that bordered it. But there was another noise, an intermittent snuffling close to the two great lichened pillars they called the Gates of Heaven. For 3,000 years these had been a gateway to the world of the dead, but lumbering back and forth through them now, nosing for roots, were two large saddleback pigs. Sadie and her daughter Molly had escaped through an open gate at the Gillespies' farm below Kilranelagh, and, wandering idly wherever the ditches and the boreens took them, they had finally found something worth eating.

The pigs were not alone. Two small figures moved through the crooked headstones towards them. Tom Gillespie, dark and eight, with a bucket of calf nuts, took up the rear; Rebecca Wall, fair and nine, his neighbour from Woodfield Glen, led the way. She had spotted them first.

They had been two hours finding the pigs, and as they had left the gate open there was an element of redemption in all this. Rebecca took some nuts from Tom's bucket and they walked slowly towards the Gates of Heaven. Tom called, quietly, 'Sadie, come on, come on', his words blurring into the 'gub, gub, gub, gub' all livestock know. Rebecca threw the nuts down in front of her. Sadie sniffed and moved closer. Whatever smelled good underground the calf nuts offered instant gratification. As she mowed along the line of nuts her daughter picked up the new scent and trotted forward eagerly. Sadie snarled; Molly stopped abruptly. Rebecca laughed.

'She's such a mean mother!'

Tom threw more nuts. Molly inched forward, eyeing her mother cautiously, and began to crunch them, only feet away. Rebecca held more food out. Sadie waddled past her daughter, pushing the outstretched hand. The children moved across the graveyard, sometimes backward, dribbling out a trail of calf nuts, calling, cajoling, encouraging, laughing.

They didn't know that they were being watched.

Heading to the cemetery gate it was slow progress through the headstones but the children were moving faster now. Once they were in the lane it would be easier. But it was dark now. Navigating their backward-walking way had already led to tumbles; the pigs were more sure-footed.

Then Rebecca fell heavily, tripping over a half-buried head-stone. She rolled down a slope, with a cry of shock more than anything, but her laughter told Tom she was fine. Suddenly a figure rose up in the darkness, almost where Rebecca had landed. A man. There was nothing to see except a shape, blacker than the darkness. He pushed past Tom, knocking him over, and in seconds he was gone. As Tom got up he heard the man crashing through the undergrowth. Rebecca was up too. They stared into the night. Sadie and Molly were unfazed, feeding on the calf nuts that had spilled on to the ground. The two children looked at each other and ran.

The cemetery gate was close now and as the two children ran headlong towards it the path was clearer. At the gate they could see a light moving, coming towards them. And there was a voice Tom knew well.

'Tom! Are you here? Tom!'

They reached Stefan at the gate. Tom threw his arms round him.

'There's someone there, Daddy!'

'No pigs?' laughed Stefan.

'We found Sadie and Molly, but there was a man!'

'There was, Mr Gillespie, he was hiding!'

Stefan saw that something really had frightened them. Then across the graveyard came the sound of an engine. It was a motorcycle, in the line of trees that marked the track heading towards Cloghnagaune. He saw the sweep of a headlight. Someone had been there. Not odd in itself; there was always something of Christmas that was owed to the dead. Stefan would be there himself in the morning to put a little of it on to Maeve Gillespie's grave.

'Well, it's quite a welcome home anyway!'

There was a grunt and a snort and the sound of slow, heavy feet. The two pigs, still munching on the last nuts, lumbered irritably towards them.

'Well, whoever it was, if you two didn't frighten the life out of him, I'm sure Sadie and Molly did. I'd have run myself if I'd seen you all coming through the Gates of Heaven across the graveyard! The Children of Lir and the Black Pig of Muckdubh, or is it two Black Pigs of Muckdubh?'

Tom and Rebecca laughed, reassured enough to feel a little foolish.

'Come on ladies, we'd better get you home.'

'I dropped all the food, Daddy.'

Stefan held up a bucket of grain, and grinned.

'Do you think I never left a gate open when I was your age?'

The stranger in the graveyard was soon forgotten. Neither Tom nor Rebecca had any real fear of the place, even at night, and there was more than enough going on to drive away a momentary fright. Even as the two sows settled in their sty, Christmas had taken over, sweeping everything before it. And when Stefan and his son came back up to the farm after walking Rebecca home, it was Christmas that was the only thing on Tom's mind.

It was the memory of what Stefan's grandparents had brought to Ireland from Germany, years ago, that meant the Gillespies kept Christmas on Christmas Eve. The presents round the tree, which Tom and Stefan's father had cut down the day before, were for opening after the Christmas Eve meal. For now, the kitchen range was full of cooking, and Stefan's mother was flustered, not because cooking flustered her, but because Kate O'Donnell did. There was an impression to make, even if it only truly mattered to Helena Gillespie.

Kate had been pulled into the rarely used sitting room where a fire blazed and candles burnt. Tom was finishing decorating the tree, which was by long tradition just too big to fit in the corner by the fire. There was a new decoration each year that Tom chose in Clerys but this year there was a second, a glass reindeer brought by Kate. He wanted it with his own new one, a bright wooden soldier with a drum. When he was satisfied with the tree they returned to the kitchen and the smell of cinnamon and cloves from the Glühwein on the range. Kate sat at the table realizing any offer to help Mrs

Gillespie would only make Helena more self-conscious. Tom smiled. It wasn't often his grandmother was like that, but he knew why of course.

In the barn the four shorthorns ate hay in their stalls, side by side. Stefan and his father sat on stools milking the last two in the light from oil lamps. The only sound was the rhythmic spurting of milk into pails. Stefan had not forgotten the stranger at Kilranelagh as easily as Tom. It was a puzzle that echoed another puzzle about his wife's grave; the flowers that were left sometimes, the white lilies. The last had been that autumn on his return from America. It had left him with the feeling that someone was watching his life. It had happened before, of course; each time he forgot about it till the next time, but he remembered now that once before he had found a lily on the grave at Christmas.

'You're very quiet,' said David.

'I'm sorry, Pa. You know how it is.'

'Do I?'

'I'm clearing the smell of Special Branch out of my head.'

He did need Christmas to clear Dublin out of his head, and above all he needed it to be what Tom wanted. He needed Kate to feel easy at Kilranelagh too. She had only been to the farm three times since she first came there to find him, after they met in America at the end of the summer.

'So Gregory's giving you a hard time?' There was a hint of amusement in David Gillespie's voice. 'I did warn you. It's what the Special Branch is about, to be a pain in the arse. And it takes a royal pain in the arse to run it.'

'You know I don't like what I'm doing, Pa.'

'I'd be more worried if you did. What about this arms' raid?'

'The IRA didn't get far beyond a show. We're picking it all up.'

'Jesus, it was some show though!' said David.

Stefan said nothing. He wanted that conversation shut off too. David could tell. He had been a policeman himself. He still knew that when it came to the job silence was usually a request for silence in return. He poured the milk into the churn behind him. He turned to clean the cow's udder. Stefan poured his milk in and clamped the round top on to the churn.

'I'm glad Kate's here for Christmas,' said David.

Stefan bent down again to clean off the last shorthorn.

'Ma's told me that half a dozen times. I have got the message.'

'Have you?'

'What does that mean?'

Father and son took the churn by the handles and carried it through into the dairy. David put it under the tap and left cold water to run over it and cool it. The two men washed the smell of the milk from their hands.

'You'll need to be quick on your feet to stop her asking what's next.'

'For God's sake, I've only known Kate a few months.'

'She'd say that's long enough at your age.'

'Should I be glad we're not here long, Pa?' laughed Stefan.

'You've got her parents Stephen's Day. They'll think the same.'

They walked out into the yard. The sheepdog Tess followed, then thought better as her nose hit the crisp air; she went back to bed in the barn.

'Well, if Ma wants my intentions to be honourable, Mr and Mrs O'Donnell might be hoping they're not. It has to be better than their daughter marrying a policeman, a Protestant policeman into the bargain!'

'Is it that way then?' said David more quietly.

'It's no way, except we don't need to get too serious about it all.' Stefan smiled. 'There is the question of what Kate wants to do as well, Pa!'

'Jesus! If you don't know, you're a bigger fool than you look!'

Stefan and his father came into the kitchen, both laughing. Kate and Tom brought them a glass of the mulled wine. Helena called out across the room.

'We'll be eating in about an hour. One present each first!'

Tom grabbed Kate's hand and dragged her back to the sitting room.

Helena walked over from the stove and picked up her own glass.

'Do you think she's all right, Stefan?'

'Of course she's all right, Ma!'

'I'm glad she's here, though,' she said in a meaningful whisper.

'You never are, Ma! I wouldn't have guessed!'

David Gillespie snorted into his glass.

'Don't be drinking too much, you two. She won't think much of that!'

Stefan and his father adopted their most serious expressions; Helena began to laugh. The door burst open and Tom and Kate returned, each bringing two small packages from under the tree. Helena took an unusually large gulp of her Glühwein, and crossed her fingers. Tom distributed the presents to be opened now. On the radio a choir sang 'The Wexford Carol'.

Good people all, this Christmas time,
Consider well and bear in mind
What our good God for us has done,
In sending his beloved son.

8

La Prisión Central

María Fernández Duarte walked from the station at Burgos across the bridge over the River Arlanzón. It should have been a three-hour journey from Salamanca but she had waited four hours at Valladolid for a connecting train. Although the Civil War was over, trains, like everything else in Spain, were only just beginning to work again. She was lucky on Christmas Eve to find one at all. But she had been dry and almost warm. Now it was wet, no more than drizzle, but on the prison road the wind would rise and the rain would be heavy. She had money for a taxi but she knew no one would take her. The drivers would see, just by looking, why she was there. It didn't pay to associate with visitors to the Central Prison. A driver who made a habit of ferrying them would be talked about; being talked about was only the beginning. One driver got out of his cab. María smiled and shook her head. She walked on. Over the bridge she turned away from the city into the darkness beyond. Already the rain was harder.

The Republic was gone. In much of Spain it had gone long before the Nationalists' victory. In some places it had barely existed. The holy city of Burgos was such a place. The Gothic cathedral at the centre of the old town was more than a monument and a place of pilgrimage; it was the heart of Castile and a Spain that looked back three hundred years for its place in the world, to a past that made the present inconsequential and shabby, as squalid as the slums that pushed up against the walls of Burgos and crept into its narrow streets, hidden behind the city's medieval splendours and its gleaming modern banks and hotels. It was a place where the pulse of Spanish Catholicism, unbending and overweening, beat so strongly you could hear it in the streets, just as you could smell the incense.

When the King left Spain in 1931 the people of Burgos felt they could tolerate a president in his place if nothing else changed. The President's visit to Burgos was encouraging; he switched on the electric lights that now illuminated the cathedral at night and made it more than ever the definition of what the city was. If the President concerned himself with celebrating what had been created between the eleventh and sixteenth centuries there was little to worry about. The city's governor was a Republican by then, of course, but as a respectable businessman he could be forgiven his eccentricities. It was better, even under the Republic's godless yoke, if power remained in the hands of people of the right sort.

Unfortunately, in 1936, with a new government of socialists and communists that had every intention of changing things, the burghers of Burgos became part of a conflict they thought would leave them untouched. And when the opponents of the Popular Front launched a military coup that would lead to the Civil War, the sleepy plains of Castile were sleepy no longer. In Burgos the army took over. The governor, who had been the right sort for a time, was arrested with his Republican administrators and shot.

The day the army took over, the cathedral bells rang into the night. Civil Guards and magistrates inspected the bodies of the executed officials and concluded they had been killed by persons unknown. Within days the unknown death squads were acting with the authority of a military tribunal. Over the next two years, thousands in Burgos would die or simply disappear. When bodies were there to find there were the same marks – Mauser bullet to the body, two or three more to the eyes or the temple. But on the first day the men who carried out the first executions joined those who had instructed them, with the city's prominent citizens, the military and the Guardia Civil, at High Mass in the Catedral de Santa María de Burgos.

As they sat in the cathedral a silent procession moved through the Arca de Santa María, across the cobbles of the Plaza Rey San Fernando. A procession that could have been seen a hundred years before, even three hundred. It was the old pulse of the city, slowed by the Republic, beating at its fullest. A quiet stream of men and women in black, wearing scapularies and sacred medallions; they carried crucifixes and the banners of the ancient sodalities and confraternities of the city; shepherding priests walked beside them; nuns and brothers from the convents and monasteries followed. Heads were bowed in prayer in that steady, black stream. It was the black of celebration and triumph. The silence was a kind of electricity.

María Fernández saw the lights of Burgos as she crossed the river, but she was going the other way, following the river out into the country, to the one contribution the Republic had made to the life of Burgos that still lived on.

The Prisión Central stood to the west of the city on a barren slope above the Río Arlanzón. It sat alone like the fortress it was, a squat, square structure inside a high outer wall. At the front was the great courtyard, the chapel and the quarters of the prison governor. It was the finest prison in Spain. Besides ordinary criminals it housed thousands of political prisoners. One of the first acts of the military government after the coup, once the prison governor had been shot, was to replace the old regime's prisoners with Republicans who could be driven out to the surrounding countryside, on a daily basis, to be shot as well. It was a bleak place, buffeted day and night by wind. There was one rough track to it that had never been metalled. When it was impassable, as it often was in winter, squads of prisoners went out to repair the damage in the storms that had caused it.

It was three kilometres from the station to the prison. The rain slammed into María's face; the wind bit harder as the sheltered parks of the city's outskirts gave way to open fields. Away from the road there were the lights of farms and hamlets; sometimes she heard the sound of laughter. But mostly there was only the darkness and the rain and the noise of her feet.

Eventually she could see the lights of the prison. Like the cathedral it was brightly floodlit; the electric lights had been installed at the same time. Where the road ended and the stony track to the Prisión Central began were two Civil Guards; she saw them ahead, in black capes and black tricorn hats. As she approached one of them walked towards her, flashing a torch.

'Name?'

'María Fernández Duarte.'

'From?'

'Salamanca.'

'Staying in Burgos?'

'No, I shall get the night train back.'

'Papers.'

She handed over her identity card. There was no reason to inspect her papers; it would be done at the prison. This was to tell her she was there on sufferance. She took the card back. The *benemérita* put his hand round hers.

'You'll have a few hours before the train.'

She met his gaze, but she knew better than to show her contempt.

'You'll need warming up by then.'

'You know I'm in your hands, señor. If you want to take the clap back home to your wife for Christmas, I'll be at the station till about two.'

He let go of her hand. The other policeman was laughing.

'Fucking bitch, you'll get what you deserve! Red whore!'

She walked on to the prison at the same slow, patient pace.

She stood in the great courtyard inside the prison. It was still raining. It was cold. It was always colder within the walls. The queues of visitors stretched across the yard. Round them stood armed prison guards. The visitors exchanged few words. Even neighbours in the city said little to one another here, and it was never wise to advertise association with visitors from elsewhere. They were watched most; they would be questioned about who they knew locally too. Networks of acquaintanceship could be costly.

María waited for two hours before she was allowed into the long room, like a cathedral nave bare of colour or decoration, where prisoners and visitors finally met each other. The visit would last fifteen minutes.

As she sat down Frank Ryan was at the bench opposite her.

They spoke through metal netting and two sets of iron bars, separated by a gap of six feet in which a prison guard sat, watching and listening. They were not allowed touch. Two dozen prisoners and visitors stretched out across the room. It was hard to hear and so everyone shouted. Ryan had been growing deaf throughout the course of his imprisonment. For a while they just looked at one another. He was always thin, but she told herself not as thin. His skin, pale enough anyway, had the tinge of yellow she always feared was the beginning of jaundice, but she told herself it was clearer now, whiter. Where there was nothing to say the simplest things said everything; and ordinary words were charged with intimacy and love.

'I brought you some olives and cheese. And cigarettes.'

'Thank God,' he laughed, 'some decent fags!'

'You do get what I bring now? They do give it to you?'

'Yes, since Leo Kerney's been coming. Nothing like an ambassador to impress a Spanish prison governor, even an Irish one. The food got better after he kicked up a hooley. Altogether a superior class of shite in fact . . .'

She smiled. He always tried hard, but he did seem better.

'You're going back to Salamanca tonight?'

She nodded.

'How's your mam and dad?'

'Okay,' she shrugged.

'But Salamanca's all right? It's calmed down. Safer anyway?'

Two of her father's friends had disappeared only a week ago.

'It's safer, yes, much better.'

The prison guard lit a cigarette. He was cold, bored, pissed off.

'Joder! Habla español!'

'Come on, Raoul, you know my Spanish is fucking brutal, besides, why would I want you to be able to understand anything I'm saying, an unmitigated gobshite like you with all the charisma of compacted effluent?'

The guard glared at him, then shrugged and drew on his cigarette.

'I'll be back in January,' said María. She spoke the words more quietly, exaggerating her lips and giving the words particular weight.

'Los Reyes Magos?' He put his hand on his head, like a crown.

She was looking at him hard, as if her eyes were where the real meaning was. He smiled again, more tenderly. He understood. There was a kind of tension between them. It was something in both their faces that was brighter, even though it was nothing anyone else could have seen.

He turned to the guard, a sense of mischief on him.

'Come on, Raoul. Un poco de español!' He half-spoke, half-sang, 'Ya vienen los Reyes Magos, caminito de Belén! The Three Kings are coming!'

María shot a warning glance. He chuckled, but she didn't like games.

'Olé, olé, Holanda y olé!' Raoul laughed out the refrain.

Ryan was looking at María; the tension was there as he spoke.

'What about Mikey, is he going on this pilgrimage?'

'Yes, he always wanted to go to Santiago de Compostela.'

'Don't we all, God willing? Tell him to say a prayer for me.'

'There are a lot of prayers said for you, Frank.'

'And for you,' he said softly.

She reached out her hand as if through some invisible solidity of the air she was touching him. And then the bell rang, loud, discordant, violent.

'Se acabó! Acabó!'

Prisoners and visitors stood up. Frank Ryan looked at María and winked; it was a lightness of mood neither of them felt. There was something deeper there. It was a mix of fear and anxiety, but somewhere there was faith too, faith despite everything, and hope, and above all love.

María Fernández Duarte's mind was still full of those things at Burgos station, waiting for the night train back to Salamanca. Next time she came to Burgos it would be over, all these agonizing months; if she believed it, if they both believed it enough. Over for him, that's all she wanted in the world. She felt it so strongly that she had no choice but to believe it. She could hear the bells from the cathedral striking midnight. It was Christmas Day. She crossed herself and prayed, as she always prayed, for the man she loved.

In his cell in the Prisión Central Frank Ryan was awake too. He heard the prison clock striking twelve. In an hour it would be Christmas in Ireland too. The twelve days of Christmas were coming, ending with Twelfth Night, the Día de los Reyes Magos, the Day of the Three Kings. And then it would happen. The plans were made. That was what María had told him at the end; that was the gift she brought. He would escape Franco's gaol. He had to believe it too. He knelt and prayed. 'Today you shall know that the Lord will come and rescue us: and tomorrow you shall witness his glory.'

9

The Seven Churches

It was Christmas Day. Stefan sat at the back of the church at Talbotstown. It was part of what remained of Maeve; the agreement demanded of him by the Church that Tom had to be brought up as a Catholic. He had no real objection but it was also true that he had no choice. Yet even as a non-participant the prayers and the responses were not so different from the Church of Ireland's; they were in his head and he didn't dislike them being there. As the organist began 'Silent Night' everyone stood. It was a carol he had always known in German, ever since he could remember Christmas. That was how his grandmother had taught him to sing it; the German words belonged to it. He sang it now in German, quietly, but he sang nevertheless.

The one Christmas card that still came from Germany, from his mother's cousin, Alice, had found its way to Kilranelagh as usual. This year the news was that two of Stefan's cousins were in the army. But Tante Alice's card was a surprise; no swastikas, no flags, no red and black, but a traditional Nativity scene. It wished them all a 'Fröhliche Weihnachten und ein gutes neues Jahr', and underneath, in shaky English, 'Pliess God'. Kate could hear Stefan's voice as he sang, 'Schlaf in himmlisher Ruh', 'Sleep in heavenly peace'. Though he sang softly she could sense that the carol meant more to him than to anyone else at Talbotstown. She took his hand.

Outside the church below Keadeen Mountain, the congregation dispersed at a leisurely pace. Stefan, Kate and Tom set off along the road to Kilranelagh. When they reached the turn for the graveyard, Kate carried on to the farm, to try to help Helena with the dinner. She needed a reason to go back alone. The visit to Maeve's grave was for Stefan and Tom. She moved down the hill to the turning for the farm as they walked to the graveyard.

'No ghosts today, I'd say.'

'It wasn't a ghost, Daddy!' was the 'don't be silly' reply.

'Was he after the pigs?' laughed Stefan.

'At least we found them. I told Opa we would.'

'You did so.'

'And we'd have got them back. It wasn't our fault.'

'What, leaving the gate open or dropping the bucket?'

'Opa said you were always after leaving gates open!'

There was little German left at the farm now, though Stefan and his mother spoke it sometimes, but Oma and Opa, Grandma and Grandpa, had stuck. Stefan liked it; it was Maeve who had decided they would be the words used at Kilranelagh, before Tom even had a word for anything.

They walked on, laughing, then growing quieter as they came close to Maeve's grave. Tom bowed his head and clasped his hands, praying as pictures in prayer books had taught him. As Stefan looked down he saw the lily immediately, next to the spray of holly from the farm. The holly had been there a week; it was wilting, but the white flower had barely been touched by that morning's frost. He bent and picked it up. It hadn't been there for more than a day. His instincts had been right the night before.

Lilies had appeared on the grave for years now, the same white arum lilies with their deep green stems, always only one.

89

They appeared at different times. Often he found them rotten and slimy by the headstone. As mysteries went it wasn't much of a mystery. But the invisibility of someone who for years seemed to lay claim to a peculiar intimacy unsettled Stefan.

Tom opened his eyes and looked up.

'It's another one of those flowers.'

For Tom the flowers were just something that happened.

'This feller last night, where was he?' asked Stefan.

'I don't know, I suppose . . .'

Tom looked round with little interest, full of too many other things. He pointed at a fallen stone and the dip beyond where Rebecca tripped, where the dark figure had risen up. For Tom there was no connection to the flower but for his father it was unavoidable. The man had been hiding, hiding from two children. It was impossible he hadn't brought the lily. Stefan had no idea what the flowers meant. But he knew something now; the man who had brought them – he had always assumed a man – was no longer invisible.

The puzzle that couldn't be solved was shunted aside. The farmhouse was livelier and noisier than it had been for many Christmases. Neither Stefan nor his father obeyed Helena's puritanical restrictions on alcohol, and since Kate was keeping up with them anyway, Helena decided that being hung for a sheep was the best option. The piano had been played more than in many years. They had all sung. Helena had swept the board at Monopoly. Now she was in the kitchen with Kate and Tom, who had almost completed the red and green Meccano crane begun on Christmas Eve. Stefan had taken tea in to his father in the sitting room, but when Kate looked in to see what he was up to he was in an armchair by the fire, like his father fast asleep.

It was ten o'clock when the phone rang. Helena answered it and went to fetch Stefan.

He came out from the sitting room, still yawning.

'I didn't tell him you were asleep,' hissed his mother.

He nodded, taking the phone from her. 'Sir?'

'You weren't asleep then,' said Superintendent Gregory.

'I might have dozed off.'

'Stefan!' Helena glared and went back into the kitchen.

'Christmas is over, Inspector. Dessie will be driving down in the morning. You go straight to Laragh and find Chief Inspector Halloran. He will have a message from the commissioner to say you're coming. He'll be very pissed off. But then that's what you're there for. To piss him off.'

'That's what I'm where for?'

'You know about the Missing Postman, William Byrne?'

'What?'

'Dessie will give you the guts of it tomorrow. Your man disappeared Christmas Eve. The assumption is he's dead, and not because he fell off his bike. Ned Broy thinks something smells about it. At the *Irish Times* they already think the smell is coming from the Guards over there. Pat Halloran is on it, but he's a Wicklow man. If it turns into murder the commissioner wants to make sure Bray CID aren't shovelling shite for their friends in Laragh.'

'That's grand, sir. I'll be made very welcome so.'

Terry Gregory didn't laugh, but Stefan could almost see the grin.

'But you're a Wicklow man yourself! Just don't turn your back.'

The next day was Stephen's Day. Sergeant MacMahon arrived in the black Austin. They took Kate to the station for the early train. The day with her parents wasn't going to happen. Christmas was over. It had been too short.

Dessie and Stefan drove into the mountains in a grubby mist that thickened as they climbed. Dessie had little to add to the story of William Byrne, except that the only thing Chief Inspector Halloran had ruled out was the fairies taking him, and that might have to be considered if no other explanation was forthcoming. Dessie wasn't happy about being dragged out of Dublin. A bit of countryside went a long way. He had seen more than enough hunting for arms in the bogs of Kildare. The climb up into the mountains on the Military Road behind Baltinglass left him unmoved.

It wasn't a journey Stefan relished either. Seven years on from Maeve's death in the Upper Lake at Glendalough, he didn't avoid the Valley of the Seven Churches, but he wouldn't go there by choice. Work had taken him into the mountains sometimes, when he was stationed in Baltinglass, though rarely as far as Laragh and Glendalough. In seven years he had never taken the road out of Laragh to the Seven Churches and the lakes. He hadn't thought about it that way before, but he did as the car crossed the Avonmore River into Laragh and stopped at the Garda Barracks.

A Garda sergeant lounged at the desk smoking a cigarette. A group of men stood in front of a map on the wall while a uniformed inspector pointed at the dense contours that marked the mountains. The countryside was being searched and the search was on a scale the barren landscape demanded. This was another search party setting off. Stefan walked up to the desk.

'Detective Inspector Gillespie, Sergeant MacMahon.'

'You're the Special Branch fellers so.'

'Do you know where Chief Inspector Halloran is?'

'You think the IRA had him then?' said the sergeant, grinning.

'It's "You think the IRA had him then, sir."'

He said it quietly, but his smile held the sergeant's gaze.

'I don't know where Mr Halloran is, sir, but Inspector Grace—'

'Take your fag out of your mouth and find him then.'

'Yes, sir.'

'Is Sergeant Chisholm here?'

The desk sergeant looked uncertain.

'In the mess room, sir. I don't know if you should talk to him.'

'Don't worry, I won't ask him anything I shouldn't.'

The sergeant hurried outside. Stefan walked through a door into a corridor. Dessie followed him. Across the hall was the station mess room. Stefan stood in the open door. Three men were there. Two uniformed Guards played draughts. A uniformed sergeant was reading the *Irish Times*.

'Not out scouring the mountainsides today, George?'

Sergeant Chisholm was in his mid-fifties. His uniform was neat; his moustache was neat; his dyed hair was neatly plastered with Brylcreem.

'You should remember me. Inspector Gillespie.'

'Baltinglass. Last time I saw you it was Sergeant Gillespie.'

'Dublin Castle now.'

'Ah, the Branch. Halloran will be pleased.'

'So what have you been up to, George?'

'Ask the Chief Inspector, Mr Gillespie, he's the detective.'

'And here comes Laurel!' Dessie spoke quietly.

A tall, thin, angular figure was standing behind them. Detective Inspector Grace looked from Stefan to Dessie with ill-disguised irritation.

'I know MacMahon. And you are?'

'Stefan Gillespie.'

'Fintan Grace. Chief Inspector Halloran said he'd catch you when he can. You may make yourself useful in a search party. We need anyone we can get. We're up beyond St Kevin's Road now, working up from the lake.'

Stefan looked at Dessie. 'You see what's going on there, Sergeant.'

'Thank you, sir.'

'It'll do you good, Dessie, and you might even find something.'

Dessie gave a shrug of resignation and walked out.

'I think I'll just have a look around, if that's all right, Fintan.'

'The chief inspector said you're to join the search.'

'Don't worry, I know my way about. I won't go missing too.'

Stefan left. For a moment Fintan Grace looked at a loss. His instructions were to keep the Branch out of the way. Inspector Grace always did what he was told; he assumed everyone else did the same. Bitter experience hadn't knocked it out of him. Pat Halloran would be pissed off. He looked up to see Sergeant Chisholm grinning at him happily from the mess room.

'There's a man who knows a bollix when he sees one . . . sir.'

He stood at the east end of the Upper Lake, looking out at the water and the fold in the mountains beyond, where the Glenealo River flowed into the lake. He knew he would have to come here at some point, where he and Maeve had pitched their tent, where they spent their last night, their son sleeping between them. Along the shore was where Maeve's body was pulled from the water. Nothing was very different. It was a still day; the mist had gone.

For a while there was only the silence of the past. It was a long time since it felt so close. Its proximity wasn't hard but he was unused to it. Some of the things he had left behind, that he thought were quietly put away, were not as neatly divided from what he had chosen to keep and cherish as he believed. A death had brought him to Glendalough; it could not but open closed doors. Perhaps he had left coming here too long. It was less than a year ago that Tom had asked to come. He knew where his mother had died; it was a place in his head he needed to come to terms with as he grew older. But when he tried to speak to his father about it, Stefan had avoided the conversation more firmly than he realized. There had been nothing unkind in what he said, but even now, questioning how he had dealt with the past, he didn't ask himself if he had helped his son cope with it.

There was traffic on the road he had walked along; the noise of feet, the sound of voices. It pulled him back into the present. That was where he needed to be. He took his binoculars and swept the slopes of the Vale of Glendalough. He saw the line of searchers working through heather and gorse above the treeline; Dessie would be there now.

If the Missing Postman had wandered up St Kevin's Road into the mountains, drunk in the darkness, as one explanation had it, there was a point in this. Leaving the Garda Barracks Stefan had seen the enthusiasm for the search. From Glendalough and Laragh and down the valley in Rathdrum, there were people everywhere, coming to join the search parties; Guards, detectives, farmers, men, women, even children, all committed to finding William Byrne. Yet he had already heard that what was facing Chief Inspector Halloran, up and down the valley, was a lack of information that felt like bloody-minded obstruction.

Everyone was busy, but no one was talking.

He walked back to where St Kevin's Road stopped and a track climbed higher up the valley through the trees. There was an almost festive air about a gang of men tramping along it. The Missing Postman had gripped not only Wicklow but Ireland itself; on the third day it was edging out the IRA arms' raid on the radio and the newspapers. Now, beyond the treeline, past the ruined cottages of the miners who once worked lead there, past the crumbling mine buildings and the carcases of steam engines and pumps, past the sterile spoil heaps, hundreds of people were scouring the hills. Stefan didn't know much about Byrne, but from what he had heard mountain climbing in the dark seemed unlikely, drunk or not.

Stefan looked back up the Miners' Road then stopped, seeing a man on horseback, riding through the trees towards him. He recognized Alex Sinclair straightaway, even though they hadn't seen one another for many years. As the tall, fair-haired man, a little older than Stefan, came level with him, he reined in the horse. Men walking past touched their caps.

'Someone said you were about. It's a long time, Stefan.'

'It is. So they've got you out looking too?'

'I thought I'd better put in my six-penn'orth. Everyone else is.'

'It's thorough, certainly.'

'Is that a lack of conviction, Inspector Gillespie?'

'I don't know far they think the man got, but his bicycle was half a mile down the road, whatever that means. They're working out from there, which sounds like sense. But up here, if you don't find anything, you keep going, anywhere. And it's a lot of anywhere. Did you know him, Alex?'

'I've discussed the weather and the price of stamps. But I'm never here these days. I've been in England for years. I'm with the RAF now.'

Stefan knew. He had not seen Alex Sinclair in seven years but it was only a month since he read his name on a list at Dublin Castle: Alexander Sinclair, Mullacor House, Glendalough, Flying Officer in the RAF, 43 Squadron. It was a list he had put at the bottom of a file. Not that it mattered much. There were degrees even in the treacherous activities Stefan was rooting out. Not everyone warranted the same attention when it came to the British forces. The Sinclairs owned a lot of land. They possessed healthy nationalist credentials too, since Alex's grandfather abandoned his Anglo-Irish connections abruptly in 1884, but they still had close ties to England. There was a great uncle who was a Royal Artillery colonel, though he lived

south of Dublin, outside Naas. He belonged to the side of the
family without nationalist credentials; he still wouldn't be on
any Special Branch lists.

Alex Sinclair got down from the horse. They shook hands.

'So are you still in Baltinglass? That was the last I heard.'

'No, I'm working in Dublin now.'

'And here to put in your six-penn'orth too then.'

'To stick my oar in as far as Bray CID are concerned.'

'Oh, it's like that, is it?'

Alex took the mare's bridle; they walked in the shadow of
the trees.

'So do the Guards have any idea what happened to Billy
Byrne?'

'The short answer is no,' said Stefan.

'The long answer is presumably not for my ears.'

'I'm not sure it's for anybody's so far.'

'I'll tell you one thing,' said Sinclair, looking at another gang
of eager searchers heading past them to the Miners' Road and
the hills, 'if he's dead then he's got a lot more friends now than
he had when he was alive.'

Stefan nodded; he had already heard that.

'I hope life's been kinder to you, Stefan, over the years.'

'Kind enough.'

'What about your lad? I'm sorry, I should know his name.'

'Tom's grand. He's eight now. Still at the farm with my
parents. It's not the way I'd want it to be, but it's how it has to
be. It works, sort of.'

'You've not married again?'

'Well, let's say it hasn't happened yet.'

Alex registered the hint of a smile. 'Does that mean it's going
to?'

'It's . . .'

'It's not my business!' laughed Alex.

'I only meant,' Stefan smiled, 'if I knew what was happening,

I might have an answer. I don't even know if . . . with the times we're in . . .'

They walked on again, the horse following behind.

'Anyway,' said Alex suddenly, 'I joined up. I'm in it!'

'How long?'

'Three months. ASAP. I've been flying for five years, you know. I had to get something out of that! I got my wings. Now I'm actually paid to sit in one of the fastest crates you can fly. They even started a war for me!'

'I'm glad something makes it worth fighting, Alex.'

Stefan smiled. Alex Sinclair looked more serious.

'I think the English know why they're fighting, most of them. At least they've got a better idea why they are than we have why we're not.'

Stefan didn't answer. Sometimes he felt that too.

'Isn't one of your parents German? Have I got that right?'

'My mother's family.'

'So your loyalties are torn.'

'No, my loyalty is here. Someone has to guard our neutrality.'

Stefan gave a slightly ambiguous smile, as if what he was saying wasn't serious at all. It was hard to make it sound convincing at the best of times, especially to someone he sensed would not want to be convinced.

'You believe all that, Stefan?'

'I believe we haven't got a choice.'

A look of impatience passed over Sinclair's face.

'I don't think there's a choice either. You have to be in it.'

'If it was that easy—'

'Nothing that matters is easy. My grandfather converted to Catholicism because he was a nationalist. He didn't care about the Church, but you have to show people who you are. It cost him every friend he had. People he'd known since school wouldn't talk to him. And my grandmother never forgave him. He never doubted he did the right thing. A country needs to show what it is too. What do we show, skulking behind England's skirts to see who comes out on top? God forbid we choose the wrong side!'

'Is that what they think in the officers' mess?'

'Surprisingly not. The English are more generous than I am.'

'What would happen if British troops came back to Ireland? Would a war in Ireland help England, or anyone? The side we've picked is our own.'

'I'm sure you're right,' said Alex, laughing. 'Maybe we should be grateful there's somewhere a postman disappears and a nation holds its breath. Grand to hear such passion for doing nothing. Dear old Ireland!'

As they walked on they heard the sound of a plane.

'I doubt they'll spot a postman's uniform from up there.'

'It'll be to do with the IRA raid,' said Stefan. 'I'm sure you know. We've had planes out since before Christmas. Two crises at once. The Magazine Fort and the postman! But you're still right. They won't spot a box of .45 calibre cartridges either. I think it's what's called reassurance.'

Sinclair shook his head. 'It's what I do every day, planes. I love them. I still can't say I find them reassuring. I was coming out of the Café Royal, before I left, and I heard one. I could tell it was some old transport nag, somewhere over Regent's Street. I'm flying a Hurricane. The noise is always there. I don't notice it. But that day I wondered what it would sound like when there are hundreds of them, of bombers. The way it must have been in Warsaw, and all over the place now. That's the way it has to be.'

'And you think that's what's on its way?'

'Isn't that what war is now, Stefan? The funny thing is, it's all quite cheerful over there. England I mean, London. I was living there before it started but I don't think I ever enjoyed it so much as now. Maybe it's because I'm flying. Maybe it's just how you have to be, in the middle of it all. Like flying. No before, no after, only now. You know you're alive.'

They had reached the metalled road. The Special Branch car was parked there. Alex Sinclair stopped and climbed back on to the mare.

'I'll be back to England in a few days, so come up to the house!'

Stefan nodded. 'I'll try.'

He wouldn't go. Alex probably wouldn't expect him to. They knew one another because of Maeve. The only long conversation they ever had was in the aftermath of her death. It was a conversation that mattered to Stefan because it was a step towards finding his way back to himself, when he had almost lost any sense of who he was. It was that exchange that connected them and only that. When they ran out of words about the postman and the war there would be a silence in which Stefan would not want to restart a conversation that had ended seven years earlier. Even worse would be polite chitchat with Mrs Sinclair, a woman he had met only twice, at his wedding and Maeve's funeral. He disliked her both times. To make him notice he disliked her as his wife was being buried was a considerable achievement. There was also the prospect of Alex's older brother, Stuart. For three years after Maeve's death he had written to Stefan, from Glendalough and from the Central Mental Asylum, to say not only that Maeve was an angel in heaven but that he was in communication with her. Through the blessed intercession of St Anthony he had even seen her.

Alex would understand all that. He was saying what he felt he had to.

'How is your brother?' Stefan asked the question in the same vein. He said it because Maeve would have wanted him to. She had cared about Stuart.

'Still getting himself into trouble. Just for Christmas he managed to have himself knocked down by a car in Aughrim, but apart from that—'

'He's not hurt?'

'I think the car came off worse. He's up and down. He's home now but he's in and out of hospital. Nothing changes. My mother needs to get him away sometimes. She sends him off and believes some new treatment will make him normal. Then she feels guilty and brings him back home.'

'I'm sorry.'

'I'm not sure he doesn't come out of the bin worse than he goes in. But I don't have to live with him. Sometimes I'm not sure they didn't do things better a hundred years ago. If we simply locked Stuart in the attic . . .'

It sounded like a flippant laugh, but Stefan knew enough to understand the pain behind those words, a pain that was simply an ordinary part of Alex Sinclair's life.

'You will come up and see us, though. And argue! I'm sure you're precisely the feller to persuade me neutrality is a grand thing altogether!'

Alex grinned to show that he didn't think that at all, and rode off.

Stefan watched him as he walked to the car. He smiled. The past wasn't easy to escape here but he needed to push it away again. On the way to the Upper Lake he had passed the post office in Glendalough. William Byrne had lived there. All he knew about the Missing Postman was that he was last seen drunk on Christmas Eve in Laragh and that nobody liked him much. Since he was stuck here, like it or not, he had better know more.

10

St Kevin's Road

The post office lay to the right of St Kevin's Road as Stefan drove out of Glendalough, the smaller of the two towns in the Vale of Glendalough. It sat below the road where the valley sloped towards the river. At the barely legible 'Oifig an Phoist' sign he turned down a track to a low stone building that looked like a farmhouse because it was. A dozen hens and a bad-tempered Muscovy duck scattered across the yard. The green door of the post office opened. A uniformed Guard emerged, his jacket off, his sleeves rolled; he was finishing eating. He looked at the man getting out of the car. He didn't know him but he had to be a detective.

Stefan smiled amiably.

'I'd like a look round. Don't let me interrupt you at your dinner.'

'Mrs Casson was after having a bite, sir . . .' 'Sir' seemed a safe bet.

'Mrs Casson is still the postmistress, is she?'

The Guard looked puzzled; why wouldn't she be?

Stefan walked into the dark room that was the post office. It was a long, narrow room with a heavy mahogany counter at one end. There was a wall of pigeonholes, empty except for a few letters. A black chest of drawers was piled with the dusty papers and forms that were a post office's stock-in-trade. Faded posters on the walls advertised the Great Southern Railway and the Irish Army; 'Oglaigh na hÉireann – Join the Volunteers'. A fire burned in a small grate. At a round table were the Guard's meal and a glass of Guinness. The man stood awkwardly, pulling on his uniform tunic.

'Is it the bike you wanted to see, sir, Billy Byrne's bike? They found it up the road, past Glendalough, heading up towards the Seven Churches.'

'Don't worry, I've seen bicycles before.'

This lack of interest in the GPO bicycle was puzzling. A photograph of it, in situ on St Kevin's Road, was in that morning's *Irish Independent*.

'The fingerprint men were here yesterday. If you haven't seen it—'

Mrs Casson, the postmistress was suddenly, noiselessly, behind the counter. She was in her sixties and, like all women with government jobs, a spinster. Had she married she would have lost the position she had held for thirty years. She knew Stefan was a policeman; he didn't look like a man who would own a car. There had been a string of them in and out of her post office, to no purpose she could fathom. People had to be seen to do their jobs, but they irritated her. There was nothing she could tell them.

'Detective Inspector Gillespie, Mrs Casson. Down from Dublin.'

Mrs Casson peered out through thick glasses, unimpressed.

'How are you, Mrs Casson?'

'Do I know you?' she asked.

'I was here, years ago. My wife was Maeve Joyce. You'll remember her. She used to stay with her cousins. Her uncle was the doctor in Laragh.'

'Yes, I remember. There are no Joyces here now.'

'No. They'd moved away, even before Maeve and I . . .'

He stopped. It was the idle conversation you might have in any country post office, but he could see she had no interest. Perhaps it was no time for idle chat. Billy Byrne had worked for her; he lived in rooms there.

'I'd like to see Mr Byrne's rooms.'

'Garda Boyle has the key. To the right outside, the door at the end.'

Stefan looked round. The Guard reached into his pocket for the key.

'Will you want me with you, Inspector?'

'I'll leave you to it. Don't let your dinner get cold.'

Stefan walked out. The Guard took his jacket off again and resumed his meal. Mrs Casson was looking thoughtfully at the space Stefan had occupied. She walked through the door behind the counter. She closed it firmly. She went to the small switchboard and picked up the telephone.

At the top of a flight of unlit stone stairs a door led into a big room. The room was well furnished. A chesterfield, a leather armchair, a round oak table, a mahogany desk that was not old and had not been cheap. Against one wall was a small iron range, next to a kitchen cabinet and a basin. Stefan stood at the desk, priming the pressure pump of a brass Tilley lamp. He lit it and took in the tidy, comfortable space. He walked to an inner door and peered in at a bedroom containing a single bed and a wardrobe.

Back in the living room he looked at the shelf above the range. There were several photographs, old and stiff, the products of a studio; parents and grandparents. There was a sepia photo of three children. William Byrne was forty-five, but there was enough resemblance between one of the children and a newer portrait of a man in a postman's uniform to identify him and suggest he had brother and sister somewhere. There was another picture of Byrne in uniform, with five other men. It was crumpled and stained, but it was the only photo in a silver gilt frame. The uniform was curious. It was military but Stefan didn't recognize it. The men wore caps that perched on their heads and had a fold in the middle. He didn't know the word for them but he had seen them. They were nothing the Irish Army wore and the uniforms were not British. It was no species of IRA uniform. In black and white the colour of the tunics could have been any kind of grey-green khaki. At the centre was an officer; lapelled jacket, shirt and tie, Sam Brown belt, riding boots. One of the men was Byrne. The picture was taken outside; the background was sky and rock. It didn't look like Ireland.

Stefan knelt at a low bookshelf. A lot of newspapers, mostly local, a few books. He recognized Zane Gray's *Riders of the Purple Sage*; he had read it as a boy. There was a Missal, a *Pocket Oxford Dictionary* and a battered grey paperback, *Dent's First Spanish Phrasebook*. He looked back at the mantelpiece and the men in uniform. It was Spain. He had seen the caps in newsreels of the Spanish Civil War. He guessed the uniforms were those of the Irishmen who went to fight for Franco with General Eoin O'Duffy. He knew little about it except that the expedition had been a disaster. The silver gilt frame suggested the Missing Postman thought otherwise. He already seemed a more interesting postman than the man who drank too much and wasn't liked for no reason anyone could think of.

On the desk was a walnut Marconi radio. It was very new; like the furniture it had cost good money. He looked down at several copies of the *Wicklow People* and the Christmas Eve edition of the *Irish Times*. There was also, more surprisingly, a copy of *Iris Ofigiúil*, the *Irish State Gazette*. It wasn't something Stefan often read, but every Garda station received it. It made obscure reading for a country postman, mostly listing state legislation and appointments. Byrne's copy was open at bankruptcies and court cases.

Stefan turned to the drawers; more newspapers, including

more copies of the *State Gazette*. As he leafed through the papers he saw that items had been ringed; deaths, marriages, bankruptcies, court convictions, addresses. Not everything ringed related to Wicklow, but much did; he assumed it all carried local connections. In the middle drawer were some Manila files; some contained receipts, including furniture and the radio; others held newspaper cuttings and scribbled notes. There was a chequebook in William Byrne's name; an account at the Bank of Ireland in Rathdrum.

A bank account wasn't unusual but for a postman in the Wicklow Mountains it was noteworthy, and what people did with their money said a lot. There was a folder of bank statements, the latest dated 23 November. Two transactions; a lodgement of £9.00 on the 17th, and the transfer of £15.00 to a savings account the same day. The statements went back two years; sums were intermittently paid in and transferred to the savings account. The amounts varied, £5, £8, £15; on one occasion in September 1938, £25, in April, £28. Occasionally cash was withdrawn.

In an envelope he found statements for the savings account. Byrne was saving surprising sums; often what he paid in was more than he could have earned. The total at the bottom of the sheet told a story, though Stefan could not know what it was. There was almost £700, accumulated in two years working as a postman. Even if he had found a way to live on nothing, it was over twice what he could have been paid.

Next, Stefan opened a file that contained envelopes full of newspaper cuttings; the contents were like the ringed items in the newspapers. Some cuttings were attached to pieces of paper, with handwritten notes, names, dates, addresses. On one was a name he recognized: Marian Gort, a childhood friend of Maeve's. She died in an accident before he and Maeve met, but not long before. He couldn't remember much about it. Inside the envelope were more cuttings. The first was clipped to a piece of paper with the words 'Church of Ireland Gazette' and a date. It all came back to him.

> The funeral took place on Friday, at St John's, Laragh, of Miss Marian Gort, daughter of the Reverend and Mrs Cyril Gort. Miss Gort died tragically in a walking accident, close to the beauty spot known as the Spinc, in the hills above Glendalough. The funeral was attended by many family and friends from all parts of Ireland and Britain. The Reverend Gort was assisted by the Most Reverend John Gregg, the Archbishop of Dublin, who was Miss Gort's godfather.

There were more cuttings about the death, the accident, the funeral, the inquest. Byrne's interest in this was odd, but something written below one cutting showed he had found reasons to think about Marian's death, to collect information and to want to question what had happened to her.

> Hushed up because she topped herself is what a lot here said at the time. Handy enough for him. But bollocks I say. She was number 2.

It was the next envelope that changed everything. As he took it from the folder he saw another name he knew. The name was Maeve Gillespie. His curiosity was replaced by a moment of almost physical nausea. Instinct told him he was on the edge of something that was no longer intriguing but strange and disturbing. Something in this seemingly random collection of facts and dates and names was about Maeve. In the envelope there were cuttings as before; there were scribbled dates, the dates of Maeve's death and of her funeral at Kilranelagh. He didn't need to read them. He needed to know why they were there. The last cutting recorded the inquest that had been only a formality, and its verdict: misadventure. But next to it William Byrne had added his own dismissive comment on that verdict.

Did anyone see it? No. He drowned this one. So it is number 3!

Stefan stared uncomprehendingly at the piece of paper. Then he heard the door downstairs. He closed the file and stood up. It was a reflex. There was nothing to hide but he couldn't begin to talk about what he had just been looking at. There was a link forging in his head, inexplicable, senseless, but somehow already undeniable, between his wife's grave at Kilranelagh and this man he knew nothing of, who had now disappeared.

A man entered the room. He wore a grey trench coat, slightly too small, and a trilby, slightly too big. He had a round face and a dark complexion; when he smiled, as he did now, he showed a set of teeth too white and regular to be anything but false. He was short and thickset. The man behind him, ten inches taller, was Fintan Grace. Stefan forced his mind out of the confusion filling it. As Chief Inspector Halloran eyed him coldly, despite the smile, he found a focus to bring him back to the present in Dessie's description of Messrs Halloran and Grace: Laurel and Hardy.

'You're Gillespie?'

'Yes, sir.'

'Terry Gregory tells me you're here to lend a hand.'

'Something like that, sir. It's up to you.'

'Up to me, is it? Jesus, is that from Terry himself?' Halloran looked round at Fintan Grace. 'They've put some manners on the Special Branch. Gone are the days they'd shoot you in the back without even apologizing.'

Inspector Grace laughed; it was part of his job.

'You're here because Ned Broy smells nefarious goings-on among the Laragh Gardaí, and he wants to make sure I'm not sweeping it under the carpet. If I didn't know, I'd think he had us confused with you fuckers.'

'Yes, sir.'

'What do you mean, "Yes, sir"?'

'Yes, sir, that's about it.'

Detective Chief Inspector Halloran laughed.

'You're right, Fintan, this one is the clever bollix altogether.'

Inspector Grace was unsure if he should laugh at this.

'So why are you in here, Gillespie? Didn't want mud on your shoes?'

'You're not short of volunteers up above.'

'We have looked here, Inspector. He's not under the bed.'

Fintan Grace chuckled; this was safer ground.

'I thought I'd see who this feller was exactly, sir.'

'And what did you find out?'

'He was careful with his money, for a man who spent most of it in the pub, I'd say. There's close to £700 in his bank account.'

'I know, I have looked. So what else?'

'That's as far as I got, sir.'

Stefan didn't want to draw attention to the contents of the desk. He had to know more. What he didn't need was Halloran blocking his access to this room. But the chief inspector seemed to have no problem with Stefan looking through the evidence here. His initial hostility was softening.

Stefan took a few steps towards the mantelpiece. 'Is this in Spain?'

'It is. Billy Byrne was with O'Duffy's boys. He even picked up a war wound. He'd a grand story about it they say and the more he drank the grander it got. If they'd left him there he'd have seen off the Reds sooner than Franco. Though some say he broke his leg falling off a balcony in a whorehouse. But you'll get begrudgers in any line of work, Inspector.'

Stefan grinned; it seemed to be what Halloran expected.

'So are you getting any closer to what happened, sir?'

'Closer to what happened, but not closer to who did it.'

'You think someone killed him then?'

'I think he's dead one way or another. Your man was a nasty bit of work. I don't know if that's why no one's saying anything, but there's a holy hush along the valley like nothing since St Kevin was in communion with the angels. Yet there's no hiding what people thought of Billy. I'd say he had a way of ferreting out bits and pieces his neighbours didn't want ferreted. Some tax-fiddling here and there, some stock missing on the hill that ended up at the butcher's back door, a poteen still doing too much business, a box of contraceptives sent from England, some dirty postcards from Paris. He was probably a great lad for the kettle and steam too.'

Halloran had decided to engage the interloper. With or without a body he felt he was on top of it. He wanted that message to get to Garda HQ.

'And I'm sure it got nastier. Who was at it with who, always a song worth knowing, plus what goes with it. The baby delivered down the country no one knows about, or the one on the wrong end of the knitting needle and gin. The girl in London who's really in a Magdalene Laundry.'

'So all this money – you think he was blackmailing people?'

'A grand word for it, but you've been looking through his desk. I don't know what he got from the papers, but he must have turned up something now and again. He certainly used what he knew to avoid bills or pay for drinks. I had that much from Sergeant Chisholm. But he was getting money too, putting a bit away, setting up very cosy here. And who's going to say anything about that now? "I didn't kill him myself, Mr Halloran, but let me tell you how he blackmailed the bollocks off me." Not very likely.'

'So perhaps someone had finally had enough?'

'Could be. One Christmas box too many.'

'Any candidates?' asked Stefan.

'I've a good idea what happened. And I'm not alone. Half the valley knows, including the Guards. Who, is another thing altogether. Because where are they, these gobshites who know what went on? Searching the mountains with faces so long you'd think they wanted to find him. There's more than one could tell where Billy delivered his last Christmas card.'

Stefan could hear Halloran's frustration; it was real enough.

'So what do you want me to do, sir?'

'I don't care much if you keep out of my way.'

'There has to be something here,' said Stefan, 'along with his bank statements, the papers, the cuttings. There's a lot of it. It might be worth going through it all in detail, just to see if it can tell us anything more.'

'You'd be here till next Christmas, Gillespie, and no better off.'

'Well, if no one else is doing it . . .'

'I never knew Terry Gregory's fellers were so thorough. What's the matter, is beating the shite out of people not getting the results anymore?'

'I'd be no use up a mountain – I'd never keep up with Fintan.'

Halloran was laughing as he turned to Fintan Grace, who wasn't. It was another part of Grace's job to confirm decisions he knew his boss had already made. He nodded. The less he saw of Stefan Gillespie the better.

'All right,' said Halloran, 'since Terry was generous enough to give us a detective who can actually read, we might as well make use of you.'

When the Bray detectives left Stefan went back to the desk. He looked at the files again. There was more. A dozen sheets of paper clipped together, covered in the writing he now recognized as Byrne's, carefully formed like words in a school copy. The first sheet was headed with another woman's name. It meant nothing to Stefan: Charlotte Moore. As he read he realized the words were not the postman's. Byrne must have found this material somewhere and copied it. It had involved considerable work. He looked at the date on the first sheet. Not the date Byrne wrote it down but the date of the *Irish Times* article he had recorded. More articles followed, covering months. It was a story Stefan didn't know anything about at all.

Charlotte Moore had gone missing on 3 March 1919. She was fourteen. Her body was never found. She lived in Glendalough. Her father was a farm labourer, her mother cleaned at one of the big houses. The search went on in the mountains for weeks, starting with a surge of public concern that echoed what was happening with the Missing Postman. But the search was fruitless. Before long it petered out. It wasn't surprising, even twenty years on. In Ireland the end of the First World War was marked by the start of another war: the War of Independence. The Royal Irish Constabulary were on the front line even in Wicklow. It was inevitable the search for the girl's body would be abandoned. Besides, everyone knew what had happened.

Not many days after Charlotte Moore's disappearance someone else disappeared from the Vale of Glendalough; a man of twenty-seven, Albert Neale, a forestry worker who had already been questioned. Outbuildings at the farm where he lived were searched; articles of Charlotte's bloodstained clothing were found. But he had already fled. There was one sighting of him on the mail boat from Kingstown, but Albert Neale would never be seen again. In the margin of his notes William Byrne had added something:

Never did find her. Nor him. They lost their 'murderer', so they looked for no one else. But it was the first he done. His number 1.

Stefan leafed back through the cuttings and notes. A girl murdered in Glendalough twenty years ago. A woman dead in an accident eight years ago. A woman drowned seven years ago. He forced himself to look at Maeve as the third woman in a list. One. Two. Three. Charlotte Moore. Marian Gort. Maeve

Gillespie. The postman saw something that brought them together. There was not one murder for him, there were three. Maeve was the third. He believed they had all been killed and by the same man. Stefan already knew the evidence was almost nothing. In the cuttings about Marian and Maeve evidence was to the contrary. But he could not dismiss what he was looking at. For seven years he had believed his wife drowned, swimming in the waters of the Upper Lake. There had never been a reason to think anything else. But William Byrne, now missing presumed dead, a man who, in Chief Inspector Halloran's words, had a way of 'ferreting things out that people didn't want ferreted', had not only been convinced that Maeve had been murdered, he believed he knew who had killed her.

Did anyone see it? No. He drowned this one. So it is number 3!

It was so matter of fact it sounded real; it had been real to Byrne. One. Two. Three. The postman was good at finding things out. He made money from it. Even Halloran had to wonder if he was so good it might have cost him his life. Somehow the fact that Byrne was probably dead gave credibility to it. If he died because of the way he pushed himself into people's lives, their errors, foibles, mistakes, into their secrets and their tragedies, into their crimes, then surely the things he believed were real.

There were more pieces of paper but none of it related to the three women. There was another envelope. Inside were photos, the two-and-a-half inch prints from a Box Brownie. Stefan recognized the Upper Lake, the mountains, houses and shops in Laragh. Sometimes a date was on the back. Then he was looking at five photographs of headstones, two headstones in what felt like the same cemetery. The pictures had been taken in winter and summer. In one the name Marian Gort was legible. But it wasn't the name Stefan was looking at. In each photo there was a single white arum lily.

11

Laragh

Stefan stopped the Austin beyond the Garda Barracks. It was not quite dark. He had passed lines of people heading in from the Seven Churches. The day's search was over. There was mist again, but no more than the meeting of damp air and freezing temperatures. He walked the Trooperstown Road to the wrought-iron gate that led into the Church of Ireland churchyard.

It was a familiar space, not because he knew it, but because it was so like the Church of Ireland churches in Baltinglass and Kiltegan he did know. He had only been here once, the day before Maeve died, when he left her bringing flowers to her friend. To one side was the square tower and the grey building that was St John's church, its arched windows glazed only in clear leaded panes. On the other side of a pebble path was the graveyard.

He walked through the black, lichened stones and the scattering of brighter, yellower newcomers, looking for Marian Gort's grave. He saw the lily first, on the grass beside a wreath of red-berried holly. It was still only a flower; he could not read what William Byrne had read. The postman knew who put it there. But Stefan would have to find a way to read it now. There was some relief in the clarity of that. In all the confusion and disbelief there was a kind of calm around him. He could see the beginnings of the night sky above the churchyard. It was where he stood, on the edge of the dark. He had to step into it. Nothing could be the same until he knew the truth.

As he walked back he saw the other lily, by a small stone set against the ivy-covered churchyard wall; not quite a headstone. He recognized it from Byrne's photograph. 'Suffer Little Children to Come unto Me: In memory of our lost daughter Charlotte Moore.' Hearing footsteps, he turned. A man, little older than him, was watching him from the church.

'Good evening!'

He saw a glimpse of a clerical collar under the man's overcoat.

'Hello, my name's Gillespie, Detective Inspector Gillespie.'

'Ah, no news of Mr Byrne?'

'No.'

'It's an unpleasant business. It's sad. It must look as if he . . .'

Stefan registered the word 'unpleasant'.

'Did you know him, Mr . . .?'

'Campion. I knew him as one knows a postman. At such times one realizes how little we do know about so many people we see every day.'

The platitude eased the Reverend Campion's slight discomfort.

'I was looking at a grave just now, someone I knew. Knew isn't right. A friend of my wife's when they were children, Marian Gort.'

'Ah, you know the Gorts?'

The vicar had recognized him as one of his own, if not for exactly the right reasons. His tone was softer. It wasn't that he had been unwelcoming, but now there was more trust, even in a conversation in which no trust was required.

'My wife did. I didn't realize Mr Gort had left Laragh.'

'He's in England now. Mrs Gort was English. Sadly, she died.

He did call in last week, though. Over for Christmas. He has a son in Greystones.'

'He brought the wreath?'

It was an odd question, though Campion didn't seem to notice.

'I imagine so.'

'There's a single arum lily, just next to it.'

'Is there? Well, quite possibly he brought that.'

'It hasn't been here more than two or three days.'

The vicar was looking at Stefan with some bewilderment now.

'There's another lily too, on a memorial to a girl called Charlotte Moore.'

The Reverend Campion frowned; he didn't understand.

'Have you seen lilies here before, by those two headstones?'

'It's quite possible, Inspector. I don't know. Why do you ask?'

'What about the girl's family, the Moores? Do you know them?'

'I don't at all. I think they left the area quite some time ago.'

'You do know what happened, though?'

'The girl isn't buried here. She disappeared, I'm not sure when. I think after the war. She was never found. I think her people left in the twenties. A lot do now. You're not from here. Does your wife's family—'

A change of subject felt like a good idea, but not to Stefan.

'Have you seen lilies like this here before?'

The Reverend Campion was now showing signs of irritation.

'Is there a reason for these questions, Mr Gillespie? I really can't answer. Possibly. It isn't something, even if I noticed, that I'd remember.'

'Does anyone else come to Marian's grave or the girl's stone?'

'I don't know. Probably not as far as the Moores go. But everyone knew Miss Gort. I'm sure there are often flowers on her grave. Why are—'

'Did you ever see the postman here, William Byrne?'

116

'He would have had no reason to come in here.' The vicar spoke coldly now. 'He would have passed the churchyard, on his way to the vicarage, but I can't see why he would come in. You can ask Father Malone, but I think you'll find he was a stranger even in his own church.'

When Stefan Gillespie returned to the Garda Barracks it was dark. The last search party was dragging in along Laragh's main street; most of the volunteers turned at the Green to Whelan's Bar. Dessie MacMahon was walking up to the barracks when Stefan saw him. He did not look happy.

'Nothing?' said Stefan.

'My arse! You could walk past a dozen bodies up there.'

Stefan caught the breath of beer. 'You found time for a pint.'

'I was visiting the scene of Billy Byrne's last performance.'

They walked into the police station.

'And what did that tell you?'

'Missing postmen are good business. You can't get in the place.'

'Anything new on what happened?'

'You'd think that would be all the talk in a pub.'

'Isn't it?'

'It is from fellers who came up from Rathdrum or Arklow. But if you start a conversation with any of the local lads you'll find yourself standing on your own. Maybe I'm just not used to country ways like you, Stevie.'

As they came into the station there was a crowd of detectives and uniformed Guards, most of them covered in the filth of the mountains.

'But there is something on,' Dessie spoke quietly, 'here.'

The noise suddenly stopped. Detective Chief Inspector Halloran had entered behind them, the gaunt Inspector Grace at his shoulder. Pat Halloran's teeth showed more than ever in his smile, a smile of satisfaction.

'Get Chisholm and the other two, Fintan.'

The inspector disappeared into the mess-room corridor.

'All the Bray men in Sergeant Chisholm's office. The rest of youse get off home, because you'll be back out on those fecking hills tomorrow.'

Fintan Grace reappeared with Sergeant Chisholm and two Guards.

'You can do something for me, George,' said Halloran.

'And what would that be, sir?'

'Bugger off.'

'And where will I bugger off to, sir?'

'Go home, and your two Guards as well. If you're in the barracks keep to your quarters. You're all suspended. There'll be letters tomorrow.'

Sergeant Chisholm smiled.

'A bit harsh, sir, for a drink on Christmas Eve?'

'Sorry lads, harsh is the last thing I'd ever want to be to you,' said Halloran, 'but even with Christmas over, I'm still making my list, I'm checking it twice, I am going to find out . . . who's naughty . . . or nice.'

He walked away. Chisholm looked less cocky than he had been.

Stefan was watching Halloran, uncertain whether to follow him.

The chief inspector turned as he reached the sergeant's office.

'You'd best shift, Inspector, or do you prefer listening at the door?'

'The search goes on till we find a body. There's a limit to how far away it can be. There are places round the town to check again. And some of the mineshafts up there go very deep as well. I've spoken to the commissioner about special equipment. There's the lakes too. There'll be divers tomorrow.'

There were murmurs of frustration, but the general silence from Halloran's officers reflected the scale of the search and the slim chances of success. Looking where they had looked was an admission of how slim.

'But we have a lot of statements now. Some contradictions to dig at too, but not many. Not as many as I'd expect if I asked a couple of dozen people to tell me what happened when half of them were too pissed to remember. But out of that we do have what we might call, for now, the authorized version of Billy Byrne's movements on Christmas Eve.'

Halloran picked up a piece of paper.

'He left the post office at Glendalough around eight in the morning. He'd been sorting letters with Mrs Casson since six. He cycled into Laragh and started deliveries. He finished in the town at twelve-thirty, two hours later than usual, then set off on outlying deliveries at the Laragh end. He'd have gone back to Glendalough after that and finished with the farms along St Kevin's Road. He didn't even finish in Laragh. I don't know how many deliveries involved a Christmas tipple, since no one wants to say, but when he left the town he was as pissed as you like. He got to Trooperstown where he gave up and cycled back to Whelan's. The pub was closed but they were still drinking. I don't have all the names. Some I know were there still say they weren't. And despite their indignant denials, partaking of this session behind locked doors were our colleagues, Sergeant Chisholm and Garda McCoy.'

There was some laughter; Chisholm's involvement was no secret.

'But as the story goes, Byrne was in Whelan's no more than fifteen minutes. He had one whiskey, then Mary Whelan, concerned she says about the drink he'd taken, ushered him out. Her word, "ushered". A helpful woman. Billy wasn't keen to go. He got a bit argumentative, but two friendly Guards were, at that moment, walking across the bridge and Mrs

Whelan asked for assistance. I don't want you lads thinking this is a fairy story. In Laragh there's always a policeman there when you want one.'

The laughter was louder.

'Garda McCoy put a comradely arm round Mr Byrne and carried his post bag. Sergeant Chisholm wheeled his bicycle. When they got to the Green, in all of three minutes, your man had sobered up. He was grand. So they put him on the bike, wished him safe home and a Nollaig Shona, and waved him off. The bicycle was found on the other side of Glendalough, on St Kevin's Road, late that night, by Mr and Mrs Lee, on their way back from Mass. And Billy Byrne, as we know, became the Missing Postman!'

Chief Inspector Halloran now picked up a heavy ledger.

'This is the station diary, which helpfully records George Chisholm's encounter with Billy. No reason why it shouldn't if George was the kind of sergeant inspectors dream of. But a quick flick through this shows nothing but roll calls and officers arriving for duty and finishing shifts. In the last two weeks we have two traffic accidents, a drunk who spent a night in the cells, and a burglar at Knockfin who turned out be a man locked out by his wife for reasons Sergeant Chisholm is too delicate to go into. The sergeant doesn't usually write down every time he helps old ladies across the street. But he does alter the record to falsify when he and his men are on duty. He doesn't do it very well. One entry for Christmas Eve has been erased and rewritten. Times have been changed. The details of Byrne's departure from Whelan's were written in later, over something else. And by later I mean after he went missing. Or maybe that just jogged the sergeant's memory.'

Pat Halloran turned to Inspector Grace.

'Have you got Dearing's statement?'

'Yes, sir,'

'We have one statement that doesn't fit the rest. Paul

Dearing, the blacksmith. He was at the session in Whelan's. He says Byrne was in the pub much longer than anyone else does. There was poteen one of the Whelan girls had from Glenmalure. That was why there were so many there. Byrne was drinking it. I'd be confident Dearing's is the real version.'

He nodded at Grace, who cleared his throat self-consciously.

'This is from Dearing's statement: I got into Whelan's through the yard as Mary had closed up. The front was locked but Mary said her girl had some good poteen and to come in anyway. I went down the back hall. Daisy Whelan was in the kitchen playing the piano and Sergeant Chisholm was singing. The sergeant's soft on Daisy, so you'd know not to go in.'

There was some sniggering; Fintan Grace glared and continued.

'Garda McCoy was with a crowd at the bar. Billy Byrne was well gone. He was arguing about paying. Mary said he could pay or fuck off. Nobody took any notice. Then he starts laughing to himself. He looks at me and asks was I getting a Christmas box. He says, I'll be getting mine. I'll be on the pig's back, and the Devil fuck all here! I sat down. All of a sudden it went quiet. People were looking at Billy and Shamie Tyrrell. Shamie has a half-crown. You want this, Billy? Billy says, it'll do, bring more next time. Why? says Shamie. You know, says Billy, only your missus doesn't. Shamie drops the half-crown. Pick it up, Billy. I will, says Billy, I'm not proud. No, you're not, says Shamie, and as Billy bends, Shamie knees him in the face. Billy flies back at the fireplace and hits his head. Then Mary Whelan walks out and says, Jesus, you have killed a man in my house! Garda McCoy comes over to Billy. The others is crowding round, saying he's breathing and he's not breathing. I didn't want trouble, so I left.'

As Fintan Grace concluded, there was a buzz of conversation. The bleak prospect of the search for a body was pushed aside. That would continue, but the wall of silence in the Vale of

Glendalough was broken. Now there were real facts. The rest would follow. One statement would lead to another; every new one would chip away at what was being hidden.

Stefan Gillespie caught Pat Halloran's eye, surrounded by his own men, reinvigorated by all this. The job wasn't done yet, but he was confident it soon would be.

It was late when Stefan got back to Kilranelagh. Tom was waiting, still on the coat-tails of Christmas. But the farmhouse wasn't the place it had been for Stefan when he left that morning. Nothing had changed for anyone else. His father sat in the armchair in front of the range, the radio on, half-asleep. His mother was knitting. Tom was at the table with his Meccano set.

'There's some dinner in the oven,' said Helena, getting up.

'Don't worry, Ma.'

David Gillespie sat up, yawning. 'Any sign of this postman?'

'No, nothing, Pa.'

Stefan sat down, tousling Tom's hair. Tom looked up, smiling. For a moment Stefan let his hand stay on his son's head. He didn't like what he had brought into the house with him. It was a new grief when grief had long gone. Tom was a part of Maeve; Stefan always saw her in him. That should have been reassuring, but he felt the weight on him now. He couldn't share it with anyone.

Helena put down a plate of dinner.

'Kate was on the telephone, she's back in Dún Laoghaire.'

'Oh, good.'

'They have a telephone there.'

'I know they do, Ma.'

He hadn't thought of Kate all day. He wanted to hear her voice, yet he didn't know how to talk to her. He wanted to put the content of William Byrne's head back in his desk. If it was true the thought of how Maeve died was not just new pain, it was guilt. If it was true he had failed her even after her death, failed her all these years. If she had been murdered the how was hard enough, but there was no why. There was a kind of vertigo inside him, as if he was falling in empty space. How could he not have known? A postman in Glendalough knew. And Stefan believed it. He couldn't make believing it go away. Somewhere in that valley, where he had been all day, somewhere there was Maeve's killer. The man who had drowned her.

Next morning Stefan left the farm before dawn. His father was in the barn, milking. It was a time of day David Gillespie liked, as much in the darkness of winter as in the light of summer. He emerged to watch his son drive out of the farmyard, the lights of the car filling the lane below for a few seconds and then disappearing. Perhaps it wasn't surprising that Stefan was in an odd mood. Investigating a death where his wife had died would unsettle him. But he knew his son's varieties of quietness. This one was strange. There had been something in Stefan's mood that he had not seen for many years. It wasn't unusual that he had nothing to say. The two men had worked together on the farm since Stefan's childhood, too closely not to appreciate each other's silence. But it wasn't only that his son was preoccupied. It wasn't only that he seemed to want to get away so quickly that morning. It was what David sensed but could not comprehend. It was a kind of rage.

12

The Spinc

Stefan stood high above the Upper Lake. The search parties were already out. He had followed them towards the Seven Churches, but as they started up the slopes on the northern side of the lake again, he took the climb to the south, past the Poulanass Waterfall, beyond the ruins of Temple na Skellig, and the cave that was called St Kevin's Bed, high on to the steep cliff that looked down at the long water. All this had been searched already, on Christmas Day. He could hear voices across the lake, but he was alone.

He stood at the top of the ridge known as the Spinc. The sun was visible in the sky today, a cold, white sun, but enough to bathe the Upper Lake in light. He held two of Byrne's photographs. This was where he took them; one looking down the track Stefan had climbed, the other looking from the edge of the Spinc to the water below. This was where Marian Gort died; where she slipped and fell, climbing on her own. That was what Maeve had told him. It was what everyone knew. But was it? William Byrne had found an announcement in the *Irish Times*; the engagement of Marian Gort of Laragh, County Wicklow, to Oliver Stanford Crosbie of Boroughbridge, Yorkshire. The cutting was dated 21 April 1930. Below it he had written: 'Engagement broke off July'. Marian died on 8 August. Byrne had got another version of the story; she killed herself. But what had Maeve really believed? She was very close to Marian. She must have known there was gossip. Yet the Missing Postman didn't believe either story. He thought someone was with Marian that day, someone who killed her.

Stefan had climbed the Spinc as much to clear his head as anything else. He knew what the photos showed. What he needed to do was take hold of it, to step out of the darkness and deal with it as a policeman. He had evidence; it wasn't much but surely it was real. He had what his instincts told him; whatever Billy Byrne was, he was no fantasist. Everything showed him piecing together tiny, vicious puzzles. Why was this different? He looked at the shoreline at the eastern end of the lake where Maeve's body was found. The two women died in almost the same place. It was an odd coincidence. It was a favourite saying of Terry Gregory's that when you had to call something a coincidence it meant you didn't have all the facts.

He returned to the postman's rooms and set about gathering everything together. He noted the items and put them in a box file he had brought from the Garda Barracks. This was what he had told Chief Inspector Halloran he was doing. It was evidence, even if Halloran had no real faith in any connection to Billy Byrne's death. But Stefan was less interested in Byrne as a victim than as witness; even dead he was the only way to the truth. Some things were clearer today. They were not things that would make Halloran listen, but Stefan had to tell him. He wouldn't like it.

He reached up to the mantelpiece to take a photo down, the one of Byrne in the uniform of O'Duffy's Bandera. It marked a before and after in the postman's life. Stefan had pieced together some facts in conversation with Mrs Casson. It had been hard work but he knew that before 1937 Byrne lived in Rathdrum, working as a painter and decorator and occasionally doing jobs in Laragh and Glendalough. He had never married; he had a reputation as a bad worker and a drunk. When Stefan asked the postmistress why she gave him a job she seemed to forget about that reputation. Then she clammed up. Given his habitual ferreting it was likely Byrne had something on Miss Casson. It was obvious she despised him; yet despite that, on his return from Spain, she employed him as her postman.

There were two Christmas cards on the mantelpiece, one signed 'Joey', the other 'Eileen', with the words 'All well with us over here'. They were probably from the brother and sister; Halloran would know about that. Stefan felt it was unlikely to matter to him. As he put the cards back an envelope fell to the floor. It had a Spanish stamp. He took out the letter. It had been sent a month earlier from the Irish College in Salamanca. Spain seemed important to Byrne. Almost the only personal things in the room, bar family photographs, were the picture of the soldiers and now this letter.

Dear Billy,

I am sorry to return your letter to Jim Collins. The Rector passed it on since we were pals while you were convalescing. Jim threw in his job here six months ago and moved closer to his wife's family, now the Republicans are gone. He left no address. The war has made the country a mess, as you would expect. We thank God it is done. The college is still closed, but the German Army still have offices here, the way you will recall. I help the Rector keep the old place ticking. But I may have to bite the bullet and come home to train for the priesthood. In Salamanca we are weary even talking of war. We want to forget it. But it doesn't look bright anywhere else now. I hope old Ireland keeps out of it all. We pray Franco does the same for Spain.

All the best in Holy Ireland, Mikey Hagan

It struck him how isolated William Byrne had been, amid all his drawers of information. Even this letter had an element of disconnection about it; a letter about another letter, a letter that hadn't been delivered. But somewhere it had to connect to the Bandera photograph. He looked at the envelope again. There was something else. It was the thinnest, lightweight paper, an air letter, still sealed. It was addressed to the Irish College, to Jim Collins. The writing was Byrne's and his address was on the back. Stefan opened it with a paper knife.

Dear Jim,

Hoping this finds you as it leaves me in Ireland. It is looking up in Spain from what the papers say, with the Commies run out, and all over bar the shooting, eh! I have meant to send you cash, like I said, but I am saving to do it right. A promise is a promise. I won't let you down. But our chum in Glendalough is not clever at paying dues, though what I have now means them dues must see you and me in easy street. There is more to it now, but a letter is not safe to tell. He knows I have him by the throat. He needs to remember you are there, that is the thing. It is hard to keep that in his head. I don't know if he forgets or is after codding me, but I don't let him get away with shite. After all we know our friend 'Bert Neale' never touched her! Write him a letter. That is the business for you. Anonymous is the thing, but if it comes from Spain he will have no doubt. Give 'fond' regards. Say you will come home to talk 'old times'! There is money, I promise, and not shillings. Do it square, Jim. I will see you right.

Your old comrade, Billy

Detective Chief Inspector Halloran turned the pages of the short report Inspector Gillespie had put in front of him. They sat in the sergeant's office in Laragh. On the desk was a pile of Manila folders and box files Stefan had brought from the post office. Halloran had a pipe in his mouth. He chewed it but it had gone out ten minutes earlier. It was dark outside now. Again the day's search was done. There was nothing. Billy Byrne remained invisible.

'Apart from the fact that it's thorough, what do I say?'

'I'm not sure what I've got to say myself yet, sir.'

'Let's divide it in two. The first part. No one's ever going to make head nor tail of that. God knows how many rings round God knows how many bits in newspapers. Names, addresses, dates. Half of it has nothing to do with Glendalough or Laragh. Maybe it might if we understood it. But what would it tell us? If we spent a month at this we might put some dates next to what – someone's spell inside, a bigamous marriage in England, an inheritance someone else should have got, an illegitimate birth? Is that it?'

'I'd imagine it's that kind of thing, yes, sir.'

'Do I need to know? It doesn't give me the names of more fuckers in Whelan's on Christmas Eve. It doesn't tell me who took the body into the mountains and dumped it. None of this is going to do anything but confirm Billy Byrne was a nasty gobshite. The second part – about these women?'

'Yes, about these women.'

Halloran put the pipe to his lips and relit it.

'That's how I have to look at it. There's no disrespect to your wife.'

Stefan nodded. Halloran turned the pages of the report again.

'Billy Byrne thought three women who died here, years

apart, were killed by someone, and he knew who. We've got hundreds of pieces of paper about things he found out or thought he did. So was everything he suspected true? The man was a chancer! How many times did he get two and two to make five? Look at what you've got. Yes, one of those women was murdered. There'll be an RIC file on the girl in Dublin Castle. They had clear evidence to hang a man if he hadn't hopped it. The other two died in accidents that were never questioned by anybody, even by you as a husband mourning his wife and as a policeman. I have to put it that way.'

'I understand that, sir.'

'What else? Someone puts some flowers on the graves. Someone remembers these women. You don't know who. And Billy writes to a feller in Spain and he says what? That he's trying to get money out of people.'

'Out of the man he believed murdered . . . these women.'

Pat Halloran shook his head.

'On Christmas Eve in Whelan's Seamus Tyrrell hit Billy Byrne so hard he fell and cracked his skull. Either he died then or soon after. Then whoever it was, because Tyrrell didn't do it on his own, put him where no bugger would find him. And "whoever" included Sergeant Chisholm.'

'What if he wasn't killed?'

'Are you telling me he's not dead?'

'What if the rest of it's true? The authorized version. He cracked his head and passed out, then he came to and left, with a hand from George Chisholm and Garda McCoy, more or less the way they tell it. But when they all knew he'd disappeared, no one wanted to admit what happened.'

'Jesus, you're not a man for making life easy, Inspector!'

'Someone had a reason to kill him, someone who's already killed.'

'You don't really have any of that, just Billy's ramblings.'

'And what if I get it? What if I find more?'

The chief inspector frowned. He had the man he believed killed the Missing Postman, whether intentionally or not. He knew some of the people who conspired to dispose of the body. He simply had to make those people crack. But Stefan had opened something else up. Halloran wasn't convinced by it but it was there, on paper; he couldn't shut the lid. He was still being watched. He had to demonstrate all the ground had been covered. He didn't want to waste his time on it, but he had a man who would dot the 'i's and cross the 't's, and then some. There was always the possibility something might go wrong with the case. George Chisholm worried him; too cocky when he shouldn't be. If something did go wrong, the more shite and confusion he could throw about the better. Inspector Gillespie's shite might do no harm. But it wasn't only that. Somewhere there was the recognition that 'these women' really did include Stefan Gillespie's dead wife. It would do the man no harm to know that what he had got in his head wasn't true.

'I told you to keep out of my way before. Keep doing that and don't expect my men to have time to waste on it. But I won't stop you looking.'

Outside the Garda Barracks a dozen men stood in the road, talking quietly. The conversation was whispered but as Stefan came out from the police station it didn't take much decoding. It was the conversation Dessie MacMahon had recognized no one wanted to have in public the night before. It would be a conversation that was everywhere up and down the Vale of Glendalough, everywhere there were no outsiders to hear.

Stefan stood in the light from the blue lamp. He knew Pat Halloran had been questioning the customers who were in Whelan's on Christmas Eve again on the basis of the one statement that contradicted their stories. The Bray detectives would be pushing hard to find anyone whose name wasn't yet on that list of customers. He could guess the interrogations were still getting nowhere, that nothing was forthcoming, lips were becoming ever tighter. But everyone knew there would be more now. There would be charges. Yet the Guards couldn't stop people comparing notes. No one could stop them cementing their stories. Stefan walked past the villagers to the Austin 10. As he passed them the conversation stopped. He smiled.

'Safe home, lads!'

'Safe home, Mr Gillespie.'

Some people knew him; some remembered him.

He didn't notice a big man at the edge of the group, watching him.

The man stared as Stefan walked on and got into the car. He kept staring as the car pulled away. He moved out from the crowd, following in the car's wake while Stefan drove over the bridge. The man recognized him now. He had heard that the Guard who married Maeve Joyce was there, the woman who drowned in the Upper Lake. He had seen Stefan before, but a long time ago. It was strange he was here. The man didn't like it. There was no reason another detective wouldn't come. But why this one? He couldn't feel easy. It shouldn't matter. He was no different to the other Guards. It wasn't as if they would find Billy's body. And if they did it wouldn't tell them anything. He was dead. He needn't have been. The man had told the postman to stop; it's all he had to do. But Billy wouldn't. Now he was gone. The man hadn't wanted him dead, but he did feel relief. It was a sin, he knew, but he needed to be quiet again, in his head. He needed it to be over. It had been over once. Then it started afresh, when Billy Byrne got back from Spain. He couldn't let that happen again.

The red tail lights of the car had gone. The man had watched till darkness swallowed them. It wasn't right. How could he clear his head with Stefan there? He told himself it was only about the postman. He told himself it would stop as it did before. But there was too much of it in his head. It wouldn't stop. It wouldn't stop at all.

13

Los Tres Reyes Magos

It was Epiphany at the Central Prison in Burgos. It was not a day like other days. The Three Wise Kings of the East were coming to the gaol; the prisoners were allowed into the outer courtyard to see their wives, their mothers, their children. The courtyard was full as it never was. On one side, beneath the cloister-like arches surrounding the stone-flagged plaza, warders and Civil Guards looked on, but the atmosphere was relaxed. They talked and laughed with the children, looking at the toys they had brought to show their fathers and grandfathers: drums, trumpets, toy soldiers, dolls, pictures, coloured crayons, books. There were parcels of food and cigarettes and today they would reach the men they were intended for. But the real gift of the Three Kings was something more precious, to be able to touch, to kiss, to hold, to speak without being watched, even if only for an hour.

Expectation was building. The prisoners were coming. A brass band started to play, slightly out of time and tune. People began to sing quietly.

> Ya vienen los Reyes Magos,
> Ya vienen los Reyes Magos,

> Caminito de Belén,
> Olé, olé, Holanda y olé,
> Holanda ya se ve, ya se ve.

Then more were singing, louder, and the children's voices loudest of all.

> See the Wise Men, riding, riding,
> See the Wise Men riding, riding,
> On the road to Bethlehem,
> Riding to the Holy Land,
> Oh, you can see it close at hand.

There was a round of applause. For a moment the children had forgotten where they were as the Three Kings walked out from the arches of the colonnade, bearded and turbaned, in flowing robes; Melchior, Caspar, Balthazar, each with a sack. The children gathered round and the Three Kings gave out the gifts they had brought. The gifts were all the same; a single postcard. On it a picture of Generalissimo Franco with a stern but benevolent face. He wore the pale brown uniform of Spanish Africa, decorated with stars and a sash in yellow and red; on his shoulders was the wolfskin cape of the warrior. Behind him were soldiers in the uniforms of the Nationalist Army, brandishing weapons, on horseback, wounded but proud, draped in the flags of Spain and all its provinces and colonies. At the bottom a golden plaque said: La Guerra Ha Terminado; The War is Over.

The singing stopped abruptly. The chapel doors opened; through them came the prisoners. As they emerged, some stumbling, they halted. When they walked on they were marching, slowly, line abreast, their heads up, until the crowd in front of them rushed forward. Then the lines broke. Prisoners and their families flung themselves into each other's arms.

One of the Three Kings, Balthazar, heavily bearded and turbaned, stood to one side anxiously. This king was María Fernández Duarte, waiting for Frank Ryan. Everything was ready. But he wasn't there. She was under the colonnade now, close to the chapel doors, surrounded by people. It was here that Frank Ryan would put on the robe and the turban and the beard. María had her own clothes underneath. Today there was no scrutiny of papers. Women and children had come into the courtyard uncounted. When they left María would be one of them. But Three Kings had entered and Three Kings would leave. Frank Ryan would walk out of the Prisión Central. His escape was planned. The way out of the prison, the car to take him from Burgos, the clothes of an Irish priest on a pilgrimage to Santiago de Compostela, the road to the Portuguese border. People were ready, waiting. But he had to be in the courtyard. He had to be there now.

Frank Ryan walked from his cell into the quadrangle with the other men. He was calm. There had been other plans. They had all failed. Some had been too complex. Some depended on finding a prison guard to turn a blind eye and in the end no one could be trusted. Other prisoners had made other plans. They had died, every one of them, in front of a firing squad. This plan had the benefit of simplicity. That's what gave Ryan hope. The more complicated things were the more to go wrong. But it wasn't only hope that had persuaded him to listen to María; it was, finally, desperation.

He had been a prisoner in Burgos since his capture in 1938 when, after a court martial lasting five minutes, he had been sentenced to death. At intervals he was taken out with other prisoners to be shot. He would stand in front of a firing squad as others died and then be returned, spattered in their blood, to his cell. It was a long game, designed to break him, but the game had saved his life. And it had stopped. There was a new governor who let him have food parcels from the Red Cross and letters from Ireland; he had been allowed to write home. There was an Irish ambassador in Spain now, who had finally been allowed see him. After Leopold Kerney's first visit the food had improved. He had received treatment for the medical conditions that were part of the prison's regime. His death sentence was commuted, though it was still a death sentence: thirty more years in the Prisión Central.

The feeling that he would die in gaol was often with him. He held it at bay, both for himself and for the other prisoners. He was the last of the International Brigade officers. All they had left him was to be undefeated.

Yet while other prisoners were released, while a campaign was fought in Ireland, Britain, America, for his freedom, nothing happened. No one knew why he had been singled out. It seemed as arbitrary as the beatings and executions that were daily life in Burgos. The visits of the Irish ambassador kept hope alive, but he had started to feel a new certainty about what was going to happen. He would die in the Central Prison, this year, next year. He had never wanted María to put herself at risk for him. But he wanted to live. That was the one hope they had not yet taken away.

On the far side of the quadrangle two warders watched the line of prisoners. One of them stepped in front of Frank Ryan and stopped him.

'Come on, lads, I've a visitor waiting.'

'The governor wants to see you.'

'Couldn't he find a better time?'

There was no point arguing. To argue was to draw attention.

The governor sat behind a huge black desk in a high white room that contained nothing else except an armchair, a chaise longue and a dark oak cupboard. As Ryan entered the governor stood up, which was unusual. He reached across the desk to pick up a bottle of Bushmills Irish whiskey.

'Your ambassador, Señor Kerney, brought this when he last came to see you.' The governor's English was better than Frank Ryan's Spanish, and he liked to show he could speak it. 'So, with your permission, Ryan, I thought we would share a little bit of Ireland and toast the Three Kings!'

'I can't refuse my own whiskey, Señor Escovedo.'

The governor waved at the chair on the other side of the desk. Frank Ryan sat down. Escovedo opened the bottle and poured two full tumblers.

'Strong stuff!'

'I'll drink to that!' said the Irishman, lifting his glass.

'What do you hear about the war, Ryan?'

'Not much, only what the warders say.'

'Nothing from Mr Kerney?'

'Ireland is neutral. Not a bad thing.'

He was unconvinced the governor was interested in the conversation. It was something to say, but whether to accompany a glass of whiskey or to keep him there, he had no idea. He could not show he wanted to get out.

'And Spain is neutral too. A very good thing,' said the governor.

'Then here's to neutrality! Sláinte!'

'It can make no difference, of course,' continued Escovedo. 'The French will collapse when Hitler bombs Paris. The English don't want war at all. For what? Poland! The solution is simple. The future of Europe is the new way, Hitler's way, Mussolini's way, Franco's way. Britain should join the war against communism. But they will see sense one way or another.'

'I don't know if the English have ever been very strong on sense.'

'And when they see that Hitler won't be stopped?'

'They would have to see it first.'

'Even the Russians have seen it, even the communists!'

The governor delivered this with satisfaction. He knew what the Russian pact with Germany meant to the Republicans in his prison, a pact with the country that had armed Franco and bombed their cities. It was an act of betrayal they could not understand. Frank Ryan felt it as deeply as anyone else. Escovedo picked up the bottle of whiskey and poured more.

It was an hour later that Frank Ryan left the prison governor's office. The whiskey was gone. The governor gave no sign that he wanted anything from him. The Irishman in turn revealed nothing of his anxiety. Half a bottle later he felt none of the effects. He had no idea what was happening in the main courtyard. When he returned to his cell block with the other prisoners he couldn't ask. No one else knew anything of the escape. He could only pray María had left with everyone else. His concern for her was too great to let him feel the despair of their failure. That would come tomorrow.

María Duarte had realized that Frank Ryan wouldn't come. She whispered it to the other two kings, then waited as darkness fell and the clock on the tower ticked away the time. It was quieter now. The last embraces were being exchanged and the last kisses. The prisoners came together in front of the chapel without any orders. The women and children watched them go, and as the great doors shut they turned in silence to leave, along with the Three Kings. Beyond the prison was the long walk back to Burgos. María stood by a small bus with the other two kings. She slipped off her robe, her turban, the black beard. It should have been Frank Ryan taking them off.

'Don't go home tonight,' she said to Caspar and Melchior.

As the two kings got on the bus María walked on with the crowd, away from the prison. The glow of the floodlights was behind her. It was very black now. Abruptly, she turned off the road. A track led out into a field below the road. The clothes she wore were dark and no one noticed; soon she was invisible, walking through the fields towards the village of Villalonquéjar. A line of rocks and bushes marked a field boundary; she followed it until she reached a road. The lights of the village were to her left, to the right was the warm glow of Burgos itself. She crossed the road. There was a wall ahead, all that remained of a barn. She listened. She gave a low whistle. A man emerged from behind the wall, running towards her.

'Jesus, this is some game!' He spoke in English. 'Where is he?'

She shook her head.

'What happened?'

'He didn't come, Mikey, that's all. He didn't come.'

'Are they on to it?'

She walked a few more yards and then staggered and fell. Michael Hagan put his arm round her, lifting her up. The first tears were in her eyes.

'What the fuck do we do now, María?'

Hagan looked up across the road and the fields towards the prison; its floodlit outline was bright on the black horizon at the crest of its low hill.

'We better just get away, María, somewhere, anywhere.'

With his arm still round her he pulled her with him. Behind the tumbled wall was a small grey Peugeot. María had frozen. The Irishman opened the car door and pushed her in. He started the engine and backed out from where the car was hidden, then drove up to the road. It was little more than a beaten track. The headlights blazed. He thought better of the lights and turned them off. Then he set off towards the village, trying to think.

'Back to Salamanca, straight back. That's it. I can pick up the road to Valladolid later. Just get me there, María. If we get lost here we're fucked.'

He reached down and picked up a map. He pushed it on to her lap.

'There's a torch in the glove compartment. We want the road from Villalonquéjar to San Mamés. It'll be to the left. It's a dirt road but it's fine, I came in that way. I think I'll recognize it. We'll have to use the lights after that. So, San Mamés, then Buniel. Right? That's the main road. Come on!'

When the bus carrying the two kings reached the junction with the road into Burgos there were torches ahead. A gang of Civil Guards stepped forward to stop it. A Civil Guard pulled open the door and climbed in. Another policeman followed, a rifle on his back. The first *benemérita* looked along the rows of seats at the women and children. He turned to the driver and nodded. The driver stepped down from the bus. The policeman walked on and grinned at Caspar and Melchior. Their beards had gone but one still wore a turban and the other a gold crown of cardboard. The second Civil Guard was covering them with the rifle. The kings got up as the driver had done. They followed the policemen off the bus. Another policeman got in. He shut the door and took the driver's seat, turning to the silent passengers.

'Don't worry, we'll have you back in Burgos in no time.'

As the bus pulled away, women and children were still on the road from the prison. They passed the Civil Guards with their guns trained on the bus driver and the two kings. No one knew why; why never mattered. Within minutes the men were marched away, not to Burgos, but towards the line of trees that marked the Río Arlanzón. The men made no attempt to resist. The end was not in doubt. The shots rang out in the darkness. The first bullets were to their heads, with shots through the eyes for decoration. Caspar, Melchior and the bus driver were left by the river for days before their families could take the bodies. There had been no angel to warn them.

14

The Round Tower

In the days following Christmas, Stefan Gillespie did little more than ask questions nobody seemed to understand let alone have answers to. He had persuaded Chief Inspector Halloran to let the suspended Sergeant Chisholm back into the station to dig out records from the mildewed cardboard boxes that filled one of the cellars underneath the barracks. The contents of the boxes sometimes related to the year scrawled on the top, but it was hit and miss, and it was impossible to know if information was missing. There was RIC material about the disappearance of Charlotte Moore in 1919, including statements and the maps used in the search. The search was a mirror of what was going on outside in the Vale of Glendalough, both in scale and in the growing conviction that no body would ever be found.

George Chisholm thought most RIC records had gone to Dublin Castle in the twenties and Stefan spent a day there, avoiding anyone from Special Branch except Dessie MacMahon. He found some of what he was looking for, including the reports of the CID investigation. None of it told him anything he didn't know. But it did make the case against Albert Neale hard to refute. And if Neale really had killed Charlotte Moore, then everything the Missing Postman believed about her death, and about the subsequent deaths of Marian Gort and Maeve, was already falling apart.

There was little in Laragh about either Marian's death or Maeve's, and no reason why there should be as far as the Garda Síochaná was concerned. There were a number of statements about Maeve's drowning, one of which was Stefan's own. All the statements were about the discovery of the bodies; Marian's below the Spinc, Maeve's at the edge of the Upper Lake. There had been no post-mortems; the coroners' reports merely formalized the accidental deaths no one had questioned. Sergeant Chisholm had been stationed in Laragh at the time of both deaths, and remembered them well. The only contribution he made to Stefan's line of questioning was that there had been gossip about Marian Gort and suicide.

After reading all the records he could find, Stefan had discovered nothing to add independent evidence to what William Byrne believed. He had not even formulated real questions he could ask locally about Charlotte, Marian or Maeve. The only ones he could see needed to be asked in Spain, of the man Billy Byrne had written to, Jim Collins, and even he had disappeared.

It was Twelfth Night. Stefan had not gone over the mountains as usual. He was taking Tom to Dublin to meet Maeve's parents, along with his uncle, aunt and cousins, to see the pantomime at the Olympia. He had seen Kate only once since Stephen's Day. She was with her parents in Dún Laoghaire, still without a job, uncertain what she was doing, and uncertain what she and Stefan were doing too. She spent New Year's Eve at Kilranelagh but she had hardly been on her own with him. He arrived late from Glendalough and dropped her at the station in Baltinglass for the early train. He was fond, even loving, for a time when they went outside at midnight, but when the moment was gone he came back in as if he was avoiding something, full of banter that wasn't how he normally behaved.

On Twelfth Night, Stefan got to Dublin with Tom at midday and left him with Maeve's family in Bewleys, saying he would see them at the Olympia. He drove from Grafton Street to the Quays. He crossed the river at Kingsbridge to McKee Barracks. Commandant de Paor was expecting him.

De Paor began with the politenesses that went with the time of year, but Stefan was unresponsive. He was tight-lipped, ill-at-ease and abrupt.

'I'm here to ask you a favour,' he said.

'Is that a favour for you or a favour for Special Branch?'

'Me. I'm not at the Castle at the moment, I'm in Glendalough.'

It was an explanation of something; de Paor didn't know what.

'Isn't that a little off the Emergency track?'

Stefan smiled; he felt slightly easier now he was saying it.

'Don't tell me you haven't heard about the Missing Postman. There's a theory at Garda HQ that G2 did it to get the arms' raid out of the papers.'

'It's done the job, I'll give you that, Stefan. So, missing postmen now. Is there anything Special Branch don't get their noses in these days?'

'There are some – you might want to call them irregularities, I suppose. The commissioner wanted someone from Dublin down there.'

'Quis custodiet ipsos custiodies?'

'Something like that.'

'Well, we're not big on missing people or guarding the Guards.'

'What were you about before Christmas if it wasn't guarding the Guards? Or are you happy Special Branch isn't mounting a coup now?'

'Happy enough,' de Paor grinned, 'though things still puzzle me. I see the Curragh filling up with every Republican Tom, Dick and Seamus you can shake a stick at, but a distinct absence of top men. It crossed my mind to offer to pick up Hayes for

Terry Gregory if he was short staffed. But if he can send you to tramp the hills for a postman it can't be that bad.'

Stefan didn't know what was happening at Dublin Castle. He didn't really want to. De Paor had pushed some of that back into his mind again, but it wasn't why he was here. The rest of them could play those games.

'You'd know a bit about General O'Duffy's Bandera, Geróid?'

The G2 man was puzzled.

'You'd know the men that went, I mean.'

'It wouldn't be on the tip of my tongue exactly.'

'The Missing Postman was in Spain with O'Duffy.'

'Is that a line of inquiry? A Spanish barman looking for his money?'

'It doesn't matter what it is.' Stefan's reply was blunt.

'I see. I'll be serious then. It is a line of inquiry?'

'Spain is, as far as I'm concerned. The postman's name was William Byrne. He went to Spain with O'Duffy, I guess in 1936. He was injured at some point. Probably in a bar or a brothel. He said he'd been wounded, but that was a lie. He did break some bones. He spent time convalescing at the Irish College in Salamanca. That's what I'm interested in. You'd know it?'

De Paor looked at him oddly for a moment.

'I do know it. I know priests who were there. And I think there were some of O'Duffy's men who ended up recuperating there. Some of them might even have seen a bullet fired in anger. They were at the battle of Jarama briefly.'

'I thought you'd know something,' said Stefan.

'That's not the level of detail you're looking for, though, is it?'

'You know people who know people. You've just told me that. Salamanca is where your man Byrne was. He was pally with another one of O'Duffy's men there, a man called Michael Hagan. And Hagan is still at the college, working or training for the priesthood. I have a letter Hagan sent to Byrne, and a letter Byrne sent to someone else at the college. He may have no connection with the Bandera, I don't know, but he's Irish. It's the relationship between Byrne and this other man that matters. His name is James Collins.'

Stefan passed across a piece of paper with the names and details.

'We have lists of men who went to Spain with O'Duffy but that's it, if you're talking ordinary soldiers. What you have is already more than we'd have. As for the Irish College, I think it was closed up, moth-balled during the Civil War.'

De Paor watched Stefan, who seemed about to say more, but stopped as if suddenly thinking better of it. He could see Stefan's awkwardness had returned. He could tell a lot wasn't being said. And he could feel there was something very personal behind all this.

'I'll see what I can find. It might help if I knew what it's about.'

'It's about murder. Three murders. Probably four murders.'

'Is that all you're going to say?'

'And it's about me, about something I didn't see, a long time ago.'

There was nothing more Stefan had to say. A few minutes later he left. Geróid de Paor sat at his desk looking down at the piece of paper that had been put in front of him. It wasn't interesting in itself, but he read the names with the same thoughtful frown he had shown when Stefan first started to explain what he wanted. He picked up the telephone.

'Can you get me Colonel Archer?'

He waited.

'It's Geróid, sir. It's just something odd that's come up, out of the blue. I don't know if it could be useful to us. It's this Kerney business in Spain. Shall I pop in, sir?'

Tom and Stefan spent the afternoon in the Olympia Theatre with Maeve's parents, Jack and Sally, and with her brother Dermot, his wife Kathleen and their three children, Tom's cousins. They were all staying with Jack and Sally in Malahide; Tom would be going back to spend two days there.

Stefan wanted to talk to someone, to ask if there was anything at all that could begin to make sense of the idea that Maeve had been murdered. He knew it might come to that eventually. But how could he start that conversation? And if everyone else was right, if it was nothing except Billy Byrne's imagination, or if it was true yet there was no killer to be found, what was the point of pushing this tumour into the heart of Maeve's family?

In the darkness of the Olympia he was surrounded by laughter, and he laughed himself as the two Ugly Sisters burst on to the stage at every opportunity to scream: 'God save all here, it's an Emerrrgency altogether!' with the audience roaring in unison with the word 'Emerrrgency!' It still wasn't the time to speak. Till he knew something real he could say nothing.

After the pantomime they ate at Hynes's along Dame Street. Oddly, for Stefan, it felt like one of the most successful of the Christmas outings they had been on together. He watched them all talking over one another, and the children, in hushed, giggling whispers, repeating the words, 'It's an Emerrrgency', endlessly. If he was unusually quiet no one seemed to notice it. But he was glad when they set off, the children still full of noise, heading for the tram to Malahide. He walked back up Dame Street to Dublin Castle.

In the detectives' room they were still working, among them Dessie MacMahon, waiting for Stefan. He had telephoned Kilranelagh the night before. It was no more than a message about catching up, but Stefan knew where Dessie was phoning from; he was being careful with his words. And it was about more than catching up.

Stefan and Dessie walked down Parliament Street, over Grattan Bridge, to the bar at the Ormond Hotel. Stefan ran through the details of what he had found in William Byrne's rooms in Glendalough and what else he had put together. Dessie was never a man to say much; what he took in stayed in until, unexpectedly, he put it together with some unlikely, inconsequential piece of information in his head and saw something everyone else had missed. His silence tonight was a deeper one than usual.

The Ormond was not a bar that invited you to stay. A man played the piano but his music added nothing to the frigid atmosphere. Stefan and Dessie sat at the back of the bar. Dessie stubbed out one Sweet Afton and lit another. Stefan took out a cigarette too. It signalled the end of an unsatisfactory conversation about events in the Wicklow Mountains.

'So what's going on at the Castle, Dessie?'

'It's all bringing in IRA men. No evidence needed. If Gregory says they're IRA, they go to the Curragh. I don't know who the informers are, but the Boys are easy to find. I'd say the IRA's leaking like a sieve.'

Stefan was waiting for Dessie to say what he was there to say.

'Terry Gregory's been asking about you, Stevie.'

'Asking what?'

'He's never said a word to me, but there's others he's talked to.'

'I don't have a lot to hide, Dessie. He can talk all he wants.'

'If he was walking round saying, what's that fucker Gillespie up to, I wouldn't think twice. But it's quiet. When he's quiet he's digging. Some of the lads don't like that. You mightn't think they'd be watching your back . . .'

'You're right,' laughed Stefan. 'So who told you this?'

'Never mind who, I'm passing it on. He wants to know the usual things, who you spend your time with, where you drink, who you talk to.'

'In the Wicklow Mountains?'

'No, but I'm not sure he minds you being out of the way just now.'

Stefan nodded. He had thought the same thing after Christmas.

'There is one thing. I was talking to Aidan Fogarty—'

'Garda Fogarty? What would he know about me?'

'He was in the mess, and he says, for a bit of craic, "Tell that inspector of yours to watch his arse, Gregory's on to him!" I asked why and he said he seen you one night before Christmas, coming into the Castle, with too much whiskey inside you.' Dessie grinned. 'His words! He said the boss was asking about you next day. Had Fogarty seen you in the Castle the night before, late? He made a joke about you having a report to give him so, and how he'd have your bollocks if you'd been off on the piss.'

'And what did Fogarty say?'

'He hadn't seen you.'

'Fair play to him, I owe him one.'

'Fogarty didn't think the boss believed him.'

'You'll want another drink, Dessie.'

As Stefan went to the bar Superintendent Gregory was walking towards him. The superintendent smiled. There was nothing accidental about the meeting.

'Fresh enough out there. A hot whiskey would do the trick. Don't worry about one for Dessie, I'd say it'll be time he was on his way now.'

Gregory walked across to the table where Dessie MacMahon was sitting and sat down beside him. A moment later Dessie got up and walked past Stefan.

'Well, you know he wasn't just passing by.'

Stefan carried the drinks to the table and sat down.

'It's a while since I was here,' said the superintendent. 'It's always been a shitehole. But maybe you'd be more a cocktail-bar man yourself?'

What Gregory said idly was never idle. It seemed he knew something about the drink with de Paor before Christmas too. Stefan didn't answer.

'Still, where a man drinks and who he drinks with is his own affair.'

The superintendent sipped his whiskey, looking at the pianist.

'I remember coming in with my father, thirty years ago. I'd say that pianist's the same feller. You'd think he'd have got better. But if he had he wouldn't still be playing here for drinks. Some people do the same thing all their lives, badly. Most people. I swear it's the same fucking tunes. Another couple and he'll give us "The Croppy Boy". But who cares? Who's listening?'

Stefan shrugged. It was a prelude to something.

'Two more of the same, Mina!' Gregory called to the barmaid. 'I did read your report from Laragh. I passed it to the commissioner, but Ned Broy's happy enough with what Halloran's doing now. The papers want a body. That's what it's all about. If there was a fecking body they'd all move on.'

'I'd have my doubts they'll be getting one, sir.'

'Jesus, you're hard fellers in Wicklow. A few too many on Christmas Eve and you're beaten to death in the pub and dumped on the cold hillside!'

'You know what I think about the pub. I'm not sure he died there.'

'I'm impressed with how you rattled Laurel and Hardy. I take my hat off. Pat Halloran has a handle on how your Missing Postman went missing and you give him three more murders besides. If you had any evidence for it he'd be in those mountains so long he'd be the one to be searching for.'

'Halloran doesn't think there's anything in it either.'

'I didn't say there wasn't anything in it, did I?'

Terry Gregory's real reasons for being in the Ormond Hotel were pushed aside for now. What he had read in Stefan's report had stuck in his mind. Putting unlikely things together was what he did; it interested him.

The barmaid put the drinks on the table.

'So have you got any more, since your report?'

'I'd be stretching it if I said I had, sir.'

'I've never been a great man for coincidences. If a feller's on to three killings no one knows about, and he's trying to squeeze money out of another feller to keep it quiet, and then he disappears, presumed murdered, well, you'd want to look very hard before you decided he died after a lad knocked him over in a bar. But the word is "if". If it happened, if anyone knows about it, if any bastard in the Valley of the Squinting Windows is going to tell you anything. Not a big word "if" but there are a lot of them.'

'There has to be a way in,' said Stefan quietly.

'Maybe, maybe not. But tell me, how is Commandant de Paor?'

The diversion was over.

'He's well enough, sir.'

'It was seasonal of you to drop into McKee Barracks to see him.'

'I had a reason.'

'And what would that be?'

'A way in. You've seen the report. Billy Byrne was in Spain with O'Duffy's crew. I think it's where he found out about the first murder – Charlotte Moore. Somehow that's how he knew your man Neale wasn't the killer and someone else was, someone who was still in Glendalough. It's where it started. He was writing to your man Collins in Spain last year. I don't know if he met him in Salamanca or where that comes in, but it's the point of contact now. It's where he tried to reach him again.'

'And what's that got to do with Geróid de Paor?'

'G2 have got information about who was in Spain with O'Duffy.'

149

'And before Christmas? You weren't asking him about Spain then.'

'We were working together after the arms' raid. It was a drink.'

'Good,' smiled Gregory, 'simple answers are best, and simple lies. You're an honest man, Stefan. There's room for at least one in Special Branch. It's why I'm reluctant to see you go. There may even be room for an honest man in Military Intelligence, but don't make the mistake of thinking it's Geróid. I doubt there's much that goes on in G2 that doesn't find its way into British Intelligence . . . sooner or later. Be careful with de Paor.'

'I doubt British Intelligence will want what's in Glendalough.'

'A privilege of rank, Gillespie, is that I do the jokes. What someone like Geróid de Paor might call "droit de seigneur". As a man of your education knows it's French for "fuck me about and you will be fucked".'

He got up without another word and left. Stefan drained his glass. As he walked out the barmaid smiled goodnight to him, idly singing as the pianist played, barely aware she was doing it, in a tuneless, cracked voice.

> We hold this house for our Lord and King,
> And Amen say I, may all traitors swing.

The following evening, Stefan Gillespie drove in fading light back from the Garda Barracks in Laragh to the Seven Churches. Another fruitless day. The rope Chief Inspector Halloran had given him was just long enough for him to trip himself up on and he knew that Halloran's men were waiting for him to do it. If Pat Halloran had started out feeling that what Stefan was doing was useful in some way, to cover his back, he was now tempted to feel it might be much more satisfying if a Special Branch man made an arse of himself.

There had been a message for Stefan at the barracks. Someone had phoned for him. The sergeant filling in for Chisholm had taken the call.

'Feller by the name of Neale, a Mr Neale. He said you'd know.'

'Is there anyone called Neale here now? Do you know the name?'

'You'd have to ask George. But he wasn't local. He was calling from Rathdrum. He said he was on a tour. He'd been abroad. He said it was years since he'd seen the Round Tower and he was heading there now, and he'd wait a bit before he went back to Dublin, so if you had the time to talk . . .'

The only Neale Stefan knew was the man who had been wanted for the murder of Charlotte Moore, twenty years ago. He didn't for a moment believe Albert Neale was in Glendalough waiting to talk to him, but someone wanted to talk, someone who knew why he was asking questions, someone who knew enough to use Neale's name. It wasn't a secret, of course; he had asked a lot of people about Neale now, as well as about Marian Gort and even about Maeve. Chief Inspector Halloran knew the questions; other detectives knew them too. If it wasn't common knowledge it was at least known that he was trying to find evidence that the postman's disappearance had another explanation than a drunken row in Whelan's.

The light was dimming as he pulled into the car park by the Lower Lake. There were no other vehicles. It didn't seem such a good idea to be here on his own suddenly.

He hadn't been thinking as he left the Garda station. He assumed someone might have information and was using Neale's name to prove his credentials. It even occurred to him that some of Halloran's detectives could be having a joke at his expense. The possibility that this was the man Billy Byrne had been blackmailing only entered his mind as he reached Glendalough. It seemed far-fetched now, but it couldn't be ignored.

He leant across to the glove compartment and took out the Webley. He had the gun in his pocket as he walked through the neat, clipped lawns that led to what had been one of Ireland's great monastic centres. The English had little use for Glendalough's bloody-mindedly Irish variety of Christianity and eventually they destroyed it. What remained were the ruins of several small churches, little more than heaps of stones, and the grassed humps that marked the monks' cells and the communal buildings. Stefan walked through the arched gateway and looked out at the Cathedral of St Peter and St Paul, with its bare, roofless walls, and at the distinctive, needle-like Round Tower, echoed by similar buildings all over Ireland. All around there were gravestones, ancient, old, new; in the 500 years since the end of St Kevin's monastery, it had become a place that was only populated by the dead.

He walked to the Round Tower and paced slowly past. He lit a cigarette and sat on the wall behind. There was still enough light to see, but there was no one there. He sat for half an hour. He knew nobody was coming. He had known as soon as he arrived. It was a game. But nothing told him what the game was. The weight of the revolver in his pocket made him feel foolish. It was still possible the joke was on him, that Halloran's men were behind it. Making a fool of a Special Branch man would go down well, and if that was true, he'd soon find out.

Stefan drove away from the Round Tower and the Seven Churches, back through Glendalough and out of Laragh, on to the Military Road across the mountains to Rathdangan and Kilranelagh. The car wound up the slopes of Derrybawn, over Cullentragh and Carriglinneen, where the road dropped down to Glenmalure at Drumgoff. There was a slight drizzle. It was cold and the road was starting to freeze as he climbed.

He was conscious he was pumping the brake pedal ascending Carriglinneen, but barely. It was a slow ascent with little need to brake, even on the hairpins; the gears did the work. As he crested the highest point on the road and began the steep descent towards Drumgoff his mind was elsewhere, still trying to see if he could make any sense of what had just happened or whether to dismiss it.

He was going fast now but he would meet nothing on the road that didn't show its headlights in the darkness half a mile away. Then he hit a bend faster than he should have done. He was further down into Glenmalure than he realized.

His foot slammed the brake, but he had no brake. He wrenched the wheel. The car cleared the bend with a squeal of tyres but it was still picking up speed. He couldn't slow it.

He pumped the pedal harder; nothing happened. He wasn't sure where he was in the darkness. The wall of the mountain was hard against the road on one side; trees on the other. If he was where he thought, there was a tighter bend ahead. And then he was on it.

He crashed the gears down to slow the car, but as the engine roared he was right into the hairpin with a wall of rock in front of him. He spun the wheel and pulled up the handbrake. The car started to slide, skidding on the thin film of ice that was sheeting the road now. He had lost control completely.

The passenger-side wing hit a boulder as the car came off the road. He was thrown forward across the wheel. His head smashed into the windscreen. The car plunged into a ditch and then rolled over on its side.

The headlights still blazed into the darkness, into the rain; it was sleet now. The engine roared and raced. Stefan Gillespie lay very still, slumped against the car door. The only movement was a slow line of blood trickling down his face.

PART TWO

IBERIA

A resolution urging widespread public support for the efforts of the Irish Government to secure the release of Frank Ryan, now in prison in Spain, was passed at a large meeting held at Middle Abbey Street, Dublin. The resolution states that 'being mindful of the sterling and unselfish services rendered by Frank Ryan to the national movement for Irish independence over a long period, this meeting views with misgivings his continued detention by the Spanish Government now that the war has ended'. Madame Maud Gonne MacBride said that Spain, a chivalrous country, had released most of the foreign prisoners. Why, she asked, did they still hold on to Frank Ryan? The Irish people had long memories and a deep tradition which made them inclined to love Spain – a Catholic nation like themselves – and it would be a pity if old affection should be weakened by the unjust detention of an Irishman they all knew and loved.

Irish Times

15

Wicklow Town

It was two months since the car crash on the Military Road when Dessie MacMahon drove into the farmyard at Kilranelagh to pick up Stefan and take him to the courthouse in Wicklow, where the defendants in William Byrne's murder would have the case against them heard for the first time.

In those months, Stefan had hardly left the farm. He had not forgotten why he was on the Military Road that night but the activity in the Vale of Glendalough had left him behind. The body of the Missing Postman had not been found; the search, though never officially ended, had scaled down to nothing. Chief Inspector Halloran had built on the evidence of his one dissenting witness to events on Christmas Eve in Whelan's Bar, and if he had not broken the alibis and accounts of the other customers he had put together enough to give substance to Paul Dearing's statement. Much of it was circumstantial hearsay, but next to Dearing's story, alongside the lies that had come from the Garda Barracks in Laragh, it carried real weight. Pat Halloran was happy that once it all came into court the job would be done.

Stefan had been left with plenty of time to brood on what had happened and no opportunity to do anything about it. His investigation, such as it was, was over as far as both Halloran and Terry Gregory were concerned. There was no need to look for murders that were either forgotten or had never happened. Halloran's need to cover his back had gone. Ned Broy, the Garda commissioner, no longer required a spy in the Bray CID camp. The press too had lost interest in the Missing Postman; even if his body was still out there the mystery had become pettier and more squalid than suited the word 'mystery' as good copy. The course Stefan was pursuing interested no one now. Chief Inspector Halloran could see the finish, but he was not so confident that he wanted a defence lawyer asking if there were other lines of inquiry and finding out there were. Stefan pestered him by phone in the weeks after the crash; he pestered Gregory when the chief inspector told him his leads led nowhere. Gregory's message was the same: forget it.

There was, of course, the issue of that night on the Military Road. The car had been found by a farmer cycling home from the Glenmalure Inn. Stefan had been lucky; skidding sideways, the Austin 10 missed the wall of rock it was heading for. If it had hit it head-on and he had gone through the windscreen the outcome might have been different. In the end, the damage was a fractured tibia and broken ribs. He was home in days, but the process of healing meant he was stuck at the farm. Now he was ready to go back to work. He couldn't forget, however, what everyone else had dismissed. And he was still convinced that the brakes of the car had been tampered with.

It was the only explanation for the summons to the Round Tower and the subsequent no-show. The car was out of sight and unattended for half an hour while he waited. He had pushed for the Austin to be examined when it went back into the Garda garage. There was no doubt a brake pipe had come away from the master cylinder and the fluid had drained away. But nothing suggested this hadn't happened accidentally, even if it was unusual in a well-maintained Garda vehicle. There was no sign of any deliberate break or cut, yet with little knowledge anyone could have detached the pipe in minutes. The idea that someone wanted to kill him or at least frighten him off impressed no one. In fact, it was enough to persuade Terry Gregory that he had tolerated his inspector's obsession for long enough.

At Kilranelagh Stefan continued to live with what was inside him and to put on the face he needed to show to his family and Kate. For them, it had to be an accident, and an accident he tried to minimize. Tom, however concerned, moved like any child in a kind of perpetual present. After the shock he was glad his father was at home for so long. For David and Helena too, the present soon put off their greater sense that this had been a near thing. It was the same with Kate, but she was the one who couldn't quite get rid of a feeling that something else was wrong. When she came down from Dublin, Stefan worked hard to keep her from seeing there was a distance between them that could not quite be bridged, yet she felt it.

In two months the only additional information Stefan had about the Missing Postman was a letter from Geróid de Paor. He had it as Dessie MacMahon drove him to Wicklow for the court case. He had used his last credit with Terry Gregory to batter him into sending him to the hearing.

Despite everything, somewhere in the back of Superintendent Gregory's mind he was intrigued by the loose ends Stefan had brought back from Glendalough. In Special Branch, loose ends mattered; if you pulled them, things you hadn't seen unravelled. But despite all that he felt Detective Inspector Gillespie had been out of circulation long enough. It was time to remind him he was a policeman, time he was back at Dublin Castle. But on the assumption that it would draw a line under the Missing Postman, he had dispatched Sergeant MacMahon to drive Stefan to the courthouse in Wicklow.

As they drove through Tinahely towards Aughavannagh, the outliers of the Wicklow Mountains were on Stefan's side of the car. The last time he had been on this road was the night he dropped Dessie at Rathdrum for the train, after the first day in Glendalough. If he didn't know what to do now it didn't mean things had changed. What surrounded Maeve's death could not be wished away. It had been there, unmoving in his head, all along.

'I heard from Geróid de Paor,' he said.

Dessie didn't need to ask what it was about.

'He did find out some more about Billy Byrne and Spain.'

Dessie shrugged. He knew he was the only sounding board Stefan had. Somewhere his own instincts told him there was something in it, but he had a realistic sense of what could and couldn't be done. He knew when you had to stop beating yourself over the head.

Stefan began to read.

I hear you're confined to barracks with broken bones. Bad luck and mend soon! I have asked about this man Byrne and the O'Duffy mob. Not much to tell that you don't know. He was with the third contingent of Irish Brigade men that sailed from Dublin on 27th of November '36, Liverpool to Lisbon, on the S.S. *Aguila*. 80 men, one of the others was Michael Hagan. From Lisbon they went to O'Duffy's base at Cáceres, over the Spanish border. The Brigade moved up to fight along the Jarama River in February '37, but they got in a fire fight with other Nationalist troops and lost several men. Byrne wasn't there. Injured during training. I can't confirm the brothel but from what came back here it sounds par for the course!

Michael Hagan was wounded in the friendly fire incident and he did convalesce at the Irish College in Salamanca. I do know someone who spent time at the college then. There were half a dozen of O'Duffy's men there; Hagan and Byrne didn't go back to the Bandera at all. I don't know if it is possible to 'desert' from an outfit like that, but I doubt anyone cared. Your information is that he is still at the college. Once O'Duffy's crowd disbanded we had no more interest.

My contact does remember a man called Jim Collins. He worked at the Irish College as a gardener and handyman. He was Irish, and he had been working there for some time, at least ten years. A fixture.

So that's it, not much I'm afraid. Let me know when you're back among the living. You owe me a drink. And you should tell me what this is about! You never do know what these old ears might hear . . .

'He's right,' said Dessie, 'not much more than you've got.'

'Jim Collins is the man Billy Byrne was writing to.'

'But you knew that already.'

'Collins knew the man, the man Byrne thought murdered Charlotte Moore, and Marian Gort, and Maeve. Collins was the one who told him it wasn't Albert Neale who killed the girl, Dessie. That's what he brought back from Spain with him. That's where it started. And Billy Byrne was using Collins as a threat. Whatever else he had on this man it was Collins who could put the fear of God in him and make him pay up. Isn't that what's clear now?'

'Maybe.'

'There's no maybe about the letter Byrne wrote!'

'There's no maybe about the people Pat Halloran's got in the dock. No maybe about Billy Byrne on the floor of Whelan's, dead or not far off.'

Stefan smiled, and shook his head.

'That doesn't change it. How Byrne died doesn't change it.'

'Jesus, I thought that was the whole point!'

'The point is Spain, the point is James Collins.'

'He wasn't even in Ireland when Maeve and this other woman died.'

'No, I'd say he hasn't been in Ireland since 1919.'

'Why 1919?'

'I've had two months to think about him. That's why what Geróid de Paor tells me does mean something. I'd say James Collins is the man they would have hanged for killing Charlotte Moore. I think he's Albert Neale.'

The drab grey courthouse in Wicklow Town was no less drab and grey than it always was, on a day that had the same qualities, but the crowd outside in the Market Square was much brighter. It wasn't often that any focus, let alone the nation's, was on the small harbour town. The last time a crowd had gathered in numbers outside the courthouse had been in 1799, to witness the executions of rebel leaders whose headless bodies were carried out from the harbour, in a rare flurry of activity, and dumped at sea. A statue of the rebel leader, another Billy Byrne, stood in front of the courthouse with a pike. A tricolour hung from the pike, though whether it was a gesture of support for the Missing Postman or the men and women accused of killing him and disposing of his body, no one knew. What mattered was the town was full, with reporters from the *Irish Times*, the *Independent*, the *Cork Examiner*, Radio Éireann, even the Irish correspondents of the *Daily Express* and *Daily Mirror*. The Missing Postman had found his way into the British press as light relief from a war in which, so far, little was happening.

Stefan Gillespie and Dessie Byrne didn't get a seat in the packed courtroom; they squeezed in at the back. Chief Inspector Halloran sat close to the front. He caught Stefan's eye. With him was Inspector Grace, smug and enjoying the attention. Stefan thought Halloran looked uneasy. This was the climax of his investigation. Everything needed to go right and that made him edgy. Attention was only truly welcome if it came with applause.

The court rose as Francis McCabe, the district judge, entered. The babel of chatter subsided. He looked less than pleased by the numbers there and announced that if any noise disturbed the business of the court he would clear it. Then all attention turned to the dock as the defendants were brought in, six men and two women. Stefan recognized some of them, but he had not been involved in the interrogations. The two Guards, Sergeant George Chisholm and Garda Aidan McCoy, were not in uniform. The charges were read and Thomas Finlay, leading the prosecution, stood up to address the court.

'The issue before the court relates to the disappearance of a rural postman, William Byrne, who made deliveries in the villages of Laragh and Glendalough on Christmas Eve last, and has never been seen since. That his body has not been found has imparted an air of mystery, but the facts are simple. On the afternoon of Christmas Eve, Mr Byrne entered the licensed premises of the defendant Mary Whelan, where a number of inhabitants had repaired, including two Guards, Chisholm and McCoy. Also there were the defendants Edward Fitzgerald, Martin Ellis, Charles Hignett, Seamus Tyrrell and Daisy Whelan, Mrs Whelan's daughter. Byrne was under the influence of drink and argumentative. An altercation took place between him and Seamus Tyrrell. A half-crown was dropped on the floor and when Byrne bent to pick it up Tyrrell hit him. His head came into contact with the stove. Mrs Whelan stepped forward and said, "You have killed a man in my house." There has been an extraordinary conspiracy of silence regarding William Byrne's disappearance, but painstaking work by the Civic Guards has given us clear evidence of events. The primary witness was present and saw what happened. The police have established that a conversation took place among the defendants about getting rid of Byrne. Nobody thought to get a priest or doctor for the unfortunate man. Nobody thought of whispering a prayer in his ear. The thought in all minds was: "We will get rid of Byrne and hush this thing up." Wherever he was taken is unknown. However, I will prove that the acts alleged against the accused persons bring home to them the crime of murder in the first degree. Shamefully I will prove that instrumental in his disappearance were the two Civic Guards. I have no doubt that they suggested taking the bicycle out to St Kevin's Road, to make it appear that Byrne fell and wandered into the hills. The sergeant doubtless reassured the other defendants that in the absence of a body the law would find no case. Sadly, his knowledge is less than perfect. For the case is of murder.'

The first witness called was Paul Dearing, the blacksmith, the cornerstone of Chief Inspector Halloran's case. Whatever else he had put together this was the only account of what had happened in Whelan's that didn't end with William Byrne being waved off to continue his deliveries. There were other witnesses to the subsequent comings and goings that night, but they were nothing without Dearing's description of the fight.

The blacksmith looked nervous. It was unsurprising. He had broken ranks and he had not had an easy time of it. Halloran had put a Guard outside his house and he had finally taken him into protective custody. The defendants looked at him with cold contempt, but Stefan could not help noticing that George Chisholm had a quiet smile on his face.

Dearing answered the usual questions about who he was, and then began to explain his movements on Christmas Eve. He talked about walking up to Whelan's at closing time for a drink. He described going into the pub and seeing several of the defendants there. He wasn't sure if all of them were there, but he was very sure now that Sergeant Chisholm wasn't.

The prosecutor stared at him and asked him to remember the statement he had given to the police. He then asked him to say, in his own words, what had happened next in Whelan's, up to the time he left.

'I had a bottle of stout and a small whiskey. I did have a few words with Billy, who was very merry with a good day's drinking. Then I went. I passed Sergeant Chisholm and Garda McCoy coming out of the barracks.'

Stefan looked across the court at Pat Halloran. The chief inspector was struggling to stay in his seat. Inspector Grace's mouth was wide open.

'The witness is attempting to go back on his statement!'

The judge looked hard at Dearing, then at the prosecutor.

'I have the statement here, your honour!'

'Then you had better continue, Mr Finlay.'

The prosecutor held up the statement.

'Do you see the name Paul Dearing here?'

'Yes,' said the blacksmith.

'Is that your signature, Mr Dearing? And is that the statement you made to Chief Inspector Halloran on the 27th of December last, in Laragh?'

'It is, but I may have told some lies at the time.'

Stefan's eyes travelled along the row of defendants in the dock. They looked no less tense but there was relief. His gaze fixed on Sergeant Chisholm, whose own eyes had barely moved from Dearing since he entered the witness box. Chisholm sat back. He looked round, satisfied by what he saw. He registered Stefan. He shrugged and gave a distinct wink.

At the end of the hearing the prisoners were driven back to gaol. They would not stay there long. Chief Inspector Halloran was back where he started; a series of statements no one believed and no way to challenge them. And it was even worse now. Not only had the breach in the Vale of Glendalough's wall of lies been repaired, the investigation had become a farce. As the court rose the crowd outside was noisier than ever. The pubs that circled the Market Square were heaving. Halloran left without a word.

'Jesus,' was Dessie MacMahon's considered reflection.

'Chisholm knew,' said Stefan.

'I'd say he did. Pat Halloran's in for a bollocking now.'

They stood on the courthouse steps looking down at the laughing, gesticulating, arguing crowd. Dessie lit a cigarette and sniffed slowly.

'They'll reopen the investigation, but the feckers are laughing.'

Stefan didn't reply. Halloran would be kicked off now. He would be blamed for everything that had gone wrong. Yet everything he had done would be done again; the searches would start again, with no hope anything would come of them; the same people would be interviewed again. But no one would look anywhere else. They would stick to the same course and it would lead them nowhere. No one would listen to what Stefan had to say.

A uniformed Guard stood at the bottom of the courthouse steps.

'Detective Inspector Gillespie?'

'It is.'

'A message for you, from Garda HQ.'

The Guard had a faint smile on his face. He thought Stefan was one of Halloran's men. There was already some satisfaction in the Garda Barracks in Wicklow, as there would be in stations across the county, at what was coming the way of Halloran and the gobshites from Bray CID.

'The commissioner wants to see you.'

The Guard handed him a piece of paper with a handwritten note.

'They said now, sir, straightaway.'

Dessie drew contentedly on his Sweet Afton and laughed.

'Now you can walk Ned wants you to pay for that fucking car.'

When Stefan entered the Garda commissioner's office over-looking the Phoenix Park, Superintendent Gregory was there. News from the courthouse in Wicklow Town had preceded him. Broy was furious, and although it soon became clear that the saga of the Missing Postman wasn't why Stefan was there, the air at Garda HQ was thick with recrimination.

'I'd rather we hadn't gone into court at all than a fiasco like this,' said Broy, repeating what he had said several times. 'Eight people charged with murder and accessory to it, and every one walking. What did Halloran do, beat that fucking statement out of your man Dearing? We're a fucking joke! And all orchestrated by the Guards in Laragh. It's a pity George Chisholm is on the wrong side of it. He's run rings round Pat Halloran.'

Stefan said nothing. The commissioner looked at him.

'I know you have some different ideas about this.'

'I think there's more to investigate than Billy Byrne, sir.'

'But you still think he died in the pub?'

'If I'm honest, I don't know about that.'

'What do you think, Terry? You must have a view.'

'Inspector Gillespie has a very personal concern about some of the things Byrne was doing, but it's hard to get away from what we know happened on Christmas Eve. If nothing went on in Whelan's, why would anybody be covering up anything? Pat Halloran's right, Chisholm knows what happened. They all know what happened. I don't see a way round it.'

The telephone rang. Ned Broy picked it up.

'Send them in.'

He turned back to Stefan.

'It isn't why you're here, Stefan.'

There was a connection between Ned Broy and Stefan Gillespie that wasn't only about the present. Stefan had encountered the commissioner in ways that Terry Gregory didn't altogether like, because there were details he didn't have, and details Ned Broy didn't seem to think he needed. There was another connection too. Stefan's father had been an officer in the Dublin Metropolitan Police before independence, along with Ned Broy. There was something about all that Gregory didn't know either. It was unusual for the commissioner to call an officer of Stefan's rank by his Christian name.

'It's something else altogether,' continued Broy, 'but what I'll be asking may coincide with your own interests, to put it no more strongly.'

The door opened and two army officers came in.

'I think everyone knows everyone, except for you, Inspector,' said Broy. 'You know Geróid, but you won't know his boss, Colonel Archer.'

As they all sat down, the commissioner spoke first.

'I'm lending you out, Inspector. The job's simple on the face of it. Our ambassador to Spain, Mr Kerney, is in Dublin. He returns to Spain next week. He needs someone to accompany him, and that's what you'll be doing. I know you have an interest in Spain. It's what drew Commandant de Paor to think of you. But be clear, it's at the bottom of the list of reasons you're going. That's as close to a personal matter as makes no difference.'

Stefan looked at de Paor, who smiled. Gregory pursed his lips; he was outside the conversation now. The fact that Stefan wasn't did not amuse him.

'It's not an easy journey to Spain. Going through France is still possible but the cross-Channel traffic from England is restricted, except for the military, so are the trains on the other side. You could be stuck for days. Leo Kerney's preferred route is the flying boat from England to Lisbon.'

Stefan nodded, still taking it in.

'One of the main reasons for the journey is that Mr Kerney will be travelling with money and credit notes, quite a lot. There may be problems getting funds through in the normal way before long. If the Germans go into France, who knows what'll happen? Spain itself is safe enough. For now, it looks unlikely they'll go into the war according to External Affairs.'

The commissioner looked at Colonel Archer for confirmation.

'That's what we think too. But the Germans won't sit still much longer. If it opens up, what that does for communications of any kind—'

'So Inspector Gillespie carries the money belt?' said Gregory.

'More or less,' replied Archer.

'Why don't we get down to the "more"? There is more I take it?'

'There is, Terry. There's Frank Ryan.'

'That's certainly more.' The superintendent's interest was keener.

Archer looked at Stefan.

'You know enough about Frank Ryan not to need a résumé?'

'I know what I've read.'

The colonel nodded at Geróid de Paor.

'Ryan is in prison in Burgos,' said de Paor. 'He's been there for eighteen months. A lot of noise about getting him released. Campaigns here and in England. Our government has put pressure on Franco, so did the British at one point. For some reason the Spanish won't budge. There's a feeling Franco has some personal grudge, but even getting him to commute the death sentence was hard work. Mr Kerney has visited Ryan in gaol. He got his conditions improved, but he doesn't give good odds for him surviving. He's a sick man. Kerney has also tried to negotiate with the Spanish through a number of intermediaries, including some influential lawyers. But every time he's getting somewhere he meets a wall – Franco. The government wants to find a way to get Ryan out and back home.'

'Are you sure of that, Geróid?' Terry Gregory laughed.

'Unless you know something we don't, Terry.'

169

'Talking about getting Frank Ryan home is the decent thing altogether, but he isn't exactly what Dev needs. We've got an IRA leadership heading rapidly up its own arse and Ryan may be the only man around who might just bring all the different factions together. Politically he's more astute than most government ministers. After Spain, he has more experience of war, I mean real war, than the entire Army General Staff. He's a leader too. If he'd been here when the IRA walked off with the contents of the Magazine Fort, we might all have had a lot more to worry about.'

Gregory smiled, satisfied he was no longer at a disadvantage.

'I'd grant you some of that, Terry.' It was Colonel Archer who answered. 'That doesn't mean the government can leave him where he is to rot. There is a solution, or there may be. Mr Kerney has been approached by someone with a proposal to free Ryan. It would involve the Spanish releasing him, but secretly. They would say he'd escaped. They do want rid of him but they seem to need some kind of face saver. Ryan would be taken out of the country. And yes, whether it's the right time for him to come back to Ireland is another question. It might be possible for him to stay in France. And America is also an option. That is still a viable journey.'

'Where does Inspector Gillespie come in – to carry his bags?'

'You're a very suspicious man, Terry.'

'That's what he's paid for,' said Broy curtly.

'Geróid,' Colonel Archer looked at de Paor again.

'When we say someone approached Mr Kerney,' continued the commandant, 'it was a Spanish lawyer that the Department of External Affairs uses, called de Chambourcin. He is close to the Spanish Intelligence services. Useful, but can't be trusted, well, as much as Mr Kerney imagines. The next move came from two friends of Ryan, Elizabeth Mulcahy and her husband, Helmut Clissmann. You'll know the names, Superintendent.'

'The Mulcahys are Old IRA,' said Gregory. 'She's not in the

country. And she's not so close to the IRA now. I'd put her more in the romantic school than the bombing school. Clissmann was a German agent here.'

'He's in the Brandenburg Regiment now,' replied de Paor, 'which means for all practical purposes Military Intelligence, an Abwehr officer.'

'I see,' laughed Gregory. 'Frank goes to Spain to fight the good fight against the fascists and the Germans want to save him from a fascist gaol.'

'All we know is the Germans are prepared to help. Mr Kerney is authorized to pursue it. It's unlikely there's any other way to get Ryan out.'

'And what does our ambassador think the Germans want?'

'He believes Clissmann's motives are all about friendship.'

'That's not an answer, is it, Geróid?' said Gregory.

'Honestly, he doesn't know.'

'And it may be he doesn't want to find out,' interrupted Colonel Archer. 'He may not be giving the department all the details either. Kerney knows people in German Intelligence quite well, because they've been based at the Irish College in Salamanca through most of the Civil War.'

Stefan registered the word Salamanca. He caught Geróid de Paor's eye. The commandant nodded. This was the place their interests met.

'They're still there,' continued the colonel. 'Kerney often stays at the college. It's difficult to believe he hasn't discussed this with people besides the Clissmanns and de Chambourcin. He has grown to like Ryan and his determination to free him has taken a very personal slant. To be blunt, he feels the government hasn't done enough, in particular that Dev hasn't done enough, personally, with Franco. He won't be looking for any complications. Under the circumstances we feel we need to know more.'

'More than the ambassador is likely to tell you?' said Broy.

'It was Geróid who suggested Inspector Gillespie. A police-man is a sensible escort under these circumstances. The ambassador has money to safeguard, some potentially difficult travelling and, in terms of Ryan, dealings that won't be the usual run of diplomacy. He would be suspicious of anyone from the army or the Department. If you'll excuse the insult, he won't think much of an ordinary Guard.' Colonel Archer smiled at Terry Gregory, then turned to Stefan. 'Special Branch doesn't have to come into it. You're a detective. You've been on this Missing Postman business, which even Mr Kerney will have read about. As it happens that's true.'

'But my real job is to spy on our ambassador?' said Stefan.

'It is. But he's a diplomat, he'll take it in the spirit it's intended.'

Terry Gregory drove Stefan to Kingsbridge Station. He was still taking in what had happened and working out where his own advantage lay. Stefan had more to take in; a convergence of interests he couldn't have anticipated.

'One thing straight, Inspector. Mr Kerney might not have much of a nose but the rest of us have. Whatever the Germans are up to, the IRA is in there. When you get back you talk to me, not Archer. You tell me what you know and I tell you what you give G2. You don't even speak to Ned Broy.'

Stefan saw the steel in the superintendent's face. It was the look he always had when he felt he was on the scent of something useful. But Stefan still remembered the night in the Police Yard, Terry Gregory and Cathal McCallister, the IRA Quartermaster. He remembered that Gregory had been trying to find out where he was that night. He remembered that he must have had him followed to the Clarence before Christmas. He remembered the contradiction between the ease with which the stolen arms' caches had been found and the way Terry Gregory let the IRA General Staff slip through his fingers. He

172

remembered Geróid de Paor's belief that someone high up in Special Branch was passing information to the IRA.

'You know the rules,' said Gregory, 'it's called *droit de seigneur*.'

16

The Avenida Palace

Stefan spent his last night in Ireland with Kate at the flat on Wellington Quay. The next evening a car from the Department of External Affairs, carrying Leopold Kerney, the ambassador to Spain, took him to Dún Laoghaire for the mail boat. He had met Kerney briefly two days earlier. The ambassador was polite but reserved. As anticipated, Kerney viewed him as a very ordinary policeman with an ordinary job to do, which was entirely about his own security. The sense of hierarchy was strong in the civil service and the tiny Irish diplomatic corps. Leopold Kerney called Stefan 'Gillespie' or 'Inspector', while Stefan addressed him 'Mr Kerney' or 'sir'.

On the mail boat Kerney had a cabin and kept to it most of the way across the Irish Sea, leaving Stefan to sit in the saloon. At Holyhead they had separate sleepers on the train to London. They didn't see each other until they reached Euston next morning. They took a taxi to Waterloo and an early train to Poole Harbour in Dorset. On the train, Kerney read the newspapers he had asked Stefan to buy for him and passed them on as he finished. Apart from a few words about barrage balloons over London and the sandbagged buildings in Tavistock Square and Southampton Row, little was said. The ambassador's occasional comments on the war he was reading about in much more detail than Ireland's press allowed, were mostly of the 'not much is happening' variety. He seemed to take satisfaction in this, and Stefan had a sense he believed the war would not last. The idea that 'reason' would bring it to a halt before things got too serious was nothing that needed hiding in Britain where many felt the same. Stefan's own experience of the New Germany, which he had seen first-hand, gave him a less complacent view. A German family and the German blood in his veins sharpened that view.

In Poole they hardly had time to reach the harbour and board the Imperial Airways flying boat that would take them to Lisbon, en route to British colonies in West Africa. The ambassador knew people on the flight. Although all the passengers looked like civilians it wasn't hard to see that most were connected to the war in one way or another. Diplomats, politicians, colonial officials, army officers in mufti, and businessmen whose business was likely to be the business of war in one way or another. Stefan spent some time trying to guess what they all did from scraps of conversation, but he felt apart from it in a way that Leopold Kerney didn't seem to. For most of the journey he stared down at the grey Atlantic, which on his side of the plane was all he could see. He had his own battle to fight.

Two days before he left Dublin Stefan had gone to Iveagh House in Stephen's Green for a briefing at the Department of External Affairs. He was given a diplomatic passport, and a civil servant who knew far less about what was going on than he did talked about travel, accommodation, the security of papers and money, and the modest expenses to be drawn. He met Leopold Kerney over a slightly awkward cup of coffee and then walked across the Green to meet Dessie MacMahon at Neary's in Chatham Street. Dessie had got a message to him at Iveagh House. It simply told Stefan where he was. That was enough to indicate there was something to say that was better not known about in Special Branch. Dessie knew what was going on; he knew about Glendalough and Spain. But he also had something of his own now.

'I had a message from your man Chisholm.'

Stefan was surprised.

'He said he wanted to talk to you. No one else.'

'So who knows?'

'Nobody,' said Dessie, getting up, 'he'll be here any time.'

Dessie paused to light a cigarette.

'Take it easy in Spain, Stevie.' He walked out.

Stefan waited, listening to the unintelligible buzz of conversation, breathing in the haze of smoke. He saw Sergeant Chisholm enter and go to the bar. The policeman, in the suit he had worn in court, came over and sat down.

'This is unexpected, George.'

'You can maybe guess what I'm in Dublin for, Inspector.'

'The commissioner?'

'Dear old Ned.'

'But you're free. The case has been dropped.'

'I've been at HQ this morning. First round of a disciplinary hearing. McCoy's on tomorrow. They'll have us sacked so. Not much doubt now.'

'But they're not going to get you for murder, are they?'

'There's a new man up from Waterford, Superintendent Herlihy.'

'What happened to Laurel and Hardy?'

'Still around, just, but I'd say Pat Halloran will be destined for Donegal or the Islands before long. Either way he'll be waiting a long time for his next promotion.'

'He's got you to thank for that.'

'He's got himself to thank. He got a whiff of someone who'd talk and he thought he was in Special Branch. I heard Fintan Grace was there loading a revolver and leaving it on the table through the interrogation. It's an old RIC job, that one. Anyone else would have told the gobshite to shove it up his arse, but Paul's a born eejit. He robbed a couple of houses in Arklow with his brother, that's the thing. Halloran got that from somewhere. So along with the gun was the stolen goods to be planted on him if he didn't cough.'

'But your threats came out on top. Still, what he said was true.'

'Close enough.'

'So why do you want to tell me about it?'

'Close enough till Billy went down. The rest is bollocks. Halloran's bollocks. No body, no trip to the mountains to drop him in a mineshaft. Billy hit his head. He'd a lump the size of a duck's egg and a spatter of blood. He came round cursing and swearing and we said we'd get him to the post office in Charlie Hignett's car. He wouldn't have it, roaring and shouting about what he knew and how he'd get every one of us. So I did take him outside with Aidan McCoy, and we did put him on his bike. He rode off to Glendalough with a "God fuck all here". That's the truth, and the end of the tale we thought. It was the last we saw of him. Next thing was the bike in the road by the Seven Churches and Billy disappeared.'

'It's a pity you didn't say all that.'

'Starting with me in Whelan's drinking all afternoon?'

'You might have got away with that, without the rest.'

'We did think he must have wandered off. But time went on and there was no forgetting what happened in the pub. We thought maybe it was hitting his head must have done it. That he fell off the bike and walked off, and dropped dead, or drowned in a ditch, whatever you like. The idea he wouldn't be found alive came quick enough. But it never occurred to us there'd be no body. We just thought he'd be there somewhere, with the blow to his head, and Shamie would be up for murder so, or maybe we'd all be up for something.'

'So no fight, no fall, and most of you were never in the pub?'

'We thought if the lot of us kept our mouths shut . . .'

'So you fiddled the station diary then?'

'That was a mistake, but it happens everywhere.'

'It'll still do for you, George, as a Guard. But it's not just that. You might get away with murder, but when you walked out of that courtroom a free man you made Ned Broy look like an arse. That's the cardinal sin.'

'Billy wasn't badly hurt, Inspector. The more I think about it . . .'

'So what happened to him, George?'

'That's what no one can understand. How did he disappear?'

Stefan listened and said nothing. Whatever George Chisholm had come here to say to him, he could see that this was where it really started.

'If Billy came off his bike, if he was pissed, if he was concussed – whatever it was – how far could the eejit have gone? How could he vanish? No one hid that body, Mr Gillespie. None of us did anyway, I swear it.'

'But somebody did,' said Stefan, 'is that what you mean?'

'Whatever happens we all have to live with it. This is going to go on and on. They're still at it, questioning us, over and over. Now they're digging up new graves, looking for Billy. No one believes we didn't do it, even in the valley. People will keep their mouths shut, but it's still there.'

'If you're looking for me to solve it, George, I've got nothing.'

'But you thought there was someone else who could have done it.'

'No one else does, believe me.'

'You're still looking, you'd have to be, wouldn't you?'

'Yes, I'd have to be,' said Stefan quietly.

'I've had a lot of time to think about that night. Mostly how to get out of the mess we made and keep out of gaol for what none of us did. But some of what you said, that day at the barracks, has been going round too. Nothing that puts flesh on it. But there is something – about Miss Gort.'

The sergeant had Stefan's attention; this was new.

'It was a few months before she died. I hadn't long been in Laragh. I was going with a girl who worked at Reverend Gort's, Elsie Gantley. One night she came to the barracks, hysterical. She said Miss Gort had been assaulted. She found her in the garden at the vicarage, crying, hardly knowing where she was. I went up, and there she was. The vicar and Mrs Gort were away. She was in a fierce state, covered in mud and bruised, her clothes torn. She wouldn't say anything, wouldn't look at me. Elsie was hollering about a man attacking her. She kept screaming. "He assaulted Miss Gort, George, assaulted her!" You know what she was telling me. She didn't want to say it outright. So I said, who was this? Elsie had no idea and Miss Gort wouldn't answer. Then she stood up and she turned to me and she says, "My horse threw me. Elsie, don't make up absurd stories." I didn't think about it in years, but that was it. That was the story, and it didn't change. But I don't have a doubt Elsie wasn't making up stories.'

'She'd been molested?'

'More than molested, Elsie knew that.'

'And you didn't follow it up?'

'You don't go around saying things like that about a woman. Not when she's who she is. It's not so strange. Best left alone as often as not. It's how people deal with it.'

'And you never had any idea who did it?'

'No.'

'You'd have to wonder if Billy Byrne knew.'

'Billy wasn't even there then, Mr Gillespie.'

'No,' said Stefan, but he knew this meant something.

'If you were looking at suicide,' continued Chisholm, 'a lot of people would say there's your explanation. She wouldn't be the first. It did have something to do with her engagement breaking up, I think. That's the only other thing Elsie ever told me about that night. It's what she thought anyway.'

'And what happened to Elsie?'

'It wasn't long before she left. She had a sister in New Zealand.'

'Not just round the corner then.'

'I think the Gorts helped her out with the fare.'

'Did they make a habit of that sort of thing?'

'No, the old feller was as mean as buggery.'

'When was the last time you had a rape to investigate, George?'

'Never. It would have been the first in the valley.'

'Except for Charlotte Moore. That's a long way from never, and not so long ago as far as Billy Byrne was concerned. That was what the RIC came up with, wasn't it? Albert Neale, remember? He raped Charlotte Moore and then he killed her, to shut her up. If Marian Gort was raped in Glendalough, it's something they have in common. Apart from being dead.'

That evening Stefan Gillespie and Kate O'Donnell ate a meal at Jammet's in Nassau Street. The restaurant claimed to offer more of what was real French haute cuisine than you could find between Dublin and Paris, dismissing London as if it wasn't there. It wasn't true, but Dublin liked to think it was. It was more money than Stefan had ever spent on a meal. It was a gesture he wanted to make, but like any gesture born out of something close to guilt, it wasn't the right one. He knew it was a mistake; so did Kate. Through the meal they spoke about not very much, with Stefan talking of travel arrangements and Kate of not finding a job. It was only as they walked down from Trinity to the river that she said what she felt.

'I wish you hadn't spent all that money.'

'I wanted to do something special.'

'It would be special if you told me what the matter is.'

It came more easily than he expected. Having avoided talk of Laragh and Glendalough for more than two months he needed to say something; he needed Kate to understand. He told the story of the Missing Postman and the room above the post office. He didn't tell her everything. The car crash was still an accident. But he told her what he thought he might find in Spain, at least what he was looking for. By the time they got back to the flat he had said most of what he could. Kate had been very quiet. She felt the weight he was carrying, and she understood how much harder it was than his words seemed to suggest.

'I wish you'd said before. It would have been easier. For you too.'

'I didn't know how to start.'

'I could feel you were somewhere else. It wasn't great before Christmas but I knew what that was about. I knew you hated what you were doing. I knew you had to work that out. And I thought you would. We would. But then it all got ten times worse. At least it makes sense now. I can't imagine how you feel. But I know you have to try to do something.'

'I don't know what, if I get nothing in Spain . . .'

'You need time, you need to be free to do this.'

'It doesn't have to affect us, Kate.'

'Time,' she said again, putting her finger to his lips. 'I have been thinking about going to England, to see my sister. I'm still not working and I don't see anything coming up. I haven't been over there since Niamh left Ireland. It might be a good time. You won't be here for a few weeks. When you come back you'll need to find a way to resolve all this – or to let it go.'

This wasn't what he wanted to hear, but he knew it was right.

'Is Niamh all right?'

'I think so. She has a feller in tow, but I don't know how serious it is. She wouldn't say either way, would she? But I'm not to tell Mam and Dad.'

Her smile was a welcome shift in mood.

'Well, if he's English, I might not look such a bad option.'

'Just shut up, Stefan Gillespie. They've never said anything bad!'

'Nothing at all?'

'Well, nothing very bad.'

It was an easier laugh than they had shared in some time.

'I think that's enough,' she said quietly. 'We should go to bed.'

Stefan lay awake, listening to the city growing quieter. Kate had gone to sleep. It was the first time in a long time he had woken in the night to hear her and feel her beside him in the darkness. It was true what she said; until he knew what had happened to Maeve he couldn't move forward. However much he wanted it to be different, he had to clear away the debris in his head. He had to cut his way through the darkness. He wished, as he had never wished before that this door had never been opened. Even if it was true that Maeve had been murdered that day by the Upper Lake, it would have been better not to know anything. For a moment he wondered what it was he was looking for. In his head it was 'truth', but what then? A court case, a hanging? The truth might be all there was to find. What if he knew and could do nothing? The figure of the murderer he had come to believe in now was only a black, shapeless fog in his mind, but the idea that revenge might need to replace justice was there beside it. He could not pretend it wasn't. It didn't disturb him as much as he expected. If that was where this led him he didn't feel uncomfortable. The truth would mean he would have to do something. And if there was no other way, he would have to do it himself.

Stefan stood in his bedroom in the suite at the Avenida Palace Hotel in Lisbon, a calm, green room with high ceilings and high windows on to the street. A fan turned slowly above his head. It was late afternoon. Looking out of the window, he could see the heat that was still in the air. He heard the noises of the city, the shouts and the car horns and the clatter of trams, like Dublin or any city, yet with its own distinct rhythm. He left his suitcase unpacked at the foot of the bed. The ambassador had muttered something about things to do. Stefan was still unclear about his duties. Kerney had left him none the wiser, though he sensed his presence was a slight irritation.

Through the open door was a sitting room with a large, ornate desk. Leopold Kerney's bedroom was on the other side. Stefan knocked and walked in. The sitting room was common ground but it was there for Kerney to use as an office. The ambassador was at the desk, his back to the bright windows. There were dark landscapes on the walls, brown fields and grey country houses; the sofa and the armchairs were gilded and hard and almost certainly uncomfortable. Two huge mirrors, the silvering spotted with age, filled the walls at right angles to the windows, reflecting the room infinitely back on itself. Kerney was sorting through papers and passports and tickets. He scribbled several notes in a diary, then put some of the papers into a briefcase and the others into a metal dispatch box.

'There is a safe in my bedroom, Gillespie. We will use that rather than the hotel one, I think. There are two keys, so if you take this one . . .'

He handed Stefan a long steel key.

'They will have a pass key, sir.'

'I know you have to think as a policeman, but I do stay here often. Apart from money and credit notes there's nothing that would interest anyone.' Kerney smiled. 'It is a city full of spies, as anyone will tell you. I don't know where spying features economically but I think it's taken over from tourism as one of Lisbon's mainstays. But if we don't have much to offer the world in trade now, it's even less when it comes to espionage.'

He went into his bedroom and locked away the dispatch box. Stefan had already seen that Kerney's humour was spare and rarely forthcoming, but he was content to be the slightly out-of-his-depth policeman. Kerney came back in with a crumpled Panama hat and picked up his briefcase.

'I did give you some escudos, Inspector?'

'You did, sir.'

'You'll want a wander round. If you need a map, the concierge will have one. The best thing is to walk down to the sea and the Praça do Comércio. Right out of the hotel, across the square, the Rossio, through the Baixa Pombalina. It's a maze but you won't get lost. It's a grid. We came up on one side from the harbour. Lots of restaurants there. If you don't want to venture far there's the Leão d'Ouro, past the station. Good English too.'

The detail was more than Stefan needed. But there was a message in Kerney's brusque good humour. He was being dismissed; the description of a tourist itinerary for him was the only instruction he would get. The ambassador looked at him uncertainly. He wasn't sure what to make of him.

'I have some business to do and I want to go to Mass first.' Kerney knew enough to know Stefan wouldn't be going to Mass. 'I may see you later, but no need for you to wait for me, Inspector. We'll be travelling on to Salamanca the day after tomorrow. So, well, soak up some atmosphere. And you will need a hat. I don't mean a trilby. I'd suggest you buy one.'

Kerney put on his own Panama to close the conversation, and left.

Stefan walked to the window. It was still bright, with only a hint of evening in the sky. Since he had an itinerary he might as well follow it.

He left the room and locked the door. He didn't take the lift but walked down the circular stairway to the lobby. The ambassador was still there, about to leave ahead of him. As Kerney walked out a man of around Stefan's age got up from a red sofa by the door and walked out too. Stefan registered him for no particular reason except the sharpness of the creases in his remarkably uncrumpled white linen suit. He recognized him. He had seen him at the harbour, where the same thought about the suit had struck him. He thought no more of it. He went to the concierge's desk and got a map, and asked where he could buy a hat. Then he went out to see if he could find his way through the city to the Praça do Comércio and the sea.

He was hungry as he came out past the carved and sculptured façade of the Central Station that dominated this corner of the Rossio. He ate in the blue-tiled Leão d'Ouro as Kerney had suggested. It was early and he was the only customer. For the moment what was on his mind was the fact that it seemed unlikely Leopold Kerney would let him know anything about anything, let alone the Germans and Frank Ryan. He left an hour later and crossed the Rossio to make his way towards the Tagus, but the huge square was a sea of people, blocking his way. A procession filed across the far end.

Close to the front was a statue of the Virgin Mary, held high on a dais, glittering with stars. Behind came a line of embroidered banners and statues of saints. There were clerics in purple and red; priests followed by brothers in grey and white habits; men in tailcoats and top hats; army officers in uniform; men in hoods and high-pointed hats. A line of choristers in white and red sang. There was the smell of incense as priests and altar boys swung their censors. Behind them men, women, children, streamed into the square. He couldn't get through. He would have to wait for the procession to pass. He turned back across the Rossio towards the colonnaded building that was the National Theatre. He had only drunk water in the Leão d'Ouro and, though the air was cooling now, he was hot. He went in search of a beer. He needed an antidote to all that holiness.

To the right of the theatre he passed the white façade of a big church where another crowd was spilling out. It was then that he glimpsed Leopold Kerney, who had been to Mass in the church. Stefan didn't want to be seen. There was nothing wrong with being there but he had no doubt about the way the ambassador had dismissed him. One way or another it would look as if he was following him, which would be no help in gaining confidence and trust. He stepped into the shadows of the building opposite, turning his back. Kerney was heading in the opposite direction. He wouldn't see him.

Only a few yards away, sitting on a wall, was the man in the white linen suit, its creases as sharp as in the lobby of the Avenida Palace. He was reading the *Daily Mail*. He had to be English. It wasn't only the newspaper; something about him said he couldn't be anything else. He got up, stubbed out a cheroot, and sauntered away. There was a studied ease about his movement that was so self-consciously casual that it wasn't casual at all.

Stefan watched him walk past the colonnades of the theatre. Kerney was just ahead. He had seen this man three times now. That held Stefan's attention along with the odd way he moved. The ambassador stopped. The briefcase under his arm had fallen. As he bent to pick it up the man in the white suit stopped. He turned away and took out a cheroot, as if pausing to light it. Seconds later the ambassador walked on. The man lit his cheroot and followed. There was no doubt; he was following Leopold Kerney.

17

O Elevador da Glória

Stefan followed the Englishman. The Englishman followed the ambassador. The man kept assiduously to the distance he had been taught. Stefan imagined him counting the optimum number of passers-by between him and his quarry. But the man struggled with Kerney's pace. The ambassador was walking too slowly to be easy to follow; his pursuer was too impatient to amble and had to keep stopping instead. Stefan kept back in the double pursuit. He knew the ambassador was heading for the Avenida Palace.

He saw them both cross the road at the Central Station and carried on towards the Praça dos Restauradores. At the Avenida Palace, Kerney spoke to the doorman who hailed a taxi. As the taxi drove off the Englishman was unperturbed. He went into the hotel. Stefan crossed over and did the same.

Inside, Stefan stood in the lobby and lit a cigarette. The Englishman was at the concierge's desk. Conscious that the lobby was almost empty, Stefan stepped into the bar. He picked up a copy of the London *Times*, several days old, and gazed at the front page dense with small advertisements, not reading but watching the man in the linen suit in conversation with the concierge. When he turned away Stefan saw a banknote passed across the desk. The way it was palmed told a story about how it had been earned.

The man in the linen suit stepped across to the entrance and went out. Stefan put down the paper and walked after him. He stood back as the door was held for a small, round woman in her sixties. She wore a grey suit and a grey hat decorated with pheasant feathers. Her face was flushed from the day's heat. She carried an easel, a pallet, paints, an unfinished canvas, a large handbag of great age. Stefan smiled politely as she passed; she took no notice of him. Her eyes were fixed determinedly on the reception desk.

When Stefan emerged from the Avenida Palace the Englishman was getting into a taxi. It turned right towards the Rossio, the opposite direction to the one the ambassador took. Apparently the surveillance was over.

Back in the hotel Stefan approached the concierge's desk. The man was no longer there. He waited a moment then turned to reception, where a tall, spindly man peered down with unconvincing patience at the grey woman clutching her painting accoutrements. She had the sharp, clipped English accent that identified her class rather than where she came from.

'It's a question of light. The window is extremely unsatisfactory.'

'It is the only window we have available, senhora.'

'I was outside the hotel just now. There are windows everywhere.'

'But the hotel is full, senhora. It is the war, of course. Desculpa.'

'Light is important to me. I am here to paint.'

The receptionist looked down at her equipment and nodded.

'We have light outside, everywhere, a great deal.'

She narrowed her eyes.

'I don't expect sarcasm at your prices. If you would look again.'

The receptionist turned the pages of the register mechanically.

'Do you have good light?' The woman looked at Stefan.

'Good enough, I suppose.'

'But you don't paint?'

'No, I don't paint.'

She regarded him with a stern, teacherly look.

'Light feeds the mind. You must have felt that sometimes.'

The receptionist shut the register loudly and shook his head.

'Perhaps in a day or two.'

'I shall be gone then.'

'Desculpa, senhora.'

She turned towards the lift. The receptionist raised his eyebrows.

'Mrs Surtees,' he said, as if the name was sufficient explanation, then resumed a static, obliging smile. 'How can I help you, Senhor Gillespie?'

'I'm looking for the concierge.'

'Agostinho is in the baggage room. I shall fetch him.'

'I'll find him, don't worry.'

He moved to the concierge's desk and lifted the counter flap.

'Mr Gillespie, we prefer our guests do not—'

The concierge was sitting on a chair, surrounded by cases, bags and trunks, with a bottle of beer and a ham roll. He stood up as Stefan opened the door.

'Desculpa, Senhor Gillespie, if you ring the bell—'

'A little business needs a little privacy.'

The concierge frowned; the Irishman was not in search of baggage.

'There was a gentleman in earlier. You were talking to him. I know him from somewhere. I just can't place him and you may know his name.'

'A guest, senhor?'

'I don't think he's a guest, but he was in the hotel this

afternoon. More than once. In fact, he left only a few minutes ago. An Englishman, in a rather good linen suit. About my height, my age, fair, a little tanned.'

'Not a guest? Then I don't know him.' Agostinho smiled, but it was an uneasy smile, the one he kept for questions he didn't want to answer.

'But you were talking to him.'

'It is possible, senhor.' The concierge shrugged as if to say he talked to so many people that no one could expect him to remember them all.

'I doubt your memory is as bad as all that, Agostinho.'

Stefan took out his wallet.

'There are a number of ways we can do this. One is that I tip you for the information you're going to give me. Another is that I raise hell with the manager about the information you've been giving to this man you can't remember, about the Irish ambassador to Spain. We have an honorary consul here. He may feel it's worth raising with your foreign ministry. I don't know who looks into that sort of thing, but not the traffic police.'

Stefan pulled out a dollar bill and put it on top of a trunk. The concierge put a hand over the dollar; when he moved it the note was gone.

'The man is English, is that right?'

'Sim, Senhor Gillespie.'

'And his name?'

'Senhor Chillingham.'

'Do you know why is he so interested in Mr Kerney?'

Agostinho shook his head. Why, was outside his remit.

'I'm not sure I can top what he paid you, Agostinho, but I can make life more uncomfortable for you. What did he ask? What did you tell him?'

The concierge wasn't sure how far the Irishman would push. People who bought information didn't normally want the authorities involved; they didn't want scenes. But he was unsure where to put the Irish in Lisbon's industry of information buying and selling. This was his first Irishman.

'He wanted to see the register after you arrived. He knows Mr Kerney but not you. He wanted to see your passports, to know how long you were staying, where you were going to. What train you were taking.'

'He talked to the receptionist as well?'

'People want information in Lisbon, it is normal.'

'Good. If it's normal, what do you know about him?'

Agostinho's eyes were on the wallet. Stefan took out another dollar.

'He is from the British Embassy, senhor.'

'And what did he want when he came back just now?'

'To know anything Mr Kerney had asked me to do for him.'

'And had he?'

'To book a table this evening. Tavares in the Rua da Misericórdia.'

'Is that it?'

The concierge gave something between a shrug and a nod.

'Shall we say if Mr Chillingham wants information from now on, it would be a grand thing if you don't know anything, whether you do or not?'

'Of course, senhor,' said Agostinho with wide-eyed sincerity.

'Is this restaurant far?'

'In the Barrio Alto.'

The concierge gestured vaguely over his shoulder. Stefan took out the map of Lisbon he had in his pocket and put it on the top of the trunk.

'Quickest is to the Elevador da Glória, the tram to the Jardim de São Pedro, here. Out of the hotel and to here. At the top go left on to the Rua da Misericórdia and Tavares is on your right. You will see a balcony and then the wooden doors. Very elegant.

Very discreet.' He marked the restaurant and then looked at Stefan. 'It is not a cheap restaurant to eat in, Mr Gillespie.'

'Don't worry, I won't eat. I'll get a sandwich on the way back.'

Stefan took the yellow funicular tram up the steep cobbled lane to the Barrio Alto. He set off along the winding Rua da Misericórdia. It was a narrow street full of tiny shops and bars, busy in the bright evening. He was aware that the man from the British Embassy knew who he was; he had seen him, probably at the harbour coming in off the flying boat, certainly at the Avenida Palace Hotel. But he had been unnoticed outside the Igreja de São Domingos when Kerney came out after Mass, and he wanted to remain unnoticed. However, if the man was watching the Tavares restaurant it would be a static surveillance. It was very different. He was the one who would be drawing attention to himself if he spent too much time there.

Stefan saw the wood and glass doors of Tavares ahead on the right. He kept to the left. He strolled idly by, not changing his pace. He glanced through the restaurant window and saw only gold and a glittering chandelier. There were three cars parked on his side of the Rua da Misericórdia near the restaurant; a grey limousine, the chauffeur lying back asleep; a red coupé surrounded by teenage boys; a soft-top Citroën taxi with a young driver immersed in a newspaper. He saw no sign of the linen suit.

He stopped at a café with tables outside but decided to sit inside. He ordered a coffee and sat on a stool by the window. He could see the front windows of Tavares to his right and just enough of the street on either side.

After half an hour he came to the conclusion nothing was going to happen. He assumed Leopold Kerney was in there but there was no obvious surveillance outside. Then he saw the man he now knew as Chillingham, a cheroot clenched between his teeth, strolling towards the restaurant from the other end of the Rua da Misericórdia. The Englishman stopped and got into the taxi. He spoke to the driver for several minutes. It was a relaxed conversation; they were both laughing. Chillingham took out his wallet, then he got out of the taxi and started to stroll back the way he had come.

The restaurant was being watched but only by a taxi driver. It could even be the taxi that brought Kerney there. If it was then Chillingham was better than Stefan had thought. And it was Chillingham he decided to follow now. He walked back into the street. It was almost dark now though the Rua da Misericórdia was bright and loud. He saw the Englishman turning down to the lower town ahead of him. There probably wasn't much to gain from following except to demonstrate that he was better at it. The chances were he would get no more than a walk through the city and end up at the British Embassy. A better option would be to confront the man. He increased his pace till they were parallel then turned with an affable smile.

'A beautiful evening.'

The Englishman returned the smile. Stefan could see that Chillingham thought he should recognize him. He was trying to place him.

'We get some rough stuff off the Atlantic now and again,' said the Englishman, 'but it usually is a beautiful evening, which makes discussing the weather pointless. If you're English, it leaves nothing to talk about.'

'Or if you're Irish,' replied Stefan.

'Or if you're Irish, ah!' Chillingham repeated the words and grinned. He recognized Stefan now; the Irish policeman from the Avenida Palace.

'You do know who I am, but we haven't been introduced. It's Stefan Gillespie. You have seen my passport already so I don't need to expand.'

'Simon Chillingham,' said the Englishman, then burst out

laughing. 'That little rat, Agostinho. He would sell his grand-mother for a dollar.'

'I shouldn't have wasted two on him then.'

'Two dollars? My God, man, you can't go off hiking the prices like that. It'll be round every hotel in Lisbon. I don't know about the Jerries, but HMG can't afford bribes at such stiff rates. There is a war on, old fellow!'

'Your war, Mr Chillingham, not ours. Our Department of External Affairs won't like you following Irish ambassadors. Any reason for it?'

Simon Chillingham ignored the question and took out a packet of cheroots. He offered Stefan one. He shook his head. Chillingham lit his.

'You're right, they're disgusting. The mosquitoes think so, which is a help. I took you for some kind of plod, if you don't mind my saying. A plod of no account. My mistake. But you are a policeman, though, an inspector?'

'Special Branch.'

'Oh, your version of that mob. They didn't tell me that.'

'What are you, Military Intelligence?'

'A lowly attaché, third secretary – general dogsbody.'

'Isn't that the same thing?'

Chillingham blew out a cloud of acrid smoke.

'Well, it is all hands to the pump. I'd better buy you a drink,'

'As you've cost Ireland two dollars we can't afford, you had.'

In a corner of the Praça do Comércio the two men sat under the stone arches of Martinho's café. Inside it was dark and cramped but here, where the Rua da Prata met the Pombalina, you could see, usefully, in every direction. The grand square of the Praça do Comércio was full of people.

Walking through the square, Simon Chillingham had chatted idly about the city and its sights, and its new population of refugees fleeing the war in Europe; as he reminded Stefan often enough to make him regret saying it, 'Our war, not yours.' Mostly the refugees were from Germany and Austria, Jews in large numbers, but all sorts of people the Nazis didn't much like, for whatever reason, and they had a lot of reasons. They came from Czechoslovakia too, and from Poland. They were there from France as well, from Belgium, the Netherlands, trickling in from all over Europe; those with the money or the vision to read what was coming if things went wrong. And if things did go wrong the stream of refugees trying to get a boat to the United States or South America, anywhere that wasn't Europe, would turn into a flood. Chillingham referred to the possibility of a flood only once, but he said 'if things go wrong' a number of times. The idea that Hitler's planes and tanks were unstoppable, as they had been in Poland, was everywhere in Europe. Stefan felt it in the night air of Lisbon now, as he had felt it in Dublin and in a railway carriage rattling through Hampshire.

'Favor, uma garrafa de Vinho Verde,' said Chillingham.

The waiter gazed at the Englishman and Irishman with mild irritation.

'You don't mind that? Cheap and very cheerful.'

'I'd say cheerful would be grand,' smiled Stefan.

'Ignore me! What the hell did we talk about before we had a war?'

The wine arrived and Chillingham poured it out.

'I hope we can drink to the end of you following Mr Kerney.'

'Well, I'm out of it anyway now. Well spotted!'

'We've done the jokes, Mr Chillingham. Do you want a complaint made?'

'That would be rather tedious, old man. These things are. But do bear in mind HMG's own complaints wending their way across the Irish Sea.'

'About what?'

'Your ambassador's peculiar taste in dinner guests.'

'Why do you care who he eats with?'

'You'd expect us to be interested in what German Intelligence is up to, wherever they're up to it. Old Lisboa in this case. Well, that's the game. So if the Irish ambassador to Spain is chomping away in a restaurant one evening with a chap who's an Abwehr colonel, it's entirely reasonable we raise our eyebrows. I happen to be the eyebrows chosen to be raised.'

It was news to Stefan, though Chillingham clearly didn't think so.

'We assume it's all to do with this chap Ryan.'

'Which chap Ryan would that be?'

'Oh, you can do better than that. We know Mr Kerney's been talking to the Jerries about lifting Ryan from prison in Burgos. Frank Ryan's no secret himself. He was always splashed across the newspaper before the war interrupted such things. All sorts of grandees trying to get Franco to let the poor bastard out, here there and everywhere. Questions about him in the House of Commons and all that. At one time HMG was even giving a push behind the scenes. Although there is a little rumour that some of your fellow countrymen aren't as keen to have him home as they say. Unfortunately for Mr Ryan, the world has other things to think about now. I doubt he's even much of a priority for Mr de Valera these days. But we have a natural curiosity about why the dear old Germans would want to spring an International Brigade officer who hates the Nazis worse than the plague.'

'And do they?'

'Oh, come on, old man!' Simon Chillingham laughed and shook his head. He took the bottle of Vinho Verde and poured two more glasses.

'Ryan is of a red complexion naturally, but not a commie. Less keen on commies than he was perhaps, after their antics in Spain. Still, more red than IRA according to our people.'

'I'm just a policeman making sure Mr Kerney gets to Madrid.'

'Via Salamanca and Burgos?'

'Don't you like the route?'

'Franco hasn't entirely moved his cohorts out of Burgos yet. It was his HQ, of course. And Salamanca is where German Military Intelligence set up in the Civil War. They're still there too. They must like it. And they're based in the Irish College. I don't doubt you'll stay with the rector there. Mr Kerney always does, you know. Bit of an Irish home from home.'

Stefan drank the light, fizzy wine and said nothing. The Irish College was already in his head, but for reasons that made the British Intelligence man's interest in it seem unimportant. Simon Chillingham was looking for reactions. He was showing how much he knew and implying he knew more. It was clumsily done. And it was not hard for Stefan to look as if what he was saying had passed over him and didn't matter. It didn't, not yet. All that mattered to him about Salamanca was that he had a reason to go there.

'It's a curious business,' continued Chillingham. 'Abwehr chap for dinner here, Abwehr chaps for dinner at the Irish College. You may not know the colonel Mr Kerney is entertaining tonight. The Abwehr are a fairly decent bunch as these things go, next to the Gestapo and their ilk. Military types for the most. Oberst Melsbach is Military Intelligence too, but he isn't liked, I mean by his own crew. They're wary of him. That's the word.'

'I see. Do you have a glass of wine with the Abwehr chaps too?'

'Not quite, but we all know who's who in Lisbon.'

'There must be worse places to follow each other around.'

'Well, I'm damned if I want a posting anywhere there's a real war.'

'There's always Dublin.'

'That wouldn't be so bad, apart from the bloody weather.'

'You have our own sentiments about our country in one.'

The Englishman laughed.

'I'll be serious, Gillespie. The Ryan business is odd but Melsbach makes it odder. He met your Mr Kerney last time he was in Lisbon. He's an officer in the Brandenburgers, the Abwehr military set-up. He was in Spain in the Civil War. The view in London is that shallow graves all over España testify to his activities. Which makes his concern for an International Brigade officer, even an Irish one,' he poured more wine, 'sehr wunderbar.'

Stefan took in the new information. The Brandenburgers were already part of this. Frank Ryan's German friend, Helmut Clissmann, was in the regiment. If an Abwehr regiment was involved in Ryan's release it was unlikely Clissmann hadn't been acting on orders, whatever about their friendship.

'I'm sure you'll be repeating all this to your ambassador.'

Chillingham looked at Stefan with an arch, colleague-to-colleague grin. Stefan knew what was behind it. In there was a version of what Terry Gregory had told him to hold fast to at all times; never tell anybody everything. And the Englishman was right. There would be things about this conversation he wouldn't tell Kerney, as there were things Kerney wasn't telling him. Instinct, not logic, decided what those things were.

'You might want to warn him to look out for Oberst Melsbach.'

'There are a lot of people he needs to look out for.'

'Oh, we're a fairly harmless bunch. Don't worry about us.'

'No bodies in shallow graves where you go then?'

'I can see you have a very low opinion of the British Empire.'

'It must be what comes of having been a part of it.'

Stefan walked back to the Avenida Palace Hotel through the streets of the Pombalina, along the Rua Augusta. It was less busy now in the restaurants and bars. Shops had closed. He bought a postcard to send to Tom. It was as much for something to do as anything else, while he thought through his conversation with the British Intelligence officer. He didn't know what time Kerney would be back but he decided he would avoid the suite's sitting room and go straight to bed. He needed a clearer head before he tackled the ambassador, starting with an explanation of why he had been following him through Lisbon. Kerney would be embarrassed. Stefan knew that when you had to embarrass the man you worked for, it required careful handling.

Simon Chillingham stayed at Martinho's for one more glass of wine. He had enjoyed his drink with the Irish policeman. Inspector Gillespie was clearly no fool but he knew less about what was going on than he pretended; he certainly had no idea how the game was played in Lisbon. But Chillingham wasn't convinced any of this mattered much. The intrusion of amateurs only hammered it home. It was the station head's view that the Irish ambassador to Spain was neither as naive nor myopic as he appeared, but he was still an Irishman soft on the IRA. Weren't they all? That message had gone to London; from London it had found its way by commodious recirculation, as these things did, to Colonel Archer in Irish Intelligence. Yet Kerney was back on the Iberian peninsula doing whatever he was doing with the Germans. The Irish appeared happy for him to pursue the Abwehr's plan for Frank Ryan if it didn't embarrass Irish neutrality, and Chillingham's masters seemed to have no strong objections, if they could keep an eye on it. There was no intelligence without letting things happen. If the Germans thought springing a defunct IRA leader from gaol was a good idea, allowing them get on with it might reveal something useful. From what Chillingham knew Ryan seemed a decent fellow, as that sort of Irishman went, and Franco's prisons were filthy enough that you couldn't blame a chap for not being choosy who opened the cell door to let him out.

As the British Intelligence officer left Martinho's he was unaware he was being followed for the third time that day, by another man who was better at it than him. He reached the little alley where the grey cast-iron lift of the Elevador de Santa Justa would take him up six storeys to the Barrio Alto. He would pay off the man he had left to watch outside Tavares and call it a day. Apart from the bare fact that Leopold Kerney's dinner with Oberst Melsbach had happened there would be no more to learn in Lisbon.

He watched the Santa Justa elevator clattering down from the Barrio Alta. He did not notice a blue sedan pulling past on the Rua Áurea.

Two men got out of the car. The agent who had followed Chillingham up from the Praça do Comércio got in. The two men walked to the elevator and stood behind him. As the lift doors opened the Englishman and half a dozen other passengers got into the carriage in a haze of cigarette smoke. The doors closed. The lift hissed and rattled upwards. At the top Simon Chillingham was the last to exit, with the two men from the car. One stepped in front of him and asked for a light, in English. He obliged with a few words about the cold air tonight, registering that the accent was German. He walked on, aware for a moment how quiet it was. He stepped into the dark lane that led to the Barrio, squeezed in by the brooding, skeletal ruins of the Carmelite Convent. Quite abruptly the two men were on either side of him, hemming him in. The muzzle of a Walther M4 pushed hard into his ribs.

18

O Trem Noturno

In the breakfast room of the Avenida Palace Hotel Stefan Gillespie sat by one of the big windows that gave on to the Praça dos Restauradores and the tree-lined boulevard of the Avenida da Liberdade. There wasn't a lot of liberty in the *Estado Novo* created by António Salazar after his military coup in 1926. Portugal's politics, such as they were, were a ragbag of fascist clichés and cherry-picked Catholic social doctrines. They didn't matter much; it was what the New State was against that defined it, not only socialism, communism and liberalism of any shade, but anything that smacked of democracy. The New State had come about in an almost bloodless revolution by comparison with the slaughter that had engulfed Spain in its civil war, but it affirmed the faith that had swept through Europe in the aftermath of the Depression, the one thing that united the deceptively distinctive gospels of the right and the left: Democracy Doesn't Work!

On a sunny spring morning on the Avenida da Liberdade, Portugal didn't feel like a state run by its secret police force. Lisbon didn't look like a city whose population was being watched by the secret police either, but it was. Meanwhile, the British and the Germans were watching each other too, as well as the hotels, boarding houses and bars packed with migrants and ticket hustlers, passport forgers, information peddlers and fabricators, and amateur spies. The city fed off the desperation and abandonment that made even hope a saleable commodity, and if the Portuguese showed little interest in all this, apart from its usefulness in generating income, it was because they were too busy spying on their own citizens to notice.

For Stefan Gillespie, however, the view from the Avenida Palace Hotel was full of light. But the view from any grand hotel was only a postcard of something that had already gone. Like everywhere else in the Europe, the light in Lisbon was growing dimmer.

'A good evening?' Leopold Kerney sat down.

'I'm not sure, sir,' said Stefan.

'What did you eat?'

'Pork.'

'Stick to fish by the sea, meat in the country, in Spain particularly.'

He took a copy of the *Times* and turned to the crossword.

'Coffee, waiter, and some scrambled eggs and toast.'

He peered down at the crossword. 'Did you get a hat, Inspector?'

'No, I'll see to it today.'

'Fonseca's is the place, and keep the receipt.'

After a moment he pushed the newspaper away.

'I've a meeting with our honorary consul this morning, then I'm at the foreign ministry. We're thinking of opening a full embassy. They're going to suggest some properties. I need to get them down from the various palaces they'll be offering us to something more like a two-room office.'

He smiled, then turned back to the crossword.

'I guess you don't know you were being followed yesterday, sir?'

Kerney looked up, frowning. 'What on earth does that mean?'

Stefan's next sentence was in Irish.

'You were followed from the hotel to Mass, then back to the hotel. You weren't followed to the Tavares restaurant because the man who had you under surveillance knew you were going. Someone was outside, though. If your meeting with the Abwehr officer was meant to be a secret, it isn't.'

Kerney waited as the waiter poured his coffee. He looked at Stefan, too surprised for a show of indignation. When he spoke it was in Irish too.

'Who the hell would be following me?'

'A British Intelligence officer, a Mr Chillingham.'

'And how do you know all this, Inspector.'

'I saw a lot of Mr Chillingham yesterday. I saw him waiting for you outside the São Domingos church. I saw him watch you leave here in a taxi. I saw him ask the concierge where you'd gone. I saw him by the Tavares when you were eating there. He's not that good at his job, but he's good enough to know you were with a German Military Intelligence officer.'

'I see, so you were following me too.'

'I thought it was something you ought to know about, sir.'

Kerney felt both irritated and embarrassed. Stefan's calm tone was calculated not to make him feel foolish, but it wasn't entirely successful.

'I don't think you'll see Chillingham again.'

'And why is that?'

'He knows he was spotted. I had a drink with him last night.'

'And what the feck was that for, Gillespie?'

The waiter put down a plate of eggs and a rack of toast.

'I thought I'd ask him if it was good for the British Embassy to be trailing an Irish diplomat. He took the point, but he did wonder if an Irish diplomat having dinner with an Abwehr colonel was altogether in the spirit of neutrality, as His Majesty's Government saw it.' Stefan smiled. 'His words, sir. And I assumed you'd want to know why he was following you.'

'And did you find out?'

'Proinséas Riáin.'

There was no one listening to the conversation, but if anybody had been, a language that was incomprehensible in most hotels in Dublin was certainly unintelligible in Lisbon. And Stefan bore in mind Lisbon as it had been described to him the previous night; a name a surprising number of people seemed interested in was best, even on its own, unrecognized.

'I see.'

'They have a whiff of what's happening. This arrangement with the Germans to get Frank Ryan out of prison and out of Spain, I mean. They'd like to know what it's about. I doubt it amounts to more than that. He was an IRA leader and the English are still clearing up the IRA bombing campaign.'

'If he was still an IRA leader there wouldn't have been a bombing campaign. I know it made him as sick to the stomach as the rest of us.'

'Whatever about that, they've put you and Ryan and the Abwehr together, sir. Why wouldn't British Intelligence want to know more?'

Leopold Kerney nodded and finally produced an awkward smile.

'The Department thought I was getting out of my depth, is that it?'

Stefan understood but looked as if he didn't.

'You, I mean,' said the ambassador.

'I don't think they anticipated a British Intelligence tail, Mr Kerney.'

'Well, they did suggest diplomacy isn't an ideal training for all this. So are you here to protect me from myself or Irish diplomacy from me?'

Stefan still looked as if he didn't quite understand, but Kerney was now under no illusions that he understood perfectly. He sat and ate, looking out at the Avenida da Liberdade. When he spoke again it was in English.

'Since you haven't got that hat, I'll come to Fonseca's with you. If they do follow, they can watch. I underestimated you. Let us start again.'

Leopold Kerney took Stefan to the hat shop in the Rossio, then crossed the square to meet the honorary consul for coffee in the Café Nicola. They continued to the Portuguese Ministry of Foreign Affairs. Stefan was satisfied the ambassador was no longer being followed, but since Kerney's movements in Spain were already known it wasn't necessarily the end of the game. That evening the two Irishmen would take the night train that would split along the way for Madrid and the French border. It was the train that would take Stefan to Salamanca and to the Colegio de los Irlandeses.

It was early evening when they left the Avenida Palace for the Central Station. The luggage had gone ahead to the train. As they walked along the crowded platform to the sleeping car the ambassador talked about Salamanca and its churches. It was a city he clearly loved but Stefan had learned that conversing about interesting things, interesting places, was an artful way of saying nothing, and was a part of who Leopold Kerney was. It was probably a part of what any halfway decent diplomat needed to be. There had been similar conversations through the day since the ambassador had decided he was now a help rather than a hindrance. Although Kerney now accepted him, he showed no sign of taking Stefan into his confidence.

When they reached the sleeping car, Agostinho, the Avenida's concierge, was waiting. He had brought the bags himself. Kerney thanked him, slipped some escudos into his hand, and stepped up into the carriage. He was unaware of the concierge's nervousness. Stefan could see it immediately. Agostinho had attempted to hand the money back to Kerney, though Kerney had not noticed. It wasn't every day a concierge did that.

'Thank you, Agostinho,' said Stefan.

The concierge spoke in a low voice, glancing furtively around.

'You have heard, senhor? The Englishman?'

'What?'

'Senhor Chillingham. His body is found in the Tagus.'

'Jesus!'

The concierge crossed himself and nodded; Jesus was the word.

'Do they know what happened?'

Agostinho shrugged and drew his finger across his throat.

'Os alemães; the Germans.'

He grabbed Stefan's hand and pushed into it the dollars from the previous day, along with the ambassador's escudos. Then he was gone. Stefan watched him disappear into the crowd. He turned back to the train.

'Mr Gillespie, could you kindly take my easel and paints?'

He looked round at the smiling face of Mrs Surtees.

'I'm bad with steps. I lost a canvas under a train in Nuremberg once.'

'Of course, Mrs Surtees.' He took the easel and the paint box.

'I managed to get the cathedral here in an unusual pinkish light.'

Inside the sleeping car Stefan offered her back the easel and the paints, but Mrs Surtees was busy leafing through a battered sketchbook.

'It's a Latin cross, you know.'

'What is?'

'But the façade is like a boy's drawing of a fort.'

She thrust her picture in front him.

'It's very simple. I like that, don't you?'

Stefan sat in the sleeper he would be occupying for the night, looking out at the darkness that had abruptly replaced the countryside beyond Lisbon. The way Simon Chillingham's surveillance had closed wasn't easy to understand. He had to assume the concierge was right about the Englishman's death; the fear on the man's face left no room for doubt. He also had to assume German Intelligence were responsible. It wasn't information he could hold on to. Kerney had to know. He had felt a growing sense through the day that the ambassador, having accepted that he did have a use for a Special Branch detective after all, had still managed to soften any real concerns that might be emerging about the conflicting interests of German and British Intelligence in Frank Ryan's release. Stefan imagined that Leopold Kerney probably saw the intelligence services as the adjuncts of diplomacy they often pretended to be; diplomacy pursued, as it were, by less gentlemanly means. It might be the job of a diplomat to believe all that, but what Kerney had stepped into now was not diplomacy; what was on his shoes was blood, not bullshit.

'My God, but how?' The ambassador shook his head in disbelief.

'I don't know how, Mr Kerney. The question is why.'

'The concierge couldn't be sure the Germans were involved.'

'I think he could have a very good idea, sir.'

This wasn't what the ambassador wanted to hear.

'For God's sake, surely no one's going to kill a man for knowing I ate a meal in a restaurant with someone. I was exercising discretion, but no more. A level of secrecy is important, mostly in respect of the Spanish response to Ryan's release. They don't want this to appear as anything but an escape. The reasons are not significant. It's about saving face, no more than that.'

'I doubt Mr Chillingham is dead so that Spain can save face.'

'All right, Gillespie, you've made that point. I know what Lisbon is. German spies, British spies, and the rest, Spanish,

207

French, Italian, Russian, American. I don't suppose the Germans and the British have trouble finding reasons to attack one another's agents. You can't assume it's about Ryan.'

'I'm a great believer in Occam's razor, sir.'

'What?'

'With competing theses choose the one with the fewest assumptions.'

'Yes, I do know what it is.'

'I prefer the explanation I can see to the ones I can't.'

'You do understand why I am helping Ryan in the way I am?'

'Because there's no other way.'

'There isn't. I can't get to the bottom of why Franco slams the door on releasing him. I've spent months with lawyers, politicians, people close to Franco, trying to negotiate. Our government has tried other avenues. It always ends the same. This is the only chance. Frank won't survive another winter in Burgos. Helmut Clissmann and some of Frank's friends started this. They have contacts in German Intelligence and the German and Spanish Intelligence services have done a deal. When he gets out, he leaves Spain. That's it.'

'Except that it probably isn't it, with all due respect, sir.'

'So let's say you're right, Gillespie. What is it then?'

'If it's about what's staring us in the face, the Germans helping get Ryan back to Ireland, or to America, or wherever it is he's going to end up, that doesn't seem worth killing anybody for. There has to be something more, something the Abwehr doesn't want British Intelligence to know.'

'So I'm being played for a fool now, am I?'

'You know what you're trying to achieve, sir.' Stefan's reply didn't deny the possibility that Kerney, if not being played for a fool, was at least being played. 'That may not be what your man Melsbach is trying to achieve. People kill each other for some half-arsed reasons when it comes to politics, let alone war. We do it at home. The IRA shoots a policeman to make a

208

point – maybe the only point is, they can. And I won't pretend it's beyond Special Branch to do the same thing, for the same reason – because they can. But the posturing has to start somewhere, even with the IRA.'

Leopold Kerney was uncomfortable. Like most Irish politicians and civil servants, he was a man with close connections to the IRA, at least to the Old IRA of the days before the Civil War. Twenty years ago people who had later come to despise each other, even kill each other, judicially as well as extra-judicially, were all on the same side, fighting England. That they were no longer was something most of them, in their heart of hearts, did not believe was much more than a superficial disagreement. As long as they could all sing a Rebel Song, the great gulf between them wasn't a polite conversation to have.

'Inspector, I don't understand what's happened. I respect your judgement as a policeman but this is more complicated. You can't dismiss the fact that this man Chillingham's death is about two sides in a war fighting each other wherever they meet. That's glaringly obvious to me. Ryan has nothing to do with that. My task is simply about getting him out of Burgos. It's what the government wants and I intend to make it happen.'

Stefan could see Kerney had just put this argument together. He did not intend to believe there was anything untoward in German help or that it had any bearing on a British Intelligence officer's death. He had moved on.

'What do you know about this Abwehr man, Melsbach, sir?'

'I don't even know he is that. He's a soldier, a colonel.'

'In the Brandenburg Regiment.'

'I have no idea, quite possibly.'

'It's an intelligence regiment.' Stefan gave no explanation for why he knew. 'They might have uniforms on but they do the same job as British Intelligence or G2. And Frank Ryan's friend, Herr Clissmann, who seems to have started all this, a grand feller I'm sure, with a lot of friends in Ireland, I know, is also a German Intelligence officer, and in the same regiment.'

'Is it odd that the man's joined his country's forces?'

'No, sir, but everywhere you turn there's an intelligence officer, German or otherwise. And when we get to Salamanca, you'll be talking to German Intelligence at the Irish College. That's the Abwehr base in Spain, isn't it? They'll be the people getting Frank Ryan out of Franco's gaol.'

'That speaks for itself, doesn't it, Gillespie?'

'I think the thing to say, sir, is that in Salamanca you know nothing about British Intelligence. You know nothing about being followed in Lisbon. You definitely know nothing about Mr Chillingham or bodies in the Tagus. It really is as simple as you've said. The Germans will know I've spoken to Chillingham, but to be honest they won't think there's anything strange about me not involving you. They live in a police state. They'll assume I'm here to do two things. To keep you safe and to spy on you.'

'Which is probably not far from the truth,' smiled Kerney.

Stefan made no comment; it would do no harm for the ambassador to think that now. His only concern was to make sure Kerney listened to him.

'You don't speak German, do you, sir?

'Hardly anything.'

'I am here to protect you. You need to let me do that. And you need to keep as far away as possible from anything that looks underhand. The British are watching. They will be somewhere. And if everyone's watching everyone, you can step out of the circle. I do speak German, and you're going to have to trust me to deal with some of this. Getting close to German Intelligence isn't what you should be doing at all. You know that better than I do, sir. You need to use me. The Abwehr will trust you more with a secret policeman to do your dirty work. That's how it works in Germany.'

'You weren't idly sent were you, Gillespie?'

'No, in a number of ways, I'm not here idly.'

What was in Stefan Gillespie's mind was not what was in Kerney's. He had a job to do for the ambassador but the more independence he had, the more freedom there would be to pursue the other job he needed to do.

'A little distance would be no bad thing, sir, between you and Ryan, and between you and me. The more distance, the more you can deny too.'

However gently, Stefan was already telling Leopold Kerney what to do.

Stefan stood at the bar on the night train, nursing a large brandy. In front of him Mrs Surtees was arguing with the barman with calm, stolid persistence.

'I'm sure you can make me some tea.'

'The chef is asleep. There is coffee, no tea.'

'It's been stewing since Lisbon. I wouldn't ask a camel to drink it!'

'Um camelo?' The barman was puzzled.

'Precisely.'

'Boiling a kettle is not my job, senhora. I am the barman.'

'Well, if there is no tea I'd better have a large brandy.'

The barman smiled; it was a small victory. Mrs Surtees turned.

'Are you going to Madrid, Mr Gillespie?'

'Salamanca.'

'A beautiful city. I have the Plaza Mayor here.' She took her sketchbook from under her arm. 'You see, quite enormous. Of course, it was fortunate to be out of the way of the conflict. Two cathedrals. The Romanesque is glorious! Wonderful simplicity. I'm doing cathedrals. Burgos is my next. Vast and Gothic, not simple at all. Burgos is more intimidating than Salamanca and rather overrated. I don't know why Franco wanted it as his capital in the Civil War. Salamanca is much pleasanter. Still, I don't suppose pleasantness featured very much in his calculations.'

'The Plaza Mayor,' said Stefan handing back the sketchbook.

'Yes, don't miss it.' Mr Surtees sipped the brandy.

'A bit on the rough side,' said Stefan.

'Spanish, not French,' she replied. 'I prefer it.' She held out the glass to the barman. 'Another one in there, dear. I might as well be hung for a sheep as a lamb.'

'A sheep, senhora?'

'Por uma ovelha como um cordeiro.'

He took her money, looking at her blankly, and didn't pursue it.

'You wonder sometimes if there's any point speaking anything other than English, Mr Gillespie. I know we should all make the effort, but is anyone any better off?'

When Mrs Surtees had gone Stefan sat for some time looking out at the night through the carriage window. Occasionally there were lights, but very few. They were in Spain, heading for the central plateau. The line was through dense woodland on either side of the train. He had been given little time to think about events in Lisbon. His first concern was to make sure Leopold Kerney waded no further out of his depth. But the ambassador wasn't alone. It had all seemed light-hearted, the walk along the Rua da Misericórdia and the Vinho Verde in the Praça do Comércio, but the lights of Lisbon, like Dublin's, were at the edge of the darkness descending over the darkling plain of the continent beyond. Simon Chillingham was like him, just another kind of policeman. Kerney had never seen him, of course, but after the proper expression of shock the Englishman had been filed where diplomacy and war pursued common ends in terms of necessity, expediency, gain. It wasn't his business. Perhaps it wasn't Stefan's either. But he felt less satisfied than he had at breakfast in the Avenida Palace Hotel. It was hard not to think that if he had not made the man in the linen suit his business, he might be alive.

213

19

El Colegio de los Irlandeses

When the train reached Salamanca the city was waking. A taxi took Stefan Gillespie and Leopold Kerney to the Colegio de los Irlandeses. The ambassador was silent. The subject on both their minds was exhausted. Kerney had accepted that there were things it was better for Stefan to deal with. He didn't like it. He liked even less the idea of what the Special Branch man would report to Dublin. But for now there was no more to say.

Stefan took in the streets of pale, old stone. The driver occasionally mentioned something they passed. The words 'iglesia' prefixed most of his comments; it was a city of churches, as Kerney had already told him. And as the taxi negotiated a street full of trucks and horses and men unloading baskets of fruit and vegetables, the taxi driver gestured across at a dark arch and said 'Plaza Mayor'. Stefan looked round, but all he could see was the day's business starting at the Central Market. The taxi climbed up through narrow, quiet streets to the high walls and pillared entrance of the Colegio de los Irlandeses, once a bishop's palace.

Stefan and the ambassador mounted the steps to the dark entrance.

An old man in a dirty white jacket bustled from the porter's lodge.

'Buenos días, Señor Kerney.'

'Buenos días, Chávez! Cómo está?'

'Bien, bien!'

The man scurried out to get the bags. A soldier in the grey-green of the German Army watched. He clicked his heels and then spoke in English.

'A good journey, Herr Ambassador?'

'Oh, not so bad. This is Mr Gillespie.'

The soldier looked down at a clipboard he was holding.

'Willkommen in Salamanca, Inspector Gillespie.'

The room at the Irish College was less a room than a monastic cell. There were no Irish seminarians at the college now; the last left at the start of the Civil War; but the small bed, hard chair and bare table advertised that the building was there to house would-be priests. Above the bed was a picture of Jesus holding a red heart streaming with light; Batoni's 'Sacred Heart of Jesus'. Stefan knew it; it sat on the walls of thousands of Irish homes. He had met no one except the porter and the German soldier yet, but he had heard German along the college's galleried cloister. The simple cells now accommodated the young German Intelligence officers who had replaced the priests. He walked back along the arched gallery, looking down into the cloister. It was a peaceful place; the presence of the uniforms didn't sit easily with it. As he came down the steps a man in his early twenties was waiting, in black trousers and shirt, a clerical outfit but with no collar.

'It's Mr Gillespie, is it?'

'It is.'

'Good to meet you, sir. Michael Hagan, a Tipp man myself.'

They shook hands. Stefan looked at Hagan with a harder, more curious stare than he could help. This was the man he knew from a letter in Billy Byrne's room. This was the man who had really brought him here.

'Wicklow myself.'

'I'd know it a bit. And how's old Ireland, sir?"

'Hard to say,' Stefan smiled. 'I'm not sure we're sure how we are.'

'You're out of it, like we are, that's the thing. God keep it that way.'

Stefan nodded.

'It's Mass at nine. There's a bit off breakfast in the refectory now.'

'I'll happily go for the breakfast, but I'll forgo the Mass.'

Hagan looked surprised and a little put out.

'It's in the chapel, specially. It always is when Mr Kerney comes.'

'I'd like to have a look at the chapel later.' Stefan gave a mock-serious frown. 'I'm afraid you've a Protestant within your walls, Mikey.'

Hagan looked slightly awkward, then laughed as Stefan grinned.

'It is Mikey, isn't it?'

Stefan remembered the signature on the letter to Billy Byrne.

'It's a good guess! It's what everyone always calls me, Mr Gillespie.'

Michael Hagan left Stefan at the door to the refectory. Stefan watched him go. There would be a right time. He wasn't sure if it should be sooner rather than later; maybe he should try to win some confidence first. It would depend how quickly they left for Burgos.

The refectory was a dark, vaulted room with little natural light. Several men sat on benches at a long table, all German, uniformed and in civvies. They looked up curiously. One stood up and walked towards him.

'You're with the Irish ambassador? Inspector Gillespie?'

The man spoke in English; Stefan had decided that for now he would appear to know no German. He had a sense the German was gauging him.

'Mr Kerney tells me you'll be joining us later for a chat.'

'Then I'm sure I will, Herr . . . I'm sorry I don't know the rank.'

'We don't worry about rank. We're not at home.' He still gave his rank. 'Konrad Eckhart, Major. That makes us the same, I think.'

'More or less, I suppose,' said Stefan.

'Help yourself to what you want. The ham is excellent. We live on it here. There's not much else. If you want some eggs, simply tell Chávez.'

He turned to the man in the grubby white jacket behind the counter. Stefan recognized him as the Spaniard who brought the bags from the taxi.

'Inspector Gillespie es un invitado del rector, un policía irlandés.'

Chávez shrugged; he didn't need telling.

'We will talk later, Inspector.' Eckhart left.

'You want something, señor?' asked the Spaniard.

'Any chance of a cup of tea?'

'Claro!' The old man leant forward and whispered, 'Bacon?' Stefan wasn't sure why he was glancing sideways at the Germans.

'Ireland bacon, the rector's bacon. Not for the . . .'

Chávez winked and disappeared through a door into the kitchen.

Stefan turned round and walked to the long table.

'Mein Freund, hinsetzen Sie bitte!' said one of the Abwehr men.

Stefan smiled politely, but showed no comprehension.

'Sit down, Inspector. I am sorry we do not all speak English!'

He sat down. The Germans smiled pleasantly, then resumed

their conversation, unaware that he could understand them. For a moment it was all about Kerney.

'Their ambassador's here to see Eckhart again.'

'He's coming out then, the International Brigade arsehole?'

'Apparently, but that's Eckhart's baby now.'

'You know the man's a fucking communist?'

'He must be some use, the orders come from Otto Melsbach.'

'That's all you need to know. What a tosser!'

'So who's this Irish cop?'

'Minding the ambassador.'

'He's not army?'

'Do the Irish have an army?'

'I think they have a bicycle corps!'

'If the Tommies don't ask for the bikes back!'

There was laughter as the Abwehr men headed for the door. Passing Stefan, they reined it in. The man who had asked him to sit down spoke.

'Will you be with us long, Inspector?'

'Home once the ambassador is in Madrid. Are you based here?'

'Two years, some of us, but not for much longer. The war! The real war. The English! We shall give Ireland something to celebrate, I think!' He turned to the others. 'Der Krieg, wir geben Irland etwas zu feiern, ja?'

The Abwehr men grinned enthusiastically at Stefan.

'Ah, well, of course, we're a neutral country altogether, I'm sure you wouldn't expect me to have an opinion on anything like that, would you?'

'I imagine you will all have an opinion when the time comes, Inspector.'

'I imagine we will.'

As the German officers walked out, Chávez came to the table with a pot of tea and a plate of fried bacon and eggs. He put it down and sniffed.

'Soon they will be gone.'

'Don't tell me you haven't enjoyed having them here, Chávez!'

'Señor, how can you say it? They are our allies!'

Stefan laughed. The Spaniard walked to the door, looking out after the Germans. Their voices were loud, their laughter echoing around the cloisters. As he ate Stefan heard something that could have been the old man spitting; on the other hand, he could have been clearing his throat.

Leopold Kerney and Stefan Gillespie sat in the library of the Irish College with Major Eckhart and another Abwehr officer, Oberleutnant Sebastian Triebel. Eckhart talked; Triebel made notes. The arrangements that had been only tentative in Lisbon were tangible; so much so that it was hard for Kerney not to feel that his involvement in Frank Ryan's release was over. Yet Stefan saw a harder man as Kerney and Eckhart went through the details.

'The Spanish have accepted the plan fully,' said the German major. 'Your lawyer Señor de Chambourcin has spoken to the ministry again. The ministry has spoken to the prison governor. I have spoken directly to Spanish Military Intelligence. It is agreed at the highest level. It has the approval of the Caudillo himself, though officially Franco knows nothing.'

'When will it happen?'

'In three days.'

'And what does Mr Ryan know?'

'He will know when the day comes.'

'Do you think he'll simply walk out of that gaol because the governor takes him to the gate and says, "Adiós, Señor Ryan"? What usually awaits a prisoner who's shown the door is a bullet in the head.'

'This is everything you have asked for, Mr Kerney.'

'Shall we leave the bollocks aside, Major? My concern is with Frank Ryan's freedom, so is my government's. The position the

Spanish have taken, and Generalissimo Franco in particular, gives us no choice but to take this route, but my responsibility doesn't end in this room. Ryan too has to take this opportunity, but he won't if there's no trust. And I need the proper reassurances that he's out of gaol and safely out of Spain.'

'Because of the Spanish sensitivity about Ryan, the secrecy—'

'I know what the Spanish want. That's why it's best I am in Madrid when it happens. I have discussed it with Oberst Melsbach at length. But Inspector Gillespie is here for a reason. He is my eyes and ears. He will go to Burgos to give Ryan my reassurances. And what comes next, Eckhart?'

Stefan smiled; now he was Kerney's eyes and ears!

'I need to know what happens when Ryan leaves Burgos.'

Stefan had not heard the authority that was in Leopold Kerney's voice before. The ambassador knew who he was talking to. It was a tone Eckhart understood because in his world the tone of authority produced an almost Pavlovian response, especially in a conversation with a superior. Kerney was still an ambassador, and the position of a neutral country on England's doorstep needed careful handling. There were people higher up the ladder in Berlin watching this. Kerney couldn't push it too far but his assumption that he carried real authority here was enough to mean that he did.

'He will be driven north, to the Asturian coast, to Pendueles.'

Oberleutnant Triebel indicated the route on a map.

'The Irish College has a summer house there. It is a small village. The rector has let us use it while we've been billeted here. No one thinks twice about German officers visiting. We have arranged Herr Ryan's departure from Llanes, a harbour along the coast. An Italian cargo boat will call in to take him to the Mediterranean, to Naples. There he will have several options. Italian boats still go America. But all that depends on him.'

Kerney looked at the map again. 'Lisbon is closer,'

'The Spanish don't like the idea of Lisbon, neither do we.'

The ambassador turned to Stefan.

'All right, once Ryan leaves Spain, I think we can say that's it.'

'Yes, sir,' said Stefan.

'You can see him in Burgos and you go with him to Pendueles.'

'I cannot permit that, Herr Kerney.' Eckhart pushed back his chair. 'It hasn't been easy to get Spain to agree to this, if anything goes wrong—'

'My government doesn't want anything to go wrong. We have good relations with Spain and we don't want them compromised. And as a neutral country we tread a fine line with Britain. If this got out it would be more than embarrassing. I shouldn't even be in a room with you. As far as my government is concerned I'm not. We are discussing a past IRA leader when the IRA has been bombing Britain. The Irish government is not without sympathy for Germany's position, but if helping Ryan is a small matter for you it could have real consequences for us. We need our arses covered so to speak, and Inspector Gillespie is here to ensure they are.'

Konrad Eckhart pursed his lips. Stefan felt the ambassador deserved a round of applause. He had taken all of Ireland's weaknesses in this plan and turned them into strengths. Unacceptable actions in a neutral diplomat had become his justification for staying in the loop. The argument might not have impressed anyone higher up in the Nazi Intelligence hierarchy, but for a junior officer at the outer circle of the intrigue the threat of misreading a diplomatic puzzle was enough to persuade Eckhart he had better agree.

'Do you see any problems, Triebel?' he said in German.

Triebel frowned, looking down at the map, and then shrugged.

'What about Richard I, Herr Major?'

'The cop will be gone by then. It may help that he confirms things.'

Triebel nodded.

Stefan could make no sense of what had just been said, but it was clear there were other things going on, as he suspected; there were other people involved.

'Very well, Herr Kerney,' said the major in English. 'Herr Gillespie can accompany Herr Ryan to Pendueles, and you will have all your assurances.'

As the two Irishmen walked out into the cloisters, Kerney grinned.

'I don't know about you, I could do with a fucking drink.'

That night Stefan and the ambassador ate with the rector of the college, Alexander McCabe, a grey-faced man who could have been anything between fifty and seventy. He had stayed when the seminarians were evacuated at the beginning of the Civil War, presiding over the near-empty college before German Intelligence arrived. After three years the Abwehr men were leaving too, heading for the war in Europe. Doctor McCabe had got used to them. He had never considered what the Abwehr did in Spain. He didn't have a lot of time for Adolf Hitler and Nazism or even, though he didn't say it outside his rooms, for Generalissimo Franco. But in a world threatened by brutal atheism, when the real enemy of humanity was communism, as the rector and the Church saw it, you took your allies where you could find them. Whatever his opinion of Hitler, he was on the right side in the real war, not the one between Germany and the Allies, but the one against godless atheism that had been won at such cost in Spain.

'We shall miss our Germans. They've been very pleasant to have about the place. And some are Catholics, so they've made Sunday Mass.'

'You'll have your priests back now. A new intake as well.'

'I don't know, Leo. Getting them here won't be easy. The feeling in Ireland is that opening the college must wait on the

222

cessation of hostilities in Europe. I don't know how long that will be, but our Germans here have a strong sense that the war won't last long. The British don't want it, I'm sure. We can only pray they have the sense to come to terms with Herr Hitler.'

Chávez appeared with a bottle of port on a silver tray.

McCabe shook his head. 'A bottle of whiskey – and some water.'

The conversation moved from the war in Europe back to Spain and the peace Stefan sensed neither the rector nor the ambassador believed was as pervasive as they told one another. The subject of Frank Ryan arose very naturally. Kerney had visited him several times in Burgos after staying at the college, and the rector seemed to have an unexpected regard for the ex-IRA man who had fought doggedly on the 'wrong side' in the Civil War.

'He's an odd man, very odd. I don't know him the way you do, Leo. He fought for a Republic that murdered priests and nuns. He consorted with every species of communist and atheist. But he is a good Catholic, as Mikey Hagan always says. It ought to be a contradiction. I don't know why, but it feels like it isn't. We are in strange times. The road is unclear. I think even within the Church we cannot all pretend that we really see our way.'

For Stefan, listening to the two men, there was considerable surprise hearing Michael Hagan's name in the context of Frank Ryan and Burgos.

'I think Ryan became more disillusioned with the Spanish Republic than he cares to admit, Alex.' Leopold Kerney helped himself to another whiskey. 'At least with what it turned into once the communists took over.'

'There's never a shortage of disillusion,' said the rector. 'Between these four walls I am not the kind of churchman who can applaud a regime that has replaced murderous atheism with something equally murderous.'

'Gillespie is going up to see Ryan for me,' said Kerney.

'Good. I hear he's come on considerably. You've met Hagan?'

'Yes, I have, sir.'

'He has visited Ryan himself. He has a real sense the man is on the up now. It's all because of Leo he's being treated more decently, though.'

Stefan wanted to know more about Hagan, and enough whiskey had gone from the bottle on the table for him to feel that a blunt question would do.

'So how does Hagan know Frank Ryan? Wasn't he with O'Duffy?'

'He was,' said the rector, 'that's how he came here. He's a mild-mannered feller but he was very insistent on going to see Ryan. I help him with the fares. It's an act of charity, after all. But there is a story and it's what made me reassess Ryan. Mikey was here with that gobshite O'Duffy, the only way to describe him. There were some genuine men among the drunks and wasters he brought to Spain, and Hagan was one of them, young as he was.'

McCabe reached out for the bottle and filled his glass.

'The only fighting they did was with each other. The only time they got near a battle O'Duffy was drunk somewhere and they were shot at by their own side. Some died, some got lost behind enemy lines. Hagan got lost. And Ryan saved his life. He would have been shot otherwise. He was wounded and he came here to convalesce with the other Bandera fellers.'

'And he's still here.'

'He stayed when the others went. He has it in his head he wants to study for the priesthood. If he has the vocation I'm not sure he has the ability. But he's loyal, a good Irishman, a good Catholic. For good reasons he's loyal to Frank Ryan. He has a job as a kind of secretary here. I have a weakness for lame ducks! I never had the heart to turn him out.'

Stefan wanted to ask about someone else who had worked at

the college, perhaps another Irish lame duck. But as Jim Collins was no longer there, and with no reason to bring him up, he said nothing. It would be Hagan himself he tackled about that. As the whiskey disappeared and the conversation between the ambassador and the rector turned to hurling and home, Stefan decided there would be nothing more for him to learn. The rector, starved of guests, let alone Irish ones, would not make an early night of it. Stefan left.

As he walked to his room the upper cloisters were in deep shadow, but he could see a light further along the gallery. It came from a partly open door. It would have been nothing odd if he hadn't known it was the ambassador's room. He walked slowly, keeping in the shadows, close to the line of small doorways into the cells. He was very near the light now.

He listened. He could hear drawers being opened. He imagined some Abwehr man was searching Kerney's room. But it was odd. Leaving the door ajar was sloppy, and even a junior Intelligence officer ought to be able to open a drawer silently. And since the Abwehr knew far more about what was going on than Kerney, what was the point? He heard nothing more for over a minute, then the silence was broken by footsteps. The light went off. He opened the door he was standing by and stepped into a dark cell. If the intruder came his way, he could push the door to. He needed to find out who was in the ambassador's room before doing anything. It might be better saying nothing to Kerney. They had pushed the Abwehr hard enough today.

The door from the ambassador's room opened. A man came out, pulling the door shut and locking it. He walked along the gallery to the stairs. Stefan moved out of the doorway and crossed to one of the arches that looked down into the cloisters. The man was moving quickly. When he reached the stairway there was a brighter light. For a moment it illuminated his face very clearly as he started down the stairs. It was Michael Hagan.

Next morning Leopold Kerney left for Madrid. Stefan could see he was still reluctant. Frank Ryan's release was a personal matter. That was what had led him to cross so many diplomatic lines and even to be economical with what he told his own government. It was what made him avoid asking why the Germans wanted to free a man they would, not long ago, have shot had he fallen into their hands in Spain. He had persuaded himself that people who cared about Ryan as he did, in particular the Abwehr agent Helmut Clissmann, were the force behind what the Germans were doing. Even after his conversations with Stefan he held to that. Yet whatever the ambassador told himself, Stefan could see that Kerney didn't leave Salamanca with an easy mind.

'This is a letter for Frank. It simply says you have my authority and my trust. He will know less about what's going to happen than we do. Then there's this.' Kerney had taken out a green booklet stamped with a gold harp; a new Irish passport. 'María Fernández Duarte. Miss Duarte lives in Salamanca but she was with Frank during the war. She worked as a nurse. But no one who was on the Republican side is entirely safe. There's no altering the fact that Spain's peace is vindictive and unforgiving. Her visits to Burgos gaol won't have gone unnoticed. Frank feels the international support he has received has, in a small way, kept her safe. Now he wants her to leave Spain. I'm giving her an Irish passport, I have to say without consulting anyone. And I've promised to see she gets out of the country.'

Stefan looked at a photograph of a woman with a shock of thick, untidy black hair. She didn't look like she would choose any easy way.

'So do I give this to her?'

'Once he's away. But I want Frank to know it's done.'

An hour later the ambassador was gone. Stefan had said nothing about Michael Hagan but he still wanted to know why he had been in Kerney's room. After seeing the ambassador's taxi off he walked into the porter's lodge, looking for Chávez, to check the train times to Burgos. Chávez wasn't there and he spent several minutes discussing the timetable with the Abwehr guard, maintaining the fiction that he spoke no German. He saw Hagan pass the door on his way out of the college, clearly in a hurry.

He wandered out to the street and watched the young Irishman heading down the hill towards the centre of the city. There was purpose, even urgency in his step. He had a feeling that purpose and urgency were not much in Hagan's make-up. Neither was searching the rooms of the rector's guests. The two things might go together. And he still had to speak to Hagan about William Byrne and Jim Collins. Whether in the past or the present, the more he knew about the rector's Irish lame duck the better.

Stefan kept his distance as he followed Michael Hagan. There were few people in the Calle Cuesta San Blas and the figure in black was easily visible, but as the streets became narrower and more crowded he had to keep closer. There were alleyways where Hagan turned abruptly, taking a route he knew well. Suddenly the crowds were denser, noisier; Stefan knew where he was. It was the market he had driven through the day before; he recognized the red market building and the trucks and carts. For a moment he had lost sight of Michael Hagan. Then he saw him across the Plaza del Mercado, passing under a colonnade, hurrying up a flight of stone steps.

By the time Stefan reached the steps he had lost him. He emerged from the stairway into a great open space, full of a light that not only beat down from the blue sky above it, but was reflected back from the three storeys of sandstone arcades and galleries that made up the vast square. It was the Plaza Mayor. He gazed about him, not for the Irishman in black, but simply at the great piazza of light.

The cloistered arcades of shops and cafés that lined the sides of the square were full of people but unlike the market outside the chatter of voices was calm and quiet. He looked out over the cobbled stones, trying to find Hagan again, and as a cloud of pigeons erupted up from the Plaza Mayor he saw him approach a café and sit at a table. There was a woman there. Stefan stepped under the arches of the arcade and moved round the plaza. He knew the woman's black hair. This was María Fernández Duarte. She smoked a cigarette as Hagan talked, leaning forward, tense in a way she was not. He had no doubt that whatever Hagan had been looking for in Kerney's room, that was what they were discussing. But these were not people to be wary of; they were Frank Ryan's friends. He walked to the café and sat down at the table.

'And a beer for me, please,' he said as the waiter brought coffee.

He smiled, looking out at the square.

'It's quite something.'

'I don't know you, Mr . . .?' She spoke good English.

'Stefan Gillespie, Miss Duarte. Mr Kerney mentioned you to me.'

She smiled. Michael Hagan looked embarrassed.

'Mikey's told me who you are. You're going to Burgos to see Frank.'

'He didn't need to search the ambassador's room to tell you that.'

'It was only to help María, Mr Gillespie.'

As the waiter brought his beer, Stefan shrugged; it didn't matter.

'I wanted to know what's happening to Frank,' said María.

'So what did you find out, Mikey?' asked Stefan.

'Nothing.' Hagan was tight-lipped, a look of defiant loyalty.

'I think you need to be very careful, Miss Duarte; you too, Mikey.'

'What do we need to be careful of, Mr Gillespie?'

'I'm sure you know. It's not me. It's not Mr Kerney.'

She looked hard at Stefan and didn't reply.

'I think he's all right, María.'

'Because he's an Irishman?'

'Something like that,' said Hagan.

'I know Frank is coming out of prison, Mr Gillespie. He has told me as much in his way. He won't tell me more. I think he can't. Or he can't say it where we can be overheard. But I know it's because of your ambassador. If it hadn't been for him, I don't know if Frank would be alive. I trust him. But I also know it is something to do with the Germans, the Abwehr. I know he has talked to them about Frank at the Colegio. I don't understand and I need to. It makes no sense. How can anyone trust them?'

'If you can trust Mr Kerney, isn't that enough?'

'I don't know, Mr Gillespie, is it?'

It was a question Stefan could not answer himself.

'You know Mr Kerney has got you an Irish passport?'

'Yes, Frank wants me to go to Ireland. But where will he be?'

'I don't know.' Stefan saw the doubt in her eyes; he felt it himself. 'That's for him. What matters is he's out of gaol. If that needs to be a secret, so nothing can get in the way, so what? He'll be free, that's all.'

'People have died to get Frank out of Burgos.' María spoke quietly. 'Now the people he hates more than the Falange, the Nazis who bombed our cities and gave Franco his machine guns and tanks, are helping him get away. Why? Because they're sorry for him and they want him to go home?'

Hagan was looking round nervously.

'Are those empty questions, Mr Gillespie?'

'Never mind anyone else, Miss Duarte, you have to trust him.'

'I know. There are no questions if Frank finds his way home.'

Stefan knew she wanted him to tell her that he would.

229

'He will, I know he will.' It was Michael Hagan who answered.

'I am going to Burgos today,' María continued, 'to the Central Prison. Perhaps the last time. He won't tell me that, but I know now. And you are going too.'

Stefan looked at her and nodded. It had been his intention only to discover what they knew, what they were doing, but he had to say more.

'I will be with him. I'll see him leave Spain. And I will come back to Salamanca to tell you.' Stefan finished the beer and stood up. 'But leave it alone, both of you, leave the Germans alone. I think Frank would say that.'

He walked away, across the Plaza Mayor. He wasn't sure María Duarte would leave it alone. As for the journey Frank Ryan would take, he had no idea what it would be. He had no sense if 'home' came into it. But it wasn't his concern. He glanced back across the Plaza Mayor to the café where Michael Hagan and María were still talking. He had established a relationship of sorts with Hagan now. He had waited long enough. It was time to tackle him about Glendalough and the letter to William Byrne.

A dark man in a grey suit watched Stefan idly from a café across the plaza. He had watched the conversation between Stefan, María and Mikey Hagan too, though he had not been close enough to hear anything. He had taken several photographs of the square that included them. He picked up his elegant Zeiss again and took one more picture, then called for his bill.

20

Burgos

W hen Stefan Gillespie returned to the Irish College a car
passed him on the Calle Cuesta San Blas. Oberleutnant
Triebel was driving; Eckhart was beside him. He knew they were
heading for Burgos. He would be taking the train tomorrow.

He didn't know if what had happened in the Plaza Mayor
gave him a better chance with Michael Hagan now. He hoped
he had shown he could be trusted as far as Frank Ryan and
María Duarte were concerned. Clearly they both meant a lot
to Hagan. He assumed the young Irishman was aware that
his search of the ambassador's room would not be reported
to the rector. That meant more trust. He took a postcard he
had bought on his way out of the Plaza Mayor and sat in the
cloisters, writing a message for Tom that was only about trains
and sunshine and the great square in the picture.

Half an hour later Hagan returned; Stefan went to meet him.

'I thought you might want to show me the chapel, Mikey.'

It wasn't what Michael Hagan was expecting. María said
she trusted the Irish policeman; that didn't make him easy to
be with. He had a feeling Stefan wanted something more. It
unsettled him. The detective looked at him with a curiosity he
couldn't fathom.

They didn't speak until they were in the chapel. It was a place of cold stone and quiet. It had little decoration except for the great altarpiece that filled the high east wall, sectioned off in golden stucco squares that framed small paintings of the life of Christ. As Stefan looked towards it, down the length of the vaulted knave, the young Irishman began to deliver a kind of lecture. The voice not was not really his own; the words had been learned by rote.

'The retablo is the most remarkable feature of the chapel. Begun in 1529, the paintings of the life of Christ are by Alonso Berruguete. The birth of Our Lord, the adoration of the shepherds, the Magi, the flight to Egypt—'

He stopped, aware that Stefan was now gazing directly at him.

'I have another reason to be here, Mikey. It's about William Byrne.'

Michael Hagan stared; it came from nowhere.

'Billy?'

'Billy Byrne, yes. You knew him in the Bandera, and here.'

'We convalesced at the college, yes . . .'

'You won't know he's dead.'

'No. Poor Billy, I'm sorry to hear that.'

He was being careful now. Stefan could see it.

'What happened to him, Mr Gillespie?'

'No one knows. He disappeared in Glendalough on Christmas Eve. Nobody's seen him since. I was investigating that. We presume he's dead, and that somebody killed him. But who did it is another thing altogether.'

Hagan was avoiding his eyes, confused, uncomprehending.

'But I think it had something to do with a man who worked here, a man called Jim Collins. I think the man who killed Billy Byrne was known to Jim Collins, perhaps a long time back. You knew them both, of course.'

The young Irishman barely nodded.

'Billy wrote to Collins, not long ago. You sent the letter back.'

'I did.' The reply was hesitant. 'Jim's been gone six months now.'

'Do you know where he is?'

'I don't at all, that's why I sent the letter back to Billy.'

'Would the rector know?'

'He went very sudden, Inspector, he left us no address at all.'

'I understand he'd worked here for years, hadn't he? So why?'

'It was his family, I'd say. He married a Spanish woman. They had children. That's as much as I know. And we weren't great pals. He was the gardener, the handyman.'

'What was his relationship with Byrne?'

'Billy wasn't here that long.'

'Did you know they both came from the same place, from the Wicklow Mountains, Glendalough, Laragh, Rathdrum, round that area?'

'I suppose so. We talked about home a lot, why wouldn't we?'

'Someone murdered Billy Byrne, Mikey. And other people. There was a girl twenty years back, then two women seven years, eight years ago. Billy thought the same man did it, and he knew who that was. He found out here, from Jim Collins. At least he found out about one murder. He put the others with it later. Did you ever hear of a man called Albert Neale?'

Hagan shook his head slowly.

'Is Charlotte Moore a name you know?'

'No, never.'

'So none of this means anything to you?'

'Not at all, Mr Gillespie.'

Mikey Hagan wasn't a bad liar but he was too short on bewilderment about these questions. Even a bit of indignation wouldn't have been out of place. But Stefan decided to stop. He would leave it here. Hagan needed to take it in. It wasn't over. He would be back, and back with news of the man who had saved Hagan's life. He would have no qualms about using that.

'Think about it while I'm in Burgos, about the three women who died in Glendalough. Billy was right. It wasn't Albert Neale, the man you never heard of. The police thought he killed the girl, Charlotte, but he didn't. I have a very good idea Albert and Jim Collins are the same man. He might like to know there's a policeman who believes him, even twenty years on.'

Hagan still wanted to avoid Stefan's eyes; he couldn't.

'The other women had names too. One was called Marian. One was Maeve. And there's someone else dead of course, your comrade Billy. Not up to much I know, but maybe we're a bit like the Church in the Gardaí, even a nasty bit of work deserves better than murder. And the woman called Maeve, Maeve Gillespie, was my wife.'

He gave a shrug, then turned away and walked out.

Mikey Hagan looked down at his hands. He had held them in check through it all. He didn't know how. But now they were shaking. He looked up at the altar for a long moment. He walked to a pew and genuflected. He knelt on the stone floor and clasped his hands in prayer, his fingers intertwined like a child's. He still couldn't stop his hands from shaking.

María Fernández Duarte sat opposite Frank Ryan. Between them were the bars and the netting. As always a warder sat in the space that separated them. It was a scene they had played out scores of times; the same place, the same sounds, the same sights. Although there were other memories, happy memories, they were not always easy to find. It felt at times as if there had never really been a before; this was what they were.

'So who is he?' Frank Ryan was puzzled.

'Señor Gillespie is his name. He came from Dublin with your ambassador. They were together at the Colegia. I think Señor Kerney has gone to Madrid now, but the policeman is on his way here, to see you.'

Ryan didn't know why there was an Irish policeman travelling with Leopold Kerney, but the Irish College had a part to play in what was brewing. It was where Kerney first spoke to German Intelligence about getting him out of gaol. Whatever this Guard was doing he was part of that. And a stranger coming to see him, on Kerney's behalf, could only mean something was about to happen. It would be very soon. He could feel that now. He couldn't show it, even to María, but he knew she sensed it too.

'There is nothing to worry about, María.'

'You've told me that too many times.'

'Everything will be all right.'

'You've told me that too many times as well.'

'Because I believe it.'

'I know you have to say that, Frank.'

She spoke even more quietly. He heard a few words, but enough.

'Do you trust them? Do you trust all these people?'

'I trust Leo Kerney. And there are friends I trust.'

'It will be soon then,' she said.

'Whatever happens, María, I will find a way – we'll find a way . . .'

She nodded and crossed herself.

'You know I want you to leave, María, and Leo will help you.'

'Yes Frank, you make it sound very easy.'

'It can be. Ireland is out of it, all of it. All of this too.'

The idea that she could get to Ireland was as much a fixation in Ryan's head as his own determination to find his way home. It was what was driving him now, and for that to make sense she had to be a part of it. Some of the time she almost believed it could happen herself. And if she could not do that all the time, at least she had to let him believe it.

'Nothing is easy, María. But things still happen. They're going to. We're alive, aren't we? That's not easy. Plenty of times the other option felt a fuck sight easier. But you have to be alive, even to think that. I woke up the other day and I realized how unlikely it is. I shouldn't be alive, should I?'

'I only want to know you're safe, Frank, to know where—'

She was aware of the guard, watching them. Raoul spoke a little English, which was why he was always there, but it wasn't enough for him to understand much of what they said. Today he seemed more indifferent than usual. He chain-smoked with an almost affable smile on his face. He grinned and winked at Ryan, then pursed his lips into an exaggerated kiss.

'You're a gobshite, Raoul, a fucking arse of a gobshite.'

The prison guard laughed and lit another cigarette.

Ryan looked at María in silence. He put his right hand over his heart.

'I'm here. This is where I am.'

'Wherever I am, wherever you are . . .' she said the words slowly. He couldn't hear them all but he didn't need to. She bowed her head. She would not show the tears she felt coming. She knew that this would be the last time here. He would not say it but she could see it in him. It was hard for her not to think it would be the last time she saw him at all. His smile seemed to say he didn't believe that, but he was always good at smiling.

It was dusk as María Duarte left the Prisión Central. The man in the shabby black suit who watched the visitors leave was familiar to everyone, a very unsecret secret policeman who checked the prison's visitors' lists and recorded who came and who went for the Burgos security police. At the end of each day he quizzed the guards on what they had heard and seen. He nodded at María as she passed. There was a strange intimacy between the security police and the people they watched. It was a job, after all, and they all knew one another.

But today María was aware of only one thing; this would be the last time her visit to the gaol would be counted. This would be the last long walk back to Burgos. She had to pray for the safety of the man she loved; she had to pray that in different ways they would both be delivered from this place. Yet something had ended that had been at the very heart of her life for a long time. However much she hated it, she was losing something.

Stefan arrived in Burgos after dark. It had been a slow journey from Salamanca. The railways had not recovered from the years of war and several times his train halted for half an hour and more, for no apparent reason, at some single-platform station in the middle of an endless plain of borderless, featureless, ditchless fields of grain and grass and stony soil.

He spent the night at a small hotel, the Norte y Londra, as instructed by Leopold Kerney. Major Eckhart was already in Burgos; he would contact Stefan at the hotel. Eckhart had been spare with details; all Stefan knew was that they would leave the city the next night.

There was a day to kill and although Stefan had no inclination to be a tourist it was wise to maintain the role he had established with the inquisitive receptionist at the hotel. He was an Irish Catholic pilgrim, following the Camino de Santiago, the Way of St James. It answered all questions. But sitting at the hotel doing nothing would make him conspicuous. As a visitor his business was to tramp the city's streets and riverside walks and gaze at the wonders of the cathedral. So the next morning he did as expected. He walked from the hotel along the Calle de la Paloma to the cathedral. Having gazed at the Gothic façade he left the inside till later and walked the streets and the parks, taking little in, until the morning had gone. It was time. The man in the gaol would be waiting for him now.

Back in the cathedral square, he left the city through the dark tunnel of the Santa María arch and walked across the river to the station. It was the most anonymous place to find a taxi. He was out into fields within minutes and soon on the dirt road to the fort on the hill that was the Central Prison.

He waited inside the gate until Señor Escovedo, the governor, came to meet him. As they moved through the crowds of prisoners in the great courtyard, Escovedo extolled the architecture of the prison, which he said was the finest in Spain, if not Europe. It was noisy as all prisons are; as in all prisons no one seemed to take any notice of anything yet everyone watched. Coming out of the sunlight from the main courtyard they climbed steps to the governor's office. The sounds inside were no different to the prisons Stefan knew at home. Prisoners spoke in low voices all the time yet somehow there was always shouting. The smell was the same too, even in the administration block's corridors; tobacco, urine, carbolic soap.

Stefan sat in the empty room that was Escovedo's office for ten minutes. Then the door opened. The governor muttered to a thin, gaunt man in a grey overall that hung on him like an unpegged tent. Escovedo smiled.

'Señor Ryan.'

The door closed behind the governor as he left. They were alone. Frank Ryan grinned, then walked straight past Stefan Gillespie to the desk. He opened a leather cigarette box and stuffed several handfuls of cigarettes into his pocket. He kept one back and used Escovedo's silver lighter to light it. Then he turned to Stefan.

'Want one?'

'I'm all right.'

'He's taken to calling me Señor Ryan. Used to be *coño*,

basically cunt, but he makes señor sound like same thing now. Still, that's grand.'

He stepped across and shook Stefan's hand warmly.

'What do I call you other than inspector?'

'Stefan, Stevie, take your pick, Mr Ryan.'

'It's Frank.'

Stefan took out the letter from Leopold Kerney and handed it to him.

'From Mr Kerney, it's a kind of reference.'

'Well, you come highly recommended already.'

'Do I?'

'María says you're all right, I don't know why.'

'Probably because I found a friend of yours searching the ambassador's room at the Irish College – and on her behalf I'd say.'

'Mikey Hagan?'

Stefan nodded.

'Jesus, does anyone know?'

Stefan shook his head.

'Not even Leo?'

'No.'

'Good. That wasn't too clever of Mikey.'

Stefan chose to say nothing about the Englishman who had died in Lisbon. But he thought of him again. Spying on the Abwehr wasn't clever.

'The reference seems exemplary, but what's the job, Stevie?'

'The job is to see you out of here and out of Spain.'

'And they sent you all this way, just for that?'

'They sent me for a number reasons. Mr Kerney is carrying a lot of money. There was also a feeling what he was up to with you and German Intelligence was somewhere between embarrassing and dangerous. I think a few people felt that a bit of distance, for him, would be – well, diplomatic.'

Ryan looked at Stefan for a moment; he liked the honesty.

'But they are behind Leo? Dev and the rest?'

'They want you out. I don't think they want to know how.'

'No, they wouldn't. I'm not sure I want to know myself.'

He stubbed out the cigarette and lit another one.

'Well, it's good of Dev to keep an eye on me, for whatever reason.'

'You'll be leaving tonight.'

'Tonight!'

Frank Ryan looked away as he said the word. He frowned, as if there was something about it he couldn't quite grasp. He looked more fragile now. The energy he had drawn on, coming into the room, wasn't easy to find; it was fading. He leant forward. He spoke quietly, more intensely.

'Is it real? For fuck's sake, it has to be real this time, Stevie!'

When Stefan returned to the Hotel Norte y Londra there was a note from Eckhart. It said only 'Tomorrow 01:00'. It would be an odd time to check out. It would be odder if he spent the rest of the day waiting. He resumed his role as pilgrim and walked the streets he had walked that morning. He ate and drank coffee to pass the time and, back in the Plaza Rey San Fernando, he went into the cathedral where, for a while, the overwhelming beauty of its interior and the sound of the choir singing Vespers did drive everything else from his head in a way that was welcome, for a while. But it was only a postponement.

He walked out into the Plaza Rey San Fernando. The bars and restaurants were busy now. It was an intimate space compared to the piazza of the Plaza Mayor in Salamanca, more like the centre of a country town than a great city. As he looked round the square he smiled. Across the cobbles was a figure in grey, at an easel. He ambled toward to Mrs Surtees. She was absorbed in what she was doing. She spoke without looking up.

'Estoy lo siento, señor, están bloqueando mi luz.'

'You mean I'm in the way.'

'Oh, Mr Gillespie, what a lovely surprise.'

'Can I have a look?'

'I've only really started. I wanted to catch the evening light.'

Stefan peered at the pale streaks of watercolour.

'Now, don't say "it's very good"! Am I capturing the light?'

'You're beginning to.'

'Beginning to will do,' she laughed. 'Are you here long?'

'I leave tonight.'

'Oh, what a pity! I was going to suggest a brandy later.'

'I'll have to leave you to it, Mrs Surtees. Good to see you again.'

'So where now?'

'Oh, northwards.'

'The mountains?'

'You're going to tell me there's somewhere not to be missed.'

'I am too old to be teased, Mr Gillespie. Do take care.'

He walked away towards the Calle de la Paloma. When he left the square he looked back. Mrs Surtees was totally absorbed in her painting again, staring intently up at the façade of the cathedral, then down to the easel. It was an encounter with what was ordinary, real. None of the reasons he was in Spain touched on that now. It felt like a long way home.

That night Stefan left the Hotel Norte y Londra at 1 a.m. In the Calle de San Juan Major Eckhart and Oberleutnant Triebel waited in a black Citroën limousine. There was little to it in the end. Triebel drove straight to the Prisión Central. Eckhart went in while Stefan sat in the back of the car and Triebel gazed at a map of the route he would be driving. A small door next to the prison gates opened. Two men came out; Konrad Eckhart and Frank Ryan. Ryan wore a suit and an overcoat; the clothes hung as loosely as the prison overall had.

Eckhart held the door; Ryan got in beside Stefan.

241

'Well, who would have thought it could be that easy?' he said.

Eckhart was in the front and the car was pulling away; he laughed. Frank Ryan laughed too but next to him in the back of the car Stefan could feel him shaking, almost uncontrollably, and breathing fast, irregularly.

'All right, Frank?'

'An bhfuil Gaeilge agat?' Ryan asked quietly if he spoke Irish.

'Go leor.' Enough.

Eckhart reached back, holding out a hip flask.

'There's some whiskey, Herr Ryan.'

'You're a gentleman, Konrad.'

Frank Ryan took a long, slow mouthful before he handed it to Stefan. He was breathing more easily, but the shaking had not quite stopped.

'It's hard to get some things out of your head,' said Ryan in Irish. 'When someone takes you outside in the middle of the night there, it's to shoot you. I suppose it was odds on no one would tonight, but then I never had much luck as a betting man. Still, I'm very glad you're here, Stevie.'

It was a long drive north to the mountains of Asturias. No one really spoke. Frank Ryan gazed almost continually out at the night. Most of the way he could see little in the darkness; occasionally there were farmhouses, villages, sometimes a town. Everything was silent and empty. They saw few vehicles. But even the night was miraculous for a man who had just left the confines of the Prisión Central. Stefan dozed intermittently; each time he woke Frank Ryan was still gazing out, his head sometimes pressed against the window, as if he was breathing the night air in through the glass.

At times the car stopped and the Germans argued about the road to take. Stefan picked out signposts that seemed to be repeated and then disappeared. For a long time it was Aguilar de Campoo, on a road where even the villages were few and far between. Then they drove through a town and the signs for Aguilar de Campoo were gone. The villages were bigger now; signs were for Torrelavega and finally, hours later, a name he recognized, Santander.

The land had been rising; the road was steeper, the bends sharper. When they stopped to refuel, they all got out. Eckhart and Triebel took jerry cans from the boot. Frank Ryan and Stefan Gillespie looked up. They could see the mountains of Asturias ahead, though the night was full of clouds. Among the clouds were patches of white; there was enough light to see the undulating lines that joined the patches. It was snow on the high peaks. The Irishmen were silent. Then Ryan started laughing.

'Fuck me, that's something, isn't it?'

He slapped Stefan hard on the back. Then he stopped laughing, and looked at the mountains in silence again, very still; he crossed himself.

They continued into the mountains, skirting the high peaks, and soon the car was heading downhill towards the coast. There was light in the sky as they turned off the road to Santander at Torrelavega; shortly afterwards they saw the sea. It followed them, appearing and disappearing with the bends in the road. Stefan marked the names he saw, looking for Pendueles. There were signs to Llanes, where Frank Ryan's boat would depart.

The car turned on to a dirt road and passed under a low railway bridge. Stefan registered the sign: Pendueles. They continued with the railway line above them on one side and fields and low hills on the other; the sea was visible in the distance. They stopped at the gates to a tall, square house, standing back from the road in a big garden. The sunlight picked out the white plaster walls, the red-tiled roof and the stone balconies in front of each window, and it also picked out the bright blue shutters and the blue wood of the glass conservatories the first-floor windows opened on to. The house had two names in Pendueles, the Casa de los Sacerdotes Irlandeses or, because of the colour, the Casa Azul, the Blue House.

It was a peaceful place; it was a welcoming end to the journey.

Oberleutnant Triebel blasted on the horn. An elderly man opened the gates. He was dark and balding and seemed irritated by their arrival. He was eating; they had interrupted his breakfast. Stefan smiled. The man belonged to the house, not the Abwehr. As the car pulled up at the entrance to the Blue House and they got out, a man emerged. He was in his early twenties, dressed in what passed for holiday clothes. He didn't need to speak for Stefan to know he was a German Intelligence officer. He saluted Eckhart stiffly and nodded pleasantly towards Frank Ryan and Stefan.

'You'll all want some breakfast, sir,' he said in German.

'We will, Pelka. Is Oberst Melsbach here yet?'

'He arrived yesterday from Lisbon, sir.'

'The plane landed all right?'

'The field is just a kilometre away, the way you came in.'

'And the pilot's happy about taking off from there?'

'He's a Condor Legion man, knows the area from the Civil War. He says he'll have no problem. Steinhaus and the pilot have camped up there. They'll refuel it today. And there's a Civil Guard to keep the locals at bay.'

'Did I hear "Früstück"?' said Ryan in English. 'My German hasn't got far, but it has got as far as that. Breakfast, fellers! Roll it out, please!'

Stefan registered what he had just heard. Ryan spoke barely any German; he had made nothing of it. Otto Melsbach, the Abwehr colonel, was there. He had arrived in an aeroplane. It wasn't difficult to get to Pendueles from Lisbon; the overnight train and a car would have brought him. Landing a plane in the middle of nowhere didn't make much sense, unless you had a reason to. Stefan wondered about the boat from Llanes.

'You two had better come and meet the colonel,' said Eckhart.

'He's in the study,' called Leutnant Pelka.

Eckhart crossed the hall and knocked on a door.

'Komm herein!'

The major opened the door. There was a desk in the middle of a book-lined room. A short, bullet-headed man stood up. He wore a tweed suit that suggested he had worked at dressing casually for the wrong climate. He gazed hard at Frank Ryan, then he burst out laughing.

'No need to introduce me to Frank. We are old comrades.'

Eckhart was taken aback. Stefan looked at Ryan. The expression he couldn't hide was shock, not surprise; his face, grey and pale from the prison regime, had been drained of the little colour it had. He wasn't laughing.

'How are you, Brigadier Ryan?'

The silence lasted a long time.

'I won't say this isn't a surprise, Commissar,' said Ryan finally. 'The last time I saw you, I think it was the last time, you were an International Brigade commissar called Klein, doing the job you had to do and shooting a priest somewhere in the Jarama Valley. That seems a long time ago.'

'A lot of water has flowed along the Jarama since then, Ryan.'

'Not to mention the blood, Commissar Klein.'

'Colonel, and the name is Melsbach now. It was with regret, the priest. He died for a cause I imagine he believed in. The Spain Franco has created. We can't expect to like what we do in war. You're a soldier, you understand that. But I did have to prove myself as an International Brigade commissar, and as executing people for no good reason seemed to be spreading through the Republican forces like an epidemic, it was hard to keep up with it. And if I remember right, weren't you going to shoot me?'

Frank Ryan was lighting a cigarette. Stefan could not understand the conversation at all; Konrad Eckhart was little better off. But Stefan could see that Ryan had now absorbed what had been a considerable shock. He had a soft smile on his face. As Stefan looked from Ryan to Oberst Melsbach he could see that, whatever else was going on, they loathed each other. It was another reason to be sure that the Germans wanted something from Frank Ryan that mattered, even if the Irishman didn't know it himself. Stefan had his own reasons to be wary of how dangerous Melsbach was. And he wasn't alone. He could almost see Ryan's tension as he drew on a cigarette and tried to look as if he had merely had an unexpected jolt.

'You've changed sides anyway, that's quite an achievement.'

'I didn't change. I was always on the right side. Germany's side. You don't get information just peering in. You have to be in the shit to find the shit. What we do for our country may not be pleasant but we do it because it is a sacred duty. I don't hold grudges. That's why you're here. Finally, you're on the right side too. Now Ireland's side is Germany's, yes?'

Only now did Oberst Melsbach turn his attention to Stefan.

'Welcome to Pendueles. Triebel will find you both some breakfast.'

It was a dismissal but as the two Irishmen walked into the hall the colonel called Eckhart back, still in the quiet, amenable tone he had used to Frank Ryan. But the German words that followed were far from amenable.

'What the hell is going on? What is that fucker doing here?'

21

El Camín de Santiago

Stefan Gillespie and Frank Ryan sat in the kitchen of the Casa Azul and ate breakfast. They could just hear loud voices from the study, or at least one loud voice, Oberst Melsbach's. Stefan knew at least some of it was about him. He had heard Eckhart reply when the colonel had asked who he was. 'Kerney insisted, Herr Oberst. I didn't have a choice.' It was obvious Melsbach knew him by now. Stefan had no doubt that he had been identified in Lisbon. But the Abwehr man hadn't expected him in Pendueles. The other German officers who came and went, in and out of the kitchen, were ill at ease, but Stefan had the impression Oberst Melsbach's temper was a familiar hazard. When Leutnant Triebel came in for a cup of coffee, Frank Ryan looked up and asked him how long they would be staying there. Triebel said he thought they would be gone the next day, if everything went according to plan. Ryan nodded mechanically and said he wanted some sleep. Triebel said there was a bedroom upstairs. As Ryan passed Stefan at the kitchen table he seemed almost unaware he was still there.

When Major Eckhart appeared, uncomfortable and angry, he suggested Stefan might want to get some rest too. He was less interested in his welfare than getting him out of Melsbach's sight. Stefan asked him when they would be leaving too, to see if he got the same answer as Ryan. Eckhart's reply was short, 'Not long.' As Stefan walked out he spoke again.

'You will be going to Madrid to report to your ambassador?'

'That's the idea, once Frank's on his way.'

'Trains from Pendueles are for Santander. There you can take a train to Madrid. If you leave tomorrow afternoon you will make the connection.'

'Do you leave tomorrow too?'

'We leave at some point.'

'When does the boat arrive in Llanes?'

'The precise times are in Oberst Melsbach's hands. You will find the bedrooms on the first floor. You can use the one to the right of the stairs.'

Stefan walked up from the hall. The study door was open. He heard the hissing of a radio. Looking back, he saw one of the Abwehr officers at a table with a radio transmitter. It wasn't impossible that Frank Ryan's departure would be by boat but with a plane waiting it was questionable. Yet there was something about it all that was still unresolved. Triebel's words had been, 'if everything goes according to plan'. None of it seemed to need much planning now. Where Ryan would go was, as always, not discussed, but it was unlikely Stefan would learn much more. All he could do was report to Kerney that Ryan had left Spain. He would not see it but it was clearly going to happen. Yet none of that explained why things were still so tentative in the Blue House.

He stood at the bedroom window, looking down at the garden. Triebel and Eckhart walked up and down, smoking. Eckhart was still angry; Stefan had no doubt it was the way Melsbach had hauled him over the coals. But there was more going on. There were other things to talk about, not talk about. There was expectation. They were awaiting something.

He lay down on the bed. He could hear Frank Ryan in the

next room, pacing restlessly. Ryan had not slept on the journey from Burgos; evidently he couldn't sleep now. After a time, Stefan drifted into a light sleep himself. When he woke the house was quiet. He heard movement next door. Ryan was still pacing. Then he heard someone on the stairs; a knock on Ryan's door, mumbled voices on the landing. Frank Ryan was going downstairs.

He left it a while before he went down himself. The door to the study was closed. He could hear voices. Ryan was in there with Melsbach and Eckhart. He could make out nothing of what they were saying.

'Something you need Herr Gillespie?'

Triebel was watching him from the door to the kitchen.

'A cup of tea wouldn't go amiss.'

Stefan followed the Abwehr man into the kitchen. Two other men were sitting at the table. He knew one as Pelka, the Abwehr officer who was at the house with Melsbach when they arrived. The other was evidently the pilot of the plane no one had mentioned, at least in English.

'Guten Abend! So, ich werde fliegen Sie,' said the pilot. He looked at Triebel and grinned. 'Richard das zweite?'

'Das ist die irische Polizist, Gillespie!'

The pilot shrugged and got up. 'You are good, Mr Gillespie?'

'I'm not so bad.'

The pilot chuckled and left. Stefan had the impression he didn't think much of the Intelligence game. But if there had been any doubt about how Frank Ryan would leave Spain before, there was none now. It wasn't the first time he had heard the word 'Richard' either. He heard it in Salamanca. It amused the German pilot, but not Triebel; it had to be code for Ryan.

There was no proper meal at the Blue House that evening. The Spanish caretaker and his wife had appeared briefly to put food out on the table in the kitchen. The Germans took what they wanted and disappeared. Melsbach made an attempt at polite conversation over a glass of beer with Stefan, as if the idea that he didn't want him in Pendueles had never entered his head. He talked about Spain and its return to peace and about the peace that would come to Europe once England and France saw sense. As part of what seemed idle chatter he made it clear again that Stefan would be taking the afternoon train to Santander the next day. He said Frank Ryan would be leaving shortly afterwards, with Eckhart and Triebel, while he would head to Salamanca, where the Abwehr base at the Irish College was being dismantled. Spain's war was over. He joked that if nothing else it had been, 'good practice'. He made a point of mentioning the plane that had replaced the boat, though Stefan had no doubt the confusion over arrangements had been deliberate. Ryan would be flown to Italy, to Milan. Italy was another neutral country, of course, like Spain, like Ireland too, added Melsbach.

Stefan asked what would happen after Italy, since Leopold Kerney would want to know. He didn't expect to get a real answer and he didn't. Otto Melsbach shrugged and smiled, and said all that would be up to Frank Ryan himself; wasn't he a free man now?

Frank Ryan had kept himself to himself most of the day, either in his room or walking in the garden. Stefan had watched him pacing the lawn, close to the high walls, as if he was still in a prison yard. He had been shut in the study with Melsbach and Eckhart at times too.

It was almost dark when Stefan Gillespie came up the stairs and saw Ryan sitting alone in the big first-floor conservatory at the back of the house. He was smoking, gazing out through the windows. Stefan stood for a moment, following his eyes to the low hills and the small fields that led to the sea, which was still just about visible.

'Did you get any sleep at all, Frank?'

'Like a log, Stevie.'

Stefan knew that was untrue.

'I did snatch a bottle of brandy from the kitchen too.'

Stefan sat down. Ryan handed him a glass and looked back outside.

'That's the Bay of Biscay.'

'I suppose it is.'

'A straight line north, north-west would get you to Waterford.'

'Not Italy.'

'No, but Italy will be another way to get there.'

'Colonel Melsbach told me there's a plane now,' said Stefan.

'Well, it'll be quick enough so.'

'Wouldn't Lisbon be quicker, for America anyway?'

'They have to play this game with the Spanish. I've escaped, you see. That's what they'll be putting out. I don't know who'd recognize me in Lisbon, but it's too close to Spain. Keeping up appearances is the thing . . .'

'Are they hiding you from the Spanish or the English?'

'I don't much care. Leo has it in his head the English don't want Franco to let me out, but it was going on before the war. Who knows?'

Stefan sipped at the brandy.

'This isn't my game, Stevie. I don't know the rules.'

'So who is Colonel Otto Melsbach?' asked Stefan.

'Not who I thought he was.'

'I gathered that. How do you know him?'

Frank Ryan looked round and spoke more quietly.

'He was an International Brigade commissar, my comrade in arms, a communist, and the reddest of the red. You must have picked that bit up.'

'I picked it up but it didn't make much sense.'

'No, it doesn't, except that he was always a German agent.'

'You didn't realize he was behind getting you out?'

'I heard the name from Leo, but Melsbach didn't mean anything.'

'Does it make a difference?'

'I feel as if it should. But what sort of fucking difference? Do I tell them I don't reckon much to the calibre of Nazi they have working for them? Ask them to take me back to Burgos? It's a shock. Still, I've survived worse.'

He looked out of the window again.

'If you sup with the Devil you can't complain about the people he asks to dinner. Klein or Melsbach, Melsbach or Klein? I thought he was a murdering communist bastard and it turns out he's a murdering fascist bastard. Maybe he's both. Maybe he's got more honesty about him than the rest of us. I didn't only lose my friends in battle, I lost some of them to the communists, in the cellars of Madrid and Barcelona, as they made sure the war was being fought the Soviet way. And there were times, God help me, I told myself it wasn't really happening, or we had to live with it because of the United Front. You see when our secret police boys blew our comrades' brains out in cellars, they were different cellars altogether from the ones Franco's boys used. Didn't our fellers have their hearts in the right place?'

Frank Ryan got up; he laughed, looking out towards the sea.

'Bless me, Father, for I have sinned. Will we go to Mass tomorrow?'

Stefan was surprised, not for the first time, by the change of tone.

'You know where we are, don't you, Stevie?'

'I'm not with you, Frank.'

'El Camino de Santiago, the Way of Saint James. We're right on the pilgrims' route to Santiago de Compostela. Jesus, you're not going to call yourself a Catholic and tell me you don't know what that is, Inspector!'

'I don't call myself a Catholic at all, Frank, but I do know.'

'Good God, they'd let anyone join An Garda Síochaná now! What's Dev doing to Holy Ireland? Well, you'll come anyway.

I poured my Catholic soul out to Otto to get the permission slip. He's convinced the two of us are on our knees day and night. And sure, wouldn't a Mass on the Camino even get a Protestant to heaven? Nothing like hedging your bets.'

He walked off to his room abruptly.

Stefan sat alone in the dark on the glassed-in balcony. The lights were on downstairs. The study door opened. He heard the crackle of the radio as it tuned through stations in Spanish, English, French; then a voice in German.

'This is Berlin and this is the news from the German Reich.'

'For fuck's sake, will someone turn that shit off?'

It was Leutnant Pelka who shouted. Laughter; the radio stopped.

Stefan finished his brandy. He walked to the open window and stared down at the garden. He could hear two men talking. There was an outside light on. He saw Oberst Melsbach and Major Eckhart walking, Melsbach smoking a cigar. They were not speaking loudly but as they halted below the conservatory, Stefan could hear. He was invisible.

'The ship will dock in Santander around eleven,' said Melsbach.

'You'll be there to collect him, sir?'

'Make sure you're ready. No reason to stay another night. Once we have Richard I, you can leave. So Italy tomorrow night – and then home.'

'When will we see you, sir?'

'Next week in Berlin. And get our friend Gillespie on the train.'

'I'm sorry, Herr Oberst, I did what I thought was best.'

'You should have known the Irish ambassador didn't matter. You certainly shouldn't have let him intimidate you. He was a go-between. He ceased to be important when Richard II walked out of Burgos. What mattered was ensuring the conclusion to this wasn't compromised by the English poking their noses in, in Lisbon, or by Irish sentimentality here.'

'You haven't told Ryan what's happening, though?'

'He'll know about Richard I soon enough.'

'And how will he react?'

'All you need to know about the Irish, Major, is that they hate the English. They make Pavlov's dogs look positively sophisticated.'

Eckhart clicked his heels and walked back to the house. Melsbach's cigar had gone out. He took a match to relight it. It blew out and he twisted round to strike another, away from the north-westerly breeze that was blowing in from the sea now. A cloud of smoke wafted up and for a moment Melsbach glanced up too. If the light had been on he would have been looking at Stefan, but he could see nothing. He sauntered across the garden.

Stefan turned back into the house and walked to the landing, heading for his room. His instincts had been right. It wasn't over. There was someone else. The Germans were waiting for another man to arrive at the Casa de los Sacerdotes Irlandeses. He was coming by boat from outside Spain. Frank Ryan was Richard II; now they were waiting for Richard I.

The next morning Stefan and Frank Ryan walked to the other end of Pendueles to the church of San Acisclo, chaperoned by Oberleutnant Triebel, the only Catholic in Melsbach's entourage. He seemed pleased to be going or at least pleased to get away from Oberst Melsbach; Eckhart looked like he wouldn't have minded going too. The colonel was in an irritable mood. Stefan knew he would be driving to Santander; the conclusion of what he assumed was the colonel's own project was imminent.

The small church was crowded when they arrived, only minutes before Mass. They attracted attention as strangers but it was not the first time Triebel had been there; Abwehr officers had used the Casa Azul before. He told the Irishmen to say nothing the Mass's Latin didn't demand.

This was a community not so different from the one Stefan knew at home. A familiar space; the smell of old stone and old wood. The statues were simply the holy family; Christ on the cross, Mary and Joseph on either side. And as Mass began, with words as natural to Stefan as any Catholic, it could have been any country church anywhere. The strength of a language no one spoke; always the same. 'Ostende nobis, Domine, misericordiam tuam.' Show us thy mercy, Lord. 'Domine, exaudi orationem meam.' Lord hear my prayer. 'Et clamor meus ad te veniat.' Let my cry be heard by thee.

Stefan sat between Frank Ryan and Triebel, but he was aware of an intensity in Ryan that was almost palpable. It wasn't hard to understand. What he had been released from was a death sentence, even after his death sentence was commuted. Yet it wasn't only about giving thanks. Whatever he said, whatever about the smiles and jokes, his prayers were troubled.

When the Mass ended and the congregation dispersed, Triebel waited until the church was empty. Even without words the Asturians had seen the two men were not German; they thought the Irish priests were back. Ryan seemed amused by the smiles and nods; he had smiled and nodded back.

'You're very popular in Pendueles, Sebastian,' said Ryan.

'They think you're priests, the two of you, from the Irish College.'

'So I don't pass for German just by keeping my mouth shut?'

'Apparently not.' Triebel laughed and got up. 'Let's go.'

'Well, Stevie, it's not every day you'd be taken for a priest.'

'I'll take it as a compliment, Frank.'

Ryan grinned. He walked to a shrine where a row of candles burnt. He took one from below the rack and lit it. He bent his head and then peered up at the statue of a young man painted in green and gold. The neck seemed just too long for his body, and there was a blood-red line round it. Triebel was walking quickly back towards them.

'Do you know this feller at all, Sebastian?'

'It's his church, he's Saint Acisclus.'

'He's a new one on me, and what did he do?'

'He was a martyr, in Cordoba, when Diocletian was trying to wipe out Christianity in the Roman Empire. They cut off his head for his trouble. Naturally it was stuck back on – when he reached his reward in heaven.'

Leaving the dark church Frank Ryan stopped to light a cigarette.

'At least you get your head put back, that's the main thing. But times don't change, do they? There's always some fucker wanting to cut it off!'

Ryan made a point of walking slowly on the way back. He said nothing to Stefan for some minutes, drawing on one cigarette then another. When he spoke it was in Irish. Triebel, as he slowed at intervals to let them catch up, knew they weren't speaking English, but he decided to ignore it.

'I hope you don't take me for a fool, Stevie.'

'Why would I do that, Frank?'

'I can play the fool, and the Irish eejit if required.'

'Is that what you're doing?'

'I know they didn't pull me out of gaol for love. I haven't thought much about it. Why should I? It's my way home. Didn't you think you could be at home, sitting in that church? Whatever happens, it's still my way back to Ireland, if I keep my head down. But my old comrade Herr Klein-Melsbach doesn't leave me the luxury of looking the other way. He hated my guts in the Fifteenth Brigade. He won't hate me any less now. I can keep my mouth shut about what I think as far as the others go. But he knows who I am.'

'So what does happen, Frank?'

'I don't know. I've been fighting the fascists a long time. I've sent too many men to die fighting them. A lot of them were English. They wouldn't have died without Hitler's guns and bombs. That doesn't change what England is to Ireland, yet it changes something. I doubt the English ever decided to fight fascism, but now they're fighting the war I fought here.'

'I don't think that's the line the Abwehr's looking for.'

'I can give them as much shite as they want. They think the IRA is important and I'm important to the IRA. Sooner or later they'll come to the conclusion I'm not what they think, and it's all bollocks anyway. If I'm just another Irish gobshite spinning a line they might as well let me go home.'

Stefan nodded.

'You don't think much of it, as a plan, Stevie!'

'Well, you're out of gaol.'

'I know you're not here by chance, whatever Leo thinks. You will be reporting back. I am no traitor to Ireland, even if I don't much like what Dev's made it. But I had to get out of Burgos. Just tell them that, will you? Tell someone. This isn't my side.'

They were walking along the track that would bring them to the back gate into the Casa Azul's garden. It was the end. Stefan knew he would be leaving soon.

'Have you heard them talk about Richard I and Richard II?'

'What?' asked Ryan; the words meant nothing.

'Any of the Germans? Have you heard those names?'

Frank Ryan shrugged and then spoke briefly in English.

'You mean, "This blessed plot, this earth, this realm, this England"?'

'You're Richard II, that's your code. Richard I is someone else.'

'So who the fuck is Richard I then?'

'I don't know, but your friend Melsbach is collecting him off a boat that docks at Santander today. And when he gets here, that's when you leave. I don't know if it helps but you might as well know. You're waiting for someone. Do you know anything about that?'

'No, nothing at all. How do you know this?'

'I speak some German.'

'I see, so we're neither of us the eejits they think we are.'

'They killed a British agent in Lisbon last week. It didn't make a lot of sense at the time, but if there's always been more to hide, more to hide than you've said. . .'

'Getting topped wouldn't be a bad reason for me not to tell you?'

Two hours later Stefan Gillespie stood on the platform at Pendueles station, along the road from the Casa de los Sacerdotes Irlandeses, waiting for the train to Santander. Major Eckhart was with him to confirm his departure personally to Oberst Melsbach, who would now be on his way back from Santander by car. Nothing more had been said that gave any hint what Melsbach was doing; there had been no mention of his being in Santander. On the platform Eckhart talked about the Asturian coast and his breaks at the Blue House. It didn't sound as if he was as enthusiastic about getting to the real war as he kept saying. When the train came he shook Stefan's hand as warmly as only a man who is glad to see the back of someone can.

He waited until Stefan was on the train. He returned along the platform to the steps down to the road. He stopped and watched a moment longer.

The train was almost empty. There were three people in the carriage Stefan got into. He walked on and opened the door into the next. He could see the head of only one passenger, at the far end. He pushed down the window of the carriage door on the opposite side to the platform, then he reached out to turn the handle. As the door opened he jumped down. The train was starting to move. He slammed the door and ran across the track. He dived into the bushes in case Eckhart was still watching the platform.

He waited long after the station was empty and silent. There would be no more passengers for some time. The next train to Santander would not be there for three hours; the next one to Llanes and Oviedo would not arrive for two. He stepped out on to the track. The Casa Azul was a five-minute walk; the railway line ran past it, just across the road, looking down on the house and the garden. On either side of the track there was a scrubby growth of trees and low bushes. He could hide easily enough almost directly opposite the gates. He would have a clear view down the embankment, across the road to the house itself. Melsbach had left for Santander two hours before he and Frank Ryan had set off for Mass. Six hours had passed. If he kept to the times Stefan had overheard he would be back in an hour, as it was getting dark.

He scrambled on to the embankment from the track. He was invisible from the road and from the line now. He could see the Casa Azul. He sat on his suitcase and watched. He saw no one outside, though figures passed across the windows. The Citroën in which he had arrived from Burgos was at the front door. At one point Pelka and Triebel came out to pack suitcases and bags into the boot. An hour had gone. Whoever the Abwehr colonel was bringing back from Santander it was someone who mattered. Stefan assumed that something in all that would matter in Ireland too. He wasn't sure why he was so determined to do the job this way. He had done what the ambassador asked. It mattered, that was all he could tell himself. Frank Ryan mattered too. Ryan was in trouble, perhaps more trouble than he realized. It might help no one in Ireland to know that, yet he still felt someone should.

An hour and a half had passed when Melsbach's car returned. Stefan saw the lights before he heard the engine. The driver stopped at the gates and blasted the horn. Pelka and Triebel ran from the house. The car swept in. Melsbach got out. With him was a taller man in a trilby and a dark overcoat. Stefan could see no more than that. Konrad Eckhart shook the stranger's hand and they went inside. He had to get closer. Darkness would

259

make it easier. He watched the lights go on in the house. No blinds were drawn, no shutters closed. He could see a lot of movement. After ten minutes Pelka came out with Melsbach's driver and more bags were packed into the Citroën. Stefan recalled that they were splitting up; the colonel to Salamanca and Abwehr HQ at the Irish College; Major Eckhart to Italy with Richard I and II.

He walked further along the railway embankment, feeling his way in the growing dark. Across the road he saw the track that led to the rear of the Casa Azul and to the back gate they had used going to Mass. He clambered down and crossed the road. He followed the track past farms and houses. As it turned towards the sea there was a path to the left. He was soon at the back wall of the Blue House. When he reached the gate it was unlocked; no one felt vulnerable now, whatever the secret. He stepped inside and slid along the wall behind a woodshed built hard up against it. He was close to the back of the house now. He looked up at the blue paintwork of the big first-floor conservatory. The lights were very bright. He could see Ryan with Eckhart and Melsbach. The tall man was there, his back to the window.

The two Abwehr officer were talking with great animation. Ryan and the other man, Richard II and Richard I, were very still. Melsbach moved forward and slapped Frank Ryan heartily on the back, laughing. Then the colonel walked away; Eckhart followed.

The two men who remained didn't move at all. It didn't seem as if they were talking, though they were looking at one another. Frank Ryan walked forward, closer to the window, and spoke. Stefan felt he knew what he was saying as he looked out. Ireland, Waterford; a straight line, north, north-west. The other man turned to the window. He stood next to Frank Ryan, looking the same way, to the sea. Then Stefan knew exactly who he was looking at.

It was a man he would have recognized from photographs in Special Branch but he knew him better than that. He had met him barely six months ago in New York.

It was Seán Russell, the IRA's exiled Chief of Staff.

Russell had gone to the USA to raise money for the bombing campaign in England and had, disastrously, got mixed up in an attempt on the life of the English king, who was visiting America then. He had been on the run in the States ever since, though no one believed the FBI, let alone the Irish-American police forces of a dozen great cities, were trying very hard to find him. His absence had plunged the IRA at home into infighting and incompetence. Now German Intelligence had brought Seán Russell back to Europe.

Stefan was still gazing up as the back door opened. He ducked behind two rubbish bins. He heard the voices of the lieutenants, Pelka and Triebel.

'You wouldn't say they looked pleased to see each other.'

'Fuck it, as long as the colonel's pleased, I'm pleased.'

'He's never pleased, not for long.'

'All that matters to me is that in two days we'll be in Berlin.'

They tipped buckets of rubbish into the bins only feet from Stefan, then went back in.

When Stefan looked up again the light in the conservatory was out. He moved along the wall to the gate. As he stepped through it he heard a car start. The last light in the Casa de los Sacerdotes Irlandeses was switched off. The engine of the second car turned over. He walked out and followed the lane. He would cut back to the railway station later. There was no shortage of darkness to hide in now, till the train to Santander. By that time the Germans would be long gone from Pendueles. Frank Ryan and Seán Russell would be over Spain, heading for Italy. But it was only a stop. Whatever Frank Ryan was hoping for, wherever he really believed he was going, in two days he would be in Berlin.

22

El Río Tormes

Below the city of Salamanca, the Río Tormes spreads itself lazily through a patchwork of mudflats and reed beds that shrink and grow as the river rises and falls with the seasons. At times the dark waters are almost lost from sight when the trees are at their thickest and the reeds at their highest. Where the river bed is widest the vegetation pushes out from the banks on either side and almost meets. It is here the Romans built a bridge across the Tormes to the gates of the city they called Salamantica. The twenty-six arches of the long, low bridge approach the city from the south. Once a cluster of temples rose up ahead, including the shrine of the virgin goddess Diana. Rising up 2,000 years later, dominating everything else, were the Old and the New cathedrals, each dedicated to the Virgin Mary. It was among the reeds below the Roman Bridge that the body of María Fernández Duarte was found. A bullet to her forehead killed her but the shots through each of her eyes ensured that everyone knew why she died.

In one respect, María's parents were lucky; they had a body to bury. The habit of disappearance was hard to break in Spain and the bodies of those still taken in the early hours of the morning were rarely found. The death squads of Franco's

Falange, led frequently by the Civil Guards who might also pretend to investigate the disappearances later, were still busy, ferreting out people who needed killing for the sake of good order in the New Order. But there was a point to the discovery of María's body; it was nicely made.

Señor and Señora Duarte lived in a small terraced house hard up against the old city wall, below the cathedrals, directly opposite the Roman bridge. The windows of the house in the Calle de Ribera del Puente gave on to the bridge and the river; coming out of the door they were the first things to be seen. They were the things María had seen every day of her childhood. They would still be the things her parents saw every day, and for the rest of their lives they would also see their daughter's body in the reeds below the bridge.

When Stefan Gillespie arrived in Santander from Pendueles he stayed the night at a hotel in the station square and travelled on to Madrid the next day to see Leopold Kerney. He saw little of Madrid apart from the Norte station and the big white house in the Calle Zurbano, which was the Irish Legation. But the short drive from the Estación del Norte told its own story. The station had been cleared of debris but the rubble from the years of siege was still piled up round it, and there was barely a pane of glass in its vast cast-iron roof. In the streets beyond there were roofless buildings, collapsed walls, apartments with their fronts blown off. There were bomb craters still to be skirted round; heaps of stone and brick were being cleared by gangs of workers. The fact that the work parties were watched over by armed Civil Guards left little doubt who was doing the clearing. It reminded Stefan of what Otto Melsbach had said about the war in Spain; it had been good practice.

The account Stefan gave Kerney of the journey from Burgos

to Pendueles ended with Frank Ryan finally leaving Spain for Italy on a German plane. It did not include the walk along the railway line to the Casa de los Sacerdotes Irlandeses, nor an account of the man he had seen there; he did not mention Richard I. What the ambassador wanted to know was that Ryan had left the country and he had. It was up to others to decide if he needed to know more. The ambassador was satisfied Frank Ryan was safe; he had no interest in speculating about where he might end up. If he had an opinion, he kept it to himself. And after a quiet evening at the Legation, and a dinner with Mr and Mrs Kerney at which they all left the world outside well alone and talked mostly of home, Stefan took the train back to Salamanca.

He had one thing more to do for Frank Ryan, which was to give María Fernández Duarte her Irish passport. He discovered, as soon as he arrived at the Irish College and saw Michael Hagan, that the passport was surplus to requirements. The young Irishman was distressed for himself, and more distressed for Frank Ryan, but he also seemed to accept María's death with a kind of resignation that was a part of what it was to live in Spain. The murderous brutality that went with the Civil War had achieved a kind of normality, and the fact that it hadn't stopped surprised no one. For Stefan, though he hardly knew María, it was harder to find anything like resignation to set beside sorrow and anger. He felt a responsibility he knew he didn't have but could not shake off. Whatever danger he might have faced in Pendueles, there was a sense in which it was still a game, a game they had all played. It was no game for the dead woman. Her death would be no game to Frank Ryan.

However, there was another thing to do, which was the real reason Stefan was in Salamanca now; to face Hagan again with the question of Billy Byrne and Jim Collins. He was still unsure how to handle it but he was convinced Hagan knew where Collins was. But it was easier than he had expected; something had changed in the young Irishman. Perhaps what Stefan had said in the college chapel had left its mark; perhaps his role in Frank Ryan's release had combined with a sense of conscience and obligation to force Mikey's hand; or perhaps María Duarte's death had hit him harder than it seemed. In the end the door was open now. Michael Hagan had spoken to Jim Collins and Collins had agreed to see Stefan.

Stefan Gillespie sat in a café in the square of a small, nondescript town upriver from Salamanca. The bus there had taken an hour, following the river through flat yellow fields and grey olive groves. Alba de Tormes had a particular distinction; Saint Teresa of Avila had died in a convent there. Seeing the statues and pictures in the shops of the town's Plaza Mayor, Stefan was unaware she was the patron saint of those in need of grace. It may be that Jim Collins wasn't.

Stefan had been there for almost an hour and was now wondering if Collins would appear after all. But finally a thin, dark man approached him. Stefan had registered the man several times already, as he had registered others, but none showed any sign of being anything but ordinary Spanish men about their business.

'You're Mr Gillespie.'

'You're Mr Collins.'

'Mikey said I should come. I didn't want to. He said it was right.'

Stefan could hear the accent of Wicklow clearly enough in the man's voice but it was coloured now by the years he had spent speaking Spanish.

Collins sat down. 'Billy's dead then?'

'That's what we assume. The body hasn't been found, at least it hadn't when I left Ireland. No one holds out much hope it will be now.'

There was a faint smile on Collins's lips.

'Maybe he was just dragged straight down to hell.'

'That's not an uncommon response, I'd have to say,' replied Stefan.

'I was never any friend of his, you should know that.'

They stopped as the waiter brought a pot of coffee.

'I don't live here, Mr Gillespie, not even near here.'

'I see.'

'You won't find me again, and I won't be going back to Ireland.'

'Do you think I'm here to take you back?'

'You're a policeman.'

'I'm not only here as a policeman.'

'No, Mikey told me about your wife. I know who she was. Maeve Joyce. I do remember her a bit, as a girl I mean, when she'd be staying in the valley with her cousins.'

Stefan took out a cigarette and offered one to Collins.

'You are Albert Neale, aren't you?'

'I'm not sure I know who Albert Neale is. It's twenty years since I was in Ireland. I've lived in Spain a long time. I have children. The only place I'd even speak English at all was at the college.'

'Are you going to tell me what happened?'

'With Billy, when he was here?'

'Start where you like, but it began with Charlotte Moore, didn't it?'

'I didn't kill her.'

'No, I'm assuming Billy was right about that.'

'I had no choice but to run. If I'd stayed they'd have hanged me.'

Stefan nodded.

'They had me down for it from the start. I'd always been friendly with the young 'uns. I worked in the forestry the Sinclairs had up on Mullacor sometimes, and there was always gangs of kids playing up there. Charlotte was a sweet girl. Not too clever, but friendly, that's all. And I worked with her father, for God's sake. It was true she had a bit of a crush on me, the daft way of the age she was. She'd follow me sometimes. She liked to talk. Maybe I had time for her, I don't know. It was a joke so, the way she followed me about, harmless. Even her dad laughed about it. And I never thought anything of it. I'd never have touched her.'

'But somebody touched her,' said Stefan, 'and you knew who.'

'No one would have believed me. And I'd told lies, you see. Who was going to believe the truth after that? It was then I saw them behind my house, digging. I never knew what they found till after, but I saw they had something. It was clothes with blood on them. I never put them there. But I didn't wait to see what they were doing. I ran. I got to Dublin and then I got across to England. I was away while they were still looking for me in Wicklow.'

'So then you came here?'

'No, I was in London for a year, working in pubs, using another name. But wherever I went there'd be Irish fellers, and I knew the peelers were still looking. They wouldn't give up, would they? I met a feller with a pub in Gibraltar and he said he'd give me a job if I was ever there. I took the money I had and I went. Jesus, it was worse than London. The size of the place, like living in fecking Glendalough, everyone knowing everyone, and the peelers still walking round in helmets. And fecking Irishmen off the ships by the bucket load again. Jesus, we're everywhere!'

He laughed, then stopped, taking tobacco out to roll a cigarette.

'One day there was an Irish feller in the pub. I knew him. He was from Arklow, I think. He knew me. Least he thought he did. He asked me where was I from. I made something up. I knew he'd remember in the end. Then he'd remember what they said I done.'

'So you ran again?'

'Into Spain. I had no real papers, hardly any money. I ended up on the tramp. I was picked up for begging in Salamanca. When they found I was Irish the Guardia Civil took me to the college. The priests gave me a bed. I was there a week, so I started working in the garden, mending things, to say thanks. The rector offered me a job to get me on my feet. I stayed. And I met a woman. I settled down. I forgot it all. I thought it was over.'

'And then Billy Byrne turned up, and Billy knew you.'

'He knew me straight away. I had no idea who the fuck he was. I must have met him, but he was younger than me and he lived down in Rathdrum. But he'd worked in Laragh and Glendalough. I don't know how he recognized me. He had a nose for it. I said he was talking bollocks . . .'

'So what did he do?'

'He didn't do anything. I thought I'd have to run. If he went to the rector, he'd go to the police. I was a suspected murderer. He couldn't ignore it. But I had a family. Running wasn't easy. So I told Billy what really happened. I thought if he knew I didn't do it he'd leave me alone. He believed me, but he wouldn't let go. I offered him money. It wasn't much. He said, "We can do better than that, Jimmy." He said it was good as a pension for us both.'

'Because you told him who really killed Charlotte Moore?'

Collins said nothing, staring down at the table.

'And now you need to tell me,' said Stefan quietly.

'He wasn't much more than a boy himself when it happened. I helped him, God save me. I helped him hide her body. I believed him. I believed it was all an accident . . .'

'So who was it?'

'The man's name was Stuart Sinclair. You wouldn't know him.'

Stefan stared. He knew Stuart Sinclair. He had met him only a couple of times, a long time ago; once at his wedding. But he knew him well enough. He knew him above all as a childhood friend of Maeve's. He was the brother of Alex Sinclair, the man he had met on that first day in Glendalough after Christmas, searching for Billy Byrne.

'I know who he is. What happened, Jim?'

'I felt sorry for him.'

'So sorry you helped him hide a dead body?'

'It's hard to say it after all these years. He was sweet on her. He was a bit older – and he wasn't right – if you know him, you'll know that. When he got angry he couldn't always control what he did. One time he attacked the young lad, Alex, and nearly cracked his skull with a shovel. Other times he wouldn't talk to anyone. He'd be on his own in the woods or walking the hills, like he was frightened of people. I'd say it got worse once they started sending him away, in and out of asylums. He didn't understand how a girl like Charlotte . . . he said he loved her. He wanted . . . he thought she wanted the same. And he couldn't control – I know that's not a reason – but he was with her in the woods, by the Upper Lake, and he tried to make her . . . she must have been terrified. He said she ran into the lake, out of her depth. She couldn't swim. He saw what he done – and he tried to get to her, but she . . .'

Stefan saw the shore of the Upper Lake, and a body.

'I found him there,' continued Collins, 'with her . . . drowned. He was talking to her – crying, shouting – he wouldn't believe she was dead.'

'So why didn't you go and tell someone?'

'I knew what they'd do. They wouldn't hang him, but they'd lock him up for the rest of his life. There was no bringing Charlotte back – and it was an accident – I believed that then – if she hadn't gone in the water . . .'

Stefan could see the pain in those words; he said nothing.

'We took her up above the mines, on a pony. I don't know

where we put her. An old shaft I think. I wanted to turn back. I knew I shouldn't be doing it. There was a part of him that did too. But we didn't turn back. You know the rest. Maybe the peelers could see I done something. I gave them different stories, where I was, what I was doing – I couldn't remember what I'd said. When I saw them digging . . . I was right to go. I would've hanged.'

'So who put the clothes there?'

'Stuart wasn't right in his head. It didn't make him stupid. Who'd have believed me? The Sinclairs owned half the valley. What was I? A murdering child molester trying to blame a halfwit? I had no chance.'

'And you told Billy Byrne all that?'

'I told him, yes.'

'And he went back home to get money out of Stuart Sinclair.'

'I couldn't stop that. It was nothing to do with me.'

'And what about Maeve and Marian Gort?'

'I thought it was over. Then he started writing about things he found out, talking to Stuart, watching him. He came up with this story about Miss Gort and another woman. I didn't know it was Maeve Joyce. I hardly remembered her. I ignored the letters but they kept coming, going on about the Sinclairs and their money, and how Stuart would cough up to keep us quiet. I burnt them. I didn't want anything to do with it. But I was the threat, see. He told Stuart I'd come back and point the finger. I'd tell where Charlotte's body was, and then they'd start on the other deaths, and he'd hang so. Billy wouldn't go away. The letters kept coming. So I did what I said I'd never do. I took my wife and kids and ran. No address, no way to contact me. I only told Mikey. He knew what an evil bastard Billy was. I thought I'd got rid of it. But it's still here. I did forget, for a long time. I can't now. It's not just what Stuart did to Charlotte. I believe every word Billy wrote about him. Charlotte wasn't an accident. Two other women are dead because of me, because I never said what happened.'

As Stefan walked up the hill to the Colegio de los Irlandeses there was a military truck outside being loaded with boxes and files. Stefan knew what it was. It was information; names, addresses, contacts, connections; copies of letters and lists of informers; lists of people's friends and acquaintances, families, lovers; lists of those on the wrong side, even the right side, who needed spying on or were ready to spy on each other; lists of the dead who no longer needed spying on but whose families did. There wouldn't only be lists of enemies, socialists, communists, Jews, German exiles finding their way through Spain to Portugal, British agents, French agents, Soviet agents, American agents; there would be lists of friends who could be bought and blackmailed too. Watching it all being carried out of the Irish College by the Abwehr officers, it smelt too much like Dublin Castle, only more rank.

He had already seen Otto Melsbach, who was in Salamanca to supervise the Abwehr's departure from the city. Melsbach was happy to chat as if neither of them knew each other and had never been on the Asturian coast with an Irishman called Frank Ryan. What made Stefan so ill at ease, talking to the colonel in the college cloisters, was the feeling that it could almost have been a conversation with Terry Gregory. Whether Melsbach had always been an Abwehr plant during the Spanish Civil War, or whether he had played both sides until he knew where his best interests lay, the image of the superintendent in the Police Yard, handing information to the IRA's Quartermaster, didn't seem so far away. Stefan felt that his silence about that made him Gregory's man, just as Eckhart and Triebel were Melsbach's.

He turned away from the college and walked back the way he had come, thinking about what faced him in Ireland. He had what he came for. He had done what had been asked of him too. He had the information his government wanted. He knew why Frank Ryan had been pulled out of Burgos by German Intelligence; he knew what the real secret was. They were rebuilding an IRA leadership that was in ruins in Ireland, cementing its fractured pieces. What they could do with that he didn't know. It was for other people to fathom. He had something else to do now. In his head was the man who had killed Maeve. He could barely remember what he looked like. But he knew Maeve had seen him only a day before she died, taking flowers to Marian Gort's grave. It seemed nothing at the time, but it was everything.

He turned over the little he knew about Stuart Sinclair. Maeve had cared about him, as she cared about all wounded things. She remembered him as an ordinary boy she played with on her summer holidays. She had watched him change. Stefan recalled her saying it. She had seen him become a confused, disturbed young man, torn in some unfathomable way, not by anything anyone could see but by what was inside him. That was it; that was all Stefan knew. He tried to think back into those last days at Glendalough again. He had not been surprised that seeing Stuart troubled her. He was sick; clearly worse rather than better. But there had been something she wanted to say. It hadn't seemed important then; it seemed so unimportant that he made no connection to her death twenty-four hours later. How did that happen?

He walked through Salamanca, seeing not its bright, sunlit stone, but the dark waters of the Upper Lake. He reached the river with no real intention of doing so. He walked out across the Roman bridge. Traffic still used it but it was quiet now. A few cars passed; a few pedestrians; a horse and cart. He stopped halfway across where the wall curved out into a bay and he stood looking down on to the muddy Río Tormes and the dense beds of reeds. Somewhere there, only days before, María Duarte's body had been discovered. Whatever the reasons, all he could feel now was that she was another woman who should not be dead.

The noise of birds was everywhere. There were swallows nesting above the arches, sweeping the sky overhead to feed in the afternoon heat. The chatter of the year's first broods came up from the stonework below. He took the Irish passport from his pocket. He opened it and saw the intense face and the bright eyes and the black, unbrushed hair. He leant over the parapet and let it fall into the water. There was a flash of gold from the embossed harp.

It was as he turned from the river that he realized Otto Melsbach was only a few yards away, watching. The Abwehr colonel stepped towards him.

'I followed you here. I saw you outside the college.'

'Well, now you can see me here too, Colonel.'

Melsbach's next words were in German.

'Why don't we speak in German?'

Stefan didn't answer, but he knew the colonel knew.

'You intrigued me. Nothing much to say except to Ryan, but always watching. I'd say watching too much. I am a very thorough man. I don't like loose ends. I took the trouble of asking someone in Dublin about you. There wasn't much but I discovered you speak good German. My mistake. The name should have told me. Stefan, not Stephen. I'm irritated that I didn't pick that up when I looked at your passport. You have German parents?'

'A German grandmother.' Stefan spoke in German too.

'There were no great secrets, Inspector, no need for subterfuge.'

Oberst Melsbach was looking hard at Stefan despite his amiable smile. He was confident there was nothing for the Irish policeman to know. Stefan had been on the train to Santander when the real business was transacted in Pendueles, the meeting between Frank Ryan and Seán Russell. But he wanted to reassure himself. He wanted to confirm nothing had been overheard. His opinion of himself was high enough that he believed he would know immediately if it had been. It was information that should not reach Ireland, not yet. German Intelligence suspected that anything that got to the Irish found its way to the English eventually. And he was irritated that Stefan had fooled him too, even if it achieved nothing.

'My government wanted to know that Frank Ryan was okay,' said Stefan. 'We weren't convinced you just wanted to get him out – and set him free.'

A little bit of truth carried more conviction than a lie.

'And are you convinced now?'

'It's no secret you want to use the IRA against Britain. Ryan was a senior IRA man. We can't have any truck with that as neutrals. If our citizens play any part in the war, on whichever side, they are still subject to Irish law.'

The Abwehr colonel shook his head. It was enough truth to convince him; enough truth to make it impossible to suppress a sneer. He laughed.

'There will be no neutrals in this war, you all know that.'

'Well, when that day comes, I'm sure I'll do my job differently.'

Stefan looked back at the river.

'Someone should tell Frank that María Duarte is dead.'

'I'm sure someone will, Inspector.'

'It wasn't necessary, was it?'

'Nothing to do with us, I can assure you. The Spanish manage their own housekeeping. But there is a price to pay for choosing the wrong side.'

Neither Stefan nor Otto Melsbach noticed the dark van that drove by, heading into the city. At the end of the bridge it turned and stopped in the Calle de Ribera del Puente so that it was facing back the way it had just come.

'Have a safe journey home, Herr Gillespie.'

Oberst Melsbach walked back along the bridge towards the city. As Stefan watched him a taxi approached and stopped. The door opened; he saw Mrs Surtees.

'You look like you're in search of a lift, Mr Gillespie.'

'I appreciate it, Mrs Surtees,' he said, startled, 'but I'd rather walk.'

'You misunderstand me. You really do need a lift. Please get in.'

She wasn't smiling; she was deadly serious.

'Get into the bloody taxi, man!'

Her voice was so commanding that Stefan Gillespie did exactly as she said. He pulled the door shut. The taxi drove off, quickly passing Otto Melsbach.

'It's always awkward dealing with the police in a foreign country,' continued Mrs Surtees, now quite relaxed, 'especially if they don't speak English, and so few do.'

The van that had crossed the bridge passed back unnoticed.

'Mr Kerney wouldn't want you involved under the circumstances.'

'What circumstances?'

Stefan spun round, hearing the rattle of a machine gun behind him. He looked through the back window. Mrs Surtees didn't turn her head.

He saw the van in the middle of the bridge. The back doors were open. A man was firing a machine gun at a body on the cobbles. It was Otto Melsbach's.

'You don't only paint pictures then, Mrs Surtees.'

'Death has an awful intimacy, why not call me Florence?'

'I take it that was for Simon Chillingham?'

'You met him, of course. The powers that be in London decided the Abwehr had overstepped the mark. There is a war on, as they keep telling us, as if somehow we're all about to forget. The Germans can't be allowed to do what they like on the Iberian peninsula, not without consequences.'

She spoke in a faintly scolding way that reminded him of a teacher he once had. He said no more. It was still their war, after all, just about.

'I gather Mr Ryan is no longer a guest of the Spanish government.'

'I have heard that too, Florence.'

'I hope he's in a better place.'

'He could hardly be in a worse.'

'Possibly not. So your business in Spain is done?'

'Yes, it's done.'

It was done, but it wasn't finished.

Part Three

Hibernia Quieta

Turning to the internal situation, Mr de Valera said that the fact that at the moment Ireland was saved from the major consequences of the war should not blind the people to the fact that they were going to be seriously affected by it. No work that could be done by the Government here could shield the community from many of the evil consequences of the war.

Irish Times

23

The Dove

Stefan Gillespie returned to Ireland from Iberia the way he had come. He took the night train from Salamanca to Lisbon and the flying boat from Lisbon to Poole Harbour on the south coast of England. He telegrammed Kate O'Donnell to say he had time to spend a night in London on his way to Holyhead for the mail boat, and he met her outside the underground station at Hammersmith. She shared a rented house with two Irish women working in London, close to the river in Chancellors Street. They called in at the house briefly and then walked down to Hammersmith Bridge and along the Thames towards Chiswick. It was not long since they had seen each other in Dublin, the night before Stefan left for Spain, but it felt longer for them both. Stefan's mind was full of everything that had happened, and even more of what would happen next. Kate had been in England for less than a fortnight, but she had found a place to live and had started a job. They were both preoccupied with things that were not about each other, and were not, in the usual way, about Ireland and home. There was an awkwardness, as if the separation had been one of months not weeks.

As for what Stefan might or might not have learned about

Maeve's death, the question was whether he wanted to talk about it. Kate realized that much had happened, but whether it was to be the subject of conversation she had to leave to him. Instead, as they turned under the bridge into Lower Mall, she spoke about the job a friend of her sister's had pushed her way. She was working for an advertising agency on artwork for Ministry of Information posters and propaganda. She already had a sense of being part of something that was more than just the job itself, a feeling that was everywhere in London now. She pointed out a 'Walls Have Ears' poster in the window of the Blue Anchor and laughed. It wasn't her work, but similar posters soon would be; she had been working on 'Walls Have Ears' designs all week.

It was busy along the river; a bright, clear Saturday with the warmth of spring in the air. People spilled out on to the pavement in front of the Blue Anchor and the Rutland Arms. Stefan was conscious how many men were in uniform; it was something Kate no longer noticed. A fortnight in, she already seemed to belong to this world of rationing and Air Raid Precautions, gas masks and blackout regulations.

The Thames at Hammersmith felt as if it was at the very edge of London, though it wasn't at all. The river was wide here and on the other bank acres of invisible reservoirs meant there was only a line of trees to see behind the towpath, and what felt like emptiness beyond. Kate and Stefan turned into the narrow alleyway that led to the next pub along the river, the Dove. It was as they went into the low, dark bar that her words startled him.

'I met someone you'll know. He's popping in for a drink.'

'Oh, who's that?'

'Alex Sinclair. I bumped into him last week, and he knows you.'

They stood at the bar as Stefan ordered drinks. Kate wasn't sure what the look on his face told her, except that she had said the wrong thing.

'I'm sorry, isn't he someone you'd want to see?'

'It's unexpected, that's all.'

There was a heavy silence as they walked to the back of the pub, out on to the terrace that looked along the Thames to Hammersmith Bridge.

'It's a nice spot.'

'He's only dropping in. I'm sure he won't stay long.'

'It doesn't matter.'

'I can see it does, Stefan.'

'It's unexpected, as I said. So how did you meet Alex?'

'I'm not sure. Someone who knew someone who knew him. There was a party full of dribs and drabs of Irish exiles like me, and someone introduced us. Then the other day he was in the Blue Anchor with Helen. She's one of the girls I share with.' She smiled. 'I was talking about you, as I occasionally, reluctantly do. I found out he knew you, well Maeve, when he was young. And he said he saw you at Christmas in Glendalough. That's it.'

'I see.'

'What does "I see" mean?' She laughed. 'He's pleasant enough.'

'I know he is. I will explain – I will tell you later.'

She watched him more seriously; something really was wrong. At that moment Alex Sinclair appeared, pushing his way through the crowd, a pint in his hand, smiling broadly. He was in the grey-blue of the RAF.

'Good choice, Kate. "Sweet Thames run softly" and all that.'

'Well, I'm only along the road in Hammersmith.'

'Oh, yes.' Alex looked at Stefan. 'So, back from the sunny south.'

'It was more than sunny enough for me.'

'Where were you?'

'Lisbon, Salamanca, Madrid.'

'A proper Cook's Tour?'

'Just carrying our ambassador's bags.'

'What about the famous Missing Postman? Last time we met we were both scouring the mountains for the poor bugger. Was he ever found?'

'No, and I doubt he will be now,' said Stefan.

'And not even a clue as to what happened to him?'

'All the clues lead to a fight in Whelan's Bar in Laragh on Christmas Eve, but with the whole population of the Vale of Glendalough behaving like the three wise monkeys, the last attempt to get anyone into a courtroom ended up in a farce. The Garda commissioner won't want that repeated.'

'It's all died a death then, if you'll excuse the expression.'

'The case stays open, but there isn't a lot left to investigate.'

Alex was not aware Stefan was choosing his words with care, and that in some way he was uncomfortable saying them, but Kate could see it.

They spoke for an hour and the conversation soon moved away from Spain and the mountains of Wicklow to life in London and life at war, and some of the same things Stefan and Kate had already talked about. Under other circumstances Stefan might have felt excluded but he was happy to let Kate and Alex take over the conversation. What he carried in his head, and what it would mean when he returned to Ireland, was hard to handle, sitting across a table from the brother of a man he would soon be questioning about four murders. When Alex found that out, he would know Stefan had lied to him. He wasn't lying, but saying nothing was much the same thing. Whatever Stefan felt, whatever had to be done, he knew what it would mean to Alex. As the pilot finished his drink he turned to Stefan again.

'Spain doing all right now?' he said, more serious for a moment.

'All right's probably about it.'

'You saw the results of the bombing?'

'In Madrid. It was only a few streets, but I saw enough.'

'We haven't had any yet,' said Alex.

'I gather not. All I've read about is fighting in Norway.'

'It's coming, Stefan, whatever they say.'

Stefan felt an odd sense of anticipation in Alex's voice.

'People still keep telling me there'll be peace,' said Kate.

'It doesn't feel like that,' replied Alex, 'not when you're up there.' He glanced up at the sky and then just laughed. 'Still, fingers crossed, eh!'

He got up. He shook Stefan's hand and pecked Kate on the cheek.

'Have fun you two. Don't do anything I wouldn't do!'

And he was gone, disappearing back into the noise of the pub.

'There,' said Kate, 'that really wasn't too bad, was it?'

'It wasn't the greatest thing, Kate.'

'You really can be hard work, Stefan Gillespie!'

'There is a reason. It's not Alex's fault he's the last person I wanted to see. But I very much doubt he'll be wanting to meet for a chat again.'

Leaving the Dove, they carried on along the river towards Chiswick, and Stefan told Kate what he had found out in Spain about Stuart Sinclair. It was a relief to tell someone. The shocking seriousness of it seemed to push away the awkwardness between them. But what he knew was not only the answer he had been searching for, it was also a burden. He didn't want it to be Stuart Sinclair. Kate could see that in his face as he recounted the story.

They returned to the Dove and sat outside again, even though the evening was cool now. They watched the dusk falling over the Thames beyond Hammersmith Bridge and drank more than was entirely good for them.

They went back to the house in Chancellors Street and made love. And Stefan slept well, conscious when he woke that it felt as if he hadn't slept like that in a long time. Later that morning he left Kate at the entrance to the Underground, and began the last part of his journey home.

When Stefan Gillespie disembarked the mail boat at Dún Laoghaire, he saw a car he knew immediately was waiting for him. By it stood Commandant de Paor. Stefan had not forgotten what else he carried back from Spain by way of information, even if it was now Stuart Sinclair and the murders in the Vale of Glendalough, above all Maeve's murder, that were at the front of his mind. Geróid de Paor's presence told him he had other things to do first.

'If you're waiting for me, that's not a bad guess altogether, Geróid, or do you just come here every day to see if I'm on the next mail boat?'

'We did hear you'd left Lisbon.'

'I take it Superintendent Gregory didn't?'

'Colonel Archer thought it would be better for you to talk to us first.'

'Terry won't like that.'

'No, he won't,' de Paor smiled, 'but every cloud has a silver lining.'

'Well, I can tell you, then I can tell him. It doesn't matter to me.'

'What you can tell him may not be everything you tell us.'

'I see. He will know that.'

'I imagine he will. I'm sorry. Every silver lining has its cloud.'

Stefan got into the car. De Paor drove away towards Dublin.

'So, there is something to tell us, Stefan?'

'There's enough.'

'Frank Ryan is out of gaol. We know that.'

'I left Burgos with him. He left Spain in a German plane.

From the north coast, a place called Pendueles. Do you want this blow by blow?'

'In a minute. What I want now is anything else. Anything that tells us why Ryan was released in the first place, where he was going, what the Abwehr is doing.'

'The main thing is that Frank Ryan left Spain with a friend.'

'I see. Someone we know?'

'Oh, you know him. A friend from America, Seán Russell.'

They drove for several minutes in silence. Then Stefan spoke.

'Is that something Superintendent Gregory should know?'

'No, I doubt Colonel Archer will think so.'

'Why not?'

'Things have a way of finding their way out of Special Branch.'

'Won't the IRA know anyway, from the Germans?'

'Maybe, maybe not. We'd rather they didn't know from us. I think we'd prefer other interested parties not know either, mainly the British.'

As they drove on into Dublin, Stefan outlined the events surrounding Frank Ryan's release in more detail. Geróid de Paor took them in and simply listened. When they reached the city he dropped Stefan at Trinity.

'Gregory shouldn't know we've spoken. He may suspect, but that's different. He can send your report to me. That way he won't feel he has to mark his territory. You're his first port of call. There's nothing to leave out, only Russell. You got your train from Pendueles. And you didn't go back.'

Stefan nodded.

'Oh, what about the other thing,' asked de Paor, 'Glendalough?'

'I got some of what I needed. Perhaps I got most of it.'

'Well, that's a considerable result.'

'I don't know. I think I have the truth. What I don't have is evidence.'

Stefan crossed the road into Dame Street and walked to Dublin Castle and the Police Yard. As he walked into Special Branch there was a crowd of detectives round Superintendent Gregory, who seemed to be giving one of those speeches he occasionally indulged in, telling his men what grand fellers they all were. Most of the time he told nobody anything but the bare minimum needed to accomplish a task. As far as information went he was a receiver, but Stefan could see a mood almost of celebration now. Even in the time he had been away the Curragh Camp outside Kildare had been filling up with ever more IRA members and Republican hangers-on; the numbers were the measure of how well Special Branch was working. Stefan was greeted with good humour in an unusually good-humoured office.

'The wanderer returns,' called Terry Gregory. 'Good holiday?'

'Not so bad, sir.'

Dessie MacMahon nodded at him.

'Anyway, with Gillespie back,' continued Gregory, 'we can expect the Curragh to be bursting at the seams before long. Right so, Inspector?'

'Isn't it already, sir?'

'Always room for more.'

The superintendent turned back to his detectives.

'There was a tip off yesterday about Cathal McCallister being in Kilmainham. He was seen in a pub. And a sighting of the Quartermaster brings me to the IRA General Staff and why we haven't pulled more in. I know it's a question that's been asked. Well, the first thing is they're moving about a lot, as you'd expect. But the other thing is that it's not in our interests to lock them all up yet. Some of them are giving us the goods. That's why we know so much about what the Boys are up to. No point arresting people we've spent a long time turning. So bear it in mind. If an IRA leader seems to slip away easy, there may be a reason.'

286

As the other detectives returned to their desks, Dessie hovered, waiting for whatever news Stefan had brought from Spain. But Stefan was looking at Gregory, remembering the night before Christmas when he had seen the superintendent in the Police Yard with McCallister, the IRA Quartermaster. Now he had as good as announced he was an informer.

'All right, Gillespie,' said the superintendent sharply, 'in my office.'

Within minutes Stefan was telling Gregory the story he had told de Paor, ending it the first time he stood on the station platform at Pendueles. It was thorough enough to convince Terry Gregory, because it was more or less what he expected to hear. He assumed, like everyone else, that the IRA and its relationship with Germany was behind the Germans' interest in Frank Ryan, which was true. It was disappointing not to know how that might affect the IRA at home, but Gregory had never anticipated that detail. He was content with the information he had and apologetic that Military Intelligence might want to pore over it all again. Stefan felt, for the first time, that he had the trick of not telling Gregory the truth, and doing it convincingly.

'Write it up. Give the report to me. No one else sees it except for the commissioner. It was all sunshine and cold beers. I don't know if this Ryan business will open up at all, but for now the government wants a lid on it. I'll pass your report to G2. They can deal with the Department of External Affairs. If Archer wants to talk to you, there's nothing you can't say.'

'That's not all there is, sir,' said Stefan. He took several closely written pages from his jacket pocket. 'A conversation I had with a feller called James Collins. Twenty years ago he was Albert Neale, wanted for the murder of Charlotte Moore. You might remember a letter Billy Byrne sent him from Glendalough, about blackmailing the man Collins says really killed her. The

287

man who killed Marian Gort and Maeve too. He may also have killed Billy.'

Superintendent Gregory read the account of the meeting in Alba de Tormes without a word. As he finished he pushed it away slowly.

'Obviously you believe this man, Collins?'

'Yes, he's telling the truth.'

'But you don't know where he is. You can't call him as a witness. In fact, you'll never see him again. No great shakes for making a case, is it Inspector?'

'This was the one time he was going to tell his story. That's why I know it was the truth. It was a confession, a real confession, by a man who was looking for absolution.'

'Absolution? You're a Guard of many talents.'

'I don't think he took much away with him.'

'You do know the blunt reality about this, don't you, Gillespie?'

'It's not worth the paper it's written on.'

'Not unless you produce James-Collins-cum-Albert-Neale in court.'

'Stuart Sinclair doesn't know that, sir.'

'If his people have money, his lawyers will know soon enough. Even if every word's the gospel truth, he only has to keep his mouth shut. A feller who's been running from a noose for twenty years tells you this in Spain, in the middle of fucking nowhere, and promptly disappears. The other two deaths, the Gort woman and your wife, remain accidents. And if there's still no one up for killing Billy Byrne, you won't find a detective on the case, from Halloran down, who doesn't believe he died in Whelan's Bar.'

'But you're not going to stop me questioning Sinclair?'

'He's not the full ten shillings, is that right?'

'Whatever is wrong with him, he's not daft. He knew enough to plant the evidence that would have seen Neale hanged. If he could do that—'

'All right, I'll talk to Ned Broy. He can tell whoever's running the case now. They'll have to know. As far as you can, keep it quiet. Bring him in on your own. If it's going nowhere, drop it. Ned won't want another fucking fiasco. You won't have long. If the man is gaga, don't kick it out of him. Sometimes it's the only way, but it never looks good with halfwits.'

24

Mullacor

Close to the Upper Lake at Glendalough was a dirt road leading up to the Lugduff Brook that flowed from the slopes of Mullacor and Lugduff. It crossed the small river and became a narrow track that climbed Mullacor more steeply, to a low stone house halfway up the glen. The house, named for the mountain, sat on a flat pan of land with a sharp slope behind it. From a distance it looked as if it had been built into the hillside. It was an isolated spot. Mullacor House had started life as a hunting lodge in the eighteenth century. It was a hundred years since one of the Sinclairs decided that the valley where their original family house stood was too closed in and too full of people. He wanted to sit closer to the top of the wide mountains he owned. The hunting lodge was extended, stables and barns added; high and wild as it was, Mullacor became the Sinclairs' home.

The road up from the Vale of Glendalough didn't take long in a car, but as it emerged out of the trees and approached the house, the high slopes were stark and empty. The estate was no longer farmed by the Sinclairs; it was let to others. The family had little to do with the life of the valley. Year by year the money to keep up the house grew less as investments were eaten away by the business of living. The staff were few and growing fewer; only the housekeeper lived in now; the rest cycled up from the valley. Margaret Sinclair, now over sixty, led a solitary life when she was at home. Her husband had been dead for ten years, broken by the estate he could not make pay and could never face selling. His wife's friends were in Dublin and London. Alex, her younger son, was just an occasional visitor. Only her elder son, Stuart, really belonged to the house and the mountain, and he, like his mother, no longer lived there all the time. His absences had been spent over the years not with his friends, as he had none, but in mental institutions the length and breadth of Ireland and Britain.

Stefan Gillespie and Dessie MacMahon drove through the grounds of Mullacor. Stefan had sometimes been close to the house long ago, walking in the hills, but that was all. He didn't know it. But for Maeve, as a girl, it had been a part of every summer when she was staying with her cousins in the Valley of the Seven Churches. Stefan still had a vision of a gang of children with the run of the Vale of Glendalough and no one ever to harm them. It was not so different from some of his own childhood, with Kilranelagh, Keadeen and Baltinglass Hill taking the place of Mullacor and Lugduff. She had always remembered Mullacor House as a happy place, he did recall that, driving towards it, but even when he first knew her she had put a distance between herself and those childhood years. There were no real reasons for that, at least none he ever knew about. It seemed only what time did.

As the two detectives got out of the car there were dogs all round, barking furiously; a Jack Russell, two black Labradors, a cocker spaniel and a mastiff which was, despite its size, the least interested. Dessie was uneasy with dogs in numbers.

'You just ignore them,' said Stefan.

'They'll understand that, will they?' Dessie eyed the mastiff. Stefan walked on to the front door. Sergeant MacMahon followed more tentatively. The dogs crowded round Stefan, sniffing at his legs and finding the scent of Tess at Kilranelagh. Only the Jack Russell followed Dessie, suspicious of any human who didn't smell of some dog or other.

Stefan hammered on the front door as Dessie lit a Sweet Afton.

'Jesus, why would anyone want to live up here, Stevie?'

'There's worse places.' Stefan laughed and knocked hard again. There was no answer. He tried the handle. They stepped inside to a square hall, full of dark, heavy Victorian furniture; black, sombre pictures lined the walls, paintings of the mountains and lakes that surrounded the house, of hunts and dogs and stags at bay. A dark oak staircase led upstairs.

The dogs had followed them in.

'Hello! Anyone at home? Anyone here?'

A door opened under the stairs and a short, elderly woman appeared.

'God save us, you let them dogs in? Do you not know better?' She walked past them, shooing the dogs back outside.

'Mrs Sinclair is out,' said the woman. 'There's no one here now.'

'I'm looking for Mr Sinclair, Mr Stuart Sinclair.'

The woman looked at Stefan with her head slightly tilted to one side, as if she couldn't really think of a reason why anybody would be doing that.

'You may find him in the back garden. Are you from the hospital?'

'No, we're not.'

'You'd be better waiting to see Mrs Sinclair, I'd say.'

'If we could have a word with Mr Sinclair now, that would be grand.'

She frowned and then shrugged; it wasn't her business.

'Go round to the back of the house. You'll see the garden wall.'

She walked to the front door and held it open.

'Well, go if you're going, or we'll have them dogs back in.'

Stefan took a guess at where they were supposed to go and turned a corner around the house. There were trees to the side and back, oaks barely in leaf now and high Scots pines, and between them dense, green, tree-like rhododendrons. The grass by the house was cut, but beyond that it was brown and choked with weeds. There was a wire enclosure of broken, moss-covered tarmac; a sodden piece of netting still sprawled across the centre; it had been a tennis court. With the mountains behind and the darkness of the trees and rhododendrons, it was a tight, closed-in space now. The plantation round the house had crept in, closer and closer, as years of neglect let it take over borders and flower beds and much of the lawn. Behind the house a range of square stone buildings made up a stable courtyard. A Dutch barn was full of mildewed hay. There was a rusting tractor, an array of broken farm implements and carts. From one of the stables came the sound of a horse, but it was the only sign of life except for the continual cawing of the rooks.

Stefan stopped, looking at a motorcycle, clean and bright, in the doorway of one of the outhouses; he remembered the noise of the motorbike at Kilranelagh Graveyard on Christmas Eve. He walked on. Beyond the stables there was a long, rough-rendered wall with a wooden door. He nodded at Dessie. It seemed to be what they were looking for.

They walked through the door in the wall. Inside was something very different from the neglect everywhere else. It was a small walled garden, given over mostly to vegetables; there were rows of them, neatly tilled and free of weeds. Things were just beginning to grow but the green leaves that would soon be rows of potatoes, turnips, cabbages, carrots, kale, beans, peas, were already showing. Against one wall a glass hothouse sloped up at an angle from the ground; inside were espaliers of plums and peaches and cherries, some in blossom. Beyond this, tucked into a corner, was a wooden greenhouse. They could see no one.

They carried on to the greenhouse and went in. It was hot and humid; there were benches full of trays of seedlings, ready for planting out. On one side, where the glass had been whitewashed for shade, there was a hotbed. As Stefan walked by it he stopped, staring down at a bed of thick, dark green leaves, and at the small white flowers emerging from them that were only just beginning to turn into the waxy white trumpets of arum lilies.

Then he saw a man watching him, smiling. A big man, in his mid-thirties, maybe older. He was balding; his features, round and fleshy, were deeply lined.

'Do you like those?' he asked.

'The lilies? Yes, I suppose . . .'

'They don't want it too warm, but I try to get some early ones.'

'You're Mr Sinclair?'

Stuart Sinclair hesitated, as if unused to being addressed like that.

'Did you want my mother?'

'No, we were looking for you.'

'Do I know you?'

He looked harder at Stefan, puzzled, not because he didn't recognize him now, but because he shouldn't be there. He had seen Stefan in Laragh after Christmas, and he had placed him then, easily enough. There was no reason for him to be at Mullacor though.

'You won't remember me. My name is Stefan Gillespie.'

Stefan knew that Stuart realized who he was now, and that he was uneasy.

'You'll remember I married Maeve Joyce, a long time ago.'

Stuart still looked baffled; he didn't like things that didn't fit.

'Yes, it was a long time.'

'Perhaps you remember I'm a policeman. I need to talk to you.'

'Why? Why would you need to talk to me?'

'Because I think you can help us.'

'I don't think I can. Not at all. What would I help you with?'

What Stefan and Dessie could both see now was fear.

'I'm sure you could try, Mr Sinclair.'

'Can you make me? Are you arresting me?'

'Is there a reason we should arrest you?'

Stuart Sinclair shook his head vigorously.

Stefan looked down at the lilies again.

'I've seen these in a few places. The places you put them.'

Stuart frowned, then he shook his head again.

'I need you to come to Dublin with us, Mr Sinclair.'

'I can't. I have work to do. Work to do here. In the garden.'

For almost a minute there was silence. Stuart was trembling.

'I've spoken to Albert Neale, in Spain. You know who Mr Neale is?'

The interview room in the basement of Dublin Castle was a large cell with a table and chairs, almost entirely below ground. The only natural light was from a small, square window close to the ceiling, so dirty that it let in barely any light. The paint on the walls could have been green. The light from the bulb above the table was harsh but didn't reach the room's dark corners. Stefan sat opposite Stuart Sinclair. Dessie sat on a chair a little way back.

'I mentioned Albert Neale before,' said Stefan. 'Did Billy Byrne ever tell you he calls himself Jim Collins now? I was in Spain a week ago, I saw Mr Neale. You'd have a good idea what he would tell me about you.'

Though Stuart Sinclair had said nothing, Stefan spoke as if

he was simply discussing what they had already talked about and agreed on.

'He told me how Charlotte Moore died all those years ago.'

'I don't understand what you mean, Mr Gillespie.'

'Well, I'll go over what I know and you can put me straight.'

'You can't keep me here.'

'This is the statement from the man you knew as Albert Neale. At one time he worked for your father at Mullacor House, I think. But you'll know who it is I'm talking about. Shall we start with his statement so?'

It wasn't a statement of course, simply a story, but as Stefan told that story he had no doubt Sinclair knew every detail and more. Few people can hear the full truth of their actions, face to face, and look as if they have no idea what is being said. Stuart's face, his whole body, could hide nothing. His knowledge of what Stefan was telling him was in every gesture. And he was terrified. But none of it mattered without a confession. He had to admit everything to Stefan. In the quiet, relentless build-up of the detective's words he had to see there was no other choice. It had to feel as if there was nothing that wasn't known. And what Stefan could only imagine about the death of Charlotte Moore had to be hammered home as certainty. There were so many things he didn't know still, that he could only imagine, but he would concentrate on what he did know, saying the same things over and over, sometimes one way and then another way, until Stuart Sinclair saw there was no way out.

Stefan had taken three small lilies from the greenhouse at Mullacor. He had put them on the table in front of him. There were few solid facts; the lilies were solid. He would make Stuart Sinclair feel as if he had seen him place lilies on the memorial to Charlotte Moore and the headstones of Marian Gort and Maeve, and so many times. He wasn't going to beat a confession out of him physically, but in a way, gently, insistently, continually, and relentlessly, as the hours passed, he would beat it out of him mentally. There were times as he looked at the man in front of him, trembling, sometimes sweating, barely answering except to keep saying 'no' over and over again, that Stefan Gillespie felt almost sorry for him.

The story of Charlotte Moore's death was repeated in all the detail Albert Neale, as James Collins, had given. Stefan could see how vividly it brought that day in the woods by the Upper Lake back. That day had marked Stuart's life; it was being relived now in his head. But as Stefan moved on to Marian's death on the Spinc, and Maeve's drowning in the Upper Lake, he was on unsure ground. He didn't know exactly what had happened; he didn't know what had motivated the killings. Some kind of sexual assault had to be behind what was done to Marian. But whether Sinclair had attacked her again, or wanted to stop her revealing the original assault Stefan knew about from George Chisholm, was unclear. He kept to what did seem clear. He focused on the Spinc. He felt he had that right. When he gave Stuart his version of events, an argument, a struggle above the Upper Lake, a push that was too hard, perhaps something unintentional, he stopped shaking his head. He stopped saying 'no'. It was as if he was seeing it all, as if everything Stefan was saying was exactly what had happened.

There could have been no sexual assault when Maeve died. What Stefan believed was that she had found something out. She had discovered the truth about Marian or at least a hint of it. Stuart had revealed it, or confirmed it, or said something that made her suspicious, when she met him by the grave in St John's churchyard. That was what she must have wanted to talk about when they left the Vale of Glendalough. However it came about, Maeve suspected Stuart. Stefan would never know what she heard unless Stuart told him, but it had to be why she died. She had seen into the darkness that he kept hidden away; she had to be silenced.

As Stefan described how he thought Stuart had drowned Maeve, he kept coming back to what he assumed the man in front of him would want him to believe, that these deaths were accidents. That was what, as little more than a boy, he had persuaded Albert Neale to believe about Charlotte Moore. Perhaps it was what he believed himself. The lilies suggested that. They were a peculiarly sentimental gesture for a murderer; and he had kept it up for years. The lilies seemed to speak of a place inside that could not live with what he had done.

Dessie MacMahon said nothing throughout. He smoked and provided Stuart with cigarettes. At times he went out for tea that only he drank. He knew what Stefan was doing, and as a policeman not averse to beating things out of suspects, he still felt uncomfortable. Stefan's determination was a kind of attack; at no point did he let up. His only concession was to tell Stuart that he knew he never meant to harm the women. Apart from that the words kept coming; when they were used up, there were more. Time and again Stuart Sinclair sat with silent tears streaming down his face, shaking, burying his head in his arms, while Stefan Gillespie kept talking, talking, telling him what he had done and how he had done it.

When Stefan came to the death of William Byrne he gave his own version again. He implied that there was far more was in the postman's notes than was true. He made more of the letters to Spain than there was to make, and let Stuart Sinclair infer they were damning proof of guilt. He described the Missing Postman's journey from Laragh on Christmas Eve, drunk, dazed from the brawl in Whelan's. At some point Stuart had found him, whether he stumbled on him or came looking for him, and he took the opportunity to rid himself of the man who was not only blackmailing him but tormenting him. And when Billy Byrne was dead, Stuart had found a way to get him up into the mountains. He hid the body as only he knew how, as he and Albert Neale had once hidden the body of Charlotte Moore.

'This isn't the end, Stuart. It's only the beginning. Unless you tell us everything. All of it. It's not just what I say, or what Albert Neale says, or all the things we know about Marian and Maeve and Billy Byrne. We have that. But we need to put the missing pieces together. You have to give us those pieces. I don't know why you're holding back. It's too late. You don't want it to be like this. Once we know, it can stop. So the sooner you say it all, the sooner we end this. All you have to do is to tell the truth, now. There's no other way.'

As Stefan spoke he pushed the three lilies across the table to touch Stuart Sinclair's trembling hands. Stuart gazed at them with a look somewhere between sorrow and disgust, then he swept them to the floor. He put his head back and let out a sound that wasn't fear, or rage, or self-pity, but all of them somehow. It was like the noise Stefan had heard as a child, when he and his father took cattle into the slaughterhouse in Baltinglass. He had never been convinced that the animals didn't know, didn't smell what was about to happen to them.

Then Stuart Sinclair bowed his head. He crossed himself and looked up at Stefan.

'Yes,' he said, 'everything you said is true. I did kill them.'

25

The Central Asylum

It was two days later that Stefan Gillespie arrived in the Police Yard to find several messages on his desk from Kate O'Donnell. She had been trying to contact him urgently. There was no privacy in the detectives' room and as Superintendent Gregory was out Stefan went into his office. He put a call through to London and waited five minutes to be connected. A woman he did not know answered at the other end; she was expecting the call, and Kate was there almost immediately. He could hear immediately that something was very wrong.

'I'm sorry, Stefan, I had to talk to you.'

'You don't have to be sorry. Are you all right?'

There was silence for some seconds.

'I've been attacked, assaulted, whatever I'm supposed to call it.'

'When?'

'The day after you went back.'

'Are you hurt?'

'No, not . . . I didn't call . . . I had to think. I need to tell you . . .'

'Yes, I understand.'

'You don't understand.' She hesitated. 'It stopped, that's the first thing. In the end he – he didn't – he went. I've a few bruises, that's all. But I don't know what would have happened if Helen hadn't come back. I was on my own at Chancellors Street, there wasn't anyone else at home—'

'So you know him? You know the man?'

'I know him. You do too. It was Alex Sinclair.'

Stefan didn't reply. This would have been a shock at any time. Now it was not only that; the echoes in his head were as disturbing and confusing as the facts.

'Tell me what happened, Kate.'

It was a policeman's question as much as a shocked friend and lover's.

'I'd been working late, so I was coming home – in the blackout. I walked from the Broadway and he was there at the top of the road, in the dark. There's a seat and a little . . . he was waiting. He'd been drinking but he wasn't drunk. He said he was at the Blue Anchor – he thought he'd call. I wasn't easy – I didn't have any reason but . . . I don't know him . . . I thought someone would be here, so I said come and have a cup of tea. It didn't seem so odd.'

She stopped; he could still hear panic in her voice.

'But it was difficult – because I knew about his brother. I didn't know what might have happened – with you back home – if he knew . . .'

'His brother's under arrest now, but he couldn't have known then.'

'It was like when we saw him in the Dove at first, talking in the kitchen, I don't know what about, then he started asking about you and Spain. He made a joke of it – what did you get up to? – did you say more about where you'd been? I couldn't think what to tell him. It was as if he suspected something. Then he was talking about Maeve . . . when he was a boy, how they'd been friends. It was quite ordinary – funny stories – yet it wasn't right. Then he suddenly said, if it wasn't for you she'd still be alive.'

The last words separated themselves from all that went before.

'If it wasn't for me? What the fuck did he mean by that?'

'I don't know, Stefan. How the hell would I know?'

'I'm sorry, Kate, I don't understand what this is. I don't—'

'That's what he said. Then he came very close, saying he'd liked me, as soon as he saw me. He backed me into a corner – trying to kiss . . .'

'Jesus Christ!'

'I pushed him, but he wouldn't move. He was laughing. He said, "You don't want me to stop." I tried to get past – he was too strong – he had my wrist. Then he slapped me. He said, "You do want it, and he's not good enough." He was staring the way I thought . . . I thought he'll kill me.'

There were tears behind Kate's words but her voice was calm now.

'Then I heard the door – and it was Helen. I kicked his shin as hard as I could – and then he just stepped back . . . and he grinned. And he left.'

'I don't know what to say,' said Stefan very quietly.

'It wasn't only about me, Stefan.'

'I know that, Kate, but I don't know what that means.'

'I think you need to find out.'

'That's not as important as you—'

'It's over for me, I promise you. Nothing else happened.'

'Have you been to the police?'

'I won't be telling the police, Stefan.'

'You need to, Kate. You shouldn't have left it.'

'How long are you a Guard?' It was the first time he felt a smile in her voice. 'Don't most women ignore it, even if it's more? And here, now? Isn't he one of their brave boys in blue ready to save us when the Luftwaffe comes? Helen knows a girl who was raped by an Irish Guards officer, a hell of a grand feller everyone says. She went to the police. The sergeant told her she should be careful what she said about a man fighting for his country. But he did give her a bit of advice so. A bit of comfort for a man like that wasn't the worst thing a fucking Paddy bitch could do to help Britain.'

'I don't have an answer for that, Kate.'

'There isn't one, Stefan. I'll mend soon enough. I'll thank God it stopped when it did – and forget it. It means more to you now than me . . .'

The line went dead. The connection was broken. The operator couldn't tell him when there would be another. But Kate had said what he needed to hear. He didn't even see Terry Gregory opening the office door.

'Comfortable there, Inspector?'

Stefan stood up. 'I'm sorry, sir, I had to phone England.'

'Something else you've fucked up?'

'I'm not with you, sir.'

'Are you ever with us, Gillespie? Let me have my desk back and I'll fill you in. You know your man Stuart Sinclair is in the Central Asylum?'

'No, I thought he was still in the cells here.'

'He was trying to hang himself from the bars on the window, when they brought him his tea and jam sandwich this morning. If he'd had anything better than a pair of trousers to use he'd probably be dead.'

'Shite.'

'Shite indeed. And whatever else he did, he didn't kill your man Byrne.'

Stefan was startled by the certainty of it.

'You've seen the confession, sir.'

'Yes, and I'm glad I sat on it before I sent it to the commissioner. It's about to turn into the confession of a madman who wasn't even in Glendalough when our friend the Missing Postman disappeared. You've said he was in your graveyard at Kilranelagh that evening, delivering his Christmas lily?'

'On his motorbike. He had plenty of time to get back.'

'You're right about the motorbike, and probably right he was there, but at seven o'clock that night he drove over the bridge in Aughrim and hit a car going the other way.'

Stefan remembered Alex Sinclair mentioning the accident.

'He wasn't badly hurt, but by the time the doctor patched him up and they got a message to his mammy, he'd spent most of Christmas Eve with the Guards in Aughrim Barracks. His brother picked him up at one a.m., by which time the Missing Postman was well and truly missing. You don't need me to tell you that if death number four is a good, fat, solid lie, then any lawyer will knock the others down like a row of skittles. And if you ask, why did he say it? – well, he's barking mad and some bastard Guard with an obsession about his dead wife wrote it all out and made the eejit sign it.'

'Whether he's mad or as sane as me, nothing I said surprised him.'

'Don't push your sanity, Inspector. If this got to court a good barrister would have a field day proving you need to be in the Central Asylum more than your man does. But it doesn't matter. It won't go near a fecking court now. You'll drop it, and you'll be lucky if that's the end.'

Stuart Sinclair sat on the floor in the corner of a small room with a barred window, in the Central Lunatic Asylum in Dundrum, a leafy suburb of Dublin. He wore a straitjacket, but he was calm. He kept his eyes closed, though he was awake. With him were Stefan and John McEvoy, a doctor.

'He hasn't said anything?' asked Stefan.

'Not since he came in. I don't think he needs the jacket now, but we do have to make absolutely sure he is not going to try to harm himself again.'

Stefan sat down on the bed, not too close.

'Do you feel better here, Stuart?'

Sinclair did not move his eyes from the floor.

'Well, they're people you know, aren't they?'

Sinclair looked round at Stefan, then at McEvoy.

'I want to stay here now, Doctor.'

'You know you can do that, Stuart.'

'My mother was here. And a man. I didn't want to talk to them.'

'There's no need.' Doctor McEvoy smiled amiably.

'Do you remember what you said yesterday?' asked Stefan.

Stuart turned back to him with a barely perceptible nod.

'I thought it was all true, Stuart.'

Sinclair frowned. He was confused but he didn't want to deny it.

'It is true, Mr Gillespie.' He looked at Stefan with an almost childish expression of accusation. 'You said if I signed it there wouldn't be any more questions. I wouldn't have to talk about it. You said it would be over. That's all I wanted. For it to be over.'

'Why did you try to hurt yourself?'

'There were still questions. I didn't want to say any more.'

'Someone said you couldn't have killed Billy Byrne?'

'I did. I signed the paper to say I did.'

'But you were somewhere else when he disappeared.'

'I told you what you wanted, Mr Gillespie.'

'I wanted the truth, Stuart.'

'It doesn't matter about me. That's the truth. Isn't that enough?'

There was agitation in Stuart Sinclair's voice now. His eyes were fixed on the floor but he was shaking, trying to push himself further back into the corner he had already pushed himself into. He shook his head over and over again and muttered unintelligibly. McEvoy touched Stefan's arm and shook his head. It was time to go. Stefan got up. The doctor held the door open for him, and as he walked out he heard Stuart Sinclair beginning to sob.

Stefan walked towards the main doors of the Central Asylum. In his head were the last words Stuart Sinclair had said. It doesn't matter about me. He remembered the housekeeper at Mullacor, two days earlier, before she knew he wanted to speak to Stuart. There's no one here, she said. But there was someone there. When he mentioned Stuart, she told him. He was no one, somehow, even in his own home. He didn't matter. Stefan could not help thinking that there was someone who mattered more, much more; so much more that he had to be protected. Someone who, despite the fact that he was everything his older brother was not and never could be, Stuart had been protecting for twenty years. He had protected him when he was little more than a child himself. He had taken the responsibility for Charlotte Moore's death in Albert Neale's eyes even then. And all those years on, when William Byrne discovered what Neale knew, and used it to worm his way into the secret places in Stuart's head, he had taken the responsibility for two more deaths. He had paid the Missing Postman to keep silent. He had been battered into revealing things to Byrne, but he never revealed the real truth. The confession made no sense unless it was there to protect someone else. What had happened to Kate in London told him who that was. He had heard the echo of what George Chisholm had said, about the night Marian Gort was attacked and raped. The arum lilies were not in expiation of Stuart Sinclair's sins; they were there for his brother's.

Leaving the asylum, he saw a tall, elegant woman in her early sixties walking towards him. Beside her was a shorter man in a dark jacket and pinstriped trousers. He recognized the woman, though he hadn't seen her since Maeve's funeral, and she knew him too, in almost the same instant.

'You have seen my son again.'

'Mrs Sinclair.'

She turned to the man Stefan assumed was her solicitor.

'You told me this would cease.'

'It will, Mrs Sinclair. I will be talking to the Department of Justice.'

'Then find a telephone in the hospital and do it now, Mr Welby.'

'There is a statement, Mrs Sinclair. The police do have legitimate—'

'You're paid to deal with people like this. Please get on with it!'

The solicitor smiled patiently and went on into the hospital.

Stefan Gillespie and Margaret Sinclair looked at one another.

'My son could have died in that cell.'

'From what I understand, I don't think so.'

'You're as complacent as you are unpleasant.'

'No one is indifferent to your son's welfare.'

'I never liked you very much, Mr Gillespie. I didn't like what I heard about you years ago, and I didn't like what I saw when I met you. You didn't belong in the places you insinuated yourself. I knew you were extremely ordinary, but I hadn't realized what a nasty little man you are.'

Stefan ignored her; he tried to talk about what was happening now.

'Do you have any idea why Stuart tried to kill himself?'

'Are you entirely stupid as well? He is frail, very frail mentally. For reasons I can't imagine you bullied him into saying the most despicable things. Do you think it's hard with a man whose mind is broken, to fill it with horrific things, to terrify him until he says anything to make you stop?'

'He didn't say just anything. He said some very specific things.'

'And why? Because you told him to.'

Stefan held her contemptuous gaze.

'I don't understand you, Mr Gillespie. Don't you think my son's illness has been enough of a burden to bear down the years? Surely when you knew Maeve Joyce, you knew something about him, something of what it meant to us all. No family is unaffected by these things. Maeve was a dear girl. She cared about Stuart. What would she think of your behaviour?'

'I'm sorry you see it like that. None of this is easy for me.'

'She would be disgusted. Maeve had no business marrying a man like you. It was a dreadful mistake. Didn't you do enough damage then?'

'Enough damage? What do you mean?'

'I mean the poor girl's life was over, even before she died.'

He saw how deeply Mrs Sinclair felt what she said, how simple it was for her. He could not but hear an echo of what Alex had said to Kate about Maeve.

'I mean the life she should have led was gone.'

'I didn't know there was a life Maeve should have led.'

'You caused more hurt than you knew. She would have found out. But it was too late. At times, I have thought it was almost a blessing in—'

Stefan thought he had heard enough not be shocked.

'You are some woman, Mrs Sinclair.'

'You must hate us, that's all I can imagine. But your superiors will put a stop to this. You won't come out of it well. When this ridiculous business of the postman began, Alex said he saw you. He said he asked you to the house. I'm sure he was only being polite. I was relieved you didn't come. Now Alex has had to come back from England, of course. When Stuart falls into his depressions, Alex is the only one who can handle him.'

Stefan's attention was no longer on what Mrs Sinclair thought.

'Alex is actually doing something, something real, something that matters. But his squadron has been considerate enough to give him a week's leave. He's better out of Ireland, though. This country has been inherited by the begrudgers and the gombeen men. What else is there? My husband believed in it all, poor man, the blood-sacrifice, the glorious future. I can't say I ever did. I knew the dregs would come to the top. And now they have.'

Stefan was in no doubt he was one of the dregs, but Margaret Sinclair's insults interested him only because they told him where Alex was.

'I see. So is Alex in Ireland now?'

'He arrived this morning. He'll be at Mullacor now. I shall take Stuart home soon. I think the lies on your scrap of paper have been disposed of. Knowing his brother is waiting will make all the difference. They love each other. I doubt you're familiar with such depths of feeling. I've always seen through people. And I did tell Maeve what I thought of you.'

'I never have met anyone quite like you, Mrs Sinclair. I only hope I won't again. I don't know who to feel sorriest for, you or your sons.'

It was less than two hours later that Stefan Gillespie pulled up at Mullacor House. He had taken a car from the Special Branch garage without asking. He had no intention of explaining himself to Superintendent Gregory. The dogs raced round from the side of the house and leapt up against the car doors. There was another car, a navy blue MG. It was the kind of car Alex Sinclair would have. Stefan leant across to the glove compartment of the Austin 10 and put the Webley into his jacket pocket. He walked to the front door, ignoring the dogs.

He knocked once and opened the door. As he walked in he could only hear the ticking of a grandfather clock. He crossed the hall and looked into the dining room. The table was huge, running half the length of the room. There were silver candelabra; there were more hunting scenes on the walls; a high gilt mirror reflected the room back at him. It was a room

that had the casual order of a country house, but it felt dead.
No one had sat in it for many years. He walked across the hall
to the drawing room. It was brighter, full of comfortable sofas
and books, yet it had the same smell as the dining room, too
much polish and not enough people. As he moved back into the
hall again he waited for a moment, then called out.

'Is there anybody at home? Alex, are you here?'

'There's no need to shout, Stefan.'

Alex Sinclair stood in the front doorway behind him, the
dogs sniffing about him. He cradled a rifle casually in his arm,
as only a man used to shooting does.

26

Poulanass

'I saw the car coming up,' said Alex Sinclair, walking into the hall. 'I was surprised when you got out of it, Stefan, in the light of what's just happened.'

'In the light of what's just happened, perhaps you shouldn't be.'

'I had to come back, for my mother as well as Stuart. It's irritating, but she can't cope with him at all. God knows the state you left him in. He's harmless, of course, except to himself. All he wants is to be left alone.'

'I did make a mistake about Stuart,' said Stefan softly. 'Probably one I had to make. And I'm not alone. There's a man in Spain who made the same mistake twenty years ago. He almost hanged for it. And somewhere there's the body of a postman who made that mistake too. I don't know if Maeve made the same mistake before she was killed. You'd know, Alex.'

If Alex doubted what Stefan knew, he doubted no longer.

'So did he say something to Maeve, that made her think he—'

'I'm sure he said a lot of things to a lot of people. Has no one told you there is little profit listening to the ramblings of a madman? However much I care for my brother that is, to put it crudely, what he is, old man.'

'But he's not a murderer.'

'Is anyone but you suggesting he is?'

'He knows you are, Alex. He is the one person who knows.'

Alex smiled; he had no doubt of his invulnerability.

'I guess some allowance still has to be made for the loss of your wife, but isn't it all a stretch, unless you have a complaint – of the Stuart variety.'

'I don't think Kate O'Donnell's mad, do you?'

'Not at all, but she certainly is a piece of action worth having.'

'Were you going to rape her too? I assume that's what happened with Charlotte Moore when you were a teenager, and later with Marian Gort.'

'What a grubby turn of phrase you have, Gillespie. Do they teach you that in the police? Sorry, old man, but your lovely lady was asking for it, and I mean asking. Don't imagine you're the only man she wanted it from. That's not how women are. But she panicked at the close. They do. It did get a little rough, but isn't she the kind of woman who likes a bit of that?'

He spoke with calm assurance; he believed what he said.

'You didn't meet Kate by chance, did you?' said Stefan.

'Not quite. When you started poking around at Christmas, I did find out what I could about you. I found out who your tart was, and when I learned she was coming to London, well, our Irish Mafia is small, within a respectable class. She knows some quite decent people. It wasn't difficult.'

'But why? What was the point?'

'Keeping an eye on you. I got a whiff of this trip to Spain. That was a surprise, I have to say. And ambassador or no ambassador, I couldn't believe a bloody-minded feller like you wouldn't follow his leads – apt word, for policemen and dogs. Following the scent of Billy Byrne's trail.'

'You knew all about Byrne from Stuart.'

'Of course, sooner or later he does tell me everything.'

'The brakes on the car – you tried to kill me first.'

'No need to be overdramatic. I was still home when you began stirring up the past. I hoped a warning would be enough. You've got people to think about, your brat, etc. I thought you just might see sense and leave things alone. Leaving things alone is usually the answer. But you were never welcome here. There are people who belong. You never did.'

'Yes, I heard that from your mother.'

'Maeve belonged here in more than one sense. In every sense.'

As Stefan looked at Alex he could see pain in his face.

'Jesus, you mean – she should have belonged to you?'

'I don't owe you any explanation. I know exactly who I am. I know how life is to be lived. It's nothing unless lived at the edge. The moment is more than the before or after. "The years to come seemed waste of breath, A waste of breath the years behind. In balance with this life, this death." You know the words? If you do, how could you even understand them?'

Stefan knew; from Alex they were the words of a precocious boy.

'You're a very ordinary man, Gillespie.'

'I have no problem being an ordinary man.'

'That's what's wrong with you. It's what's wrong with everything. To be ordinary is to be nothing, one of millions and millions of nobodies.'

'I'm not sure you're fighting on the right side in this war, Alex.'

'The sides don't matter. Being in it matters.'

'This shite isn't why I'm here, Alex. You know why I'm here.'

'There's nothing you can do, old man, you must realize that. Even if everything you think you know is true, everything I did, every little mistake I made, no one's going to believe you. A policeman who forced a mental case to confess to other people's murders and say he killed two women who died in tragic accidents? My brother will never speak against me. I have to give you some credit for tedious persistence, but in the end it's worthless.'

Stefan didn't reply. It was true; what he had was only in his head.

'You could shoot me, something like that, if you had the guts.'

Stefan was holding the revolver in his pocket.

'I can't say it's not in my mind, Alex.'

'You've a bit more about you than I expected. Not much, but a little.'

'Do you really think this is over?' said Stefan.

'Yes, I do, because it is. You'll have to leave it to the Luftwaffe.'

'I have a feeling you're a survivor, Alex.'

'Yes, I rather think I am. Goodbye, Stefan. It's finished now.'

The front door of Mullacor House closed shut. Stefan got into the car, not knowing what he could do. It wasn't the end, whatever Alex Sinclair believed, but what the end was, he couldn't know. He wanted to believe he could use the gun he carried, if not now, eventually. But even if Alex hadn't had a rifle, could he have simply taken out the revolver and killed him there and then? There was a part of him that said he had a right to, but there was too much that told him he didn't. Yet what else was there? He turned the ignition. Nothing happened. He tried again. It was dead. He got out and pushed up the bonnet. He saw that the distributor cap was off; the rotor arm was gone. He knew that Alex had taken it, and that he could have only one reason. He did not intend to let him leave Mullacor. Stefan recalled the rifle Alex had almost been caressing. He heard his final words: 'It's finished now.'

Behind the car was the drive and the track to the road. Beyond the gates there were straggling trees and half a mile of grass and heather. In front was the house and its outbuildings; Alex Sinclair knew that like the back of his hand. Stefan looked at the dark rhododendrons framing the lawn at the side of the house. It was all there was. He had already stood still too long. He ran, zigzagging over the grass, through the torn wire of the tennis court, out the other side into the trees. A shot sounded, very close. He heard the bullet thud into a tree. He moved into the rhododendrons, crawling. He stopped and took out his revolver. Looking back, he could see no sign of Alex. Another shot. He felt the bullet sing past him. He guessed where it had come from. He fired. But he saw nothing to shoot at; a wasted bullet.

He pushed the gun into his pocket and half crouched, half crawled further into the trees. A third shot, to his left this time. Alex Sinclair knew where he was. He was a man who had hunted all his life; he had stalked deer since childhood. Another bullet whined past, this time to the right. Stefan crawled on, sheltered by the thick green of the rhododendrons and azaleas. But he knew he wasn't taking his own course. Those shots, left and right, closer and closer, had nothing random about them. He was being driven in the direction Alex wanted him to go. He knew if he broke cover he would be dead. He was being stalked. He was being pushed through the trees. Two more shots in quick succession made it clear.

As he broke through the undergrowth that once marked the boundary of the demesne at Mullacor, there was a stone wall; beyond that a thistle-strewn field and then the rough grazing that soon gave way to the mountain slopes of Lugduff.

Ahead there were only ancient Scots pines and oaks and the tumbled stones of the broken-toothed wall. Sheep netting stretched along the demesne side of the wall. Beyond, in the field, there were a few small trees and a line of sprawling, unkempt gorse. The gorse was high in places, but once past that there was only the hillside; pale grass and the purple of new heather. He turned back into the trees. At least there was cover. In the open he had no chance against a rifle. But two shots rang out, only yards away, one biting the flesh out of a Scots pine. Alex was invisible behind him but the slightest movement in the undergrowth was enough to show where Stefan was. Back into the gardens wasn't the way he was meant to go. He was being pushed over the wall, into the mountains. He had no choice but to go. Alex Sinclair was not trying to kill him, not yet; he had to take whatever moments he had left.

Now he was at the broken wall. He was sure he couldn't be seen but once he was out on the hillside he could be picked off when Alex chose, without ever coming near enough to be at risk from the revolver. 'When he chose.' The words sounded in Stefan's head. Disappearance was what this was about. Hadn't it worked with Charlotte Moore and William Byrne? A bullet in a Garda inspector would take some explaining, but if he was never found, what did it matter? Yet he felt there was more to it. He could see the smile on Alex Sinclair's face as he left Mullacor. It was a game. There was pleasure in it. The end was inevitable, but Alex was taking his time. Whatever that time was, Stefan knew the fact he was being played with was all he had. He had to go another way to the way his pursuer was trying to make him go. He had to move down the mountain and not up it. He had to make Alex come closer.

He stepped over the sagging sheep netting and huddled in a gap in the wall that ran in a curved line between the trees of Mullacor's demesne and the rough grazing beyond. There was cover between the wall and the gorse beside it. He inched forward, looking out at the hillside. He knew this place. He had been here before. Then he remembered the time he walked in Glendalough with Maeve, before they were married, when they had only known each other a matter of weeks. They came here, following the Lugduff Brook from the Upper Lake. He remembered her talking about the house beyond the trees and her friends there. Somewhere near here they turned back, through the narrow gorge the brook had cut through the rock.

They stopped by the waterfall at Poulanass and ate a picnic. He saw the beer they put into the water below the fall to cool. He listened. There was something he heard, a low hum. The waterfall. He remembered the wooded valley. It wasn't very far away.

That was the way he had to go.

Following the wall, with the gorse on one side, he would be hard to see. Further along he knew the hill sloped steeply down to the gorge of the Lugduff Brook. If he could get far enough ahead he might make it to the trees. A shot rang out to his left as he looked along the wall. It was there to keep him on track, to keep him going right, across towards the slopes of Lugduff. Alex felt in control. He was confident Stefan was going the right way. At some point his quarry would have to break cover; all he had to do was keep driving him uphill.

Stefan ran, crouching low, keeping the wall tight on his left. The gorse was hard up against the stones, scratching and tearing at him. He was going uphill, just as Alex Sinclair expected, but soon the land to the left would drop away abruptly. The wall seemed to peter out ahead, close to a clump of Scots pines; that was where he had to turn the other way.

He would have to run for his life down that slope, hoping that by the time Alex had him in sight again he would be close enough to the gorge itself to make the trees.

There was another noise along with the sound of the waterfall. He saw another wall. It was the same dry stone that ran round Mullacor House, but there was nothing broken-down about this. The noise was sheep, a lot of sheep, packed together. The wall was one side of a sheep pen, where the hill shepherds brought their flocks for feeding in winter and for whatever else in the way of lambing and drenching and foot-trimming and shearing through the year. The hope of finding people there was soon gone. When Stefan reached the pen there were several hundred sheep, eating the dregs of last summer's hay. As he looked over the wall two shots sounded in quick succession to his left. Alex Sinclair had seen him now. He was driving him again, right, up towards Lugduff. Stefan threw himself over into the pen.

The ewes bleated more noisily, gazing round at him, but the sheep were his allies. There were two gates to the pen, one giving on to the slope up from Mullacor across to Lugduff, the other, in the opposite wall, opening down towards the Lugduff Brook itself. Stefan ran to the second gate and pushed it open, then launched himself back at the ewes, careering through them shouting, 'Go on, go on, you bastards!' He didn't need to hide his presence. Alex knew where he was, but there was a wall and there was distance and there was confusion.

As Stefan drove them across the pen, the ewes burst through the gate and streamed down the slope towards the trees that marked the gorge of the mountain brook. And Stefan was with them, driving them on. He tore down the hill, scrambling as fast as he could, stooping and zigzagging, the sheep all round him. He wasn't impossible to pick off, but with speed and the melee of dirty-grey bodies, it wasn't the kind of shot even the most practised stalker would make easily. Alex Sinclair would be running to catch up now because Stefan had gone the wrong way after all. He would be breathless, shaking, angry, because the simple process of driving a man where he wanted him to go with a rifle, had failed.

There was a shot. It was close, but not as close as before. It missed, but the next might not; the game would be over. Stefan reached an outcrop of rock; the gorge was near.

The sheep knew their mountain; they scattered away left and right, aware of another wall ahead of them. Stefan leapt off the rocky outcrop; for an instant he was a sitting target there. He fell heavily and rolled downhill, hitting the stone wall at the bottom. He clambered over it, tearing his legs on the barbed wire along the top. The noise of the waterfall was a loud rumble now. It was close. And there were trees and bushes, not thick, but new cover.

The gorge cut by the Lugduff Brook was narrow. There was no forest to disappear into, but as Stefan scrambled down to the river at the bottom the trees were thicker. He couldn't know what his hunter would do; he had to make a guess. Alex was nearer. He would know roughly where Stefan went into the trees. He would also know the only way of escape was down. He would work out Stefan's plan because it was the only obvious plan. Down was where there were farms, roads, people. So Alex Sinclair would go further down than his quarry, then work his way back up to meet him, or simply lie in wait. And it was because the only escape was down, down towards the Upper Lake, that Stefan turned the other way and went up, back towards the mountainside he had left. He could not do what Alex could do and kill at a distance, but he did have a gun.

The odds were in the hunter's favour; he still knew this place far better than Stefan. But Stefan could wait too. There were trees, rocks, small cliffs, cracks in the walls of the gorge. If he could make Alex come close, he had a chance.

Stefan walked along the bank of the stream, keeping as far as he could from the water's edge, where his footprints would show. He threaded his way through the thinly leaved beeches, alders and hazels. He moved slowly in order to make as little sound as possible and to avoid anything that might give him away. A few pigeons bursting up from the trees would be enough to tell Alex where he was, and which way he was going. But his leg was slowing him now. He could feel the pain pulsing in his left ankle; the leap off the rock had done damage there. It would make running hard, but running wasn't going to save him.

The rumble of the waterfall had become a roar. Stefan turned a bend in the gorge to see water cascading from a high, black overhang. The sun was shining. Poulanass sparkled as it

319

had sparkled many years before. He spun round as a flock of pigeons flew over the gorge some way behind him. They had been disturbed. The hunter wasn't waiting. He was working his way up the brook to find him. Stefan was looking for somewhere to hide. It had to be a place Alex could miss, or tight enough, narrow enough, dark enough that the odds between rifle and revolver would even. Stefan had five bullets; Alex Sinclair would have a lot more.

Above him there was a ledge, to one side of the waterfall. If he could get up there he would see his pursuer coming. It was narrow. He wouldn't be completely invisible from below, but he decided to try. If Alex Sinclair was working up the gorge, there was little time.

He crossed the stream and reached the rock wall, but as he began to climb his ankle gave way. Pain shot through him. It wouldn't work. He might get halfway, but the last few yards would take real climbing. If his ankle gave then he would fall. He stared at the waterfall. He would have to keep going. He would have to climb the track to find another place to hide, and it would need to be on a gentler slope.

He felt the spray on his face. And then he saw the place.

Alex would have to come this way. It was the narrowest part of the gorge.

Stefan was standing on a stone in the middle of the brook, gazing at the Poulanass Waterfall, when he heard a noise. He reached for the Webley, then stopped. A small stag was at the water's edge behind him, drinking. It had the black coat and white rump of the Sika deer that lived in the mountains. He had been standing so still that it hadn't seen him. It looked up. He didn't move. It stared a moment before walking slowly back into the trees.

He stepped straight into the water. There was a pool at the base of the fall. The water was deeper here. He was up to his thighs. The spray was heavier. He was soaking. He took the revolver and wrapped his jacket round it, then held the package to his chest. He stepped through the waterfall. Poulanass beat down on him, then the pool was shallower, the battering flow a trickle. The black rock-face sloped slightly outwards. He was still up to his knees in water as he pushed his back against the rock. The curtain of water was only feet away but in the dark he was invisible. He crouched over the package clasped to his chest. He waited, staring at the cascading water. As his eyes adjusted he found he could see. He could make out trees, rock, branches in the breeze. The water was very cold, but at least it numbed his ankle.

He stood behind the waterfall for what seemed a long time, growing colder. He had only thought about survival since running from the car outside Mullacor House. Now those thoughts were harder. Now he had time to think about other things. He tried to drive them out, especially thoughts about Tom. They didn't help here. Only what happened next could help. The cold was biting into him. He couldn't escape it. And he was shivering almost uncontrollably. The numbness was spreading up from his legs. Although he could see beyond the wall of water, he could hear nothing but the roar of Poulanass. He wasn't sure how long he could stand there. Could he wait until night? Darkness would come. Alex Sinclair would not leave until then; but even after nightfall he would be waiting for him somewhere.

There was a rifle shot. Something had made Alex shoot; he wouldn't give himself away so casually. Stefan thought of the stag by the pool. It would be enough, moving among the trees. It told him Alex was close but it also said he was on edge. He stepped forward slightly and almost fell. He rocked back and forward, pushing the blood back into his limbs. He gazed out through the curtain of water. The shot had been close, very close.

The sun was still shining. He could see movement across the pool, through the cascade, the shape of a man. He would let him pass. Alex would take the track up the side of the gorge. In a few minutes Stefan would be behind him. He had to make a choice. Did he try to escape, knowing his pursuer would follow the gorge uphill for a time, or did he go after him and try to end it? His ankle would slow him if he ran. And Alex would soon come back.

Stefan stayed where he was for a few minutes more. The cold was biting, the numbness returning; it killed the pain in his ankle but froze his limbs. He could wait no longer. He stepped out through the monsoon of water. As he reached the edge he fell. He made no sound, but the pain was fierce. The choice was made: to face Alex Sinclair.

He looked up at the track his pursuer had just taken. Alex would not know he wasn't ahead of him, yet. Stefan had to get closer, into the narrowness of the gorge, and take him from behind. Alex was moving slowly; he could catch him. He unfolded the jacket that held the revolver. He took out the gun and opened the barrel. It seemed dry but he couldn't know for certain. He closed the chamber. Something made him look up; a shadow, a sound. He saw Alex above him, close to the top of the waterfall. His back was to Stefan but he was retracing his steps, searching for what he realized he had missed. He knew Stefan had slipped past.

Then Alex Sinclair looked down. He saw Stefan Gillespie below. He smiled. There was no urgency now. He had his quarry. It was the only thought in his head as he raised the rifle. At the same moment, holding the Webley in both hands, Stefan fired. Five shots, one after another. Perhaps Alex had forgotten the revolver; perhaps he simply had his superiority in this stalk so firmly in his head that it didn't occur to him to worry about it. But a bullet hit him, the second or the third, faster than a rifle could fire. The one bullet Alex fired off shot into the air.

The rifle tumbled over the edge of the rock, down to the pool below.

Stefan's ammunition was gone. That was it. He peered at the black rock and the falling water above him. He could see nothing. Alex was no longer there.

He started up the path at the side of Poulanass, carrying the revolver by the barrel; it was some kind of weapon. At the top he saw his pursuer, lying on his back above the waterfall. His eyes were open. Stefan crouched beside him. He thought Alex could see him. The look on the dying man's face was odd. All Stefan could register was an expression of faint surprise. Probably it was not much more. Even in his last moment Alex Sinclair was puzzled that he could not do whatever he wanted; it wasn't how it should be. Briefly the two men looked into each other's eyes. Then Alex Sinclair was dead. Now it was finished.

27

Keadeen

At Dublin Castle there was a degree of satisfaction. The previous evening, coming home from Mass to a safe house in Kilmainham, the IRA Quartermaster, Cathal McCallister, had been approached by two men on bicycles. They produced revolvers and shot him several times. Although the killers had nothing to do with Special Branch, 'theirs not ours' as Superintendent Gregory put it, a senior member of the Army Council was ticked off the list and out of action. The fact that Terry Gregory had, not long ago, implied that McCallister was providing him with information didn't count for much; double-agents were the necessary currency of the business they were in, but a traitor, on either side, was a traitor.

The news greeted Stefan as he arrived at work. He had not gone straight back to Dublin Castle after Glendalough. He left Alex Sinclair's body where it fell at Poulanass and returned to Wellington Quay. He spent the night wondering what he was supposed to do. He reached no conclusion. Now he sat in Terry Gregory's office and explained. Gregory's expression was the same as ever, simultaneously intrigued, amused, irritated, and unsurprised.

'A fucking mess, Inspector.'

'Yes, sir.'

'You left him where he was?'

'At the top of the waterfall.'

'Very picturesque.'

'There wasn't much else I could do.'

'You weren't daft enough to tell the Guards in Laragh?'

It wasn't the response Stefan expected.

'They must be looking for him by now,' said Gregory. 'Will they find him? We won't have a Missing Airman to join the Missing Postman?'

'It's not far from Mullacor House. He'll be found.'

The superintendent took a cigarette and lit it.

'Who saw you?'

'I don't know. There was no one at the house.'

'You got the car started?'

'He had the rotor arm in his pocket.'

'On the road?'

'I passed a couple of cars, a tractor.'

'What about here? The leg?'

'I said I fell on the stairs.'

'You're a better liar than you were, Inspector.'

'I know it's all true, sir. Alex Sinclair didn't even deny it.'

'That doesn't matter. You can't prove a thing.'

'No.'

'Go back to Baltinglass. You're due leave after the trip to Spain. Say nothing.'

'Nothing?'

'You know how to say nothing, Gillespie, I know that.'

Stefan could not quite believe Gregory thought it was this simple.

'The other options aren't attractive. Your word against a dead man who apparently never did a wrong thing in his life. You've fucked up accusing his brother. Who's your witnesses – Billy Byrne, Albert Neale?'

'And when they find him, sir?'

'Wasn't your man up there shooting? Hunting accidents happen.'

'And if there's a post-mortem, and the bullet that killed him—'

'You can sit on anything if you keep it simple. A British serviceman and Irish landowner gets himself shot by an unknown pistol in the mountains. Special Branch is not the place you'd be looking for the gun.'

Terry Gregory got up. He took a shoulder holster on his desk and put it on. He pushed a revolver into the holster and then pulled on his jacket.

'Go home. Get rid of it.' He tapped his head. 'I'll walk up to Kingsbridge with you. I've got to go across and see Ned Broy.'

'About this?'

'Jesus, he won't want to know about this! There's an Emergency!'

Detective Inspector Gillespie and Detective Superintendent Gregory walked along the Quays towards Kingsbridge Station. Stefan was using a stick, but the ankle wasn't badly hurt. For a while they walked in silence. Stefan had expected something very different. He knew the consequences of Alex Sinclair's death could have seen him in court; he knew that his job and his liberty were at risk. There was only his word that Sinclair had been trying to kill him. And now it was over. He had to act as if nothing had happened.

'You're a hard man to satisfy, Gillespie,' said Gregory eventually. 'You look like you're desperate to be sacked or hauled away into court.'

'It's hard to shut the door on it, any of it, maybe that's all it is.'

'I can understand that. It's the way it needs to be. Not just for you.'

Stefan didn't know what he meant. 'The Sinclairs?'

'I don't know about them. I mean your own family, your wife's family. What happens when they all find out she was murdered? What do they do with that? She's got a mother, a father, brothers and sisters?'

Stefan nodded.

'And she has a son,' continued the superintendent. 'Is that what you want him to carry through life with him? I wouldn't want it for my lad.'

Stefan took this in. They walked on.

'Do we trust each other enough to clear the air, Stefan?'

'How do you mean, sir?'

'Christmas, the Magazine Fort. I know you saw something, before. I don't know how much, but something. You saw who was in the yard.'

'Cathal McCallister, yes.'

'Well, you had the sense to leave that alone.'

'Did I have a choice?'

'You did, and you made the right one.'

'It makes no odds now he's dead, does it?'

'What do you think my job is, Inspector?'

'I'm not always sure, sir.'

'It's not to keep an eye on the Boys in Sinn Féin and the IRA and make sure they don't get too many guns, or do bed and breakfast for too many German agents, or shoot more than a few Guards, or blow up anything that matters. I'm here so they mean fuck all to anything going on in this country. To make them as much of a threat as the fellers in *Oh, Mr Porter!* And with half of them in the Curragh now, I'm well on my way.'

They crossed the road towards Kingsbridge Station.

'Before the arms' raid Leinster House was full of bleeding hearts who didn't want any IRA men arrested, not till the feckers killed someone important maybe. Then they got the wind up. Now they couldn't care less.'

'So you set it up?'

'No, Hayes and his Army Council don't need me to come up with daft ideas. But I helped them along the way. I used McCallister to do it.'

'Is that why the IRA shot him?'

'I imagine they shot him for giving me information.'

'And when you told us all he was feeding you information, what was that? If the IRA have someone in Special Branch, it was a death sentence.'

'You think they do? Have someone inside?'

'I've heard it said.'

'By who?'

Stefan didn't reply; Terry Gregory grinned.

'The reason I left the IRA General Staff out there is because they're incompetent gobshites. Stephen Hayes doesn't know what time of day it is unless the pubs are open. And the less they trust each other, the more they squabble and fight, the easier our job will be. Why would I lock them up?'

They stopped outside the railway station.

'I didn't know they'd kill Cathal, but it's the business he was in.'

'Isn't it the business we're all in,' said Stefan, 'the family business?'

'You shot a man yesterday.'

'A man who was trying to kill me.'

'Is that all? There wasn't any more?'

Stefan couldn't answer that as easily as he wanted to.

'There's always more,' said Superintendent Gregory, 'don't think there isn't. And there endeth the first and last lesson. I know you're a bit of a reader, unlike me, so you will understand it when I say, the rest is bollocks.'

For a moment Stefan watched Terry Gregory walk away. It all sounded like the truth. It probably was the truth. But something in his boss's face, in the bland impenetrability of his smile, suggested that if you didn't much like that truth, or if circumstances changed, he had other truths.

Two days later Stefan and Tom sat on the long ridge of Keadeen Mountain, looking west to the flat lands of Carlow and Kildare below. It was a clear day; they could see a long way. They had climbed all morning and ate their picnic halfway along the ridge. At first they talked of what was below, starting with the tiny buildings of Tom's school at Talbotstown and the line of the Slaney River, moving west and south past places Stefan could identify, until all that remained was the rest of Ireland.

It was a long time since the earth beneath Stefan had felt so solid. And then he spoke of Maeve and a day, when Tom was still inside her, when they had taken the same climb up Keadeen and sat close to the same place, talking about the name they would give their child. More stories followed, easier, happier stories than Stefan had told his son before. He was conscious how close he had kept those things to himself; he could see how much it mattered to Tom that he shared them now, not because he had to, but because he wanted to. In sharing her with Tom, Stefan was finding his own way back to the woman he had loved so much, away from the body by the Upper Lake that had filled his mind again. Finding his way back to her; finally letting her go.

When father and son walked back along Keadeen, home to help David Gillespie with the afternoon milking, Tom raced ahead, his arms outstretched. A low buzz sounded as he ran, broken by the staccato that was his fighter's machine gun. He gave no thought to whether his plane was Luftwaffe or RAF; he was flying. Stefan came behind him, rehearsing in his head the letter he would write to Kate that evening. It hadn't been easy to decide what to tell her; in the end he knew it must be the truth, all of it. It wasn't only that he owed her the truth after she had been dragged so brutally into his past; it was the place they needed to be, to begin again.

28

53°N 10°W

Sea Area Shannon, August 1940

The U-boat had surfaced at dawn. It sat in a quiet sea-swell on the edge of the Atlantic, thirty miles from the west coast of Ireland. A wet mist cloaked the entrance to Galway Bay, but the low hills of the Aran Islands, rising out of the sea only a few miles away, were sharp in the morning light. Four seamen stood on U-65's deck, smoking; rifles were slung on their shoulders. Below the conning tower, the Oberbootsmann crouched over an irregular, lumpy piece of sacking, draping it in the red and black flag of the Kriegsmarine. The roughly sewn bag was about the size of a man. It contained the body of Seán Russell, exiled Chief of Staff of the Irish Republican Army, along with iron ballast to carry him into the darkness.

'Der Kapitän!' snapped the bosun, standing to attention.

The seamen took the rifles and formed a line behind the body.

Kapitänleutnant Hans-Gerrit von Stockhausen was followed by another Irishman. Frank Ryan was the only mourner. He stared down at the flag and the sacking bag. A thin, rolled cigarette stuck to his lips; the leather overcoat he wore dwarfed him. As von Stockhausen spoke to the Oberbootsmann, Ryan pulled the flag from Seán Russell's shroud. The bosun looked indignant, but von Stockhausen only turned and smiled.

'We don't carry a tricolour, Herr Ryan.'

'Take it as you like, I don't think he wants a swastika to see him off.'

Von Stockhausen shrugged. 'Well, as an Irishman, at least he has a choice in that.' He nodded to the bosun who stepped forward, still disgruntled, and took the flag, making a point of carefully refolding it.

U-65 had left the Wilhelmshaven U-boat pens five days earlier. It travelled north of Scotland and down to Ireland's west coast. This was the day Seán Russell and Frank Ryan were to land on Irish soil. Ashore, IRA men had been waiting for them all night. But they wouldn't come; there would be no landing. Seán Russell became ill barely a day out of Wilhelmshaven. It started with the stomach pains his ulcers had long inured him to, but the pains intensified as the journey continued. There was no doctor; the medical orderly could only offer painkillers that seemed to make things worse and, as the agony became constant and unbearable, give him as much morphine as he could without killing him. It might as well have killed him. By day three everyone on the U-boat knew Russell was dying.

Frank Ryan stayed with Seán Russell day and night. The two men had never been friends, and they no longer trusted one another as once they had. But during the time in Berlin they were bound together not by the fight for their country, which they had once fought together, but only by their love of it.

For Russell, Germany and the Nazis were a way finally to free Ireland and unite it; for Ryan, who spoke little and fell back continually on how hard of hearing he had become, and how bad his German was, there was not only an Old Enemy now, but a new one he could not embrace as Ireland's saviour. They chose not to discuss what divided them. Seán Russell chose not to betray his doubts about Ryan to the Abwehr handlers.

For the last twenty-four hours Seán Russell drifted in and out of a fitful, nightmarish sleep. When the pain cut through both morphine and unconsciousness his screams filled the U-boat's tin-can hull. He stared into Frank Ryan's eyes as he roared in agony; each time he became conscious he held his comrade's hand so tightly that even as Ryan stood on the deck, gazing down at the shroud, he could still feel Russell's despairing grip.

Kapitänleutnant von Stockhausen held up a small book and read. 'Das Volk das in Finstern wandelt, sieht ein grosses Licht; und über die da wohnen in finstern Lande, scheint es hell.' He looked at Ryan. 'Isaiah.'

Frank Ryan nodded and repeated the verse he knew so well.

'The people that walked in darkness have seen a great light: they that dwell in the land of the shadow of death, upon them hath the light shined.'

Moments later the four seamen raised their rifles and fired. Frank Ryan and the bosun pushed Seán Russell's body to the side of the hull. It slid down into the grey Irish waters with hardly a sound. And it was gone.

The Oberbootsmann and the sailors went below.

'My orders are that I can't land you, Herr Ryan. Back to Germany.'

'I know. I could only be trusted with Seán to watch over me.'

Von Stockhausen shrugged; the reasons were not his business.

Frank Ryan looked out over the sea to the Aran Islands.

'Árainn Mhór, Inis Meáin, Inis Thia. I know people there.' He corrected himself. 'I knew people there. You could almost swim it.'

'Few men could swim it. One dead Irishman is all I can afford.'

Ryan didn't move; his eyes were still fixed on the islands.

'Not long, my friend. Only a few Spitfires stand between Germany and England. The Spitfires won't stop it. The numbers are overwhelming.'

'So I hear,' said Ryan, finally turning away from the land.

'Then you'll have your country, all of it, a gift from us. If there are still people there you don't like, we'll give you the camps to put them in.'

'Perhaps we won't need those, Captain.'

'No enemies, Herr Ryan? What would we all believe in then?'

The smile was wry enough, but there was no doubt about what Frank Ryan had to do. Von Stockhausen's hand did not move closer to the pistol in the webbing holster at his side, but he had undone the clip that held it. The Irishman did not look back again. He climbed down into the hull of the U-boat. The captain followed him. The last hatch closed. U-65 dived. It slipped into the darkness of the Atlantic, and soon even its wake was gone.

Acknowledgements

The story of Larry Griffin, the real Missing Postman, from Stradbally, Co. Waterford, is told in Fachtna Ó Drisceoil's *The Missing Postman*; not only a wonderful piece of historical detective work but a recreation of an Irish community in the 1920s, where life was far more complex than fiction. Many books have left the Spanish Civil War in my head, starting as a teenager with George Orwell's *Homage to Catalonia*, but the particular atmosphere of Burgos and its prison owes much to Ruiz Vilaplana's *Burgos Justice* (1938). Vilaplana was a magistrate at the time of the Nationalist rebellion; he was a participant in the 'cleansing' of Republicans from Burgos; he was also a constant visitor to the prison. Vilaplana fled Nationalist Spain eventually, but his description of events has a rawness no historical retelling captures. There is an online account by Leopold Kerney of Frank Ryan's release to German Military Intelligence, leopoldkerney.com; variant details (and they do vary) are available in *Documents on Irish Foreign Policy 1939–1941*. The encyclopaedic *Thom's Directory* provided precise information on Dublin and its streets in 1939 and 1940. The *Irish Times* archive offered its inspirational mix of the international, national and defiantly 'parish pump'. Macmillan's period guide to Spain and Portugal allowed me to travel through time between Lisbon and Pendueles, via Salamanca and Burgos. Most of Micheál Mac Liammóir's words on the closure of *Roly Poly* at the Gate are his own, from the autobiographical *All for Hecuba*. Anyone who detects in Mrs Surtees a hint of Alfred Hitchcock's Miss Froy in *The Lady Vanishes* is quite right. Last but not least, thanks to Dermot Allen's pigs, Molly and Sadie, who escaped to Kilranelagh Hill, and began the story . . .